Praise for Reavis Z. Wortham and His Novels

"Reavis Z. Wortham is the real thing."
—**C. J. Box**

"The most riveting thriller all year!"
—**John Gilstrap**

"A masterful and entertaining storyteller."
—***Ellery Queen's Mystery Magazine***

"Entertaining and emotionally engaging."
—**T. Jefferson Parker**

"Wortham combines the gonzo sensibility of
Joe R. Lansdale and the elegiac mood of *To Kill a
Mockingbird* to strike just the right balance between
childhood innocence and adult horror."
—***Publishers Weekly***

"Populated with richly drawn characters, good
and (deliciously) evil, and propelled by some of
the best dialog you'll find in thriller writing
today. A true winner!"
—**Jeffery Deaver**

Also by REAVIS Z. WORTHAM

Hawke's Prey

The Rock Hole

Burrows

The Right Side of Wrong

Vengeance Is Mine

Dark Places

Unraveled

Doreen's 24 Hour Eat Gas Now Cafe

HAWKE'S WAR

A SONNY HAWKE THRILLER

REAVIS Z. WORTHAM

PINNACLE BOOKS
Kensington Publishing Corp.
www.kensingtonbooks.com

PINNACLE BOOKS are published by

Kensington Publishing Corp.
119 West 40th Street
New York, NY 10018

All Kensington titles, imprints, and distributed lines are available at special quantity discounts for bulk purchases for sales promotions, premiums, fund-raising, educational, or institutional use. Special book excerpts or customized printings can also be created to fit specific needs. For details, write or phone the office of the Kensington sales manager: Kensington Publishing Corp., 119 West 40th Street, New York, NY 10018, attn: Sales Department; phone 1-800-221-2647.

This book is a work of fiction. Names, characters, businesses, organizations, places, events, and incidents either are the product of the author's imagination or are used fictitiously. Any resemblance to actual persons, living or dead, events, or locales is entirely coincidental.

PINNACLE BOOKS and the Pinnacle logo are Reg. U.S. Pat. & TM Off.

ISBN-13: 978-0-7860-4178-7
ISBN-10: 0-7860-4178-1

First printing: June 2018

10 9 8 7 6 5 4 3 2 1

Printed in the United States of America

First electronic edition: June 2018

ISBN-13: 978-0-7860-4179-4
ISBN-10: 0-7860-4179-X

This one is for my girls,
Chelsea Hamilton, Megan Reynolds,
and my unofficially adopted step-daughter,
Amy Rodriguez.

Y'all make me proud each and every day.

AUTHOR'S NOTE

While researching the southern border of the U.S. for the first Sonny Hawke novel, *Hawke's Prey*, I ran across a story about the last documented Indian raid in the United States that occurred in southwest New Mexico in 1924. That's not a typo. 1924. Allegedly the descendants of Geronimo's last band came out of the Sierra Occidental Mountains, a steep, rugged, canyon-slashed world south of Arizona and New Mexico. Fascinated by the story, I looked further and found a copy of *The Apache Indians* by Helge Onstead, written in 1937. The story of his search for this last band of "wild Apaches" was fascinating and became an integral part of this book.

Chapter 1

Thunderheads boiled over the high desert peaks in Big Bend National Park as four hikers stretched out along the winding Devil's Den Trail. The experienced thirty-somethings filled the dry, cool morning air with comments and good-natured ribbing.

Trailing last as usual in the group's fifteen-year relationship, Harmony Cartwright stopped to tighten the faded Texas flag bandana she used as a headband to keep her blond hair under control. She adjusted the pack straps and, seeing that she wasn't falling too far behind, bent to pick up a 520-million-year-old chunk of quartz from the well-traveled trail.

She scratched away a few grains of sand with a chewed, unpainted thumbnail and angled it toward the sun. After a short examination, Harmony blessed it with a quick smile and tucked the rock into the pocket of her cargo shorts, where it clacked against half a dozen similar stones. The others continued at a steady pace and she hurried to catch up with her husband, Blue. He trailed behind Chloe Hutchins, who followed *her* husband, and the troop's leader Vince.

The veteran Marine stopped to take a long, deep sip of water from his bright yellow CamelBak pack. Solid as the trail under their feet, Vince was fearless, and had been all his life. After two tours in Afghanistan, he wrapped up his time in the Marine Corps and came home to sell real estate. Such a sedentary life caught up with him after months of inactivity, and he cast around for something adventurous.

Over half a dozen Friday nights and many cans of Coors, the four of them decided to hike the Devil's Den trail in some of the most rugged backcountry of the national park. The trail was off the beaten path for most hikers, who preferred to drive deeper into the park. Rated as a moderate five-and-a-half-mile hike, the trip would at least help them burn up some Yellow Belly calories and maybe lead to even more outdoor activities in the Rockies, a place he loved to visit, a few months down the road.

He swiveled to see Chloe hoofing along at a pace as quick as her wit. "Hey, Spousal Unit, how about you walk point? The view of this trail is getting boring, and that way I can watch your transmission twitch."

Chloe gave Vince a wink and pinched the blue nylon shirt from her damp skin, pumping it like a bellows to cool herself. The brunette wore a wide-brimmed straw hat exactly like the one shading her husband's head. "You wouldn't be able to concentrate then, Sergeant Hutchins. You'd probably trip on something and break a leg, and none of us can carry you out of here, so behave yourself and keep an eye out for marauding Indians."

Blue caught up with the sparring couple and tilted his Tilley hat upward. Built like a fireplug, he wore khaki shorts that revealed thick legs built for walking. "Y'all drinking enough water? This dry air's suckin' it out as fast as I can pour it in."

Chloe rolled her eyes in fun. "Not as much as Big Guy here, but he's working harder than I am."

"I'm still fresh enough out of the Sandbox to think this is chilly." Vince frowned in mock anger. "You're right though, Little Bit, y'all need to make sure you're staying hydrated. I don't want anyone on this team to be falling out."

"You should be sweating out all that beer y'all poured down last night." Chloe poked his flat stomach with a finger.

He raised an eyebrow at the petite brown-haired woman who weighed less than a hundred pounds. "Twelve little ol' cans ain't that much, besides, I run a bigger machine, so I can handle it."

Blue watched the clouds in the distance. "I wish I had one of those Yellow Bellies right now."

The quartet had formed in college, and Blue was used to the same good-natured arguments he'd been hearing in the years since. He waved a hand at the scattered scrub below the ridge above them. "Couldn't you guys find somewhere in the shade to stop?"

Vince spread both hands. "We're a little short on trees around here."

Blue scanned the sun-blasted landscape. The only sign of active life was a lazy buzzard drifting on the thermals high overhead. "Yeah, which is exactly why we should be hiking in Colorado, where there's trees, instead of this godforsaken desert. I get to pick next year, and it's gonna be a hike in Hawaii . . . from the condo to the beach."

Harmony caught up with them and tugged a bottle of water from her pack. "This is beautiful! I love all this space! Look." She picked up a twisted piece of wood. "This will look good in a flower arrangement." She brightened. "You know, I'm gonna use it to make one for Kelly Hawke. I tried to get them to come with us, but she said Sonny couldn't get loose this week."

"Honey, that'll just add weight to your pack." Blue watched the love of his life tuck the wood into a side pocket. "I've already seen you put three pounds of rocks in your britches, and besides, it's *illegal* to take anything from a national park."

Harmony winked at Chloe. "They have plenty of rocks around here. I doubt they'll miss a handful."

Chloe tore open a packet of powdered electrolytes and was pouring the contents into her high-tech BPA-free water bottle when Vince grunted, staggered, and folded in half. The sharp whip-crack report of a rifle shot reached them half a second later and echoed off the bare rocks and cliffs bracketing the trail. Shocked, her hand moved and the remainder of the powder drifted on the slight breeze in a tiny orange cloud.

Unable to grasp what was happening, Chloe sat the bottle on the ground and knelt beside her husband as he dropped to one knee. "Vince. Vince?"

The look in his eyes from under his hat brim was one of pain and confusion. He took his hand from his chest and stared at the blood-covered palm. "Oh hell. I've been shot."

Blue's head whipped toward the ridge. "Some idiot

isn't paying attention to where he's shooting! Y'all, get . . ."

A second shot hit Vince above his left ear. The soft-nosed round expanded, blowing out the side of his head. His gore-splattered hat flipped off to land in a clump of bunch grass. The man who'd survived two tours of duty in Afghanistan dropped without a sound onto the American soil he'd sworn to protect.

Recovering faster than he would have ever imagined, Blue slammed Harmony onto the dry trail in a full-body tackle. They hit the hard ground at the same instant a third round punched through Blue's pack with a *thock*. Digging in with his hiking boots, he yanked his confused wife against the rocky arroyo wall and waved at Chloe, who was petrified with shock. "Chloe! Get down!! Get over here with us"

Still not grasping that she was also in danger, she grabbed the straps on Vince's pack to drag him out of the line of fire coming from above. His dead weight and the heavy pack proved too much for her slight frame. She grunted, and jerked back on her heels. Vince's body moved an inch.

The shooter's next round plucked at the top of her shoulder. The ripstop fluttered and blood wet the nylon. Chloe gasped, lost her grip, and fell out of sight from above.

Blue and Harmony squeezed against the shoulder-high rise between them and the shooter on the ridge above. Keeping one eye on Chloe's struggle with her husband's body, Blue shrugged out of his backpack and dug into its contents. "Dammit, girl, get under cover!"

Eyes wide with fear, Harmony crouched low, her

shoulder against the bank of rocks, dirt, and scrub. "What are you *doing*?"

"That's no accident. Somebody's shooting at us on purpose!" Elbow deep in the pack's contents, Blue fished around for a long moment before pulling out a Glock 19. He would probably have left the heavy weapon home had they not planned on camping overnight in the back-country.

Vince had a Glock 40 in a Kydex waistband holster tucked under his shirt, but neither expected a sniper attack in the middle of a national park. The night before, they'd discussed their concern over illegal aliens who often crossed into the U.S. from Mexico. Though most of them only came looking for a better life, there were always a few with bad intentions.

The guy above seemed to be something completely different. Blue jerked the slide back to chamber a round. He didn't intend to let him murder them all.

Feeling a little better now that he could shoot back, Blue took several deep breaths to settle his nerves. Another chunk of lead slapped into a rock near Chloe, showering her with rock fragments and sand. It whirred away with a low, vibrating buzz.

Assuming the shooter was using a bolt-action rifle for accuracy, Blue figured it would take a few seconds for the sniper to rack a fresh round and reacquire a new target. He rose enough to peek through a scrubby honey mesquite growing at eye level on the arroyo's edge and squinted upward to locate the shooter. The ground exploded only inches away, spraying the side of his face with sand and pebbles, the echo of the shot coming half a second later.

"Shit!" Skin hot and stinging from the tiny bits of shrapnel, Blue fell hard onto the trail and gasped when he realized he was fully exposed. A round punched through his left shoulder and shattered rocks on the hard trail underneath his body. His arm went numb.

Grunting, he flipped onto his good shoulder and squirmed back to the rise, far enough away from Harmony to draw the fire and keep her safe. She screamed at the sight of blood welling from his wound.

Panting and in shock from the wound, he thought only of keeping her out of the maniac's sights. "Stay there!" He held out the hand with the Glock, muzzle pointed at the sky. She rose in a crouch, as if to race out and help. "No! I said stay down!"

Only yards away, Chloe gave up on pulling Vince's body to cover. She sat against the sheltering rise. Blood soaked the front of her shirt from her shoulder wound, but the shocked woman's soft voice floated over the bare ground with the inflection of a worried child. "Blue, Vince's been shot!"

"So have I!" He groaned and used his feet to push away and gain more distance from the women. "Stay down!" He crawled ten feet to the lowest part of the bank's taper.

Another round hit Vince in the chest. Echoes bounced from one hard ridge to the next. His shirt fluttered from the impact, but he was already beyond hurting or responding. Chloe shrieked and covered her face with both hands. "They shot him again!"

Blue reached the rise's downward slope that tapered

to a dangerously low level, ending his cover. He wondered why the sniper was shooting at the motionless body. Then the realization struck him. "Stay down, Chloe! He's trying to draw you out! Harmony, don't move, baby!"

"Why is he *shooting* at us?"

Blue ignored Chloe's question that didn't need an answer. It didn't matter *why* they were under fire. Someone was trying to kill them and that was the hard, simple truth. It was unbelievable that four people on a hike in a U.S. national park were the targets of a madman with a rifle.

The numbness of the shot was already wearing off. His arm hung limp and useless. He'd never felt such intense pain before and was swimmy-headed. Afraid he'd pass out from either the pain or shock, he gritted his teeth to keep from puking and focused on a piece of quartz to get hold of himself.

Harmony stripped the pack from her shoulders and crawled toward Chloe at the same time Blue rose just enough to peek through a different cluster of honey mesquite. Movement from above caught his eye and he saw the upper half of a man's body shift and twist in her direction.

"There you are." Drawing on hours on the shooting range back home in Dallas, he aimed the 9mm and adjusted for the elevation, hoping that the new technology in Parabellum ammo was true to the manufacturer's hype. He'd never shot uphill before, and the shooter looked to be at least a hundred yards away, but the trigonometry in his head worked out the angle for the trajectory he'd read about. He cranked off six fast shots from the 15-round magazine, thinking it was odd that his mind would register the empty brass tinkle off the rocks in such an intense situation.

The man on the ridge above threw his hands into the air and a rifle flipped end over end. "Got you, you son-of-a bitch!" Blue started to rise, but his response drew a stunning fusillade from above. The world erupted in mind-numbing noise as more than one fully automatic weapon hosed the area below the ridge.

The tiny geysers of dirt and rock exploding around Blue looked like hailstones falling onto still water. Rounds shredded the leaves off his covering brush and punched through the scant branches and lacy leaves to find flesh. His legs folded and he went down hard.

Harmony screamed over the rolling man-made thunder and reversed her direction, belly-crawling toward her husband.

Startled by the sudden continuous gunfire, Chloe spun toward Blue's body and became the next target when she involuntarily straightened into view. The rifle spoke again and Chloe's hair flew from the round's impact. Dead before she landed, she fell across Vince's legs and stilled.

Harmony's tan shirt and shorts blended well with the landscape. Knowing what would happen if she presented any part of her body above the rise, she kept her head low, grabbed Blue's shoulder, and rolled him out of sight from the rifle above.

Her husband was already gone. A single tear ran from the corner of his eye. The sight of that clear drop of liquid defined the moment, and Harmony cradled her husband's body. Trembling with fear and horror, she wept with deep, wracking sobs.

The high desert grew silent. The buzzard narrowed its spiral and circled overhead, waiting.

The day's heat rose as the sun reached its peak in the blue-white sky. Dark thunderheads to the west built to 50,000 feet, but refused to bring relief to the only survivor of the ambush. Flies buzzed the corpses and clotted pools of blood. Beyond those insects, there was no movement other than a kettle of buzzards circling in an airborne funeral procession.

No one came down to inspect the carnage. Throughout the day, Harmony had expected the shooters to come check on their victims. She worried that other hikers would stumble onto the massacre and become victims themselves, but she remained the only living human on the sun-blasted trail. The buzzards dropped lower, but wouldn't approach with one of the figures still moving.

They call them a kettle when they're flying, she thought, her shocked mind working to overcome the horror of what had happened. *They're a wake when they're feeding.*

She covered her mouth and gagged at the thought of what would soon happen if help didn't come.

Dusk arrived, bringing relief from the blazing springtime sun that slipped first behind a collapsing thunderstorm, then reappeared momentarily before settling below the bluish mountains in the distance.

Stiff and dehydrated, she released her husband's

body and risked a quick peek at the ridge above. It was as empty as the rest of the park around her. When there was no more gunfire, she gained even more confidence and knew what she had to do. She kissed Blue's cold forehead and ran a finger along the thin white line of the dried tear.

With a deep, shuddering sigh, she hooked two fingers through her backpack and swung it over one shoulder. Hesitating for a moment, she picked up his Glock that was familiar from shooting at the local outdoor range not far from their house.

A house that'll be lonely and still from now on.

She gasped at the thought and gagged, but nothing came up but bile.

With an effort, Harmony gritted her teeth until the feelings passed. She didn't need distractions right then. She needed to escape, to bring help, and tell the authorities what had happened.

Still cautious, she belly-crawled along the edge of the low rise. It was slow, painful work as rocks gouged every part of her body that scraped along the trail. Her elbows, thighs, and knees took the brunt of the abuse and were soon as raw as hamburger. After a hundred yards, her shirt and shorts were cut and torn in a dozen places, her waistband full of sand and pebbles. She paused to dig the rock samples from her pockets and drop them on the trail.

Her crawl resumed, and when her bare legs couldn't take any more, she decided she'd had enough. Hoping she was finally out of range, Harmony rose and ran in a crouch for another hundred yards without drawing gunfire. There was nothing but a brilliant orange glow over a ragged line of mountains behind her as Harmony straightened, slipped the second pack strap over her other shoulder. Grasping the Glock in a white-knuckled death grip, the only survivor of the attack jogged through the dusk to get help.

Backlit from her angle against the orange horizon and pinkish clouds, the sniper wearing a *shemagh* head scarf rose and watched the blond woman's escape. Acquiring her dim image through the scope, he grunted and asked Allah for the strength not to shoot the fleeing target.

Though the gathering darkness and her bobbing figure would have made it a challenge, he was confident it would have been an easy shot to bring her down. But then there wouldn't be anyone left alive to tell the story.

Chapter 2

The Devil was beatin' his wife several days after the triple homicide in Big Bend National Park. Chilly raindrops fell despite the bright sun casting my shadow on the rocky ground.

My horse snorted and I rubbed his nose. Red liked it enough that when I quit, the big knothead tucked his nose under my arm like a puppy looking for more attention, making me stagger sideways.

"Careful, ya big moose."

Horseback sure wasn't the way I wanted to travel, but the rugged backcountry in the Big Bend region of Texas sometimes required that we use the tried-and-true methods that worked for generations. It allowed me to move faster and sure beat walking.

The hikers' bodies had been airlifted by helicopters and the responding law-enforcement agencies were long gone. The .308 Win, and 5.56 casings from what they were calling "the sniper's nest," and the 9mm hulls from Blue's Glock were in Washington, along with the plaster casts of footprints and tire tracks from the ridge. There was nothing left but a buzzard hanging on the thermals above.

Since it was a national park, the FBI was still in charge of the case. But I wanted some time alone to study on what might have happened without the input from those guys, the park rangers, border patrol, or the highway patrol. I was friends with those folks who were murdered not far from where I stood.

There are sixteen Texas Rangers in Company E, my company. I told the boys to come on out if they wanted, but they knew I had a personal stake in what happened and said they'd be there if I needed 'em.

My wife Kelly and I were really close to the hikers. In fact, we'd planned to be part of the hike at the outset. I got a call at the last minute and we had to bow out. That thought got hold of me for a minute and I felt the hair rise on the back of my neck, wondering if the outcome would have been different had we been with them.

Kelly and Chloe had been good friends since they were third graders in our hometown of Ballard, nearly ninety miles to the northwest. Blue and I were hunting buddies. Vince was a good enough guy, but we only saw each other when he was home from the service, and I hadn't had the opportunity to spend time with the Hutchinses after he started selling real estate.

The girls spent the last month posting photos and comments about the upcoming trip on their Facebook pages, something I stayed as far away from as possible. I never had any use for social media, and didn't intend to start.

Because of our close personal connections to the

victims, I stayed out of the way to let the other agencies complete their jobs. My boyhood friend Sheriff Ethan Armstrong and I visited with Harmony in the hospital to take her statement after the FBI guys finished, but what I wanted was to be on my own.

That's how I work best. And an even better reason was my new assignment. Major Chase Parker changed my position in the Texas Rangers with a brand-spankin'-new title after what had become known as the Ballard Incident a few months earlier when terrorists took over our courthouse.

My recent Shadow Response designation was a fresh and as-yet-untried concept in Rangering, one that adapted modern investigative techniques to the tough, in-your-face tactics used by the rough old men who'd protected the Lone Star State a hundred and fifty years ago.

I was no longer attached to one particular district, but now moved about the state, supporting the district Rangers as they handled those difficult cases that defied common descriptions, but operating at my own discretion along the shadowy edge of right and wrong. I knew it'd be a dangerous balancing act, but changing times dictated a new approach.

And lordy were the times changing.

I knew why the victims wanted to hike that spring day. The air was fresh and clean. The hardpan was bursting with color in the unusually wet spring. Cactus flamed with yellow blooms. Other flowers that I'd grown up with but couldn't identify to save my life carpeted the rocky country.

Jagged ridges bristled with piñon mixed with junipers, depending on the elevation, and spread in all directions. Bare ridges in the distance were devoid of timber, but farther down, enough green vegetation grew in a fringe that reminded me of older men losing their hair. The canyons below were already starting to shadow, worming away dark and mysterious with the promise of pitch-black nights if the clouds continued to build.

I tilted the straw O'Farrell's hat up on my forehead and turned away from the crime scene below to scan the area. Black clouds towered above the craggy ridge in the distance, promising another afternoon of pop-up traveling thunderstorms that arced torrents of rain onto the hard ground until they cried themselves out.

The sudden out-of-place echo of automatic weapons bouncing off the mountains sparked a jolt of dread. The hair on the back of my neck prickled again, and I shivered as if the air had suddenly gone frigid. I angled my head, using my "good" ear to find the source of the sound. Like many hunters and gun enthusiasts, I suffered from "Hunter's Notch," a slight hearing loss on the side opposite the shooter's gun hand.

The recent firefight I'd been involved in only months earlier hadn't done my ears any favors, either, and now I had tinnitus to deal with. The steady ringing didn't block sound, but it remained a constant annoyance and despite what my doctor said, it sometimes made hearing difficult.

The best I could tell, the shots came from far away toward the west, back where I left the truck and trailer parked on a two-track trail ending in a cul-de-sac. I checked the phone in my back pocket, and as usual, there was no signal so far back in the wild territory. I wondered why I ever toted the damned thing around in the first place.

Red pricked his ears toward the west. I trusted his hearing more than mine. "That's what I thought, too."

He snorted what sounded like an agreement. I jammed the useless phone back into my pocket, stuck a boot in the stirrup, and swung into the saddle. Red knew where we needed to go and took off toward the pops like I'd reined him that way. I kicked him into a lope and settled back in the saddle as his rhythmic clatter of shod hooves ate up the rocky ground.

It was a long way back to the truck, and periodic shots sounded like a firefight. The echoes bounced off the broken land. I resisted the urge to kick Red into a full-out run. After a while, I realized it probably wasn't a firefight, unless the guys were in a running gun battle.

The truck and trailer were just as I left them, and I had Red loaded up in a matter of minutes. The shots came again, as I slapped the locking lever closed on the trailer door, sounding clearer than before. They weren't any closer than when I first heard them though, despite the distance I'd traveled, but the horseshoe shape of the canyon gathered the sound like a parabolic mike.

A single report sounded heavier, sharper. It was followed by lighter rounds that were drowned out by thunder from a curved curtain of gray rain in the distance. I slid behind the Dodge's wheel and snatched the microphone off the dash.

"Ethan, you there?"

We were supposed to use the codes I learned as a highway patrol officer, but he and I had slipped out of that habit long ago. He came back, but the storms and box canyon caused so much havoc I couldn't make out what he said.

"Ethan, I'm at the Dripping Springs trailhead. I'm hearing automatic gunfire. This may be the same bunch we're looking for here in the park."

His response was even worse. I pitched the mike on the seat in disgust and rolled the window down. I don't know why I bothered to check, but there still weren't any bars on my cell phone even after I held it up and angled it in every direction. I got to feeling like the Statue of Liberty and pitched the infernal device onto the seat beside the useless mike.

It took a second to maneuver the trailer around so I could follow the dirt track full of dips, humps, and washouts. I had to go slow on that rough old road because it wouldn't take much to bend an axle or blow a tire. Even when I intersected with the gravel road, there wasn't any driving fast on the washboard ruts, where a couple of terrapins outran me at one point. Rocks rattled the undercarriage and I ground my teeth hoping that I wouldn't punch a hole in the oil pan, or bruise a tire that'd go flat once I reached the highway.

I wanted a blessed smooth highway to make some time, but where I was headed was even rougher. It probably wouldn't do anything but raise my blood pressure, because on the way in that morning I'd gotten behind two tourists in a Jetta who were poking along at thirty miles an hour, the driver fiddling with his phone while his wife took pictures out the window. I didn't need a repeat of that. They used those same phones to take a picture of my truck as I passed them and cut back into their lane close enough for Red's trailer to scrape the bugs off their front bumper.

I figured I'd be talking to the park police about that later. Big Bend has exclusive jurisdiction within the park. As a ranger once told me, "Big Bend law is the only law inside its borders."

I could understand that.

I hoped Red was digging in to stay on his feet as the trailer bounced like a rubber ball behind my dually. The road straightened and another staccato burst of gunfire came stronger, even making me forget the rattling gravel for a second. I got to thinking it was a battle between drug dealers. There was no doubt that smugglers called "mules" hoofed their crap through the desert in primitive packs. Maybe two groups from different cartels found themselves on the same trail.

Nah, I doubted mules would come through a national park, especially the northeast quadrant. It didn't make any sense for them to hike for days only to intersect either Farm Road 2627, or worse, the well-traveled north and southbound U.S. Highway 385 that had a permanent border patrol check station up near Marathon.

I really didn't care if the cartels shot one another across the river, but this was my country, and I didn't want their troubles to deal with in the park, or anywhere else for that matter.

I shouldn't have run toward the fight. Those guys were usually armed to the teeth, but there was one thing a Ranger didn't do, and that was run away *from* anything. I remembered having that thought a few hours later and regretted it.

I slowed to stick my ear out the window. Thunder

rumbled and I sat there long enough to think it was all over until the shots came again and rose to a crescendo before trailing off. It sounded like *two* automatic weapons this time, followed by reports from the heavier rifle.

I came upon a two-lane dirt track splitting off the road and paused. My imagination said some poor sucker was holed up and shooting it out with several some*ones*. The recent murders and distinctive sounds of two rifle calibers made me think it might be a second ambush of innocent hikers. Maybe another armed civilian like Blue was fighting back. But run-of-the-mill visitors didn't hike Big Bend with automatic weapons.

Nothing made any sense.

Clearly defined tread marks in the fine sand near the highway told me someone had recently driven an ATV down the trail. The National Park Service has definite rules against those annoying little machines, so I steered off the highway and followed still another two-lane track that wound into the mountains.

It petered out into a bumpy, barely defined clear space through the scattered brush that was once a ranch road, way back when the settlers did their best to scratch a living from the desert. My sense of urgency increased and I pushed the foot-feed closer to the floorboards. The trailer rattled along behind me. "Sorry Red! Hang on back there."

The gunfire came again, but I still wasn't gaining.

It must be a running gun battle.

The phone still said No Service. Five years ago, I would have thrown it out the window in frustration, but I've learned to control some of my strongest impulses because my son Jerry has the same failings. I was trying to be a good bad example, but sometimes I'd forget and have to bear Kelly's wrath.

Instead, I bounced it off the seat so hard it ricocheted off the passenger door and into the floorboard full of dirt, stickers, work papers, and maps. Feeling better now that it was out of reach and not a factor in raising my blood pressure, I checked the radio again. "Ethan!"

Garbled sounds like a space invader gargling razor blades punched through the static only to be replaced by occasional ear-splitting squeals followed by nothing but static.

It seemed like I'd been driving for miles before the trail became too narrow for my dually at the foot of a steep, rocky ridge. I killed the engine and waited for the cloud of dust my tires had raised to blow past while I studied the tracks of at least two ATVs heading east.

Those noisy little machines are going to make the park rangers mad.

A single distant pop made me prick my ears forward just like ol' Red.

Dammit. I need to get help and come back.

But it'd be too late. Not happy about having to back the trailer into a narrow gap between two large patches of prickly pear, I glanced out the window and saw enough open space to make a circle.

Another shot.

Two more.

Once again, my impulses got the better of me. I killed the engine and backed Red out of the trailer. Thunder rolled across the Chihuahuan Desert as I stuffed my Winchester into the saddle scabbard and swung aboard.

I rationalized that at least he would get me across the rough landscape until I could get a peek at what was ahead. It might be something I could handle alone, or at the very least, I might get high enough for that damned cell phone to work.

If somebody got after me, Red was the perfect way to cut through the country and get gone. I pointed his nose toward a 50,000-foot mountain of clouds pulsing with electricity and the resulting fractures of lightning. We took off at a lope as a cool breeze washed over me from the collapsing thunderstorm. Red pricked his ears forward. I let him have his head and we went to see what was going on.

The trail we followed wound through a rocky incline leading toward the top of a mesa overlooking several tiers rising to the craggy horizon and another vein of mountains. Red's hooves made powdery explosions in the dry terrain. Thinking that the different mesas, arroyos, and cuts in the desert landscape looked like they had been created by a giant hand, I let him pick his own way around the boulders and dozens of prickly, sharp-edged plants that could cut or injure his legs.

It seemed like an hour later before the ATV tracks brought me to the edge of a steep, high-desert canyon. There hadn't been any gunshots in more than thirty minutes, and I wondered if it was over. Maybe everyone was dead and all I'd have to do was count the bodies.

The air was rich with a blend of damp earth, short-lived desert greenery, piñon, juniper, and sage. Red kept testing the wind with his sensitive nose and blowing with satisfaction. He loved the idea of a coming storm as much as I did, but I hoped it would wait until we identified the issue ahead and got our butts back to the truck.

We rounded a lacy honey mesquite and Red almost stepped on a well-worn, bright orange ball cap surrounded by several dozen gleaming brass hulls scattered around a thick clump of cactus. I reined in and stayed in the saddle, checking the area. Nothing but the cooing of a white-wing dove broke the silence, not even the hint of thunder from the distant storm. I figured no one else was around, so I swung to the ground.

Red sniffed at a clump of bunchgrass, unconcerned. I'd learned long ago to trust the horse's instincts. His ears told me there was nothing of interest within hearing distance, so I relaxed and scanned the edge of the mesa above. A white-wing dove sailed along the crest and whiffled down to land out of sight on the ground.

Holding the reins in one hand, I studied the empty brass at my feet. There was no blood, but that didn't mean anything. Footprints in a clear sandy spot pointed toward the edge of the canyon. Stepping close, I peeked over the edge, thinking the cap's owner might be down there.

I tensed at a sudden movement far below, but relaxed when I saw a whitetail deer working its way along the canyon floor. Being careful not to get too close to the edge because heights make my skin crawl, I carefully placed my boot on a solid rest at the edge of the drop-off and peeked over into the abyss. Dozens of shallow gorges and arroyos splintered from the huge fracture below my feet and spread like lightning bolts indicating random directions from which water flowed into the floodplain.

The light died behind the pulsing thunderstorm and I realized it was later than I thought. It'd be dark soon and I'd likely have to ride back without the aid of the stars or moon.

Uh oh. I'm supposed to be at the house for dinner.

Dang it. Perry Hale and Yolanda were supposed to come over for my favorite meal, homemade spaghetti. I glanced at my watch, torn between what I needed to do about the gunfire and family obligations. Remembering how many people had gone over the edges of canyons just like that one in the Big Bend, I stepped back and took my sunglasses off.

A flicker somewhere on the rocky incline leading up to the mesa caught my eye. That's how the Old Man taught me to hunt, by being still and looking for any kind of moment that betrayed the game, like the flip of a squirrel's tail, the flick of a deer's ear, or the smooth rustle of quail gliding through the underbrush. Even though it figured to be another bird going to roost, I turned and glanced up at the ridgeline above at the exact moment a white-wing dove floating past caught the bullet meant for me.

The bird vaporized in an explosion of feathers about thirty yards from where I stood. The impact with the tiny body diverted the projectile enough that it wasn't the center shot that would have blown out my chest. It still punched a hole through the big latissimus muscle under my left arm and staggered me backward.

A number of things happened at the same time the rifle's crack reached my ears. Startled not by the gunshot, but by the unnatural sight of an exploding bird, Red yanked the reins out of my hand. He spun and took off like a striped-ass baboon at the same time my foot came down on nothing but air.

I screamed like a little girl for the first time in my adult life. Anyone would, knowing they were plummeting over the edge of a canyon rim. The breath caught in my chest and I fell back in time past the strata of millions of years. Horizontal, multicolored layers of rocky soil flashed by and a useless burst of information came to me from my geology classes in college that the rock layers are ordered with the oldest layers on the bottom, and the most recent layers on top.

Yeah, that really helped.

Images both blurred then came sharp as a tack as I fell. An upside-down glimpse of the rocky wall became my boots flashing past the heavy clouds off to the southwest. The next time I saw them, they were defined against the blue sky in the opposite direction.

A strobe-like image of the sun peeking between clouds and a sweeping gray curtain of falling rain became rocks and embedded fossils flashing by. A crisp crack inside my skull hurt worse than the bullet wound when I slammed through a thick bush clinging to the side of a steep slope made up of sand and scree.

My hat cushioned the blow, but vanished as I slammed through another bush, then bounced off the hard surface of the canyon wall's acute slope. Despite all that, I was lucky it wasn't as steep as the virtually straight drop of the nearby Santa Elena Canyon.

I cut a flip and my shoulder smashed hard on the rocks, reversing the spin so that my hip took the next hard blow in an explosion of dirt and small rocks. I still had the presence of mind to try and stop my accelerating fall. It was probably a bad idea, but I spread my arms and legs to gain traction on the steep slope. The bottom of the canyon was still a long way down, and I sure didn't want to roll all the way like a meat cannonball, knocking chunks and pieces of myself off on every rock and boulder all the way to the bottom.

It seemed like a month of Sundays before I managed to grab a tough little bush with one hand and slide to a stop. Rocks jarred loose by my fall continued to rattle within earshot. I waited until everything was quiet before taking a deep breath of relief.

Thank God, I might just make it.

I closed my eyes as if that would help and rotated my numb left shoulder. Gunshot wound. Check, but nothing felt broken. My right hand was busy holding me still, so I wiggled the rest of my fingers and toes to make sure they were still functional and attached. Stuff ached, but all was still good.

One foot felt like it was hanging over a big rock, and I dug my other heel in. Stable for the moment and with a heart pounding like a jackhammer, I turned loose of the bush.

The scree stretching in all directions broke free and I slid again with the terrible realization my foot wasn't over a rock. It was another drop. I grabbed at the bush again, but missed. The dry ground melted away as the dusty flow took me over the sheer edge like a leaf slipping over a waterfall.

"Well, hell."

I dropped again. Nothing but luck kept me upright, and I fell feet first.

Kids love the feeling of stepping off a high diving board, but there wasn't anything fun about looking down past the slope and seeing the long dark shadows stretching across most of the canyonland still far below.

There was enough of an angle that I landed in the soft river of fine dirt and rocks that poured into the tops of my boots. I went down again, this time on my rear, and it was another wild ride through the gathering dusk, hearing the snap of dry branches and hoping that's really what it was, and not important bones.

There was no control, but I dug my heels into the loose ground, grabbing at everything grabbable. Material tore and my funny bone banged on a boulder. My arm went hot and numb.

I was upside down again before thumping off what felt like a rock big as a hall closet, then it was freefall city. The thought that a storm was coming and it wasn't the one in the distance was the last thing I remembered.

Chapter 3

Lying prone and almost invisible in his desert camo fatigues and tan *shemagh* wrapped around his black hair, Syrian-born Mohamed Abdullah lowered the rifle and squinted past the scope at the empty ridge five hundred yards away. Instead of racking the long bolt on his stolen M24 sniper rifle, he clenched his jaw in frustration and waited for his temple to quit pounding.

Beside him two men whose names he didn't know were jabbering like idiots in their barbaric language that seemed to Abdullah to have way too many words for what they were trying to say. The heavily tattooed members of the Coyotes Rabiosos, a ruthless Mexican gang from the rugged canyon country of Chihuahua, weren't nearly as well camouflaged. Their dusty jeans and cast-off western shirts stood out in the earth-tone landscape.

Sitting cross-legged behind him, three more similarly dressed and tattooed gangsters were waiting silently to see what was about to happen. They were listening to the conversation between Yooko Ruiz and Javier Martinez, grinning at their sideshow discussion.

The Coyotes Rabiosos were headed by a bloodthirsty man with light skin and red highlights with one name, Chatto. He was rumored to be the direct descendant of Geronimo's last band of fighters who raided across the border into the U.S. as late as 1924. It was said he was weaned from his mama's tit on spilled blood. He lived in the Sierra Madre Occidental, a range of mountains far to the west.

Yooko and Javier continued their discussion in Spanish while Abdullah lowered his head as if to pray. A full minute passed, and his anger and frustration increased with every tick of the watch on his wrist. He felt that the only thing holding his skull together was his *shemagh*, and it would likely go flying at the detonation. Talking in conversational tones, they didn't bother to lower their stupid voices. Military discipline wasn't even on those idiots' minds.

Beside Abdullah, Yooko Ruiz lowered the borrowed binoculars and spoke in Spanish to his brother in arms, Javier Martinez. "After all that, he shot through a damned bird! I bet the bullet missed the *guardabosque*. I hate this, this, what do the Americans call them, raghead? I could have made a better shot than this raghead."

Javier snorted and rolled onto his back. His wide round face grimaced when a sharp rock jabbed through his western-cut shirt. "Do you think this idiot hit the Ranger at all?" He glanced along the length of his body and past his booted feet to his *compadres* waiting in the scant shade of a honey mesquite. All three shook their heads and grinned.

Yooko crossed his ankles as if they were lying on a soft bed, having a casual conversation. His name meant Tiger in Yaqui. His innocent-looking, boyish face belied the man's ability to kill without remorse. "Probably not. It looked to me like he fell by accident."

"We wasted all that time and ammunition and he misses."

"First he says we can kill this *guardabosque* a week ago when he's hiking with the others, then he isn't there. Now we drew him in and this *idiota* misses."

"He says the first chance was based on his daughter's Facebook post, and that the target didn't come after all." Javier spoke slowly, as if trying to figure out what a Facebook post was at the same time he related the explanation.

Yooko was also in the dark about that one. "Well, I don't know what that is, but it's getting dark and I don't want to try and find the body down in that damned canyon."

"We won't find him at all until in the morning. By then there'll be a hundred *la migra* here."

"That's what I was thinking, too. I wish we were back in *our* mountains."

Abdullah considered swinging the nasty little Mexican-produced Cobra Short submachine gun and hosing them until the magazine was empty. Unfortunately, all three of the other cold-blooded gangsters squatting behind him would have no trouble tearing him to shreds with the same kinds of weapon he carried.

They carried 9x19 machine pistols illegally purchased from a crooked captain named Perez in the Armería del Ejército Mexicano, Mexican Army armory, in Torreón, the city seat of Coahuila.

Regaining control of his anger, Abdullah finally spoke in English, the common language they used to communicate. "Will you two shut *up*! Gather your weapons and let's go find the body. I am to bring his head to Chatto. If we don't, he'll drink from your *skulls*."

Even though his Spanish was extremely limited, he knew they thought he'd missed the shot, and if the truth be known, he wasn't sure he *hadn't*. It was incredibly bad luck for the bird to fly into the "short-action" cartridge's trajectory at that exact moment, but the way the Texas Ranger reacted, he was almost positive he'd hit him *somewhere*. Even if he'd only wounded the man, luck was on his side, because no one could survive a fall off that cliff. They'd been over every inch of it in the last several days, waiting for the opportunity to draw the Ranger in for the kill.

His employer Marc Chavez had been right, and the OCD-driven American terrorist's research had paid off. Even if their first attempt at murdering the Texas Ranger failed when he didn't join in the hike Chavez had learned about by monitoring the Hawke family's social media pages, the madman understood Sonny Hawke's need to work alone.

The Ranger's, or *guardabosque*'s, independence had killed him.

Chapter 4

Two months earlier, Marc Chavez was sitting ramrod stiff in a chair positioned beside the large plate-glass window in his midcentury modern house in the upscale River Oaks section of Houston. "So it was your brother who was killed in Ballard back in November?" He absently sharpened the crease in his slacks with a thumb and forefinger.

Abdullah had only been in the U.S. for a week, after crossing the Rio Grande somewhere between Laredo and Brownsville, though he wasn't new to Mexico. Before that, and like thousands of others before him, Abdullah paid $4,000 to a *coyote* with one dead eye to provide passage across the Rio Grande into Texas. The Mexican national came highly recommended from the Syrian's employers, the Coyotes Rabiosos. The price was at least a thousand dollars more than other human smugglers charged, but Abdullah didn't care, because it wasn't his money.

The Islamic terrorist's face remained stone blank, watching the OCD mastermind worry at the crease of his slacks. "Yes. Under *your* direction."

Chavez shrugged. "I gave him the opportunity to rain death and destruction on one little West Texas town, and he failed because of his own greed and arrogance."

"It doesn't matter the cause. He was my brother, and I will avenge him by taking the head of the man who killed him. What do *you* get out of this?"

"It's a twofold win for me." Chavez ran his fingers over the crease again, obviously annoyed that the material refused to remain sharp. Chavez's mental affliction was shifting into overtime in an effort to make them look as fresh as when he put them on that morning. "I get my revenge on the Texas Ranger who destroyed my operation, and his death . . . and dismemberment . . . will again show this country that there is no safe place to live, not safe, not safe. You come highly recommended by *your* employer, who, by the way, is under my employ. Don't you love the circular beauty of that?"

Abdullah shrugged, understanding only half of what Chavez was referring to and wondering when they would get to the important part of the conversation, money.

"Tell me about your experience across the river in Mexico. How did you get there?"

The Syrian's eyes narrowed, trying to understand why Chavez needed that information. "I came in with a dozen other believers from Brazil. It was nothing to pay the corrupt border guards to cross, especially in countries like Colombia, Nicaragua, and Guatemala. Panama and Costa Rica posed a few problems, but obviously nothing that stopped me."

"Then you simply drove to the first ISIS camp you heard about?"

The man who wouldn't leave his pants alone was getting annoying. Abdullah wondered why he needed so much information that didn't help achieve their goal. Saudi Arabia and Qatar were funding hundreds of Islamic terrorists to establish and operate training camps in the corrupt country of Mexico. He considered telling Chavez about serving as a training "officer" in two camps, one only eight miles from the U.S. border in an area known as "Anapra" west of Ciudad Juárez in the Mexican state of Chihuahua. The hungry look in Chavez's eyes shot a needle of doubt through the consideration.

"We have a vast network and as long as anyone has Internet access, they can find other Brothers who believe in our ultimate goal of a global caliphate."

"You didn't get what you wanted there?"

"Opportunities arise to provide *better* opportunities in establishing a network into America's New Mexico state."

Abdullah outlined how he moved to a second ISIS camp in Puerto Palomas, farther to the west, to join other fanatics working to establish a drug- and human-smuggling pipeline into the New Mexico towns of Columbus and Deming.

"Ah." Suddenly excited, Chavez stood and paced the room. "You made that decision with exactly the same criteria in mind as I had when I planned the Ballard takeover."

"And that is?"

"Small towns separated from large cities by vast distances, and the most important part, understaffed municipal and county police forces. I see we think somewhat alike. We sow terror in the U.S. by proving to Americans that no place is safe, not even rural towns with no political or militaristic value."

Abdullah's plans were much wider. He had no desire to tell Chavez that his people had better targets than small towns. His brothers already had maps and plans of Fort Bliss, the sprawling military installation north of El Paso that houses the U.S. Army's 1st Armored Division. A successful strike on a U.S. military base would send shockwaves around the world, hopefully inspiring his brothers to attack bases in other countries.

The only thing standing in his way was the need to avenge his real brother, who had shown him the light when they were kids and convinced him to join the *jihad* against the United States when Abdullah was old enough to fight.

"So tell me." Chavez glanced down to make sure the creases lined up with the center of his shoes. "You no longer help train fighters in the camps. You moved your alliances to the cartels?"

Did this idiot not know anything? Abdullah gazed out the window, as if watching for incoming threats. "I provide security for Vincente Flores, when he needs me."

Both knew that the Vincente Gonzalez Flores Cartel, the Juárez Cartel's El Machete enforcement arm, was one of the most bloodthirsty gangs in Mexico. Their Coyotes Rabiosos provided security against the Mexican Army and Federal Police. In return, the cartels paid vast sums of money, provided guns and ammunition for the terrorists, and looked the other way when the terrorist cells planned and executed missions against the U.S.

Chavez resumed pacing and thinking. "You're always looking for a better opportunity. I understand that completely. Here's my proposition. I want you to find the Texas Ranger Sonny Hawke and kill him. Once you've achieved that goal, I will provide the monetary assistance you need to bring one or more of your cells across, I presume through that pipeline you've already established near Deming, and launch the bloodiest, bloodiest, blood . . . bloodiest attacks you can plan against the U.S."

Chavez's jaw muscles flexed as he ground his molars in an effort to rein in his OCD need to repeat.

Abdullah thought only he and his closest jihadists knew the details of the busy pipeline funneling both humans and drugs into the U.S., and here Chavez spoke the specific location of their targeted area. He figuratively pulled the cards closer to his chest. This man with the glasses, oiled hair, and maddening habits was even more dangerous, and valuable, than he originally thought.

He focused on Chavez's melting crease, just for the fun of vexing the rich, homegrown terrorist. "I heard we lost several devoted followers in an operation with you behind it."

Instead of allowing himself to be pulled into an argument, Chavez returned to his original thought, but only after he obviously ignored the frustrating crease and crossed the newly installed gleaming hardwood floor to the bar. He placed three cubes of ice in a high-ball glass, covered it with Glenlivet, and placed it precisely in the middle of a round coaster, where he turned the glass three times. "It would have worked if it hadn't been for one man. That Texas Ranger who was in exactly the wrong place at the wrong time."

Abdullah shrugged, watching the process. He had no idea what a Texas Ranger was, nothing more than a vague idea that he was some kind of law-enforcement official. He threw both hands wide, wondering why the man's mannerisms annoyed him so. "So?"

Chavez's nose wrinkled and he touched the tip of each finger on one hand against the tip of his thumb over and over again, watching the glass of scotch. "Our plan was to make a statement, an impact, that nothing is safe in this country. Nothing. I still plan to do that soon, but right now I want to make an example out of that Ranger. I've heard of your talents. Kill Sonny Hawke and deliver his head to another in my employ whose name is Chatto. He will take it from there and your job is finished."

"Then what? I kill this man and where do I go?"

"Where do you want to go?"

"Washington. Make arrangements for me to get to Washington to meet up with my brothers."

Chavez snickered. "Which Washington?"

Abdullah frowned, not understanding. Heat rose in his face at the look on Chavez's face. "There are two?"

"Yes. One is a state and the other is the District of Columbia, on the opposite side of the country. Knowing your probable plans, I'd say the one with the White House and the Capitol is where you want to go."

Abdullah felt his chest swell with a fanatical flame. "How long will it take to get there?"

"How do you want to travel?"

Not understanding Chavez's need for exact information, Abdullah's shoulders tightened. "What difference does it make?"

"A lot." Chavez raised an eyebrow. "If you drive, it will be approximately twenty-seven hundred miles."

The jihadist was stunned. He had no idea America was so large. "Where does the president live? The White House? The Capitol?"

"The White House."

"That is where I want to go."

"Done." Chavez picked up a photo printed off the Internet and passed it to Abdullah with two fingers as if trying to avoid physical contact. "Kill Sonny Hawke and I'll get you there."

Abdullah frowned at the photo of a middle-aged man who looked like a cowboy. He studied the red-headed Ranger. He committed the ridiculous-looking hat, red mustache, angular face, and penetrating eyes to memory, noting the man appeared to be posing with a lever-action rifle, in front of a desert landscape. He wore jeans, a tooled leather gunbelt supporting what looked to be a .45 semi-automatic, light colored shirt, and odd-looking boots.

"Is this real?"

"It is. He has become one of the most well-known Rangers in their history. Don't underestimate this man." He pointed at a satellite phone on the coffee table. "Use that to communicate with me. Cell phone service is spotty at best in Big Bend."

Abdullah shrugged and picked up the phone. "He is a man, and nothing else. I will kill him."

The corner of Chavez's mouth rose in a slight grin. He picked up the highball glass and drained the contents in three swallows. "You do that."

Chapter 5

The crack of light peeking between the distant, rugged horizon and the electric light show to the west was going fast. Elongated shadows from boulders, vegetation, and mesa crests stretched across the national park's arid ground. Golden sunlight heightened the warm rust and brown colors in the eroded landscape, contrasting the darker fractures of canyons and ravines spreading like a broken windshield.

"Are you sure that was the *guardabosque* Sonny Hawke?" Yooko stood and adjusted the Cobra's collapsed stock to rest more comfortably against his side. "It was hard to tell through the glasses in this light. It looked like just another *norteamericano* to me."

"His face is burned into my brain." Abdullah rose from the ground overlooking the canyon. His voice was sharp with disdain for the annoying Indio-Mexicans, who in his opinion existed in a class barely above the dogs that roamed the streets of his home village of Al-Mayadan, a hot, squalid town on the banks of the Euphrates River. "Don't question me any longer. Do what I say."

The electric crackle in the air didn't come from the approaching storm, but from the tension rising once again between the mercenary and the gangsters. The other three squatting against the honey locust stood when Yooko's face hardened and Javier tensed.

The Syrian had left the scoped rifle lying on the ground, but when he rose, the slung Cobra swiveled to the man's chest. Yooko noticed Abdullah's hand rested on the pistol grip holding an extended magazine. His finger was curled around the trigger, a sure sign the safety was off and the man was as keyed up as he.

Both Yooko's and Javier's weapons were on safe and the position of their firearms put them at a disadvantage. The light flashing in the Syrian's usually emotionless eyes spoke clearly of the danger waiting there. Though the odds were against Abdullah killing them all before one of the five could bring their weapons into action were small, they weren't good.

Yooko relaxed and smiled showing several gold teeth. "I work for you, *jefe*. We go down and make sure the *norteamericano* is dead, no?"

Javier shrugged and picked up his recycled gallon milk jug of water. "I bet he didn't miss. I saw him fall. Let's go pick up the body."

The three tattooed men laughed at the joke.

Built like a bulldog with an abdomen stretching the buttons of his western-cut shirt, Calaka's skin, like that of the others, appeared to be dried by the sun and freshly oiled to the consistency of leather, but he looked nothing like the skeleton his nickname implied. "We are like the buzzards above, no?" He also had a gold tooth that flashed in the last of the sunlight.

The joke lightened the mood. Chino, who had chiseled Asian features, raised his weapon and aimed it toward the empty ridge. The teardrops tattooed from the corner of his left eye to his jawbone were the only water that ever fell from his eyes. "If he is not, I will punch holes in him until this gun dries up."

Dark clouds absorbed the sliver of sun and dusk arrived. The rugged country immediately lost its intense color, going flat and gray. Pepito, the silent one of the gang, slung a backpack over his shoulders and waited.

Abdullah pointed with a forefinger at the shortest man with a face tattooed with spiderwebs. One rough tattoo of a large spider clung to his left cheek. The remainder of the web appeared to be filled with its much smaller offspring. "That one is the smartest of you all. He is silent, but observant."

The others waited for Abdullah to start his Polaris. It was the only vehicle they had, and he'd used it to lure the Ranger deep into the unmarked Canyonlands far from where he'd ambushed the hikers. Instead of starting the four-wheeler's engine, he adjusted the Cobra across his chest for quick action and led the way on foot down to where the Ranger had been standing.

Surprised that he chose to walk instead of ride, the Coyotes Rabiosos followed the Syrian from their sniper position toward a game trail zig-zagging down the shallow slope and through the scrub brush. Yooko followed last, making a point to himself and the others that he was unafraid of anyone or anything.

Abdullah set a quick pace, hearing the armed illegals make enough noise for a company of men. He compared the slovenly gangsters behind him to the battle-hardened al-Qaeda fighters he'd worked with in the Jabhat al-Nusra outfit in his home country and found them wanting. These gangsters seemed as weak as kittens and lacked the religious fire his Islamist brothers kept stoked day and night.

Though both the gang's leader, Chatto, and to a lesser degree Chavez, said they were the deadliest of the Coyotes Rabiosos, the sullen men with false smiles seemed to be missing some vital cog in their mental machinery.

He adjusted the strap across his chest and under one arm. Abdullah's thin daypack was small enough that the .308 Win rifle rode comfortably across his back. He promised Allah that they'd search all night if they had to in order to find the body. Once they located Ranger Hawke's corpse, he'd bury most of him with these other five morons in the desert and piss on their graves.

The idea lifted his spirits, and he followed a game trail to the canyon's floor.

Chapter 6

It was darker than the inside of a casket when I finally woke up, but it wasn't nearly as comfortable. I wondered why I was laying on the ground. Rocks dug into my face, and I was wrapped in the distinctive odor of the high desert.

My left arm and side ached, and I remembered I'd been shot. I tried to blink my eyes clear, but still couldn't see. A jolt of fear ran down my spine when it occurred to me that I might be blind. I moved a foot to sit up and felt my boot bump into something.

Fine then. You're not paralyzed. That's a good thing.

The other foot moved as well. My back ached like hell, but an easy wiggle of my hips told me most of my traveling gear was working just fine. The gunshot wound throbbed, burning hot and feverish.

Fingers.

Yep, they moved.

I raised my head and the muscles that did all the work were sore as a risen. I went swimmy-headed and my thoughts got all fuzzy for a good long while. Even though the rocks added to the pressure in my skull, I had to rest again before things stopped spinning. The world came into focus, what there was of it. Glancing up, I realized it was so dark because of a thick cloud cover.

I put my hand on the ground to raise up and even that hurt. It started coming back to me, and I remembered grabbing at everything in reach when I was sliding down the mountain. Good lord! I fell off the cliff. I started to sit up and finish taking stock when I heard distant voices speaking Spanish.

It all came back to me. I remembered the exploding dove and echoing shot before falling off the edge. The fog lifted from my brain, and I finally made out the shape of a creosote bush between me and the voices.

The instincts of my Choctaw ancestors kicked in and I lay still as a nervous jackrabbit, trying to figure out where they were. The frigid desert night was so thick I couldn't see more than a few yards, and there was no way to know where they were coming from.

"Ya no volveremos a encontrar a este hijo de puta esta noche!"

It was the guys who'd shot me. They didn't know me well enough to call me such a bad name, but I knew better than to move.

The man's statement was answered by a second voice, but I couldn't make out what he was saying. They launched into a low-pitched conversation. More rocks clattered and a soft curse came from below, but I couldn't for the life of me figure out how that could be.

A third voice spoke in heavily accented English that I recognized as Middle Eastern. "You two shut up! Keep looking. He has to be *somewhere* around here."

These boys sure aren't here to help.

Boots shuffled on the hard ground. Someone kicked a rock and a startled bird flushed from the scrub. "*Vete a la mierda, pájaro. Casi me haces mear los pantalones.*" From the chuckles and harassment floating in the still air, there were more than three guys wandering around in the dark.

I raised my head and an unnatural flash of light from *below* told me I was layin' about twenty feet higher than the valley floor, right on the rim of a sharp drop. Propping myself on one elbow helped to see over the lip, but at the same time it brought a world of aches and pains. I figured that my whole body was a mass of black-and-blue bruises, but at least I was still alive and intended to stay that way.

The flashlight was intense. I had one of those new high-intensity lights the size of a dill pickle mounted onto the AR-15 back home and figured they were carrying something similar. If those guys had *theirs* mounted on the automatic weapons I'd heard, and there was no reason for them not to have them, then I wouldn't have a chance if one of the beams rooted me out.

A bright lance caught the fine dust in the air as it probed the ground at the searchers' feet, then angled up along the steep canyon wall farther down, giving me a good view of what was over there. The rocky wall was steep, and if I'd fallen from twenty yards south of my position, it most likely would have been a straight drop to the ledge.

The damnedest thing happened right then. A recollection of my old man chuckling at a Road Runner cartoon popped into my head. He always loved seeing the coyote fall to the desert floor much like the one I was in, until he landed with a tiny pop. I was lucky I hadn't ended up that way, but it looked like my luck was about to run out.

The lights played out into the canyon, illuminating nothing but scrub vegetation that disappeared into the darkness. Another beam aimed at the clouds.

The Middle Eastern voice was sharp, obviously annoyed. "He's not up in the *sky*."

Male voices chuckled again, and they spoke Spanish. This time the Mideast guy cut loose with a string of gobbledygook that I couldn't understand, but it was the tone of voice that shut the others up.

I figured there were at least three nearby, but wondered how many others were scouring the area. I'd only heard the one rifle that shot me, and two other fully automatic weapons on the way over, but that didn't mean anything right then. For all I knew, the country was alive with men carrying automatic weapons.

I thought I'd been ambushed by drug smugglers with backpacks full of marijuana and cocaine. They humped those loads weighing as much as sixty pounds or more at a time, making their way north from Mexico. Truthfully, we didn't see that many mules in Big Bend National Park, but they went through from time to time, as sure as shootin', and I'd seen the trails to prove it.

Most of the trouble down our way usually involved illegals trying to slip in to make their way north. Despite what Americans heard on the television news, the border area in Texas was infested with a steady stream of illegals crossing into the country. Every now and then the park rangers, and even tourists, would come across evidence of a trail. Most of the illegals avoided the park, though, because there are nearly four hundred bluffs and cliffs on the Rio, and that makes for hard walking.

Every now and then an illegal or two would try to cross down near Boquillas, but the roads funneled them toward places where they'd get caught. Another easy cross was at the Langford Hot Spring on the Texas side of the river. They usually found themselves sticking out like a sore thumb among the tourists.

Okay, check that. Probably not mules.

What then?

Coyotes. Not the four-legged kind, but hard, ruthless men paid to lead illegals into the country and, hopefully, to a rendezvous point that might be as far as three days away on foot. There they made contact with those who would move them farther or provide jobs. They sometimes left their clients, men and women, to die alone in the desert. Those guys didn't care if kids were with them, either. They often carried guns, but usually tried to avoid any kind of altercation with U.S. law-enforcement officials. But then again, there was always that one guy who didn't follow the norm.

I wonder if I stumbled across a whole covey of those trigger-happy idiots.

Anything was possible.

Chapter 7

Long shadows from a row of cottonwood trees and Faxon Yuccas bordering a cactus garden stretched across the Hawkes' arid front yard in Ballard. Yolanda Rodriguez and Perry Hale stepped onto the wrap-around porch of the farmhouse-style home. Yolanda stopped short of the door to let him do the knocking.

Kelly Hawke was expecting them, but peeked through the peephole just to be safe. She opened the iron door with a smile. "Hey! Y'all come on in."

Yolanda hugged her neck as she flowed inside with the grace of a dancer. That grace impacted everything she did, even when she practiced shooting outside of town with Perry Hale and his friends. Her long black hair and olive skin contrasted with a white silk blouse. Wrangler jeans and cowboy boots were as dressed up as she got.

The walls of what everyone called a "comfortable house" were filled with photos of the Hawke family dating back to the late 1800s. Several were of Sonny's dad Herman cheesing for the camera beside a number of high-profile officials and famous entertainers when he was a Texas Ranger.

Knowing Kelly's fondness for wine, Yolanda handed her a bottle of cabernet. "My mother told me never to go to someone's house without bringing a gift."

"You've been here dozens of times."

"Yep. This is my favorite cab right now. It was a good year with a hot summer and lots of rain."

Perry Hale followed them through the living room, past the leather sofa and easy chairs, and into the kitchen. Lean and roped with tendons and muscle, he looked more like a cowboy than a veteran marine. Sonny once told him that their daughter Mary described Perry Hale's walk as like that of Mr. Miyagi from the *Karate Kid* movie. Crow's-feet formed at the corners of his green eyes, listening to the women talk. "You've been here dozens of times? They've only invited me twice."

Kelly hugged *his* neck and stepped back. "Come in this house. That's because Yolanda drops by for coffee pretty regular, and you meet Sonny over at the Chat 'N Chew."

He took off his straw Stetson and hugged her back. "Fine, then. I get café eggs with a sorry Ranger and some dried-up old ranchers while y'all get to hang out on the porch and drink Folgers. That ain't right."

Yolanda raised a black eyebrow. "We drink Kona coffee, my friend."

Kelly was a teacher and had first met Yolanda and Perry back in November when terrorists held her hostage in the Ballard courthouse, along with the twins Mary and Jerry, their high school class of students, and nearly a dozen adult citizens who found themselves in the wrong place at the wrong time. Yolanda and Perry were only two of the responding citizens who rescued the hostages held at gunpoint that snowy day.

"I better get Hawaiian coffee after supper then." Perry Hale's growl didn't fool either of the women.

The two military veterans became good friends after the Ballard takeover, and had a lot in common. Yolanda and Perry Hale were part of Sonny's new Texas Ranger Shadow Response Team that didn't officially exist and hadn't yet been tested in the field. Though they weren't Rangers, they operated as law-enforcement officers under the vague umbrella that sheltered Sonny's SRT. The Texas governor issued badges to them with the admonition that they produce the authorization only when absolutely necessary, and he told Perry Hale they were never to be used to get out of a traffic ticket.

He growled that day in the governor's office in Austin and scratched his three-day-old beard. "All Yoli has to do is bat her eyes and she'll get a pass. I should at least get something out of this."

"You call me that again, I'll bat something else, Big Boy."

The governor agreed with Perry Hale's opinion. "You will, with a check once a month."

The tough military veteran hadn't known what to say to that.

The twins joined them in the kitchen. Kelly grinned when Jerry shook Perry Hale's hand, looking down on the man, who was a good four inches shorter. Yolanda hugged them before Mary sat at the table across from Perry Hale after barely saying hello.

"How's high school these days?" He leaned both elbows on the table.

Jerry rolled his eyes and dropped in his dad's chair at the head of the table. "The teachers are crazy. All they want to do is teach us stuff we don't need to know."

"Careful there, bubba." Kelly sat a platter of spaghetti in the middle of the table and juked around Yolanda, who pitched in to bring the sauce. "Remember what your mama does for a living. And don't you let your daddy catch you sitting there."

"Yeah, well, besides that, all we hear about at school is that stupid statewide test we have to take . . ."

". . . and I'd like to know more. Even in *our* class, Mama." Mary often completed his sentences. Kelly taught civics at Big Bend High, and because the campus was so small, one class of American History, which was the twins' favorite subject. Mary glanced down at the cell phone in her hand. The device glowed for a moment when her fingers flew over the screen as she answered a text and talked at the same time. "You know, no one ever told me that Christopher Columbus never really *discovered* America, and besides, the Indians had been here for maybe forty thousand years and back east they had villages and complete societies . . ."

"That's right." Jerry jumped in and they exchanged a look that revealed their connection. "Why didn't you tell us they . . . what do you call it?"

"Assimilated."

"Right, Sis. The Cherokees assimilated and owned grist mills and land by the 1830s . . ."

". . . and those were the ones left after 90 percent of their population died a couple of hundred years earlier from the diseases they caught from the first white men, and that's 90 percent of one hundred million, and I had to learn all that at the library, on my own."

Kelly thumped the open bottle of Robert Mondavi Bourbon Barrel wine onto the table. "That, my son, is the reason we have libraries, so you can take the initiative and learn on your own. That's enough, you two. We have guests, not a captive audience. Mary, try your daddy again and see how close he is, then get off the phone."

Mary punched at the screen, her thumbs flying. She still hadn't truly acknowledged Perry Hale's presence other than a side glance from the corners of her eyes. Anyone else would have thought she was being rude, but Kelly had already realized that her daughter had a serious crush on the man ten years her senior.

Her attention flicked from one to the other while Mary studied the screen. The high school junior keyed in a quick text, then switched to a different view to check two more social-media apps, all the while moving a bowl of salad from the island dividing the kitchen and the table in the open concept living area.

Yolanda raised an eyebrow. "Sonny in the middle of something?"

"He's late, as usual." Kelly poured three glasses. "He left yesterday and was supposed to be back this morning, but I haven't heard a word. Knowing him, his phone probably ran out of juice. He never plugs it in like he's supposed to."

It wasn't a surprise to any of them that Sonny wasn't there. Chronically late, his personal interest in the recent murder investigation made it different from the other crimes he handled, more intense and timely due to his friendship with the Cartwrights and the Hutchinses.

"He headed into the backcountry." Jerry jerked his head to the south. "He won't give up on what the TV calls the Big Bend Shooting. He took Red, so that means he's probably out of range."

Kelly shivered, fighting off a wave of sadness. "That's because we knew them."

Losing such good friends had been a shock. She and Sonny spent the following week grieving in their own way over the murders. Kelly stayed busy during the investigation, using her days of teaching at Ballard High to stave off wave after wave of tears.

Sonny handled it with anger at first and kept up a calm front with the family. But Kelly saw him more than once after the kids went into their rooms at night sitting on the back porch with a tall Bombay Sapphire and tonic, staring with wet eyes at the bright stars above.

The fact that they had originally planned to join the others on the hike added another level of fear and uncertainty.

"I tried to call, too." Mary punched the screen with her thumb and tucked the phone into the back pocket of her jeans. "It went to voicemail."

Perry Hale plucked a piece of French bread from a shallow wooden tray and dipped it into a bowl of seasoned oil. "You can get out of cell service pretty fast back in there."

"Well, let's eat." Kelly took her seat to the right of Sonny's empty chair at the farm table. "He'll be here when he can."

Chapter 8

"Over there. You, skinny one, Yooko, check up there on that ledge. The rest of you spread out and keep those lights in front, not in my face."

The voices told me those guys down below weren't too worried that I might be alive. Pieces of the puzzle began to fall into place. The odd man out spoke English as a common language so the Mexicans could understand.

"He has to be here somewhere."

I rolled onto my stomach, biting back a groan. The bullet wound under my arm shot jolts of hot pain down my side and into my armpit. My stomach rolled and I thought I was going to puke, but it passed. At least the nausea took my mind off the other hurts that were throbbing to beat the band. I'd knocked a lot of bark off my hide on the way down, and my right knee ached like the devil.

Getting to a position where I could see, I raised my head. At first there was nothing until I rose a little higher. That angle let me see over a rock the size of one of those old console TV sets. Six distinct flashlight beams played over the ground below, probing under bushes and behind boulders the size of my first apartment. They were working the area pretty hard, expecting that I'd rolled all the way to the bottom.

Well I hadn't. A boulder stopped my tumble and saved me from making a final long, sheer plunge. It was a wonder I'd survived as it was, but the straight drop would have probably finished me off.

I don't know how long I'd laid there unconscious in the cold, but it couldn't have been more than an hour. That's the amount of time I figured they needed to hike down from the canyon rim. I didn't know that part of the country, and for all I knew it was so rough it might've taken them two or three hours.

Look at your watch, dummy.

The Old Man's voice was loud in my ear and I took his advice, but my wristwatch that Kelly'd given me for Christmas was long gone, replaced by a pretty impressive gash that showed the white tissue below. It still leaked a little blood, but not as much as you'd expect.

I'd laid a finger open on a piece of bob-wire once when I was about twelve, and the sight of the white tendons then caused me to get swimmy-headed. I felt a little better that at least I'd grown tough enough not to swoon at such a sight.

The sounds coming from below told me those guys were getting frustrated. One of 'em finally had the sense to look up. "Maybe he stopped up there." His Mexican accent was heavy, but I'd been around Hispanics most of my life and understood his words that were clear as branch water.

His flashlight beam danced over the scrub brush

covering the steep slope over my shoulder. He kept it moving pretty fast, and soon it skipped up into the darkness.

A second beam joined his and I ducked as it explored the rocks below and above where I lay. "See anything?"

They spoke in Spanish between the two of them.

I knew enough of their language to work out that *ver cualquier cosa* meant they were looking for me. Most folks in Ballard knew a little Spanish, and I was like them, understanding more than I could speak.

"I would have said so, wouldn't I?" One of the guys launched off in a stream of curses that would have made my good friend and the Old Man's hired hand proud. Gabriel Nakai had worked for my dad as a ranch hand for years and was part of the family. He spoke English as well as most of us, but he never learned to cuss, and that kept us laughing whenever we pitched in to help work cows or fix fences.

This guy was a pro at cussin' in Spanish and only quit when the voice with the Middle East accent had enough. "Yooko! Why don't you stop talking and check it out?"

Ol' Yooko switched back to English. "You want me to climb up there in the dark?"

"We are not waiting until sunrise. I expect someone to come looking for him as soon as it's light."

"It will be easier with the sun. I am hungry. Let us sit here and eat our tortillas. Then we can get some sleep and be fresh in the morning."

The man's voice went cold. "You will do as I say, *comprende*?"

Yooko hesitated for a moment and I knew he was as

scared of that Middle East feller as I was of a bear. "*Sí, jefe.*"

My little hidey-hole was about to get real unsafe. Shivering both from fear and the cold, I crawfished backward on the sharp stones to get my back against the slope. It real fast proved to be uphill and didn't work especially well with the bullet wound catching fire every time I flexed my arm. Stifling a groan, I pulled myself up into a crouch and peeked through the brush again. A narrow beam of light worked its way to my left, darting around like a little kid playing with a flashlight.

Yooko was making slow progress. Every now and then I heard him slide and cut loose with another string of curses. It was hard work that told me there wasn't a trail to where I was hiding, so he was making his way up a raw slope, avoiding cactus, and trying to be quiet all at the same time.

They were expecting a body, not a live person, and that worked in my favor, or would when the time came. I lay still, hoping he'd fall and break his damned neck.

The one that concerned me was the leader. Ahab the Arab, as I thought of him, was in charge, and that usually made those guys the worst of them all. Oh, I really didn't think he was Arabian. He could have been Syrian, Iranian, Iraqi, for all I knew. No matter who his daddy was, he had to be a terrorist and from my experience, that made him dangerous as hell.

I remembered I hadn't checked to see if the 1911 was still in my holster. I gave the .45 a pat and found that the thumb-break had done its job. The semi-automatic on my gun belt was still there. My two spare magazines on the left side were where they were supposed to be, though the entire Ranger rig was up around the middle of my waist and not riding snug like the companion belt holding my britches on.

Knowing the snap was bound to be loud in the desert night, I waited to release the weapon until Yooko slipped and cursed again, sounding like he'd taken a knee on the steep rise. Rocks rattled to the canyon floor, and he struggled to stay on his feet. The snap was barely audible when it released. Even that slight movement pulled the gunshot wound and I stifled a grunt.

The smooth Sweetheart Grips on Granddad's old Colt 1911 were comforting and it calmed me. During World War II, American soldiers replaced the textured grips on their pistols with clear, lightweight Lucite from the viewing ports of warplanes. To personalize the handguns, they put photos of their gals beneath the grips. The photo was also an easy way for a soldier to identify his pistol from others. Sometimes they put photos on both sides, but Granddad left one side of the grip clear so he could see at a glance how many rounds were left.

I tried not to look into the lights to preserve my night vision as the men continued their search. My thumb found the cocked hammer, and I shook the pistol a couple of times to jiggle out any rocks or dirt.

It was hard to tell in the dark if the action was clear. Letting the hammer down would have been the best way, but I was afraid my thumb'd slip and fire off a round, so I stuck my little finger in the tight space to be sure there were no rocks or dirt between it and the striker pin. I ground my teeth and almost squealed when I discovered that the fingernail had been ripped off in the fall. By then I knew I'd be finding even more dings and scratches that hadn't yet woken up.

The gun was clear, and I was as satisfied as I was gonna get.

I waited and hoped they'd give up and move on to search somewhere else.

Chapter 9

They'd been searching for the Ranger's body for over an hour and Abdullah's frustration grew as dark as the night around them. He directed the tactical light on his weapon at the steep canyon wall rising into the darkness, trying to guess where the Ranger had been when he fell. From that angle, everything looked different.

The entire operation had been bad luck all around and he blamed the two idiot gangsters, Yooko and Javier, for the whole thing. They'd been a constant source of irritation from the moment he joined up with the gang down in Paso La Carmen, a ghost town southeast of the National Park, on the Mexico side of the Rio Grande. He recalled that his brother Kahn had no patience for men who weren't good at their jobs.

If he'd still been alive, Kahn would have already shot them both and left their bodies to the buzzards.

But he'd been killed months before, and that's why Abdullah was there that frustrating night. He was to kill the Ranger who'd disrupted the terrorists' plan and shot Kahn. Now Abdullah was the leader of Chavez's special cell and planned to exact his revenge, get paid, and use that money to fund their next act of *jihad*, an attack on a Kansas shopping mall in the heart of America to prove that no one was safe.

Oh sure, he'd told Chavez something completely different, but he didn't like or trust the *al ferengi* or creepy man with bizarre mental issues.

Abdullah whispered into the darkness. "Javier."

"Yes." His flashlight beam lit the brush and cactus thirty feet above the canyon floor.

"Any sign?"

"Nothing yet. We should wait . . . ."

"Yooko?" Something stirred in the darkness farther down the canyon, but Abdullah ignored it. "Yooko!" He paused when the dimming beam of Yooko's light pointed in his direction. "Anything?"

Yooko spoke in a disgusted voice. "No. I think Javier may be right. We'll never find the body tonight."

The cold seeped into Abdullah's bones and his spirits sagged. "Keep looking until I say we stop. I told you to find a way up to that ledge."

Yooko continued upward, playing his beam over the ground and scant cover, as if he were afraid the Ranger was going to pop up at any moment. He swept the vertical wall before probing the wide, cactus-covered slope. "I found a trail." It was obvious that the shelf wasn't a dead end. Deer wouldn't establish trails unless the shelf led to other access points.

Javier took a step to the side to gain a better viewpoint, and a jackrabbit exploded from its hiding place only three feet away. The gangster jumped and squeezed the trigger on his Cobra, sending a string of bullets after the fleeting rabbit.

Shouting and cursing, the other two gangsters in the line of fire ducked for cover in the bright flashes of light as the rounds came dangerously close. Calaka dropped behind a boulder until the shooting stopped. He leaned out and aimed his own machine pistol at his friend, the flashlight beam picking out Javier's shocked face. *"No me dispares, hijo de puta mudo!"*

Javier froze in the light and lowered his weapon while at the same time raising his left hand to block the light in his eyes. "I wasn't shooting at you! I thought it was that damned Ranger. And don't talk about my mother like that again or I *will* shoot you!"

Yooko's voice rose over the confrontation, cursing at the harsh desert vegetation on the rising slant leading to the ledge. *"Condenados* cactus!" The light in his hand jittered along the rocks and scrub as he plucked a needle from his leg. He straightened and steadied the beam toward a large boulder near the edge of the shelf. *"Que es eso?"*

Holding the Cobra across his belly, Pepito raised his bulldog face toward the wavering light above. "What's what?"

Yooko paused for a long moment, then reverted to his native language in excitement that turned to terror. *"Detenerse! Aquí está él . . . y él no está muerto!"*

The Syrian cursed in his language, then switched to Spanish. "What? What did he say?"

Javier quickly translated for Abdullah.

The Syrian jerked his rifle's muzzle back to the

shelf. "You see him? He's not dead?! Shoot him now! Shoot him!"

Strobes flashed overhead as automatic gunfire hammered throughout the canyon to echo across the cold, dark desert. Two distinct shots followed and there was momentary silence before the men below threw a fusillade toward the ledge overhead.

Chapter 10

The meal was long over. Two empty wine bottles and glasses were the only things left on the farmhouse table. The clock read 11:00 and cool night air flowed through the screens on the open windows.

Mary Hawke draped herself across a stuffed chair in the living room while the adults talked. She'd cleared the table and loaded the dishwasher. Jerry had done his part washing the pots and pans and was in his room.

The iPhone in her hand came alive and she punched the Snapchat icon, scrolling through the latest posts. Her thumbs flew across the screen and when she was finished, she hit Post to enter still another photo of her and Yolanda cheesing for the camera.

She snuck a quick shot of Perry Hale reclining on the couch. She sent the snap to her best friend Gillian, expecting it to vanish ten seconds later after she had a chance to see the guy who unconsciously suffered Mary's huge crush. "This guy!"

Mary also posted a photo she'd shot earlier of the table full of dirty dishes and glasses. "Finished for the day after another meal without Dad. Good news! School is almost out!"

The mood had turned sour. Kelly chewed her lip and sat her empty wineglass on the coffee table. "Now I'm getting worried."

"You and me both." Yolanda crossed her blue-jeaned legs and wiggled her boot, a nervous habit she'd had all her life. "Doesn't he have a radio in his truck?"

"He does. Ethan talked to him this morning, but Sonny tried to call in about an hour before sunset and the static was so bad Ethan couldn't understand anything he was saying."

Sheriff Ethan Armstrong and Sonny were childhood friends. They met not long after Sonny and his dad moved to Ballard. The boys had been there for each other ever since.

Perry Hale reclined on the couch in his sock feet, making himself at home on Kelly's orders. "We probably need to do something, but I don't know what."

"I sent a text to Major Parker a few minutes ago." He was Sonny's superior in the Texas Rangers. "He hasn't heard anything from Sonny in a couple of days, either. He said he was going to be here in the morning. He's worried, too."

"I guess I can try Ethan again." Country folks tend to avoid phoning each other after it gets late, and by nine, a call in the night usually spelled a disaster of some kind. Kelly sent a text. She laid the phone on the table only seconds before it vibrated with a response. She read it aloud. "I tried about an hour ago. No answer on the radio or his cell."

She started to reply when the phone's *noir* tone told her it was Ethan calling back. She answered without the usual pleasantries, grateful that he'd called so they could talk instead of text. "We're getting worried. There's more?"

"So am I, and no, but I'm all thumbs when it comes to texting. He should have checked in long ago, and you know that, but there's not a stinkin' thing we can do tonight. What's worrying you more about this time than the others? He comes in late all the time."

"This is the second night he's been out. We had dinner plans and he'd been looking forward to it. He always checks in if he's going to be late, but I haven't heard a word in almost twenty-four hours. Hang on." Kelly laid the phone on the table and punched an icon. "You're on speaker. Yolanda and Perry Hale are here. They haven't heard anything, either."

"Hey, guys. We can't do anything tonight, even if we wanted to, other than to drive into the park, but I don't know where he went."

"Knowing Sonny, he's back at the murder scene." Perry Hale leaned toward the phone and scratched his short beard. "I'm going out there tomorrow morning at first light. If nothing else, I'll find his tracks."

Ethan was silent for a moment. "I figured you'd say that."

Ethan saw Perry Hale in action back in November and knew the man was solid as a rock. Any time anyone went missing in Big Bend, the National Park Service used their team of experienced rangers to locate and rescue the individuals. In cases where the search took more than a few hours, or even stretched into

days, the Park Service often contracted other federal
resources from nearby parks such as Big Bend State
Park to send auxiliary personnel.

Local law enforcement or sheriffs had little or no
experience in wilderness locations, but Perry Hale's
military history had proven valuable in a Search and
Rescue, or SAR, mission and was instrumental in finding a missing Galveston man who'd gotten off the Mule
Ears Trail and wandered for two days in the desert
without water. Perry Hale caught a glimpse of a faint
footprint near a creosote bush. He and two other park
rangers followed tiny signs until they located the severely dehydrated hiker curled up in the shade of a
boulder.

"I'll pack the truck and be ready to go at first light."
Perry Hale swung his feet to the floor and pulled on his
boots.

"I'm going with you." Yolanda rose lithe as a cat
and stood as if they were leaving right then.

Ethan continued to talk as if ticking off a check
sheet. "You'll have to drive your own vehicles as volunteers. I can't officially take y'all with me."

"We'll come together." Yolanda glanced toward
Perry Hale, who nodded. "Is there anything else we
can do before you leave in the morning?"

The tone in his voice told them Ethan was shrug-
ging. "Not that I can think of right now. He's probably
asleep in the back of his truck. I'll see y'all in the
morning."

Never one to mince words, Perry Hale sighed. "I've
got a bad feeling about this all of a sudden."

Kelly took a long, shuddering sigh. "I wish I had the
training to go with you."

Yolanda, ever the optimist, the corner of her mouth rose. "We'll find him tomorrow, and then you're gonna have to cook supper for all of us again."

"Okay." Kelly ticked her fingers on the table. "Call me if you hear anything."

"Will do."

Ethan was gone, and Kelly opened her laptop. "You guys can stay here if you want."

Yolanda returned to her chair. "That's probably a good idea. Perry?"

Torn, he shrugged. "May as well. That way we won't be trying to do all this on a phone, but we leave early."

Relieved that they were going to stay, Kelly logged into her computer and pulled up her Facebook page. At least she could reach out to her friends and see if any of them had any information on Sonny's whereabouts. "I'm going to check here and then try to get some sleep."

She was startled when her Facebook page loaded with a new comment to her announcement two weeks earlier that she was looking forward to an upcoming hike she and Sonny were going to take with Harmony, Vince, Blue, and Chloe. Her stomach tightened and she deleted the post.

No longer tired, she swallowed the lump in her throat. "I'll get some coffee going in a little while. I think we're gonna need it."

Chapter 11

I thought the Yooko guy was going to miss me with his flashlight. The beam was bright and narrow, and he didn't seem really interested in his job, waving the light around in the air so much it looked like one of those searchlights they used when I was a kid to attract folks to a grand opening.

I almost pulled the trigger on the Colt when everything broke loose down below. Somebody must have thought he saw something, because a machine gun opened up with a nasty ripping sound. Men shouted and angry voices rose up as soon as the shooting stopped. I caught part of it again and realized they were as amped up as me.

Then when the guy approaching stepped smack in the middle of a big clump of cactus, it looked like I was home free. He yelped and danced sideways, brushing several pads of prickly pear on the way. He started cussin', too, and his beam cut the air like a light saber, finally catching the steep slope of fallen rocks behind me. It skittered there while he plucked the biggest spines out of his leg.

If there'd been a bobcat within two miles, it would have had a field day chasing that point of light across the rocks and sand. Dumbass pulled a few more spines out, cussing everything he could think of. The pain must've sharpened his mind a little bit so he could focus on why he was up there in the first place.

He probed the dark, looking under a catclaw bush, and the odds finally caught up with me when he saw my boot. It would have been comical to watch on television as he locked in on my scuffed Lucchese ostrich skins, then followed it up my leg, torso, and finally blinded me.

There was a sharp intake of breath when he saw me squint my eyes and realized I was alive. "What's that" in Spanish and it reminded me of Billy the Kid's last words, "Who is it?" before Pat Garrett allegedly shot him.

Truthfully, it doesn't matter what he said, or how he said it. I should have put him down the minute his light found my foot, hell, I should have shot him when they opened up down below and my rounds would have been lost in the blasts and echoes, but it was that niggling thought most law-enforcement officers have that maybe, just maybe, he wasn't going to really shoot me.

Fine then, I'd already been shot, but maybe it wasn't him that did it and he was there to help. See, that's how your mind can get warped when you're shot off the side of a mountain and roll two hundred feet like a snowball to find yourself lying on the edge of still *another* cliff while people with machine guns look for you.

All doubt fled when Ahab down below hollered up for Yooko to shoot me. And he didn't say it just once, he said it twice. Kinda like when a mom hollers "no, no, no!" three times to make a point to keep a little kid from doing something bad or dangerous. Emphasis by repetition.

He dropped the flashlight and yanked the trigger on a nasty-looking little machine pistol instead of squeezing it at the same time a tactical light came on his rifle. The rounds shredded a creosote bush. The .45 was already in my hand, and I pulled the trigger twice, feeling the big Colt buck.

Partially blinded by both lights, I aimed a little low and to his left, hoping the guy was right-handed. He hollered "oh!" and the tactical light went out. At the same time, all hell broke loose down below as more beams crisscrossed the darkness.

They weren't interested in conserving ammo when they opened up on full auto. They must have bought it by the truckload. Muzzle flashes down there were strobe-light-fast, flickering off the canyon walls and freeze-framing what little I could see.

I'm not sure what they were shooting at, because I was still low to the ground and out of sight, but goddlemighty did they cut loose for a good long while. Bullets whanged on rocks lining the ledge's lip and much higher on the wall due to their angle. I might could've crawled to the edge and shot at the muzzle flashes, but I had something else on my mind.

I wanted whatever automatic weapon Dumbass Yooko had around his neck.

While gunshots echoed off the canyon wall and ricochets screamed into the darkness, I snatched up the little flashlight and scuttled toward the dying man like a crab. Every movement sent lances of pain though my shoulder and side, but the time for curling up and whining was in the far distant future.

If I had one.

There was a lot of hollerin' going on down below, and Ahab was issuing orders. Dumbass was on his back, making wet, gurgling sounds when I reached him, but he was limp as a dishrag. Cupping the little flashlight in my left hand, I passed it over the solid mass of tattoos covering the man's face.

I'd seen guys like him in wanted posters and they all looked scary as hell. This one was no different. Though his black hair was long, unlike a lot of those guys in the posters, he was as tatted up as any gangster I'd ever seen. Both pupils were dilated in the light, so I knew he was gone before he did.

The first thing I did was check out the weapon lying on his chest. I'm not *that* gun guy, and don't know squat about most firearms and tactical accessories. I pulled it away from his body and something that felt like a wire slapped my forearm when I twisted the weapon. It wasn't hard to figure out it was a pressure switch that activated the tactical light. Hoping to have time later to figure out how it worked, I went to work on the hard part, getting the gun free. I'd had experience with getting a slung rifle off a dead body, but it didn't help much.

The shooting was over by the time I gave up and fished the lockblade out of my back pocket to cut the nylon strap free. There was no way to wrestle it off, and I figured my time was limited before they came charging up that same skinny slope, guns blazing again.

Sticking my .45 back in the holster, I yanked the unfamiliar weapon free. Dumbass' chest hitched one more time, and then he was gone. That was fine by me. I'd already helped several felons get through the gates of Hell, and one more wouldn't add much more time to the guilt I wrestled with on most nights.

I patted his pockets and located four extra magazines heavy with stacked rounds while keeping an eye on the beams darting every which way. Flipping him over wasn't easy with one hand, but I rolled him enough to drag the daypack off his shoulders.

I figured I was out of time. The sound of footsteps scuffling on the slope told me someone else was on the way. Ahab was shouting at people down below, ordering them to take up positions . . . like I was gonna come charging down at 'em.

Crab-crawling back to my boulder, I had a decision to make. I could stay right where I was to make my stand and wait for help to come. I could hold them off for a while from my position, but they were loaded for bear, and five mags of ammo for the automatic weapon, and my three for the .45, didn't seem like enough

My other option was to follow the ledge and find a way out under the cover of darkness. I liked that idea best. Historically, forting up never seemed to be the best option. The guys at the Alamo proved that.

Jolts of pain lit me up as I slipped my left arm through the daypack's strap. It wasn't any better when I got into the other strap and shrugged it into place.

Cupping my hand over the tac-light, I found the pressure switch and gave it a squeeze. My fist glowed, and I cracked two fingers to let out a narrow beam. It showed me the fresh rocks I'd brought to the bottom with me, and beyond that, what looked like a thin trail leading off in the opposite direction from where the bad guy came from.

"Yooko? Dónde está?"

"Ha do aai fuera!"

Two whispered voices on my level reached my ears, telling me time was up. One spoke Spanish, and the other a curious mix of that and some Indian dialect. It sounded like some Apache I'd heard, but I'm not even close to a linguist.

They were on the way. Keeping low and bent almost double, I retreated to the opposite side of the boulder that suddenly seemed much smaller now that I was standing.

The clouds above split and my whole plan went haywire when the full moon appeared, washing the world in cold blue light that filled the valley. My ledge continued along the side of the canyon and widened into a slope leading down and away from the killers. From my vantage point, I could see far into the canyon.

And so could they.

Chapter 12

The clouds parted, revealing the moon-bleached valley. Pupils slowly constricting to adapt to the silver glow, Abdullah caught a flicker of movement up and to the right.

Using his flashlight beam to show his men, he swept it across the lip. "There! I saw something move!"

Javier and Calaka were halfway up the slope when the Syrian shouted. Crouching, they held their weapons as far out as the straps would allow and slowed their approach.

When no one shot, Abdullah released the pressure switch and closed his eyes to allow his pupils to dilate. "You two, Chino, Pepito. Follow the canyon wall and cut him off if that ledge continues. There may be a way down. Be ready for him."

Chino kept one eye on the ledge above, as if Abdullah had seen a mountain lion. *"Sí, jefe!"* He took off at a jog, followed by the mostly silent Pepito, the only one of the gangsters Abdullah could tolerate.

Abdullah waited for a full thirty seconds as his eyes became accustomed to the moonlight. The clouds from a collapsed thunderstorm raced off toward the south, and the unfiltered moonlight was bright and strong, revealing the valley floor in surprising detail.

Keeping the muzzle of his Cobra pointed at the ridge where he'd last seen movement, he paced Javier and Calaka, winding between boulders and prickly vegetation. He moved slowly, alternating his concentration on the cactus-studded ground and the possibility of an attack from above, at the same time wondering how the man he'd shot off the edge of a cliff could have possibly survived.

And with enough life left in him to fight back.

Chapter 13

The huge River Oaks house in Houston was silent as Chavez paced the new mesquite hardwood floor in his bare feet. He'd realized months earlier just how filthy his house was when workers arrived to replace the living-room carpet.

It was all the obsessive-compulsive terrorist master-mind could do not to scream when he saw the under-side of what he thought was clean carpet. Several strange stains yellowed the backing.

"What is that filth?"

The hourly carpet layer looked up from his work in surprise. "What?"

"Those stains! And on the floor, where did all that dirt come from?"

"Sir, it's not unusual for carpet to have stains. It's not dog or cat pee, but you can see where something was spilled. It looks like the carpet cleaners used a chemical to get it out." He flipped the material back over. "See? There aren't any stains in the fibers on this side."

"But this carpet is only a year old."

Frowning, the Hispanic worker shrugged. "I can see that. Why are you changing it out so soon?"

"That's not the point. This is supposed to be stain-proof and antimicrobial. Look how filthy it is! Filthy, filthy, filthy."

"Sir. It's stain resistant, not stain-proof, and all carpet gets dirty. It comes in on people's shoes."

From there the argument disintegrated into a one-sided shouting match resulting in solid-wood flooring throughout the house. Now guests were required to remove their shoes upon entering, Hawaiian style, keeping the polished floors clean and unscuffed.

The smooth boards under Chavez's feet calmed him as he paced the living room, bagged TV remote in one hand and a glass of 25-year-old Glenlivet in the other. A satellite phone was squared on the dividing island between the kitchen and living room, perfectly aligned with the counter's edge and the open laptop turned so he could see it.

It was everything he could do not to dial the phone. Instead, Chavez sat the scotch down on a coaster and picked up his iPhone. He punched at the screen until he found the number he was looking for.

The heavily accented Hispanic voice on the other end was friendly, but reserved. "Yes?"

"Have you heard anything?"

"No. Your man said he would call when they have the . . . package. We have not heard from him, and I suppose you have not, either."

"He said the target was in sight the last time we spoke."

"I prefer the word 'package,' and like I said, nothing. I am sure it will be delivered. There may have been issues with the retrieval."

Why doesn't he pronounce 'head?' This is a secure phone for Chrissake. We should be able to speak freely instead of this spy shit.

Chavez placed the sanitized remote on the counter and took a huge swallow of scotch. He passed the sole of his bare right foot over the smooth floor, breathing deeply to calm himself. The 80-inch flat-panel television on the wall was muted and tuned to CNN. "It's getting late."

"Yes."

"I am concerned."

"Look, try to be patient. The call will come through. When it does, I'll get my package and you'll get your revenge."

You'll get the Ranger's head, and I'll get some relief. "I hope your people know what they're doing."

"My people will do their jobs. I brought them in especially for this one. It's your vengeful associate that is untested."

"He came highly recommended by those who trained him."

"Then there should be no problems. Relax. It will be over soon."

"Have your people taken care of the second issue? Has his family been eliminated? Remember our deal. I wanted Hawke and his entire family wiped out."

The voice hesitated. "There was an issue of too many players on the field. They had to wait and regroup, but I can promise you that by this time tomorrow night, they too will be neutralized."

"Fine then." Chavez saw something on the floor that concerned him. "I will speak to you later."

"I'm sure you will."

Chavez punched the phone off, keeping an eye on the floor.

He tapped his computer's keyboard, bringing the laptop to life. He'd long ago learned how to hack into a Snapchat feed. Using a fictitious name, Chavez's stolen information revealed him to be one of Mary Hawke's high school friends.

A common misconception is that Snapchat photos disappear forever after one to ten seconds, however Chavez had long since learned where they resided in the dim recesses of the online digital world.

Mary Hawke had posted a photo of her and an attractive Hispanic woman a few years older. The accompanying message read: Dad's late for supper again, and we're starving! The timestamp read 9:30 P.M. He grinned to himself, knowing that Sonny Hawke wouldn't be home for supper that night or any other.

A quick scan of her latest posts told him nothing else about the girl or her Texas Ranger dad. Oh well, she'd feed him more information later. It was her habit to send a flurry of Snapchat photos later in the evening before going to bed.

He jumped over to a Facebook page he'd stolen. "His" photo in the newsfeed was of a middle-aged woman by the name of Norma Wilson. She was a real person who lived in Ballard, but the remainder of the page was bogus. Chavez then scanned Kelly Hawke's most recent posts, seeing that she and Sonny planned to attend a local barbecue dinner in a week. Finding nothing else, he'd wait until eleven, when she usually posted a comment or two before turning in.

She'd have plenty to post later tonight.

That finished, a spot on the floor finally had his full attention. Chavez knelt as if sneaking up on a scorpion and dropped to his hands and knees to better see the one mesquite board that had caught his eye. A knot in the wood caused a small imperfection to show.

He stifled a whine.

It was a hole, roughly the size of half his little fingernail, that caught a small amount of fine dirt.

His eyes widened at the thought of what might already be growing in there.

He snatched his cell phone from the counter and pushed a button. He had the flooring manager on speed dial. No matter that it was late. He'd paid for quality and by-God he was going to get it.

Chapter 14

I wanted to run more than anything, but even with the moonlight bathing everything with a soft glow, it was still too dangerous.

Now just use your head before you go charging down to the bottom of the canyon. It's too dangerous to move fast. Slow and steady, Son, slow and steady.

Thanks, Pop. I'll do just that.

Jaw flexing as I ground my teeth, I forced myself to hold back to a fast walk heading southeast. I didn't like the direction worth a flip, because it was taking me farther and farther from the most traveled part of the park and well into some damn rough country.

Though I'd been at it for five minutes, the ledge kept going. At one point, it narrowed down until it was barely six feet wide and overhung by towering cliffs that felt like they could come down at any time.

Had it not been for the bare game trail winding through the plants, I never would have made it. The next thirty or forty yards scared the pee-waddlin' out of me, because the brush quit and the trail narrowed to only four feet before it widened again.

It wasn't like I could see as well as daylight, even though I could have read a book if I'd angled it just right. The ledge continued to fan out, but the landscape was full of dark corners, shadows, and holes. The bushes and cactus glowed, and for a while it was easy to avoid them. It was a good thing, too. I didn't need legs full of spines and stickers. No one could stand that for very long, and it would for sure slow me down with every painful step.

I slid stock still at the sound of a hoarse, whistling cough and brought the unfamiliar machine pistol to bear. Finger along the trigger guard, I waited.

Listen.

Check your surroundings.

A slight movement caught my attention, along with what sounded like a foot stamping the ground. I relaxed at the familiar sound and broke into a slow jog. A doe wheeled and bounded away.

The bullet wound under my arm was still firing lances of pain down my side. The worst of the bleeding had stopped while I was unconscious, but my shirt was stuck to the dried blood. Every movement pulled the material, and I felt the wound soften with fresh blood.

Dozens of other aches and pains woke up as my body warmed and chased the night's chill away. My boots sounded like horses' hooves on the hard trail. I tried jogging on my tiptoes, but that got tiring fast.

The cool night breeze helped clear my head, and the fuzziness was gone, leaving a slight headache. The adrenaline dump was wearing off at the same time, and I wondered about shock. I was functioning better than

I would have expected, but the human body can take just so much before it folds up to regroup.

Cactus crowded closer to the trail and I slowed. Succulents. I recalled the sign above a table full of one-gallon pots of cactus on sale at in the plant nursery back home. Kelly and I'd argued to a standstill that day when she wanted to plant cactus in our yard. I was against anything that could cut, poke, or stick me, and she couldn't understand why.

I crouched to pull a cactus needle out of my calf. I hadn't been completely successful at avoiding them. A coyote yipped in the distance. Another answering yip followed and seconds later a whole pack tuned up. They were chasing something, and the barks and yapping became frantic. I had nothing to fear from them, they'd probably kicked up a rabbit, but those sounds could help cover my own noise, I hoped. My lips were dry, and my tongue was already starting to stick to the roof of my mouth.

Water.

A sudden sinking feeling in my gut took some of the spirit out of me. My water supply vanished with Red when he ran off. If I had any water at all, it was in the pack I hadn't yet checked out. It was heavy all right, and if the bad guy I'd killed was from anywhere around there, he was sure to have water.

But how much?

The traditional rule of thumb is at least a gallon per person, per day, but we always carried twice that amount on our hikes. It sure didn't feel like there was more than a gallon back there. Let's see, one gallon equals seven pounds. The pack was at least twice that, so maybe I'd be all right for a day or two.

Any other time, I could have hiked out of the canyon without too much to worry about, if I knew where I was. Half a dozen mountains and pinnacles were easily identifiable from the right perspectives. But after falling off the cliff and suffering a gunshot wound, I wasn't exactly sure where I was.

That part of the country was cut up and crisscrossed with arroyos and washes, often leading to deep canyons that eventually drain into the Rio Grande. That is, if there's any water to drain, and that's a stretch of the imagination until one of those storm trains comes through that flushes the entire country.

You let 'em lead you into the middle of nowhere, dummy.

I wished I could have taken a better look at that guy I'd killed back there, but there was one thing I was sure of, the dark tattoo on the side of his neck, and those on his arms weren't from any professional tattoo parlor. I figured him to be at least an ex-con or cartel member who'd spent much of his life behind bars, or a gangster, and probably a combination of the two.

Mexican gangsters in the Big Bend spelled nothing but trouble for me and innocent civilians. I'd also gotten that brief glimpse at a tattoo on Dumbass Yooko's neck that seemed familiar, but I couldn't place it. It sure wasn't fancy, a squiggly horizontal line intersected by four lines curving downward and to the right, like those rain showers I'd seen in the distance, ending with a perpendicular convex line cutting across at the bottom.

I'd seen it on a wanted poster, maybe, or even in a photograph, and that's where my mind kept coming back to, something about an accident. The Occidental Saloon in Buffalo, Wyoming, kept coming to mind, but what could that have to with the dead guy's tattoo?

There was something about his features that wasn't quite right, either. He didn't look like most of the full-blood Mexicans I'd known. He was shorter, squatty, and slightly bowlegged, like the darker-skinned *Indios* I'd run across in the past.

I checked my back trail to see a flash of high-intensity light skittering along the boulders, shrubs, and cactus, seeking me out.

Someone was coming.

Chapter 15

Surrounded by nothing but scrub brush, I was caught in the open like a rabbit under a hawk. I did what the bunny would do. I froze, hoping the light would miss me.

Don't move, Son, and he might not see you.

The Old Man told me that once when we were walking along an arroyo, looking for deer tracks. We stepped around a bush to see a twelve-point buck with thick antlers. Pop gripped my shoulder and held me still.

The buck didn't see us, but something else spooked him and he whirled to run right past us. The Old Man reached out and the tips of his fingers grazed the deer's side. "I count coup on you!"

The buck kicked in the afterburners at Dad's shout and streaked away. Counting coup by touching the deer meant it was as good as dead in Dad's eyes, and that's how I felt standing there. As good as dead, because the guy intent on killing me and not just counting coup was about fifty yards off.

But nothing happened. I realized he'd ruined his night

vision with the flashlight. Either that, or he must've been looking down at his feet, because he never saw me. Then again, I was as still as that rabbit under a hawk.

The only thing that moved were my eyes, which flicked over the huge tumbledown boulders jumbled up at the base of the cliff wall maybe thirty or forty yards away. It's funny how your mind can work out problems in a hurry. One of those boulders was the size of a small house, and it was surrounded by dozens more of various sizes, offering protection in the shadows underneath.

I just needed to get there without trading gunshots.

He still hadn't seen me, and my luck held when the break in the clouds closed and the valley floor once more plunged into darkness. Despite the desperate need to run, I dropped to the hard ground and stifled a grunt when about a hundred cuts, bruises, and gunshot wounds shrieked in protest. Lying on my stomach, I made myself count to sixty, listening all the while. When I opened them back up again, it was a world of shapes and shadow.

Bent like Quasimodo to find a trail through the shrub and prickly pear, I moved perpendicular to the approaching beam. I concentrated on both sides of the imaginary path before me, knowing the rods in my eyes were incredibly efficient at picking out shapes if I used my peripheral vision instead of looking directly at the ground.

The guy's night vision was shot from the light on his rifle, but mine was good enough to avoid the plants. The growth tapered off close to the tumbledown, and a dozen dark shadows offered protection, but I wouldn't take it. There was no way I was going to trap myself in a hole where all he had to do was stand outside and spray into the opening.

I had a better idea that improved the closer I got. The jumble of boulders offered a way to climb, and that's what I did when I reached the pile, gritting my teeth at the shrieks coming from the bullet wound. I slung the machine gun out of the way and used my good arm to scramble from one big rock to another.

The natural stepping-stones took me around behind one of the biggest rocks, where I found I could climb twenty feet to the top. Moving like a tripod dog on one hand and two knees, I crept to the middle of a relatively flat-topped boulder warmed by the sun.

He came by five minutes later and did what I expected. He poked that flashlight into every one of the little nooks and crannies, hoping to catch the reflection of my face, or a piece of equipment. The beam flashed up the canyon wall and crossed over my boulder, but I was out of sight from below. It was a quick sweep, and he whirled to make sure no one was sneaking up on him from behind, then moved on.

A chill crawled down my spine when I caught sight of a second man. He'd been searching without a light, and I realized they'd almost outsmarted me. The point man used his flashlight to run me to ground, then after he passed, the second guy, who must've had the senses of a bat, would come along behind, after I relaxed.

It would have worked had I not gotten above them to gain some perspective. The guy riding drag walked closer to the rim's edge. Unlike the first, he was farther away, giving him a better angle. If the moon came back out, he'd see my silhouette.

I watched him dodge an ocotillo. The guy's night vision was uncanny. He threaded himself through obstacles without slowing his cautious pace and I wondered how he'd missed me at the outset when the moon caught me in the open. It must have been because I'd been a statue for a while in the moonlight, or he'd been concentrating on close hiding places in the scrub instead of farther out.

I lay like a mountain lion and rested my cheek on the rock, choking down a hiss when sand and gravel ground into a gash I didn't know about. It lit me up like a Christmas tree, screaming for attention.

With my seeping cheek on the hard surface, I became part of the rock and was just as still.

Wait for him to move on.

Wait.

Chapter 16

Mohamed Abdullah Kahn squatted in the chilly night-time air beside a creosote bush, his Cobra ready for action, and watched the beams of light make their way across the shadowed desert landscape. Chino and Pepito had positioned themselves a hundred yards away, vanishing the moment they were still.

Javier made his presence known on the ridge above by the movement of his probing lights. Abdullah sighed. If he could see their lights, then the Ranger could see them, too.

Yipping coyotes chased their prey in the Syrian's direction and he couldn't help but see the similarity between running down the rabbit and the wounded Ranger. The clouds parted and the full moon washed the valley floor in cold light.

"Señor."

The sudden voice in his ear almost made Abdullah yelp in surprise. His heart stuttered as he spun to bring the Cobra to bear, but a hand caught the weapon and stopped his response. It was Calaka.

"That kind of thing could get you killed." He was

stunned at how quietly the big man could move. It must have been the blood of his ancestor, Geronimo. It was bright enough for him to see the tribal tattoo on Calaka's neck. "Did you see anything?"

"No. We won't, either. If we see that light up there, then so can he."

"You people are supposed to be able to track across concrete."

"We will have a better chance in the daylight. He's crawled into a hole for now."

Abdullah turned his attention back to the hard-packed terrain bristling with cactus, mesquite, and yuccas. "You may be right."

"*Bien*. We will find him tomorrow and take his ears. I would like to wear the ears of a Texas Ranger. It will bring me great power with my people."

Abdullah started to tell him no, that Chavez had already given him instructions for the final disposal of the Ranger's head, but he paused. No one said the head must be *intact*. The light in Calaka's eyes frightened him, and it was the first time he'd felt that emotion since he was a kid.

He'd heard stories about the Indio tribe that was said to exist in the Occidental. Stories about their murderous raids through the mountains even made it into the Mexican newspapers from time to time. None of the local branches of law enforcement ever did much more than make a cursory investigation into the incidents, because they might come face-to-face with the descendants of the fiercest fighters in American history, Mescalero Apaches.

"Find him, and you can have his ears."

Chapter 17

I stayed on top of that boulder for what I figured to be a full hour before deciding they'd moved on. It was the guy with bat radar that scared me the most. The clouds parted for the final time that night, giving me a great view from my boulder. I rested my chin on a fist and scanned the tapering rim, watching the first guy's light fade into the distance.

By that time the sky had completely cleared, and the moon hung bright as a silver peso, setting to the west. That reminded me to check my badge, and I twisted to feel my chest. Good lord I hurt, and laying still for an hour hadn't helped. I was surprised to find the *cinco peso* Ranger badge was still on my shirt, and that made me feel better, because it had been the Old Man's when he was Rangering.

I finally had time to work my hand around to feel the hole. The entrance wound had stopped bleeding. It felt as if the bullet dug a channel across my ribs. The exit wound had me more worried than anything else. At least I hoped there was an exit wound. Yep, there it was, a hole slightly bigger than the other. The edges felt hot, and proud.

Satisfied that I wasn't going to die right then and there, I wriggled my way to the ground and waited in the shadows, listening. Still hearing nothing, I adjusted the machine pistol across my chest and headed east, exactly opposite of where I wanted to go.

Northwest of my position was the national park's headquarters and the well-traveled roads used by tourists. March and April are the busiest times of the year in Big Bend, because of the mild weather. If I could cut a road, someone was sure to come along to give me a ride back to civilization and help.

Knowing cell phone service is spotty at best in the region. I figured I was far enough away from the bad guys I could risk trying to text somebody. I reached into my back pocket to power it up and slapped nothing but material. It took a minute to realize I hadn't lost it, but had pitched the infernal device onto the truck seat when I got pissed at the lack of service.

Well, that figured. My temper once again got the best of me.

I headed back where I came with the intention of making as much time as I could in the cool night air.

Chapter 18

Javier and Pepito drew close as the descending slope opened to the canyon floor.

"The gringo vanished like a ghost." Javier shivered in the cold air. "I'm not sure if he isn't a spirit."

Pepito shrugged. "Turn out that light. You don't need it. This man isn't a ghost, he's lucky, and pretty good. We've run down better men than this, though."

"He was *hombre* enough to kill Yooko." Javier's voice was full of sadness. "He was a good cousin. We had fun when we were kids."

"Now his spirit is waiting for you. As sloppy as you are, it won't be much longer, and then the two of you can make jokes again with our ancestors." Pepito angled his head toward the stars. "Grandfather will probably beat them out of you with a stick, though. He'd prefer to live in the spirit world in peace, not listening to you two little *perritos* yapping under his feet."

It was a long speech for the typically silent Pepito, and the Lost Apaches exchanged grins, remembering their youth in the southwestern borderlands of the

Sierra Madres, in Mexico. It was where their ancestor, Geronimo, hid his last band of fighters before turning himself in to General Nelson A. Miles in 1886.

Represented by the second of the four long, curved lines in their tattoos, the mountain range was where they'd lived as their ancestors had, preying on the poor Mexican farmers.

It was when the Lost Apaches found an easier and more exciting life with the cartel gang, the Coyotes Rabiosos, back in the 1980s that their own lives improved with good food, better places to live, and women. Doing the cartel's work was nothing new, other than being even bloodier and brutal. Beheadings, mass executions, public hangings, and torture all became a way of life, putting money in their pockets.

They didn't always see things as the gangs saw them, though. Despite their background, the Lost Apaches had a rudimentary sense of right and wrong, as they saw it. More than once they'd disagreed with the gang members and backed away. Anyone else would have been executed for violating the cartel's own code, but the boss, Chatto, was loyal to his tribe and allowed them more leniency than his other soldiers.

"This *gringo* is a challenge all right." Using the moonlight, Pepito led the way. It was he who searched for the Ranger without a light. He'd told Javier to take the lead, and he hoped the Ranger would think himself safe and crawl from his hole.

The land flattened, and a figure rose from the scrub.

The Syrian stepped forward. "Nothing?"

"No. We will wait until morning and retrace our steps. He is probably in a hole, finally dead from your bullet that knocked him over the rim."

Pepito playfully shoved Javier's shoulder. "You may be right. Chino here thinks he's a ghost."

"Let the ghost wander. All I want are the ears from his body." Calaka waited for a response.

His brothers paused, then laughed.

It would be a great joke on the Ranger to enter his reward without ears. Then he wouldn't be able to hear his god's message.

Chapter 19

I made good time following a winding game trail before the clouds closed in again. I wasn't exactly running, that's for sure, but for a guy who'd been through as much as I had that night, I was pretty proud of myself.

On the other hand, I was also kicking my own ass for getting into that situation in the first place. It was a rookie mistake, being suckered into the ambush while at the same time not letting anyone know where I was. One more impulsive action that nearly got me killed went into the minus column, and it seemed like that one was getting longer every day.

I was miles from the original murder site, in country full of narrow arroyos with steep, rocky slopes. Even when they finally missed me back home and came looking, they'd be so far off it'd take at least a day to find the truck and trailer. That's where they'd start the search, and if one of those little rain showers came by and washed Red's tracks away, it might be days.

Big Bend National Park is a dangerous place if you're not careful, and sometimes even when you are.

Dozens of hikers get lost every year, though they find them most of the time. That comes from preparation. Hikers and backpackers are encouraged to check in with the ranger station, then leave a note in their car with the date, where they're going, and when they'll be back.

In my case, no one had the slightest idea where to look, and instead of staying put and waiting for a plane or helicopter to fly over, I was afraid I'd have to keep on the move. Those bad guys were doing their best to kill me, and if they failed, the desert would do it for 'em.

I figured I'd put plenty of distance between us, but the sky clouded up again, and I brushed a prickly pear. The long needles buried deep, pinning the jeans to my calf. It sure stopped me in a hurry and I backed up, hissing from the pain.

The biggest spines were the easiest to pull out, but each one felt like I was yanking a fishhook out of my skin. The problem came after those were out. Dozens, if not hundreds of hair-like needles broke off in the material and every movement was sheer torture.

I couldn't stand there all night picking needles out of my hide. Cold, miserable, and hurting, I started off again but my speed was cut in half. After what seemed like a couple of hours, an incredible thirst took hold of me and I needed water right then. I'd been hearing a sloshing sound coming from the dead man's backpack, so I swung it off my shoulders and used the flashlight to see inside. There were a number of items in there, but one I wanted most was a plastic gallon jug that once held milk.

I unscrewed the cap and took a sniff. It reminded me of muddy water on a warm summer day. Glad that I couldn't see in the darkness, I tilted the jug up and took a sip. My mouth was dry as toast, and I hadn't realized how dehydrated I'd become. I drew down several long swallows that left that same muddy taste in my mouth, but I didn't care. It was wet.

Using the flashlight hooded in my fist, I separated two fingers to release a flat beam of light. I'm sure it was as bright as aircraft landing lights in that inky darkness, but it was necessary to avoid even more cactus, so I planted one foot in front of the other and kept going.

An hour or two passed and it was still pretty dark when the ground below my feet gave way. I threw myself backward and landed hard on my wounded side, biting off a scream of pain. The inside of my head went as gray as the clouds until I swirled into unconsciousness.

An ocotillo cactus stretched its waving arms toward the gray dawn when I came back to the world. I rolled onto my good side, grunting and whimpering as I regained my knees, then my feet. Blood had seeped into the dry ground, and I wondered how deep it went.

Swaying, I looked over a steep drop-off into a deep arroyo. Cold sweat popped out on my face at the thought of how close I'd come to falling again. It was the deep, rocky gulch that gave me an idea. I figured I'd been leaving a pretty good set of tracks. Now that it was getting brighter, it was possible to use the terrain to my advantage. Panting like a hound dog, I waited a good fifteen minutes to get enough light, then skirted the edge of the sheer thirty-foot drop into the canyon, looking for a way down.

The wide arroyo below was hard-pack, full of

jagged rocks, both living and dead mesquite, and still more cactus. I followed the edge and pretty soon came to a cut that led downward where water had collapsed the bank, providing a natural path angling downward to end in a cone of rock and dirt.

More than once a big rock shifted underfoot, almost throwing me. My heart swelled up in my throat every time that happened. The last was the worst. I twisted to keep my balance and hollered when the bullet wound tore again.

Halfway down, one of the rocks broke loose and I had to jump to another. I was shaking by the time I reached the bottom and had to lean against the eroded wall to catch my breath and get another drink. In the filtered daylight, the water was cloudy through the plastic jug, but I didn't care. This time it tasted as sweet as well water.

I really wanted to find out what else was in the pack, but at that moment, I was in a precarious position. I needed to get away from the rim where the bad guys might get a clear shot at me, if they trailed me that far.

Rocky walls on either side kept the world narrow, topped by a heavy gray sky above. The fine sand underfoot was boggy, and my leather-soled boots slipped, leaving deep gashes in the silt. I felt as alone as I've ever felt in my life. I was lost, shot, and hunted by people determined to kill me, and I had no idea why, not that it mattered.

I slipped and skidded out of the low place and onto the hardpan, where I started making good time on the gravel bed. Mesquite trees had taken root, and pretty soon I felt like I was walking in a park. At times I couldn't see the rim, and then I'd break out into an opening before the gravel bed led me deeper into an even thicker stand of mesquites that had broken off more than once in long-ago floods.

An insect buzzed past my head and a second later there came an ugly whap of a bullet that splintered a green mesquite trunk in front of me. I dodged around a thick bush at the same time the shot echoed down the canyon, followed by a lightning-fast strip of automatic rounds that shredded the leaves around me.

Instinct kicked in, and I took off like a jackrabbit to get as much space between us as I could. There was no thought of shooting back. That first one was a rifle, and I knew in an instant it was the same guy who'd shot me off the other canyon rim, and the same one who'd killed my friends.

Chapter 20

Herman Hawke hung his elbow out of the open window on Sheriff Ethan Armstrong's county-issued Dodge Durango SUV. "Thanks for picking me up. I'd have been blowed up without you."

Sheriff Armstrong didn't much like the vehicle purchased with taxpayer dollars, preferring his personal Silverado pickup, but he appreciated the steel lockbox in the rear that protected his gear and firearms. "You bet. We'll get out there as soon as we can."

"Say they can't get helicopters up?"

"That's what I heard. These clouds and the storms coming up from the south have everything grounded."

The retired Texas Ranger nodded as Ethan drove them out of the flat Chihuahua Desert to climb the rocky bluffs leading to Ballard. He'd picked the old Ranger up and was taking him to Big Bend to be there when his son was found. Behind them, a low ancient ridge of eroded mountains broke up the horizon. Far to the south, and out of sight, was Mexico.

The two-lane ribbon of concrete stretched toward

the mountains. Thick gray clouds cast the country in the monochromatic light of early morning.

Ethan took his eyes off the empty highway. "Sonny didn't talk to you before he left?"

"Nope." Herman adjusted a new Colt semi-automatic on his hip to get more comfortable. He'd taken to wearing the rig again after the Ballard Incident. "Last I heard he was headed back into the park, but he didn't say much more. That killin' is worryin' him to death."

"You know him and Kelly were supposed to be on that hike, don't you?"

"Yep, and I thank the good Lord ever' mornin' for that." Herman fiddled with a pair of binoculars. "I hope I can still see through these field glasses."

"I don't think you'll have any trouble."

"I won't be much good walking a far distance, but get me up on top of a hill where I can see, and I'll go to lookin'."

Ethan grinned at the old man's grit. "Those guys are pros. They may have him found by the time we get there."

"Well, at least we know where he was headed. That's a start. There ain't no law says we can't just drive where we want."

Before Ethan could respond, the radio mounted below the dash squawked. It was Karen Anderson in dispatch. "Sheriff Armstrong?"

He'd instructed Dispatch to use codes as little as possible when they were calling him, and that included using his name instead of unit number. "Go ahead."

"You close by?"

"Fairly. We're heading out to the park to help search for Sonny. Why?"

Herman tilted his head, listening.

"Gary Collins called and said two dogs attacked his mama about two blocks from her house while she was taking her walk this morning."

"She hurt bad?"

"Cut up enough they took her to the emergency room. You want me to send Deputy Malone over there?"

"No." Ethan took an intersecting road and headed back toward Ballard. "I'm not that far away. I have an idea who those dogs belong to. I'll take care of it."

"Ten-four."

Ethan replaced the microphone on the bracket and accelerated. "I hate to do this, but I know who those dogs belong to. Gary's mama lives out on the north side of town and there's a rent house about a quarter mile from there. Couple of the sorriest guys I've ever talked to moved in not too long ago and they have two pit bulls that get out all the time. I've talked to 'em 'till I'm blue in the face, and I fined 'em, and they still don't lock those dogs up."

He checked his rearview mirror, feeling he needed to explain further. "The park has the point on this one anyway. My folks expect me to take care of things here first . . ."

Herman waved a hand. "You don't have to explain nothin' to this ol' warhorse, son."

"I know it, but it don't seem right that I can't get on out there."

An experienced lawman in east Texas, Herman was no stranger to folks labeled "sorry." The high desert flashed by as they sped past flowering cactus and ocotillo. "I believe you have an idea about how to handle this dog business."

"Sure do." Ethan pressed the gas and they cut the wind back to Ballard. "We're close and it won't take but a few minutes. Malone's headed toward Alpine right now anyway."

Ethan nodded and watched out the window. "You're right about Search and Rescue. I probably won't do much more'n get in the way anyhow."

Ethan glanced over to see the old man's face. His jaw was set, but he'd been a lawman long enough to know Ethan had a job to do. Herman would have already been on his way, but his good truck was broken down and he'd sent his hired hand, Gabriel Nakai, to Fort Stockton for the part, leaving Herman to hitch a ride with the sheriff.

Ethan's cell phone rang and he plucked it out of the cup holder.

It was Kelly Hawke, and she still hadn't heard from Sonny.

Chapter 21

By eight-thirty the next morning, Kelly couldn't wait any longer. She sent the kids to school and put in for a substitute to teach her class. She punched Ethan's name on her cell phone.

He answered with a question. "Still haven't heard from him?"

Kelly's voice trembled. "No. Even if he'd broken down, someone would have picked him up and he would've called as soon as he could get phone service. Major Parker's on the way to a command center they've set up at the park. There are a lot of folks volunteering to come help look for him."

"Well, tell 'em to wait. We don't need a lot of amateurs out there right now. I have Herman with me, and we'll head out there as soon as I take care of something that just popped up. I'll call the Park Service again as soon as we hang up. I talked to them last night and I know for a fact that they've already got a team on the ground." Ethan paused. "You realize they'd have already called you if they found him."

"I know it. I just needed to touch base with you."

"Good, like I said. Herman and I are headed out there as soon as we're finished in town."

"Perry Hale and Yolanda are here with me."

"Good. I wouldn't have expected anything else. Try not to worry."

"You know better'n that. Thanks, Ethan."

She hung up and related the news to Perry Hale, who'd spent the night on her couch. He drained his eighth cup of coffee since daylight and pulled on his boots. "I can't stand this." He stomped them into place.

Yolanda knew him well enough by then to pull on her own boots. She'd dozed in and out all night in the guest room, but looked as fresh as if she'd gotten a full night's sleep. "Kelly, we're heading out."

"Ethan says he'll be on the way as soon as he handles a call. He doesn't seem that worried."

Perry Hale rubbed his three-day beard. "He's worried all right. The Park Service is doing what they do best. He'll let them handle the first stages of the search, but I expect them to give us a holler at any time if this thing stretches out any longer."

"Why?"

"Because Ethan's a lawman," Yolanda answered. "After what happened here a few months ago, he's thinking the way we are. Sonny probably got turned around, but if it's something else, typical search parties won't be prepared for what's waiting on them. I'm afraid it might be tied to last winter."

Kelly, ever the realist, was startled by the direction the conversation was headed. "You're talking about the man who was behind the Ballard attack."

"Yep. The terrorist Sonny took out on the train is bound to have family or friends." Perry Hale rolled his shoulders to ease some of the tension. "They might want payback for Sonny's part."

Kelly's hand was shaking when she set her empty cup down. "I wish you hadn't said that."

"I shouldn't have." Perry Hale tugged a gimme cap on his head and pulled the brim down on his forehead. The emblem on the front was a cannon, and the words Come and Take It were embroidered underneath. "It's kind of far-fetched."

"So was the takeover here." Kelly stood.

Yolanda tied her thick black hair back. "But we're probably overreacting."

Kelly followed the pair to the door. "Y'all find him."

Perry Hale stopped and scanned the front yard. "Look, I'm probably borrowing trouble, but you keep a pistol handy anyway, just in case."

Kelly felt her stomach knot, but no stranger to trouble, she nodded in understanding.

Not much for public displays of affection, Perry Hale gave her shoulder a soft pat and led the way outside. Yolanda hugged Kelly's neck and whispered in her ear for a moment.

Perry Hale was in the truck with the engine running when Yolanda came out. She started toward her own car, then paused. She circled the rear of her Explorer and went to the passenger side. "I'm riding with you."

He nodded as she slammed the door and shifted into

gear. "My place." She raised an eyebrow as he steered onto the highway toward his rent house. "I have everything we need there."

"Not everything. I need to change."

He sighed and bit his lip. Another hour wouldn't make any difference in the long run. They needed to properly outfit.

Chapter 22

Chino and Pepito led the way through the subdued morning light. The Ranger's tracks were easy to follow in the sand, despite the overcast. A couple of hundred yards farther and the tracks were less distinct in the higher gravel bed. The others fanned out behind them, keeping an eye out for their quarry.

"I'm getting tired of taking orders from that *chinii*." Chino spoke in their native language that had evolved into a mix of Apache dialects and Spanish. His favorite insult for the Syrian was "dog," because the rawboned man with the ragged beard reminded Chino of the poor dogs that lived in the small settlement they grew up in, back in the Sierra Madre Occidental.

Pepito grinned at the dog reference. "If it weren't for Chatto, I would have already killed him."

"You're not afraid of Chatto, are you?" Chino's eyes thinned even more, making him look even more Asian, though his blood was a mix of Apache and the Mexicans their great-grandparents had taken in to raise.

It was easy to disregard the head of their gang, even

though both knew that if any of their discussion got back to him, Chatto would have them put to death immediately, if he didn't do it himself.

"No, but I like his money. I want to take more back to my mother. She needs a generator so she can have electricity and a television."

"There is more than money at stake here. I'm getting tired of all this. I think I would like to go back into the cool mountains where we grew up. I miss the tall trees and the water. Here there is nothing but dirt and cactus."

"Let's find this man and let Calaca take his ears, then when that *chinii* back there is satisfied, we can go home. These people and their drugs are making me tired."

Abdullah's voice cut through the morning air. "Will you two be quiet! This Ranger will hear you long before we see him."

Chino threw a look back over his shoulder and spoke in Spanish. "You have that long rifle. Maybe he'll stick his head up like a mole to hear what we're saying and you can shoot it off. Then we can go."

Javier spoke up with a laugh, using their dialect. "He'll probably miss again."

The gangsters laughed and went back to tracking while Abdullah seethed.

He wasn't the idiot they imagined him to be. A radical to the bone, he once worked in government-run prisons back in his home country, torturing prisoners for both information and enjoyment before joining in as a refugee fighter for al-Qaeda-affiliated Jabhat al-Nusra.

After refining his skills, he was sent over to join the Mexican cartels to train and establish cells destined for the U.S. He came through Germany, taking advantage of their open-border policy that turned the country into a safe haven for Islamists departing the Syrian-Iraqi battlefronts.

He joined other Islamists in Mexico. They had all been radicalized in European mosques, or in the suburbs of various countries, and evolved into battle-hardened terrorists with combat experience.

Abdullah was the worst of the lot, and he had a plan. He slung the pack off his shoulders and dug for the satellite phone Chavez had provided. It was time to tell him that he'd return alone to meet Chatto with the Ranger's head. The other four would soon be food for the scavengers and he could go to Washington, where his skills were needed.

"There!" Chino pointed at a tiny figure trudging more than a hundred yards away.

Heart pounding with excitement, Abdullah snapped the rifle to his shoulder. The Ranger disappeared behind a bush, then reappeared. The anxious terrorist's finger tightened on the trigger too soon, and he knew he'd missed as soon as he fired.

The Apaches opened up with their automatic weapons and the figure disappeared.

Abdullah cursed and refused to meet their eyes. "Go! He may be wounded."

They trotted ahead and he slung the rifle over his shoulder with a trembling hand.

The call would have to wait.

Chapter 23

Ethan's Durango slowed at Ballard's city limits and he steered around the courthouse, which was under repair. Half a dozen trucks and vans bearing the names of local businesses were parked on the lawn. It would soon look good as new.

He turned through a quiet neighborhood of stucco houses landscaped with native plants. The paved road ended and packed gravel took over. The houses thinned until they were scattered like marbles.

Gary Collins' sun-blasted Southwest-style house squatted alone amid a mix of mesquite and prickly pear. Ethan steered into the driveway between two thick cedars guarding the entrance. He and Herman stepped out and were about to knock on the front door when Gary came around the corner by the carport.

"Howdy, Ethan."

Sheriff Armstrong shook his hand. "You know Herman Hawke?"

Gary's brow furrowed. "Sonny Hawke's daddy? We've not met, but I've heard of you. You're a Ranger, too."

"Howdy." Herman tilted the hat back on his head. "I'm retired." True to his law-enforcement roots, he kept his answer ambiguous. "Just ridin' with Ethan to remember all the reasons I retired."

Gary gave him a wry grin. "This might be one of them, but I doubt it's enough to interest the Rangers."

"You can never tell what brings what."

The pleasantries were over. Ethan jerked his head toward the house. "Your mama home? She all right?"

"Yep." Gary turned to Ethan but addressed Herman. "Mama came to live with us a couple of years ago when her health got bad." He met Ethan's eyes. "She's laying on the couch. Just got back from getting her stitched up, took about thirty, and they gave her some pain pills. They're worried about rabies, and said the dogs need to be quarantined."

"She awake?"

"Let's see."

The men stepped into the cool living room. Exposed overhead beams and stucco walls echoed their footsteps on the red Spanish tiles. Carl's wife had decorated the interior with a Southwest flair that was like something from a magazine article, complete with rough-hewn furniture, Spanish tapestries on the walls, colorful horse blankets on racks, pottery, and hand-braided rugs on the floor.

Gary left the gimme cap on his head. Both Ethan and Herman removed their hats as soon as they stepped through the door. An elderly woman in a housedress and robe was laying on the couch.

She started to get up, but Ethan held out a hand and sat on the edge of the couch. "Stay there, Mrs. Collins." He introduced Herman and glanced down at the white bandages on her pale legs. They were both covered with dark bruises and scratches, telling him the unseen wounds were frightening. "Can you describe the dogs?"

"Yessir." Her voice was weak from age, stress, and the painkillers. She wiped the corner of her mouth with a white silk handkerchief. Her silver hair that had been brushed and curled that morning stuck out in several directions, making her look even older. "One was a big brindle and the other was light tan, almost white."

"Do you know what breed?"

"I don't know dogs, but they both had leather collars with brass plates. It's funny what you remember in times like that. Squinty eyes, those collars, and all that snarling."

"That'll be enough." Ethan stood. "I hope you get to feeling better. I'll take care of it from here on out."

She leaned back and closed her eyes, the hand with the handkerchief held aloft. "Thankyee, Sheriff."

They went back outside. Gary paused in the shade of the carport. "She's been walking every day, because the doctor says she needs the exercise. Those dogs have threatened her more than once, but this is the first time they've ever attacked. They would have hurt her worse if it hadn't been for that high school kid that beat 'em off her with a stick."

"You know where they live for sure?"

He pointed. "That trailer out there."

They followed his finger. A line of low blue mountains in the distance acted as a backdrop, defining a battered, dusty house trailer that would have otherwise blended into the desert. It was obvious Gary's house was built to take advantage of the spectacular view.

Ethan was sure the trailer arrived after construction on the house was completed. "That's what I thought. Who's the kid?"

"Don't know him. He moved out there in a trailer past that one over yonder. Looks like a single mother and boy is all. They moved in about a month ago."

"Fine. I'll take care of it, Gary. Y'all have the option of filing charges against the dogs' owners. This is a one-bite state and you can file for damages if you want, but those people probably won't pay up, even when the judge says so."

Gary sighed. "I guess that's it, then."

"Let me talk to them."

They were back on the dirt road when Herman finally spoke up. "Those dogs tore her up pretty bad."

A rooster-tail of dust rose behind the Dodge as Ethan pressed the foot-feed. Gravel rattled against the undercarriage, and cedar fence posts flashed past.

"Yep. They belong to that Martinez bunch." He pointed at a fence line. "That's the city limits."

Herman reached into the back pocket of his Wranglers and pulled out his badge holder. He opened it and slipped the cover behind his belt, presenting the gold *cinco peso* retirement badge to anyone they encountered.

They came to an intersection and the sheriff barely slowed before taking the corner and accelerating down the connecting dirt road. They passed two other trailers that looked more like abandoned shells than actual houses.

A young Hispanic boy was on the road, marking his pace with what appeared to be a walking stick. Ethan slowed to keep from smothering the kid in dust. He recognized the youngster when the distance closed.

He slowed to a stop. What he took for a dark stick turned out to be a piece of thin rebar. "Arturo, how you doin'?"

The high school junior brightened. "Good mornin', Sheriff. Mr. Hawke."

Arturo had been instrumental in the aftermath of the Ballard takeover. Neither Ethan or Herman knew the kid before the courthouse incident, but they'd grown to like him more and more with every encounter. Arturo was one of those kids who had the odds stacked against him, but always managed to squeak past. Sonny was intent on ensuring the boy's success achieving his dream of a career in law enforcement.

"What are you doing this far out?"

Arturo ducked his head, obviously embarrassed. "My mom lost her job, and we had to move." He jerked his head toward a barren trailer. Dented and broken washing machines, barrels, and the rusting skeleton of an Audi took the place of landscaping. "We live there now."

Ethan took stock of the trash-strewn yard and the screenless windows gaping open. The door was warped and splintered. "You stayin' out of trouble?"

"Yessir. Mr. Sonny said I had to keep my nose clean if I wanted to be a lawman."

"He's right about that. Keep your grades up, too. Why aren't you in school this mornin'?"

He shrugged. "Missed the bus. I'm walking to my friend's house. His mama has a car and she'll take me. You here about them dogs that chewed up that old lady this morning?"

"How'd you know that?"

"Because I'm the one that run 'em off from her. They've come at me before." He held up the rebar. "I took to carrying this when I'm out."

"We'll take care of it." Ethan accelerated as Herman waved good-bye.

Chapter 24

Mary and Jerry Hawke were arguing in the cloudy parking lot of Ballard High School. The twins looked alike all right, but they were as different as night and day. Slender as a willow, Mary was the planner, doing everything by the book and trying her best not to stray too far off the path their parents had set for them.

Jerry was like his dad, impetuous, solidly built, and quick to anger. It was his habit of jumping without looking that kept them from going inside. "Look, we both know Dad may be in trouble. They're putting together a search team down in the Bend, and I'm not going to sit here in class while other people look for him."

Raindrops beaded on windshields and fresh wax jobs, but spread into a dark gray paste on older cars with bad shines. The West Texas dust was quickly turning to mud. Beads of moisture caught in Mary's long, strawberry blond hair. "So, what, you're just gonna drive down there and join in the search? The first thing the school's gonna do is call Mom at home and tell her you didn't come in today. You're already busted and you don't even know it."

"I don't care. What are they gonna do? Nothing. Cutting class isn't much of a crime."

"It is right now. She's already worried about Dad, and you running off down there will just make it worse."

"I can't sit behind a desk, listening to old Miss Latimer drone on and on about American History. She's probably showing a stupid movie right now anyway since school is almost out."

"That doesn't matter . . . ." Mary stopped when their friend Arturo stepped out of a beat-up Ford Contour sedan driven by a frazzled-looking Hispanic woman.

Arturo waved and joined them. The little junior had become close to the twins after last winter's Ballard Incident in the courthouse, and often ate at their house on weekends when school was out and he couldn't get a decent meal. His deadbeat step-dad had been deported for the umpteenth time, and his mother's below-minimum-wage job barely kept a roof over their heads.

He joined the twins, seeing the anger in their faces. "What's up?"

Mary pointed a finger at her brother. "This dummy is ditching school."

"Cool. What for?"

Exasperated, she mimicked her mother's habit of tilting her head back and venting toward the sky. "*Guaaah.* You two are just alike."

Jerry threw a glance at the lowering clouds and pulled a green gimme cap low, the edges of the rolled bill resting low on his temples. "Dad's missing in the Bend. I'm going down to join the search party, and she doesn't want me to go."

"Why?"

Mary shook her head. "Because it'll worry Mom even more when the school calls to tell her he ditched class."

"I'll go with you." Arturo pitched his books in the backseat of Jerry's 1976 Bronco.

Mary spun on her heel. "You two do what you want. I don't care if you get in trouble or not, just don't drag me into it when you get caught."

"They won't say anything when we find Dad." Jerry slipped behind the steering wheel and waved his cell phone in the air. "I'll call you from the park!"

Chapter 25

Bare, dead trees seemed to keep the heavy clouds from falling on the sagging trailer and dirt yard. It appeared to Sheriff Ethan Hawke that the residents simply threw their trash through the open doors and windows. The only vehicle was a pickup on blocks.

Ethan tapped the horn. Dogs barked from the back, but no one came to the door. The sheriff and Herman stepped out and surveyed the area. Tire tracks from numerous cars crisscrossed the yard. The drive off the dirt road was thick with varying treads.

While Herman stayed beside the Dodge, keeping the vehicle between himself and the ragged trailer, Ethan knocked on the front door. When he was sure no one was home, the Sheriff returned to the Durango and reached inside, withdrawing the Remington pump shotgun that rode in the front-seat bracket. He jacked a shell into the chamber and rounded the end of the trailer.

Herman raised an eyebrow and followed him past a dusty dump ground anchored by a washing machine full of beer cans. He stopped at the corner to keep an eye on the front yard and the back. From his vantage point, he could cover Ethan on three sides, if necessary.

Two pit bulls were barking, snarling and jumping up on the sides of an often-repaired dog pen. Cinder blocks filled holes dug under the fence as a stop-gap. In one place, a chewed wooden pallet plugged a hole.

The dogs growled and backed up as Ethan approached the pen. "Herman, I see a brindle pit and a light-colored pit. Both have collars with brass plates."

"Yessir."

Ethan raised the shotgun to his shoulder, but before he could pull the trigger, Herman spoke up. "Hang on a minute." The old Ranger crossed behind the sheriff, picked up two broken cinderblocks, and dropped them into the hole under the fence where the dogs dug out.

The sheriff lowered his shotgun. "Why'd you do that?"

"I know the law says you can shoot 'em, but did you see all them tracks in the yard?"

"I noticed 'em. Why?"

"They circle around back here, too. That's a lot of cars for this shack, don't you think?"

"Now that you mention it." Ethan studied the tracks. "You thinking this might be a drop?"

"That's my thinking." Herman pointed toward the dirt road curving past the front of the house and disappearing toward the west. "Where does this road come out?"

"Well, this one don't. It runs into a couple of two-lane tracks that meet up with some ranch roads."

Huge ranches spread across the Trans-Pecos, or far West Texas. The area was so vast that many ranches were isolated and only accessed by crossing other ranches, using dirt roads and two-lane tracks. Both men knew drug smugglers used the roads to avoid the highways and border patrol.

"Looks like they're using the back roads. I'd have to check, but I think they all finally funnel everything out toward Fort Davis."

"Something's up." Ethan pointed to tire tracks that were much wider than the others.

"Yep."

"I'd say there's a lot of 'em here that match that cattle trailer settin' over there. You think somebody might be hauling more than just cows in that thing?"

"Could be."

"I'm asking, because we both know for a fact that them terrorists we tangled with showed up at the courthouse in one. Somebody might have gotten the bright idea to move meth or cocaine in there. This don't smell like no meth house, they're not cooking it here, but I've heard of 'em puttin' it in bags of roasted coffee to mask the smell. Cow shit and piss'll do the trick, too, I 'magine."

"So you think we watch and see, instead of me shooting these two dogs?"

"I would."

"Gary and his mama'll want more."

Ethan raised an eyebrow as Herman fell in beside him and returned to the Dodge. "They'll be happy if we clean this rats' nest out."

The sheriff hit the horn as they pulled in Gary Collins' drive. He met them in the yard. "I didn't hear anything. I figured you'd shoot those dogs."

"Started to, but I want to ask you, has there been a lot of traffic on this road in the last few weeks?"

"Sure enough. Trucks pulling cattle trailers. Sometimes they're full of stock, other times just empty rigs. A pump truck comes out pretty regular. They must be having trouble with their septic tank."

"Since they moved in?"

"Yep. Don't remember the folks who lived there before having any trouble. It's aggravating. We didn't have any traffic before these guys. The people who moved the trailer in there a few years ago pretty much stayed to themselves, and I didn't mind that one bit. I moved out here to get away from traffic."

Ethan rubbed his chin. "This new traffic going out and coming in the same way?"

"A few, but now that you mention it, I'd say most don't come back out. You think they're going on through to Fort Davis?"

"Could be."

"Why do you think that?"

"To get around the border patrol stops. Tell your mama I'll deal with those dogs, but to give me a few days. This might be something none of us expected."

"You bet. But I'm not going anywhere around here from now on unless I'm heeled, and you need to know, I'll shoot those dogs next time I see 'em out."

"Wouldn't blame you if you did."

The sheriff waved as they headed down to Big Bend National Park.

Chapter 26

The Ranger's tracks were distinct in the sand, and Abdullah Kahn's spirit soared when he saw blood droplets near at least two of them. "Javier!"

The gangster joined him. "What is it?"

Abdullah pointed at the track. "He's wounded. We shouldn't be too far behind. Tell your men to be careful."

"They always are." He called to them and they spread out, moving through the brush as smoothly as the deer who left their tracks throughout the region. A rabbit burst from a clump of cactus and crisscrossed the arroyo before disappearing from sight.

He lost sight of the gangsters and followed, thrilled that they were so close to their quarry. No stranger to hunting men, Abdullah pressed forward with the Cobra ready. Hawke's wounds and physical condition were sure to take their toll, forcing him to seek cover somewhere. Abdullah expected Hawke to turn and fight at any minute.

Despite his frustration with not yet having the Ranger's head, the terrorist realized he was enjoying the chase. His eyes took on a new light, and his lips spread in a wide smile behind the beard. The game had changed and his heart rose.

Not far from a rock formation was a confusion of jumbled boulders both large and small, all undercut from eons of swift water. The desert was ever changing from the causes of erosion.

Wind sandblasted the land with tiny particles it blew against the rocks and ground. Periodic flash floods picked up everything in their paths, grinding down the arroyos in a devil's brew of rocks, branches, whole trees, and sun-washed trunks.

The mesquites that had weathered the last floods, or had grown in the meantime, thickened at a bend in the arroyo. Abdullah walked alone, keeping a close eye on a particularly thick bush. The Ranger wasn't there, but a ragged skeleton was.

Despite the need to maintain caution, Abdullah slowed to get a good look at the skull with a gaping hole in one side. Bodies were nothing to him, but the sight of a human skeleton partially shrouded by rotting clothing was something else entirely.

Intent on the fatal wound in the skull, he didn't see the diamondback rattlesnake coiled nearby and blending into the sand and rocks. At least five feet long, it had the ability to strike half the length of its body. It lunged and missed by less than an inch. Human instinct took over and Abdullah screamed, jumping to the side.

The snake coiled for another strike, but Abdullah stumbled into the open and was met with a hail of bullets. In shock, he registered strikes and explosions around him before the Ranger's aim steadied. A round punched through his shoulder, feeling as if it had been struck by a sledgehammer. The terrorist dropped to his knees.

Moments later the gangsters whooped in delight. Through his shock, Abdullah saw his prey rise to his feet from behind a window of rocks and raise his hands. Despite his wounds, he felt light as a feather. *"Allahu akbar!"*

Chapter 27

I was getting pure-dee pissed.

Nobody likes to run from a fight, and no one wants to be hunted. It was time to fight back. A formation of red rocks a mile away was my best shot. They'd be cautious coming down the arroyo, expecting just the kind of attack I had planned farther on.

I was one big mass of hurt and blood, and about played out, but anger took over and drove me forward through the wide-open expanse of reddish soil and rocks carpeted with mesquite and prickly pear. All those cactus blooms and flowers weren't near as pretty as before, in my opinion. The canyons, arroyos, arches, and cliffs were a magnet for those who loved the desert away from the safety of their air-conditioned cars and well-established trails.

Those who found themselves in the wilderness had a different view in a world filled with barbs, stickers, and daggers. The desert had always been a dangerous place, and a horrible nightmare come to life for those lost or severely injured in the backcountry, but it was about to become even more dangerous for those guys following me when I reached the shelter of the high ground.

I ran as best I could, grinding my teeth at the pain from the bullet wound. I'd already knocked a lot of bark off my carcass, but I wasn't going to let those sonsabitches catch me standing still. That scoped rifle of his gave him an advantage that scared me worse than a rattler, but the odds would get better in a jumble of boulders.

The sudden dry buzz of a rattler didn't faze me. It wasn't close, and I was too mad. I spotted him about six feet away, and it was one of the biggest rattlesnakes I'd ever seen. It wasn't the rattler that had my attention, though, it was the human skeleton lying nearby.

With no way to tell if it was a man or woman without a closer examination, I thought of the bones as those of a male. His clothes were nothing but rags. Both feet still in a rotting pair of sneakers were separated and lying five feet away. A skeleton stretched out under a mesquite was one thing, but the large hole in the side of his bleached skull was another. The lawman in me wanted to stop and examine the scene, but I was hunted and had to keep moving.

The rattler buzzed again, warning me away. I wished him luck, because the other guy's had run out, and kept going.

Despite the cloud cover, the dry air was turning me into jerky. My tongue felt like a strip of leather, and I wasn't sweating. The formation of rocks didn't look any closer and I was sucking wind.

One second I was dodging around the mesquites and cactus, for the most part hidden, and the next I popped out in a flat wash scraped by water and scattered with debris and boulders. A ridge rose to my right, and halfway up was a tangled logjam of splintered mesquite trunks, limbs, and dead vegetation sunblasted to a light gray.

I broke out into a staggering, painful run, feeling like I was out there with a big red target painted on my back. A bone-colored mesquite limb caught my foot, sending me head over heels. That one almost did me in. It was as far as I could go. I regained my feet and hobbled across the wide-open space, half-expecting to feel the sniper's bullets put an end to my misery.

What would the Old Man say?

Think, dummy! You're a Texas Ranger for God's sake.

Yeah, but I wasn't trained in desert survival or warfare.

Fine. But use your noodle. Gain the high ground and evaluate your situation. Maybe this is where you make your stand. Search teams'll be looking for you by now, on the ground and with planes and helicopters. You can hold them off from there if it gives you a good field of fire. See that rim? It overhangs those rocks so they can't get above you.

They're gonna come busting out of all those mesquites just like you did, and maybe you can get a shot. If not, hang on and wait for the cavalry. You know we're already on the way.

The hair rose on the back of my neck, and I heard myself grunting and whining, straining hard to reach the tangle of debris. A covey of quail exploded almost under my feet and whirred away like shrapnel, scaring me worse than the rattler.

Go figure.

Keep moving.

Keep dodging.

Almost out of gas, I finally reached the bottom of the ridge. The drift was higher'n I thought, and I lost even more valuable time climbing with one hand to reach a small window created by two boulders that had leaned on each other for a thousand years.

The Old Man in my mind was right. That's what I needed, the high ground. I worked my way behind them and settled into the window. When I got there, I saw the top of the rim was another twenty feet higher than my position.

I checked my back trail, but they still weren't in sight. Despite the cloud cover, I was dry as a gourd. The desert air was sucking more moisture than I was able to replace. I pushed my thumb into the skin on my forearm and the dent stayed there much longer than I wanted. Serious dehydration. I was down to less than a half gallon of tepid, rusty-colored water and drank half of that, hoping it would stop the buzzing in my ears that sounded like a swarm of bees.

It was the first time I'd been able to check the machine pistol hanging around my neck. I read the name on the side. I'd heard of Cobras, Mexican-made machine pistols, but had never shot one. I unfolded the shoulder stock and gave it the once-over. The safety was easy to find. I located the fire selector and flicked it off of automatic, putting it on semi-auto. I didn't want to get overly excited and squeeze off a whole magazine.

I laid out two of the extra mags and promised myself

I'd wait until they got close enough for the 9x19 caliber ammo to be most effective.

How many hours had it been since they shot me off the rim? I was finally still for a little bit, feeling blisters on both heels. The once glossy black cherry Lucchese boots weren't made for desert travel. They looked like work boots.

It was the first time I was able to evaluate my wounds in the light. In addition to the gunshot, I had three serious gashes, one behind my right shoulder, one on that same arm where my watch had been, and another seeping cut on my left thigh. The dozen scrapes and slashes on my cheek, arms, and legs were stinging like fire.

Keeping an eye on the wash, I pulled out two dozen needles that stuck out through my jeans, but twice that many had broken off and were buried in my flesh. Sitting there thinking about it, my legs lit up with a whole spectrum of hot stings from the tiny hair-like stickers from those same prickly pears, adding to my misery.

The overcast was a stroke of sheer luck. My hat was somewhere back up that first canyon and I sure did miss it. Had the sun been out, I would have been in even worse shape. However, the clouds didn't block all the UV rays, and I could feel the sting of sunburn on my face, neck, and ears. My lips were already cracked and peeling.

Still nothing out beyond my rock window. Feeling weak and feverish, my mind was oddly clear. I settled into a more comfortable position and worked another cactus thorn free. With time to finally rest and think instead of react, I wished I was back home with Kelly and the kids. A thought crossed my mind and I jolted straight up. What if it wasn't just me they were after? Did they put together an orchestrated plan to take me out and at the same time go to my house?

Wait! Pieces began to fall into place. The one guy's Middle Eastern accent. The people responsible for the Ballard takeover had ties to ISIS, and they'd teamed up with Mexican gangsters and even one of the so-called homegrown terrorist groups from east Texas.

This had to tie in somehow. And that meant it was entirely possible that they led me right into an ambush and had every opportunity to make me pay an even higher price for throwing a monkey wrench into their takeover by kidnapping or killing my family.

For the first time since I went over the rim, I was afraid. Not for my own safety, but afraid they might kill me and then go back to Ballard, if they hadn't already done so. My hands were shaking when I took another long swallow of water.

I wondered if any of the tourists camping or hiking in the park had heard the shots that drew me like the sucker I was. If they had, then maybe they reported them to the ranger station and help was closer than I thought.

Think, boy, think!

Run due south until you come to the river, then float down to Boquillas or if you went farther, Rio Grande Village was next. There were park rangers there, and people. They wouldn't chase you into such a populated area, would they?

I studied the heavy clouds. *Who knows, Pop?*

I'd never been so thirsty in my life. The jug of water felt much lighter in my hand. I closed my eyes and wished I had half a dozen of those water bottles Kelly kept in the icebox. Cold, cold water that would make the wait in my natural stone fort more tolerable.

I took one final drink, holding it in my mouth, letting it trickle down my throat, registering for the first time the odor of creosote released by the bright green bushes all around me.

I'd barely replaced the cap when I saw movement at the head of the arroyo. Moving slow, I put the jug down, snugged the Cobra's stock to my shoulder, and tensed when a roadrunner popped into view. It scurried twenty yards before it stopped to listen and watch with one unmoving black eye. He wasn't hunting or listening to the bees. Someone or something was behind him.

Index finger along the trigger guard, I licked my lips and waited.

Two men flickered through the mesquites, moving cautiously in my direction. It was the first time I'd gotten a good look at them and I was surprised by what my imagination had created and what I saw.

They were slight. One was built like a barrel cactus, and the other like a hungry five-foot-five-inch stray dog. They wore dusty jeans and faded shirts. Both had rags tied over their heads. One wore ragged tennis shoes. The other was in some kind of lace-ups.

They were less than a hundred yards out, within range of my weapon, but I wanted them closer.

Much closer.

A shriek came to me. I'd heard that kind of scream before. It came from sheer terror.

What'n hell?

A bearded guy with a rifle strapped across his back

popped into view and took two steps into the open with another machine pistol in his hand. The long gun told me he was the guy who'd shot me, there was no doubt in my mind. I squeezed the trigger, just like I was on the target range.

Shooting with both eyes open, I saw explosions in the sand and all around him. The guy hit the ground. Already knowing what to expect, I dropped down at the same time the rocks in front and behind my position snapped and cracked from the impacts of two other fully automatic weapons. I curled into a ball, hoping none of the ricochets would find me. They quit firing at the same time, probably reloading.

I took that opportunity to rise and scan the area, hoping to see a leg, an arm, or a whole body to get a little more payback. The sound of a rock rattling down the slope behind me was startling, but not as much as the voice not ten feet away.

"*Manos arriba.* Get your hands up, my friend, and you'll live long enough to meet Abdullah, but you won't like it too much, I think."

I swiveled my head to find an even smaller version of those guys standing on the edge of the rim, with the mate to the Cobra in my hands aimed right at my chest.

Believe me, that kind of thing'll make you holler calf rope pretty quick. I laid the Cobra down and showed him my hands. "You're under arrest, you know."

His face broke into a smile after a long beat, which meant he had to translate my words. He laughed. "That's a good *joke*. Now, stand up and go with my brothers. They will want to hear that, too."

Chapter 28

Yolanda rode shotgun with the windows down in Perry Hale's 2003 Dodge truck. It was unusually cool for that time of the year. Yolanda pulled her hair through the adjustment hole in her gimme cap, and her black ponytail danced in the wind. Both wore shades and desert camouflage Marine Corp Combat Utility Uniforms, or MCCUUs. It would be easy to mistake them for on-duty marines.

Yolanda turned to cock her left leg against the center console. Arm stretched across the distance between the seats, her fingers rested on his shoulder. "All right. Now that we're away from everyone, what do you *really* think?"

Keeping both eyes on the two-lane road, Perry Hale flexed his fingers on the steering wheel. "I think something bad's happened. Sonny checks in with Kelly more than once a day. Even if he broke down somewhere out there, he'd call as soon as he got cell service or to a phone. I don't believe he's lost."

Yolanda glanced at the low mountains on her right.

"So what's the plan? I don't suppose we're joining a search party."

"Well, we need to check in with SAR to see what they know." Both were familiar with Search and Rescue terminology after volunteering in the past. "I'd rather do that at first, but if things seem to be off, then we go on our own."

"He went out to check on that crime scene. Maybe he saw something, like tracks, and followed them and got lost."

Perry Hale nodded. "He's on Red, so that means he might've gone in any direction."

She twisted to check out the gear in the back of the four-door cab. Their loaded packs took up the seat along with an RTIC cooler and cases of bottled water. A heavy water-resistant bag filled one well in the floorboard, packed so full of gear the seams stretched and the zipper looked ready to pop.

The custom-made built-in aluminum case under the back seat contained two custom AR-15s and extra handguns. Those were in addition to the .40 caliber Glock 23s on their hips.

"That bag tells me you're ready for anything."

The corners of his mouth rose. "Like I said, Sonny's impulsive, and if something else happened related to those murders last week, then he's gonna need help."

She faced forward at the same time Perry Hale's phone rang. He dug it from his shirt pocket. "It's Ethan." He punched it to speaker and rolled the windows up. "Yessir?"

"Where are y'all?"

"Coming in to Marathon."

"You're at least forty-five minutes out."

"Less than thirty."

"Funny. Don't get pulled over. I have an idea what you're carrying and it might make somebody nervous. Anyway, you'll get there first. I've talked to Tammy Rivera, the park ranger who's heading the search. They sent a two-man Hasty Team out last night to the crime scene. It was dark when they got there, so they set up a SAR cache and did a little exploring. They didn't find anything. The bad news is that Sonny's truck and trailer weren't parked at the trailhead."

"That's not good. I assume they've checked other trailhead parking lots."

"Been on that since daylight. The command post is at the ranger station.

"We'll go there, then."

"I'm a little behind, but you'll see me when I get there. Herman's with me. I talked to the Park Service, and they say the clouds show no sign of clearing up anytime soon. In fact, they think even more moisture is headed up from the Gulf and that'll increase the cloud cover."

Yolanda leaned forward to squint upward through the windshield. "That means rain."

"Hundred percent chance, and that's gonna play hell with tracking Sonny."

"You want us to wait for you then, if we need to move?"

"No, do what you need to do, but if you lose cell service, backtrack and give me a call."

They knew from experience that communications was always a problem in the remote park. The large dead spots where neither radios nor cell phones worked were a common frustration for visitors and employees alike.

"Will do."

"They're worried. They've already called in parks personnel from Big Bend State Park and are planning on asking for others, so I figure we listen in and then decide what to do on our own. The governor called TEXSAR in without asking, and I imagine the Park Service ain't too happy about that."

Well respected, TEXSAR, or Texas Search and Rescue, was a volunteer first-responder organization with teams in Austin, Dallas, and Galveston. Though the unit based in Austin primarily served most of central Texas, they often deployed anywhere in the state upon request from federal or state agencies, local law enforcement, or even relief agencies.

Perry Hale also expected a call from the governor once he heard that Sonny was missing. "I'll let you know what we find out." He ended the call and showered down on the gas.

Chapter 29

I wasn't gonna to let them see me sweat, but I was afraid and empty.

There was no doubt the little guy with the machine gun pointed at me wouldn't hesitate to shoot. He flicked the muzzle back toward the way I'd climbed up and waited for me to turn before he started down. The slope and loose rocks would force him to take his eyes off me to follow. My mind raced.

All right, he can't see the .45, so when he looks down, draw, shoot, then spin and throw a couple more at those other guys to keep them down while I pick up the Cobra.

It was a great plan, but he stayed right where he was. The next thing I knew, another voice from over my right shoulder ended that idea right then. *"Manos arriba."*

Those guys moved like lions. Another down below looked Asian and was so confident in his friend's ability to ventilate me that his weapon wasn't even pointed in my direction.

I did what he said and raised my hands.

Knees weak and shaking, I concentrated on picking my way down the rubble and to the bottom of the arroyo, all the while keeping both hands where they could see them. That's when Asia pointed the gun at me and twisted one finger in a circle, telling me to turn around. I did, and he plucked the .45 from my holster.

Another guy appeared out of the mesquites with blood running down the side of his neck. Asia said something in a language I didn't understand and laughed. It sounded like there was some Spanish mixed in there, but an Indian dialect was all tangled up with it.

The next thing I knew, somebody hit me behind my right ear and I went down like a pole-axed steer.

That kind of blow will take down even the toughest guy, and I was far from tough right then. The Old Man taught me to hit a hardcase behind the ear to knock the fight out of him, but it was the first time I'd ever been hit there.

It took a few minutes for my head to clear, but I was conscious the entire time. Someone tugging at my gun belt told me they'd pulled my handcuffs from the case. I was still seeing little bluebirds in front of my eyes when they jerked my arms back and clicked the cold metal cuffs around my wrists.

I'd been hurtin' before, but *goddlemighty*, I thought I was gonna pass out for sure when those muscles damaged by the bullet pulled and twisted. My left scapula felt like it was cracked or broken. One cuff was on that deep gash in my wrist and it burned like the dickens.

Hands grabbed my arms and yanked me upright as

if I weighed only fifty pounds, tripling the lightning bolt of hot pain in my shoulder. Another guy grabbed ahold and they pulled me into the mesquites. I let out a groan and stumbled along between them until they stopped beside a thin tangle of bushes.

The guy in the beard was sitting on the ground, holding himself upright with one hand, swaying forward and back. He spoke into a satellite phone. "We have the Ranger. Yes. I will call you again when we cross the river. Now wipe his family from the earth." He pressed a button to disconnect.

His eyes were glassy and his skin looked pale and waxy. I registered a bloom of red on his shoulder. It made me feel a little better to know I'd hit him. I was never any great shakes with a machine gun and could only hit with a rifle when I took my time.

Looks like I should've aimed better.

He rallied after a few seconds. "You are Sonny Hawke. Texas Ranger."

I blinked a drop of sweat from my eyes. "That was *my* line."

The Beard frowned at the comment.

"I never listen to my own advice."

"What is that?"

"My old daddy always said to use enough gun. It took years to realize what he meant, and you're the best example I've ever seen."

"I am an example?"

"Yep, if I'd waited for you to get closer, I could have shot you with that forty-five over there, the one that skinny little goober's playing with, and"—I raised my voice—"I intend to get it back from you."

Asia stopped looking at the photo in the Sweetheart Grip my ol' granddaddy made during World War II. He frowned in my direction and jabbered for a second. He angled the cocked and locked pistol to look at the other side of the inside grip. The clear Lucite revealed the remaining cartridges in the butt. Obviously unfamiliar with the .45, he was pointing it every whichaway.

"Hope you shoot yourself with it, you sawed-off little bastard." I turned back to Beard. "Anyway, that forty-five is enough gun to do the trick. Then you wouldn't be sittin' there."

He started to say something else, then stopped and dragged a desert-tan pack close to hand. He unzipped an outside pocket. From there he drew out a gray cloth bag and a long knife. He pitched them toward Asia.

"Esto es para su cabeza. Tómalo y ponlo en la bolsa." This is for his head. Take it and put it in the bag.

My Spanish is bad, but I knew exactly what he said. I kicked sideways and caught the Chinese-looking guy in the knee. He howled and stumbled backward. Fighting was useless, but I couldn't stand there and let them saw my head off like those poor people I've seen in execution videos.

Before I could launch myself into the next guy, an arm wrapped around my neck and yanked me backward. I hit the ground like a crash-test dummy and choked down a cry when I landed on my cuffed wrists.

Whoever'd jerked me backward grabbed a handful of hair and pulled my cowlick so hard my eyes watered. I dug both boot heels into the ground and threw my head back. His nose broke with a soft crunch and he gasped and let go of my hair. I twisted on the ground and drew my knees upward to stand. I was halfway to my feet when another grabbed my arms. A loop dropped around my neck and the next thing I knew, I felt like a calf fighting a lariat rope. They drew it tight.

My ears roared and I panicked, knowing from experience I had only seconds before I blacked out. No air. No blood to the brain. Instead of fighting it, I bucked toward the rope to get some slack. A flat-faced guy fell back, pulling the noose tighter, if that was possible.

Those guys were pros. One grabbed me around the waist to hold me still while another dug in with his feet and pulled hard.

Lights flashed. The world turned silent.

I thrashed harder, but it was a weak effort.

Then darkness.

Chapter 30

Abdullah was amped up by adrenaline from his wound and their success at capturing the Texas Ranger Sonny Hawke. Wincing in pain, he unscrewed the cap from a small bottle and shook white powder on the back of his hand between his forefinger and thumb.

He sniffed the cocaine into one nostril, then shook more powder and snorted again. Abdullah wasn't an addict, and had only used cocaine once before when he was wounded. It was the best medicine he had on hand and it would keep his mind sharp when it kicked in.

Waiting for the coke to take hold, he tucked a compression bandage under his shirt and held it in place with his right hand. Knowing his wound was grave, Abdullah had no doubt that Allah would see him through. They'd planned for such an event, and it called for one of the gangsters to strike out alone and return with the four-wheeler they'd hidden back where they shot the Ranger at the outset.

He tried to smile, but the muscles wouldn't work. They should. He was successful. Abdullah had captured the man who killed his brother and would now get his revenge.

His vision grayed and his mind wandered. The buzzing of bees on the blooming sage and creosote bushes reminded him of a swarm of locusts that had once flown over their tiny house in Qara, Syria, a remote mountain town perfumed by cherry trees. His father heard it long before the swarm arrived and shouted for everyone to get inside. The boys had been playing in the street and stopped to see a cloud approaching.

His mother rushed the brothers inside. The last thing he remembered seeing was the insects blotting out the sun. They stayed there for hours as the locusts covered their village, eating anything they could consume and destroying the cherry crop they depended on.

He blinked away tears of pain and focused on the unconscious Ranger's face. There was something he was supposed to do. Something to do with that face. Then he remembered. With an effort that almost exhausted him, Abdullah retrieved the knife and thick cloth bag Chino had dropped when the Ranger kicked him in the knee.

A long knife wrapped in a thick cloth bag was what he needed. He held them and focused on Chino, the one with features of an Asian. He recalled that some said the American Indians might possibly be descendants of Asian tribes of long ago.

He again tossed the items to Chino and repeated his order in Spanish. "This is for his head. Take it and put it in the bag."

Abdullah faded out and regained his wits to find the

Ranger still alive with Calaka squatting nearby like a vulture, spitting blood. Abdullah still had obligations to honor his brother. He issued orders again in his native language. None of the gangsters moved, and, irritated by their lack of communication, his voice rose in irritation.

They exchanged looks and turned their attention to anything but him. Their response enraged him, and Abdullah first cussed them in Spanish, then switched to his native language, getting louder as his fury increased.

Chino turned the long knife, as if checking the keenness of the blade. Apparently satisfied, he rose and approached the red-faced Syrian.

Abdullah met the man's eyes, and saw Death there.

Chapter 31

"Now what?" Arturo huddled under a tent sheltering volunteers from the most recent rain shower. He'd never seen clouds so low to the ground before. A dozen people were gearing up from folding tables, or drinking coffee from the dispenser and waiting for the rain to stop.

Jerry looked confused. "What do you think we do now?"

"You don't know what to do, now that we're here?" Arturo's aggravation rose as he stuck both hands into the front pockets on his jeans. Jerry was just like his dad, impulsive without thinking of any possible outcome. "I thought you had a plan."

"My *plan* was to get here, then figure out the next step."

"Look, if we go over there where all those people are, they'll kick us out."

"No, they won't. They need volunteers."

"With experience. We're just a couple of kids that cut school."

The frustration on Jerry's face was evident, and the

frown line between his eyes also reminded Arturo of
Sonny Hawke. He'd seen it more than once in the Ballard Courthouse a few months earlier.

"So, we'll talk to some of these guys and find out
what they know about Dad. *Then* we decide what to
do."

"Great." Arturo pointed at a group standing in the
far corner of the shelter, sipping coffee. "You know
any of them?"

Jerry studied the group and nodded. "That guy over
there's a highway patrol officer. Dad introduced us a
few months ago."

"Go on, then."

Almost as if he were reluctant to follow up on the
idea, Jerry moseyed in that direction, stopping to fill a
cup with steaming coffee before he joined them. Arturo sat on a table and waited as the rain intensified,
drumming on the taut roof.

Jerry returned with a triumphant look on his face.
"Got some news. As soon as this rain slacks off,
they're sending out more search teams."

"And how is that gonna help us?"

"Well, we can tag along."

Arturo pointed. "You're about to tag along with that
Ranger right there, right out of the park and back
home."

They watched Chief Park Ranger Tammy Rivera
duck under the tent and head straight toward them. Jerry
deflated at the look on the woman's face. "Boys, you
might be in trouble."

Jerry took a breath to argue, but Rivera raised a
hand. "Hush and listen. I know you're worried about

your dad, son, but your mama called a little while ago and *she's* worried sick about *you*."

"How'd . . . ?"

Rivera's eyes crinkled. "Because she's a mother like me, and your sister ratted you out. I know you want to help, but here's the deal, kid. You don't have any experience in search and rescue, and if you boys go out with a team, you'd slow them down because they'll have to fool with *you* and not what they need to do.

"These guys are splitting up into teams. They've all been trained, or have experience in search and rescue. Right now, it's dangerous out there, what with the flash floods and washed-out roads. Here's what I want you to do."

She grinned again, but it was forced. "Y'all come to the command center with us. You can see and hear everything that's going on. I'll keep you updated there and at the same time know you're not in any danger. Then when Sheriff Armstrong gets here, you can hang with him, and when this is over, *you* can drive your old man home."

Arturo saw Rivera almost say something else. Her mouth had already formed the words before she thought better of it, and the youngster was sure he knew exactly what she was going to say.

It was, "If we find your dad safe and sound."

Chapter 32

I woke up lying on the ground. The world was sideways, and the first thing that registered were legs walking back and forth. I swallowed and winced. Despite the pain in my throat, I was pleased my head was still nailed on.

The world wasn't clear, so I blinked a few times to clear my vision. Rocks and mesquite beans half buried in the sand came into focus, along with bleached sticks, and dried leaves leading to the Beard sitting beside his backpack. It took a few moments to register the sounds of angry voices and rustling leaves.

I was still in la-la-land and couldn't make out the words, but I didn't need to hear what was going on. Even though I couldn't follow the lingo, the Beard was giving the guys around me a dog-cussin', and rivaled the Old Man's fury that always arose around bob-wire.

Beard was still bleeding, but to be honest, it wouldn't have made any difference in the long run. His eyes flashed, and he got louder. Somebody stepped over my head and stalked toward Beard, who kept rattling away. I recognized ol' Asia when the guy walked up close to the terrorist and tilted his head like a dog looking at a new pan. Beard's eyes flicked from the others who were apparently behind me, up to Asia.

I waited for him to say something, but he surprised us both. Asia spat a mouthful of blood, then as casually as swatting a fly, he sank a big knife in Beard's chest. I recognized it as the one that was supposed to cut off my big ol' grape. The entire blade disappeared for a minute, looking like one of those toy knives we pretended to jab each other with when we were kids.

The gangster drew it out at the same lazy speed and walked away with no expression at all, as unconcerned as if he'd just killed a fly.

Now, I wasn't in the Beard's corner by any means, but it was still surprising to see someone murdered with absolutely no emotion whatsoever. His dark eyes widened in shock, and he gave a weak gasp. It must have taken everything out of him to make that little sound, because the guy wilted. Chin on his chest, it looked like he was examining the bloody wound, before he fell sideways. His head bounced against a flat rock and he lay still, blood pouring from his mouth and onto the dry ground that soaked it up like a sponge.

We lay face-to-face, staring into each other's eyes. The sight of the blood running from the corner of his mouth made me lick my own to be sure I wasn't in the same condition. I barely felt my own dry lips, but at least there wasn't any blood. His eyes widened slightly, as if realizing that I was watching something intensely personal.

I've killed enough deer to recognize when the light flickered out and his eyes filmed over.

The guy was dead as nickel coffee.

I swallowed, and the pain from my strangulation yanked me back into the world. I was next. The bag for my head lay only three feet away.

That's a helluva thing to think. I'd seen images like that, and recalled stories of the French Revolution, when they beheaded people with guillotines and some mean sonofabitch picked up the victim's heads as soon as they dropped into a basket and asked them questions to see if the brain still functioned.

I swallowed and croaked out the first thing that came to my mind.

"Hey guys, does this mean you're gonna let me go now?"

No one answered at first, but then a voice translated my words and they lifted my spirits by laughing.

Chapter 33

Sheriff Ethan Armstrong took the radio's handset from the dash bracket. "Dispatch, this is Armstrong. You copy?"

"Go ahead, Sheriff."

"Finally on the way. Anything new?"

"Negative. It's started raining, and that's not gonna help one damn bit. Their Hasty Team checked the murder site and came up empty. They found hoof prints on the way in and figure it's Sonny's horse. They're backtracking now to pick them up again, but like I said, the rain's making it hard."

"Ten-four. Keep me updated. Out."

He replaced the handset and steered around the courthouse. "You need anything before we head out?"

Herman Hawke was silent. Ethan glanced over to see the old Ranger's furrowed brow. Those and the crow's-feet in the corners of his eyes reminded him of the arroyos and canyons they were headed for.

"Herman?" Ethan figured he was so deep in thought he'd missed the question. "You need anything before we go?"

The old man cocked his head, peering from under his hat brim. "What if this is something else?"

"Such as?"

"What if Sonny ain't lost? I know that ol' horse coulda throwed him. You can't be around them jugheads much without 'em hurtin' you at some point, though they don't mean to. But what if Sonny tangled with something else?"

"I still don't get your drift."

"I can't explain it, son. I've got an itch that's tellin' me we're on the wrong track."

They drove past the Chat 'N Chew, the café where he met Sonny and Perry Hale for breakfast at least three times a week. The crowd inside looked thinner than usual, and Ethan figured some of the men had volunteered in the search.

"It'd be hard for Sonny to get lost. He knows the park and that kind of country. Even if he did, he'd sit his ass down and build a fire and wait. He wouldn't be gone far off the trail, neither."

"So what are you thinking?"

"A lot of things, but none of it sounds right."

They passed the high school on the way out of town and Herman held up a hand. "Rein up there and turn around. Take me to Sonny's house."

"What for?"

"I don't know that, either, but Kelly's still there, I bet. I need to be with her instead of stringing off to the park and getting' in folks' way." He dug a flip phone out of his shirt pocket and punched at the screen. "Hang on before you do anything." The call was answered on the second ring and the volume was turned up so loud Ethan had no trouble hearing the conversation with Herman's hired hand and unofficially adopted step-son, Gabe Nakai.

"Hello, *jefe*."

"I told you not to call me that, knothead. You're as much my kid as Sonny."

"*Sí, padron*."

"I changed my mind." Herman didn't respond to Gabe's warting. They both liked to aggravate the other when they had the chance. "Get my Winchester out of the house, that M1 you like so much, and both shotguns, then hoof it on over to Sonny's house."

The fun was over. "Trouble?"

"Yep. Grab plenty of shells for everything, too, oh, and the thirty-eight over the refrigerator."

"Remember I don't have a truck."

"Dammit. Fine." Herman spun his finger. "Call one of the Mayo brothers and have 'em bring you out." He hung up. "A man ain't no damn good to anybody when they don't have wheels. It's fixin' to rain, and they'll be headed to town anyway."

An odd pair, the Mayo brothers worked their ranch like the old-timers, from dawn 'til dusk in good weather. But if it rained or snowed hard, they headed for town like any good cowboy to blow off steam in the bars. The first sign of clearing weather, and they headed back out to their ranch.

Knowing better than to quiz the old man, because he'd been taught to do what his elders said, Ethan took a left and cut through a residential street lined with houses built eighty years earlier. Several older folks sat on the shaded porches and waved as the cruiser went by.

Herman absently threw up a hand in response, because that's what you did in the country.

"I got a feeling that I need to be here with Kelly."

"You're expecting trouble, then."

"Not expecting, but I intend to be in the way if it comes."

They pulled up in front of Sonny's house.

"Much obliged." Herman stepped out. "I got a bad feeling that won't go away, so I'm gonna stay right here."

No stranger to a lawman's sixth sense, Ethan leaned across the seat to speak. "I'll check back with you when I get to the command post. Y'all call if anything happens. Deputy Murphy's on the desk and he'll come a-runnin'."

Herman slammed the door and stood rooted to the ground, scanning the nearby houses. "Okie doke."

Chapter 34

Lying in the maze of shallow canyons, I was invisible to everyone in the world except for the four Indio-looking gangsters covered in tattoos. They were having a great time, though, jabbering at each other and talking about me.

I listened for aircraft, hoping for a search plane or helicopter. I knew enough about search techniques that they would deploy ground and search parties, but the timing was off. There was no way they could have tracked down the truck and trailer, and then pinpointed where to look from there.

The clouds had thickened since they'd knocked me in the head, and thunder grumbled in the distance. I was at least thankful for that. Had I been lying in the sun, I doubt I could have been in good enough shape to think. But then again, it made matters worse.

I'd heard the spokesman before when he told a news crew about a similar situation a year earlier when we were looking for a lost climber in the mountains.

"Our problem is this low-level cloud ceiling. We're basically socked in by these sitting on top of us, and

the higher-level clouds that are pouring in from the southwest that are providing additional cover. Right now, all this is preventing aircraft from participating in the search, so it's basically ground crews."

The problem with the spokesperson's answer bothered me the most right then. It was his way of saying things weren't good. The rain was going to hamper their search efforts, whenever they started looking for me.

Our people are doing the best they can right now.

"I need to sit up."

The Asian-looking Indio gangster squatted in front of me. "Be quiet, *amigo*."

I had another smart-ass answer ready, but one of the other guys cut me off.

"Maybe we take *this* dog's head instead, and tell Chatto it belongs to the Ranger. He is not afraid, and I like that. Let's let him live."

"No." I didn't like the speaker behind me. "Chatto will know the difference. American police don't have beards. He'll know the Ranger is alive, he will send men to kill our families and then us."

"Abdullah has already told him we have the Ranger."

"What?"

"He made a call with that satellite phone and sent our brothers to this man's house to wipe his seed from the earth."

The statement hit me like an electric shock. Twisting on the ground like a wrestler, I screamed in fear and frustration. I've never felt so helpless in my life. Trying to gain my knees, I fought harder than the time before, finding enough traction to lurch forward, trying to knock someone, anyone, off their feet. I needed to get *free!* A strange keening sound rose at the same time they put the boots to me.

They worked me over pretty good, but it didn't matter. Their kicks didn't register because I was numb with a fury I'd never felt before, spurred by the sheer horror of what I'd just heard. I lashed out with one boot. A shrill voice yelped and the others laughed as the unseen gangster behind me knelt to rub his shin. A worn-out tennis shoe caught me in the nose, flattening it with a crunch of cartilage and knocking me senseless.

I lay there, gasping for breath and struggling to stay conscious. Every second counted in getting back to Ballard to warn my family. Squatting with his elbows resting on his knees, Chinese guy laced his fingers. He dropped to one knee beside my head and picked up the bag, examining it as if he'd found it lying in the desert and wondering how such a fine bag came to be lost.

He leaned forward and dropped it over my head in one smooth motion, yanking the drawstring at the same time. I didn't like that kind of efficiency, having my head already in the bag before they went to work with the knife. I flipped like a crawdad, struggling to regain my feet, but more kicks to my ribs knocked the breath out of me.

A body dropped onto my back with one knee. I gasped and struggled for air while footsteps crunched up and stopped only a couple of inches from my broken and bleeding nose. The man put a knee to the side of my head, crushing my cheek into the ground.

I couldn't do anything except make my last words count. "You bastards can go to hell! You don't know what you're tangling with!"

Chapter 35

Yolanda Rodriguez quit tapping Perry Hale's shoulder so suddenly he noticed.

"You all right?"

Her dark eyes narrowed and she stared out the windshield like a toddler trying to wake up. "Pull over."

Knowing better than to argue, Perry Hale steered onto the shoulder, taking care not to run over a patch of cactus that had spilled through a bob-wire fence and spread out in a glacial flow onto the two-lane highway's shoulder. "All right. You forget your makeup?"

"You'll need it to cover up the bruises if you make that kind of crack again." She smiled with her eyes the way he liked, but it quickly went away. "Would you be upset if I told you to take me back to Kelly's house?"

"You throwing me over for her?"

"She's not my type. Listen, dummy. I'm not superstitious or anything. Well, my grandmother was and she believed in a lot of that old-world stuff that I never could explain . . ."

"What . . . are you talking about?"

Yolanda paused and glanced out the passenger window, as if bad guys were creeping up on them in the broad daylight. "Something's up, and I can't put my finger on it."

"I 'magine it's this gray weather and Sonny that's giving you the heebie-jeebies." Perry Hale scratched at the stubble on his jaw. "I've never seen you like this."

"Well, you haven't seen me in a lot of ways." She held up a hand to block his obvious comment. "Don't get nasty there, buddy. What I mean is I think you need to take me back. If something's happened to Sonny that wasn't an accident, it might be related to the takeover a few months ago.

"It may be just my imagination working overtime, but I was thinking about what you said when you were at the house and played the What If game. The first thing I'd say is, what if Sonny was a target for what he did in the takeover? What if he's not the *only* target?"

"I hadn't thought of that."

"Guys don't think the way us girls do. For the most part, you're more reactive."

"Like the other night."

"Stop, dang it. I'm being serious. Think about it. Ethan's on his way south, and so are most of his deputies. Lots of guys have already volunteered, and even a couple of the DPS guys are there."

Perry Hale rested an elbow on the console and rubbed his chin. "Half the volunteer fire department is gone. I get the picture."

"Good. It's not just me."

"I didn't say that." Perry Hale checked his mirror and made a U-turn. "But I've already learned to trust your instincts. I'll take you back, but Kelly's gonna throw a fit.

She wants to be at the command post, too. She's not going to like the idea of staying at home."

Yolanda rested her hand on Perry Hale's bicep. "This bad feeling's getting stronger. I can handle whatever comes our way back in town, and having me out there to search with you guys won't make one bit of difference."

"It will to me."

"That's the sweetest thing you've ever said to me."

"Well, don't get used to me being such a nice guy all the time." He studied her face for a second. "You really don't wear much makeup, do you?"

"Thanks for finally noticing."

Herman Hawke and Gabe were sitting on Sonny's and Kelly's wraparound porch when Yolanda and Perry pulled into the drive. Herman looked comfortable with his chair back against the wall on two legs. Anyone simply glancing at Gabe would have thought he was asleep with his back against a column and his legs stretched out on the wide railing. His arms were crossed on his chest, a sweat-stained straw hat shading his eyes.

Herman stood when Yolanda opened the Dodge's door. "News?"

"No, sorry." She grabbed her MOLLE pack while Perry Hale dug under the back seat and unlocked the gun box. She crossed to the steps and dropped the pack beside her. "I changed my mind and decided to stay here with Kelly. Looks like you had the same idea."

Herman eyed the MOLLE pack, then the AR-15 that

joined it. "In my day, the women usually baked or quilted when they were worried."

"I don't do those things, but I do clean weapons to take my mind off my troubles."

He grinned and winked. "I wish you'd been around when I was younger."

"Me too." Gabe thumbed his hat upward.

"Easy, boys." Perry Hale laid a heavy canvas bag beside her pack. "She's locked and loaded."

Yolanda climbed the steps and hugged Herman's.

Gabe swung his legs inward to stand and almost lost his balance. "*Hijo de puta* . . . boy of the bitch!"

Herman sighed. "It's son of a bitch, boy. You have *got* to learn how to cuss."

Chapter 36

My dome was still on my shoulders as they hauled me across the ground. Limbs crackled and rocks put bruises on top of those that were probably turning a nice shade of black and blue. It sounded like they'd pulled me under the mesquites, though the sound was somewhat muffled by the bag. The next thing I knew, my feet were tied and fingers grabbed the material in front of my mouth.

I found myself fighting to breathe through the bag's thick material.

Still not going out without a fight, I kicked and thrashed until a fist caught me upside the head again. "*Estate quieto*! Be still!" A hand pushed the bag into my face and the owner squeezed my nose and pulled the material away from my mouth. The next thing I knew, a blade punched through and cut my bottom lip. I wanted to tell the dumb sonofabitch he'd completely missed my neck when he sliced outward and quit. "*Para el aire. Respira aquí.*"

They pulled back and I did what he said. I twisted my head inside the bag, working my face closer to the material and putting my mouth over the new slit. The fresh air coming into the already stale bag was the sweetest and coolest I'd ever inhaled. My head cleared. They were going to let me live a little longer.

More sounds of rustling and I heard them drag Beard's body the same way. They dropped him next to me with a heavy thump and left. We lay side by side, but only one of us was breathing.

Chapter 37

The gangsters fiddle-farted around all day, loafing under the mesquites and napping in turn. I could tell because the tones of their soft snores were different. Even though I was scared to death, I dozed a time or two, always jolting awake when someone spoke. It was easy to tell when dusk arrived only because the inside of the bag got darker.

As far as I knew, they were staying there to avoid being spotted by aircraft. They were spinning their wheels, because based on past experience and the last time I'd seen the clouds, there wouldn't be anyone searching by air.

At least they bought me some time. The last time someone was lost in the park, I was part of a search party that involved an airplane and helicopter from the DPS, and even a drone, new technology I hadn't been around, but of course it was a clear sky.

That day in the command post we watched the monitor as the operator flew the drone over some of the most rugged country I'd ever seen, and it showed me that the world had passed me by. The drone investigated corners we could never explore on foot or by plane, and we found the hikers on the second day because they'd left their destination written down in their car.

I brightened, hoping they had one up right then, but it might take a day or two before anyone stumbled across the truck and trailer. SAR would concentrate in that area first, giving my new friends time to go or do whatever they wanted.

A light pop thumped the sack over my head, making me think one of the gangsters had thumped the bag for some reason. Another landed on my cuffed hand. That one was cold and either someone was spitting water on me like my friends did when us kids were swimming at the local pool, or it was raining.

The wind freshened and a distant rumble of thunder told me falling weather was on the way. That sounded pretty good to me, because I needed moisture. In addition to being dry as a gourd from breathing through my mouth against the slit, my stomach felt like my throat really *was* cut.

Wind increased as the distant storm moved closer. Hands grabbed my feet and those guys weren't any too gentle about dragging my carcass out from under cover. I'd been still for so long the bullet wound had settled into a low throb, and the rest of the cuts, scrapes, and punctures faded into the background. The minute I moved, my wound fired up.

I groaned when they yanked me upright. It was all I could do to stay on my feet, but I figured that if I went down, they'd take what was already bagged up and leave the rest behind.

"Water, guys. If you're planning on making me walk, I'm gonna need water and something to eat."

They jabbered with each other in their complicated language until one of them untied the drawstring and yanked the bag off my head. It wasn't full dark like I thought, only dusk, giving me enough light to make out the faces surrounding me. The one with the bag in his hand was the little sawed-off guy who'd snuck up behind me.

He held up an unidentifiable object and pushed it against my lips. "Eat."

"I'd be easier if you'd uncuff me and let me hold it myself."

"No. *Comer.*"

"So I just bite it off or hold it like a cigar in my teeth and go to chewin'?"

"Comer."

"You were the valedictorian of your class, right?"

A second voice cut in. I'd heard the name Javier, and thought it might be him. "He does not speak English. That is the only thing you will get, so do it as he says. If you don't, you won't eat."

I shrugged and bit into what the runt held. I expected some kind of jerky or homemade food, but it was an energy bar. I didn't like the consistency that reminded me of sandy peanut butter, but ate it anyway. It was harder'n hell to chew with a mouth as dry as the desert.

Gnawing on the granola bar like a cigar, I had time to check them out. It was then I noticed they were geared up for a hike. Each one of the four wore backpacks slung over their shoulders, Cobras hanging battle-ready over their chests. They were spread in a semicircle, facing outward. It was obvious they were keeping an eye out for search parties.

The Beard still lay under the bush, but there was something odd about him. It took me a second in the fading light to figure out that his ears were gone. My head spun when I saw them hanging on a leather thong around Fat Face's neck. That's what I'd come to call him. The guy was built slender, but his face was abnormally large for his body and neck with four sweeping lines. Snarling coyote tattoos faced each other on both cheekbones, their snouts against his flat nose.

Pieces clicked in my mind and I remembered where I'd seen those sweeping tattoos, on a wanted poster. My eyes flicked from one gangster to the other. Even though we were losing light fast, there was enough to see that all four of the heavily armed men standing around me had the same tattoo in the same place. What skin I could see on their arms and hands was also tatted up, and most were jailhouse art.

I was seriously in trouble, because the Coyotes Rabiosos were my captors, and they killed for a living.

Chapter 38

Darkness fell and so many volunteers and reporters filled the command post in the Panther Junction training room the CP had to be moved to three large canvas tents set up at the far end of the parking lot. One of the tents became a "media room," and the other a gathering place supplied with coffee and snacks.

Searching the maze of shallow canyons in the stark Chihuahuan Desert took organization, and that's how the park staff was spending their time in the brightly lit tent surrounded by experienced Search and Rescue team members frustrated by the weather.

Perry Hale stood to the side of the tent, out of the traffic flow, and watched as Chief Park Ranger Tammy Rivera accepted a cup of coffee from Emergency Coordinator Ronda Boyd, who served as second in command for what had become known as the Hawke Incident. Both wore Park Service uniforms. Their flat-brimmed hats rested on the edge of the table.

Boyd waved the foam cup toward the top of the tent. "Texas DPS and Border Patrol aircraft have been coordinating for a potential air rescue in the morning, but the Operations Support Manager with the McDonald Observatory says foggy conditions and low cloud cover will most likely prohibit any flights into the area, just as they did this afternoon."

The CP glowed in the dark, lit from within by electric lights served by two near-silent portable Honda generators. Sheriff Ethan Armstrong studied a waterproof, tear-resistant topographic map spread over a table. Several experienced Park Service personnel were gathered around the table as the emergency coordinator discussed possible search locations with SAR volunteers from multiple agencies.

Typical Search and Rescue teams often involved as few as four or five volunteers, along with Park Service personnel. A Texas Ranger disappearing under mysterious circumstances on the heels of a horrific triple murder brought a sense of urgency never before seen in the national park. The brotherhood of law-enforcement officers resulted in a significant turnout, so many that what they'd begun calling the Coffee Tent was nearly full.

Sonny's superior, Major Chase Parker, waited off to one side with two other Rangers, listening. All three lawmen stood out in the group, exuding what Ethan had once heard called Texas Cool. Their Silverbelly hats were the most noticeable item. The aura that only iconic Texas Rangers can project cleared a three-foot circle around the trio.

Major Chase Parker stood out from the other two in a white shirt, dark tie, and black khaki pants. Rangers Bill Gasch and Cameron Dulles wore light pinstriped shirts and dress jeans. All three carried semi-automatic .45s in almost identical Ranger Rig holsters strapped under matching tooled leather belts. Their *cinco peso* badges glowed under the lights. Different brands of polished boots were the only noticeably individualized items they wore.

None of the three had offered any suggestions or advice since they arrived. The Rangers had little or no experience in desert search and rescue, and knew the federal government, specifically the FBI, held jurisdiction. They were there for Sonny.

Holding a cup of steaming coffee not far away, Perry Hale half sat on a table with one foot on the ground, listening. Although the governor had authorized Sonny to work with Perry Hale and Yolanda, they were both instructed to fly under the radar. Only Major Parker knew of his involvement. The other two Rangers in the CP had no idea who he was.

Coordinator Ronda Boyd marked an X with a grease pencil on the topo map and pulled a stray strand of short brown hair out of her eyes. "This is the site of last week's murders. Based on information from Sonny Hawke's wife, he was most likely headed there. Now, here's the problem. He was in his truck and pulling a horse trailer and we haven't found them yet. That's a huge concern. You all have descriptions for them, including tag numbers.

"The Hasty Team reported tire tracks of a truck and trailer, but they were following them by flashlight when it started to rain. They're the only ones we have on the ground in the target area at this time because of the weather."

She glanced up at the Rangers standing nearby. "We dispatch Hasty Teams at the outset. They're our first boots on the ground and equipped with light packs to get in fast and evaluate the situation. They're prepared for a fast medical response and carry satellite phones."

Major Parker nodded his thanks and Boyd went back to her outline. "Like I said, National Park Service ground searchers were deployed to trails in the area, and the park's fixed-wing aircraft and Customs and Border Protection helicopters are standing by, but we can't get them up right now, so it's not looking terribly good for aerial extraction.

"This is rough country." She glanced up again, fighting that troublesome strand of hair and making eye contact with the Rangers. "Some of the roughest in the park, and that's what concerns us. Our SAR usually utilizes helicopters for extraction in there. Tracking was difficult this morning. I have guys walking the slickrock areas by the mile, and besides the Hasty Team, other experienced park personnel are out there with flashlights."

Chief Rivera scanned their concerned faces. "Some of them have been out there in the rain since it started. Just so you know, and this doesn't get out of this tent, and especially to the media out there, we have the Justice of the Peace and the funeral home on standby. Local game wardens called in to say they're available if we need them. A couple of those guys are experienced desert survivalists and will come in handy if this continues."

Park Ranger Boyd picked it up without a break in the beat. "I have the county emergency medical services on standby, with extra paramedics who can be here in thirty minutes. We have people checking all the pull-outs and trailheads in the park, but if this rain keeps up, and I'm afraid that's going to happen, some of these roads are going to wash out. When they start to get dangerous, I'm pulling my people in."

Sheriff Ethan Armstrong couldn't stay silent any longer. He crossed his arms and studied the map. "Since we don't have reports of the truck and trailer anywhere else, maybe someone moved it."

"Did he come out with anyone else?" Chief Ranger Rivera frowned and flipped open a small pocket notebook. "I don't have that information."

"No." Ethan hesitated. He didn't want to misdirect the SAR team. They had a proven plan to find people that worked over and over again in normal circumstances. "My concern is that this is connected to the murders in some way. What if someone took Sonny at gunpoint and drove the truck away?"

Stone faced, Major Parker crossed his arms and leaned into Ranger Gasch, who flipped a page on the small notebook that seemed to be part of his left hand. He wrote a brief note and nodded at the quiet statement, then turned his attention back to the sheriff.

Completely out of his comfort zone, the single FBI agent on-site had been stationed in West Texas for only a couple of months after his involvement with the Ballard Incident. After two years in the Washington, D.C. field, Agent Landon McDowell had yet to acclimate to the Big Bend region. His suit, tie, and white shirt were completely out of sync with the rest of those in the CP. "That's something we haven't discussed. Lost visitors and hikers are one thing, felony kidnapping is another. I worked with Sheriff Armstrong on getting an APB out on the truck, but what if it never left the park on normal surface roads? What if he never arrived?"

Boyd put the coffee down on the table and slipped

both hands into her pockets, studying the map. She raised her eyes to Sheriff Armstrong. "Does he have four-wheel-drive?"

"He does."

"That truck could be anywhere."

The cell phone in Perry Hale's tactical pants pocket vibrated. He read the text from Mary Hawke. As stone faced as the three Rangers across the tent, Perry casually rose and exited, heading straight for his truck.

Chapter 39

It was full dark when the littlest gangster with the head full of spiders took off without a word. A scattering of light raindrops came and went, bringing the odor of petrichor, the smell of rain on dry earth. The rain also released the scent of creosote from the surrounding scrub. I'd always enjoyed the scent, because it brought great memories of cool afternoons and quality time on the porch with my twins Jerry and Mary.

One of the gangsters was more outgoing than the others and I'd heard him speaking a little English, so I figured it wouldn't hurt to get him talking.

"You got a name?"

"Yes."

I waited for it, but he remained silent. "Am I supposed to guess?"

"You're supposed to be quiet and do as we say or we'll put the bag back."

"No, you won't. You boys want to make time now that it's dark and I'd slow you down too much if I can't see."

The rain increased in volume as Fat Face behind me

launched into a string of Spanish mixed with an Indian dialect. The only things I could pick out were the Mexican cusswords I'd learned in school. The way he said them, though, made my skin crawl almost as much as Runt's snarling coyote tattoos, or the terrorist's fresh ears hanging like a pendant necklace around Fat Face's neck.

It's like the guys in school who used the "F" word all the time. For some, it came as second nature, but when a couple of others I grew up with used it in any sense, it was the nastiest word I'd ever heard.

Funny, both of those high school acquaintances were in prison. I'd put one of them there myself, within a year of graduating. I was a rookie cop and got a Breaking and Entering call one night on a warehouse.

Two men were crawling out a window when I arrived. It was nothing to drag them the rest of the way and cuff 'em. When I finally got a light on my fresh catch of the day, I saw they were the nasty-talking buddies Jim Looney and James Baker, who decided to go into business for themselves by taking other people's property and reselling it.

Unfortunately for them, Looney lived up to his namesake and had a pistol on him, automatically graduating him to felony status. It was my first good arrest and conviction, though it was odd to arrest someone you'd known for years.

Fat Face cut loose with another string of complaints again, and I waited until he was finished before turning to Javier to translate. He saw the look on my face and grinned in the glow of the flashlight cupped in his hand. His gold tooth sparkled.

"Calaka says that you talk too much and I'm being

too good to you. He may be right. We were supposed to bring back your head in that bag, and that's all. He wants to finish the job and go."

All of a sudden, I felt like a mouse, knowing that if I moved or raised my eyes to Calaka, he'd kill me as quick as that rodent. I stared downward, already soaked, trying not to shiver from the sudden chill from the rain. They may have taken it as fear.

"I don't know why I don't." Javier dug in his ear. "Maybe I want Chatto to have the pleasure of killing you himself. Maybe I can get more money for you all in one piece."

My usual smart comments stuck in my throat. I was afraid to speak.

"I don't know what to do now that Abdullah is dead." Javier dug in his ear again. I hoped for a roaring case of MRSA. Maybe the staph infection would travel from his ear directly into his brain.

More silence.

"My name is Javier, if it matters." He quit digging. "Right now, I think we walk. This storm is just what we need to wash away all the tracks."

There. I was right. Now I had all their names. Asia was Chino, Calaka replaced Fat Face, and the last guy was Pepito, a name I remembered from my childhood watching *The Real McCoys* television show.

The little guy reappeared, and they leaned in together for a minute before Javier pointed with his light. I guess he'd taken over as boss, now that the Beard was attracting flies. "Calaka, *vámonos*. Chino, *deyaa*."

I was trying to figure out what language *deyaa* came from when Javier turned and led off. The Chinese-looking Indio, Chino, fell into line behind him. Calaka shoved me between the shoulders, causing my bullet wound to catch fire again, and I followed. He walked drag.

Six steps into our walk, the blisters on my feet felt as if someone was holding a blowtorch against the backs of my heels. Calaka shoved me a third time, causing me to stumble and land on my knees.

"Rapido!"

"Got news for you, partner. My top speed's gonna be half of what I figure you want."

He raised a fist and I braced myself, knowing I probably wouldn't get back up.

"Espera!" Javier came back and they launched into an argument I couldn't understand, so in response, I sat down to wait them out. It seemed to be the prudent thing to do.

Chapter 40

Marc Chavez was indecisive and despite his OCD, the obsessed man was usually in complete control of any situation. To him, every fiasco had to do with someone else, and Abdullah's failure to check in was another example of weaknesses they should strive to overcome.

Though Chavez promised himself he wouldn't call the satellite phone Abdullah carried, he couldn't help himself. He dialed the number and paced his expansive living room as it rang and rang. He snatched the remote control wrapped in a Ziploc bag to prevent contamination and flicked the enormous flat-panel TV to the Weather Channel.

The female meteorologist smiled at him and launched into the forecast for the southwest portion of the country. "This stream of moisture will continue for at least another twenty-four hours, pumping moisture from the Gulf of California up and over Mexico and into the Big Bend region of Texas."

The gray plume on her map stretched all the way to Abilene and west to Lubbock.

Chavez lowered the volume and ended the call. He dialed a second number that was answered on the first ring. "Yes."

He dispensed with normal formalities, because the gangster on the other end hadn't yet deserved such courtesy. Chatto was an employee, and nothing else. "Abdullah hasn't called in. I don't don't don't know what's happening."

His tendency toward repetition, especially under stress, was getting away from Chavez, adding to his frustration.

"We haven't heard from him, either."

"What are you going to do about it?"

"Nothing."

"You assured me this man knew his business."

"We both made decisions on the information we had at hand. Abdullah came highly recommended, and the men I sent with him are the descendants of the greatest fighters who ever lived. Let them do their jobs. They will contact you when they have the Ranger's head."

"What if they don't?"

Chatto chuckled. "Then they won't."

The phone went dead in Chavez's ear, and he carefully placed it on the granite counter instead of throwing it against the wall.

"They won't won't won't. That's what he said." He nodded at the meteorologist who smiled at him again. "I can wait. Yes. I can wait wait . . ." Chavez clamped his jaw.

I am in control.

I am in control.

I am in control.

Chapter 41

My captors' new pace wasn't as fast as when they'd started out, but it was almost too much to handle. Besides the blisters on my heels that were probably bleeding, my left side and arm felt hot. I was sure infection had already set in, and if I didn't get some medical assistance, I was gonna be in a world of hurt pretty damn quick.

The little guy led us across the slick hardpan as rain pattered my bare head, making me wish again for my hat. At first the water felt good, but the air cooled quickly as the night progressed and after a while I grew chilly in my drenched shirt and jeans. There was a moment of hope when I thought I could slip my wet hands free of the cuffs, but they'd clamped them too tight.

I had no idea where we were headed, but the little guy led the way through the darkness by dead reckoning. He had a destination, and that worried me most of all.

Memories rose as our group stretched along the

trail, reminding me of stories I'd read when I was a kid
of settlers captured by Iroquois Indians who were bound
and led day and night through the wilderness and into
Canada. I was in a modern-day nightmare of the same
kind. My mind jumped to accounts of the Comanches
who often took prisoners and traveled hundreds of
miles on horseback, but the Apaches from our area
usually walked—

Apaches! That's who these guys were. Descendants
of those little bands of fighters who ran General Crook
ragged back in the 1800s. That's what I'd been trying
to remember. Those four sweeping lines on their necks
indicated where they came from. Rabid Coyotes were
an offshoot gang of Apaches who still lived in the Occidental Mountains of Mexico and surfaced every now
and then when killing needed to be done.

There was no doubt now. Those guys were meaner'n
snakes and would just as soon kill a person as look at
them. I wondered why I was still alive. They'd knifed
Beard, or Abdullah, pretty damn quick. He must have
pissed them off somehow.

I quickly learned to stay almost under Chino's heels.
Each time I lost ground and trailed him, Calaka slammed
my wounded shoulder with his fist to push me ahead.
Each time hurt worse than the last and I promised myself that I was gonna knock him in the head the first
chance I got.

They moved like animals, dodging all manner of
plants with weapons. No one spoke and their silent communication reminded me of quail threading through the
grass. Words can't express how much I appreciated that.
I didn't need anything else to hurt. The cactus thorns

and tiny needles I'd collected earlier were still in my jeans and skin, sending waves of pain and irritation up my legs at every step.

Flashes of lighting fractured the clouds, coming closer with every minute. Rain increased, and we were soon hiking through a downpour. Desert storms are dangerous in the daylight. They're worse at night when you can't see where you're going.

Pepito flicked on a flashlight up ahead and paused. We'd come to a wash already churning with water. Hard rains run off the desert hardpan and even a shower results in a flash flood. The volume falling upstream guaranteed floods. That's why we were moving so fast. They wanted to cross as many arroyos as possible before they filled with water.

Calaka grabbed my collar like I was rushing ahead, nearly jerking me off my feet. The guy was really pissing me off, and I didn't like being manhandled. Javier and Pepito studied the stream of dark water and conversed a few feet away. I couldn't hear them, but it was obvious they were debating the depth and strength of the rushing water.

They came to a decision as lightning flickered overhead and waved us forward. Calaka shoved me and I'd about had enough. I spun to find him grinning like he had good sense. He was just hoping I'd give him a solid reason to kill me, but it wasn't going to happen at that moment.

Choking down my anger, I stumbled down the slope and waded into the thigh-deep water that immediately filled my boots. Lordy, it felt good at first, because the cold water numbed the open blisters on my heels. The problems would come later when my wet socks pulled against the boots.

Pepito waded ahead and reached the steep bank on the opposite side, but had to follow it downstream a few yards before finding a good place to climb out. It took both hands to scrabble up the sharp slope. His feet slipped, and he lost the flashlight that flickered once in the current before disappearing.

Ahead of me, Javier struggled in the muddy current and with both hands cuffed behind my back, I was getting afraid. Boots full of water and no way to swim, I'd go under in a heartbeat. The water was noticeably rising. Walking was difficult enough as it was, but Calaka kept shoving me as if I could go faster.

Javier dug a flashlight out of his pocket and shined it on the bank, then back at me. *"Rápido!"*

He didn't have to tell me twice. I had no intention of getting caught in the flash flood I finally heard. Out of sight in the dark, a low rumble and clatter of soaked wood being swept downstream told me time was almost up.

Terrified, Javier aimed his light upstream. The intense beam skipping across the surface of the water lit the garbage carried along the ripples and waves that rushed past the steep, narrow walls of the arroyo.

I broke into a splashing run, doing my best to reach the other side before the tangle of trash arrived to sweep us downstream. It's hard to run in a strong current with your hands cuffed behind you. The steep gap leading up the edge of the wash seemed miles away. I lost my footing as the high water arrived, knocking my right foot out from under me. Water filled my mouth when I went down on one knee.

Regaining my feet was one of the hardest things I'd ever done. Once upright, I couldn't use my arms for balance, and every step was a struggle. Each time the leather sole of my boots came down, the sand below melted away. By the time I was within five feet of the steep bank, I was forced to plant my left foot and lean sideways against the torrent.

There was no way to climb out without using my hands and I shouted at Javier, who had just reached the bank. "Hey! You're gonna have to help me!"

"No! Climb." He started up and had to grab a young bush growing over the edge. "Use your knees!"

It was obvious he intended to save himself first, and I couldn't blame him. The rising water was terrifying and it was all I could do to stay calm and think. I stumbled against the crumbling bank, falling sideways, my legs almost pulled out from under me. Rocks and mud caved in on my good shoulder. I pushed off and leaned into the slope, losing my balance. The current grabbed my legs and pulled me sideways.

Sliding down into the water, something big and hard brushed my shirt. Had it hit me full on, I'd have gone under. Still, my head and shoulders were barely above the surface. I turned my head, spitting water, barely remembering the word for help. *"Ayuda!"*

It seemed like I was a goner, but then Chino made it across and grabbed me from behind. He wrapped his arms around my waist and lifted me upright. Goddlemighty did things pull. I shouted in pain from the hot bullet wound and dug into the arroyo bed with my heels to help.

We tried to climb in tandem, but it wasn't working.

Pepito and Javier leaned over the edge and reached down. Chino had me far enough up the bank for them to grab me under my arms. I shrieked as the bullet wound tore open, but without my hands, I was nothing but dead weight. Rain filled my eyes and I ducked my head.

Chino managed to plant his feet and pick me up even higher. Little Guy and Javier were on their knees by then, straining downward. They each got a hold and fell backward, dragging me over the edge like someone pulling a lost swimmer into a raft. Physics took over and I was halfway up the bank, my legs dangling in space.

Chino scampered up and past like a monkey. I guess he felt he'd done his do and it was time to save himself. Bent double on my stomach, I couldn't get any traction. One foot kicked something, and I realized it was Calaka back there still in the water.

A bolt of lightning lit the world, and I turned my head enough to see his terrified eyes. The black water was up to his neck, and he had a grip on a rock jutting from the bank. His mouth was open in fear. People notice the oddest things under stress. The ear necklace he had made with a leather thong was incredibly clear, while his face seemed slightly out of focus.

Eyes wide in panic, he grabbed for anything to save himself. His free hand slapped my soaked knee, slid down my leg, and his fingers locked onto the upper leather throat of my right boot.

If he'd gotten a good hold, he would have taken me with him when a dark log rose from the water. I saw it coming in the next flash of lightning and kicked out with my free foot, grazing his face, but it was enough for him to lose his concentration and slap the boot away.

The submerged end of the soaked log caught against something underwater and rose at a forty-five-degree angle. It seemed to almost take a bead on him like a battering ram and slammed the guy in the side of the head at the same time I kicked one last time. Calaka flailed with one hand, but the Cobra around his neck got in the way and tangled his arm. His grip slipped off my boot and he gave a yelp that ended in a gargle.

Chino saw him go under. *"Izel!"*

Oh, you guys have real names.

He rose, but his face didn't break the surface of the water, just a hand and arm. Then he was gone.

Pepito and Javier dug their feet into the slick mud and pulled me onto the bank. Once I was completely out of the arroyo, Pepito crawled past, looking for Calaka, who I hoped was already playing submarine and halfway to Mexico. Chino shouted at Javier, who answered in their same ancient language.

I didn't have to know what he said, because the tone of his voice spoke volumes.

I'd have danced a jig if I coulda gotten up, but I had to stay right where I was on my side, trembling and hoping they hadn't seen my part in Calaka's drowning.

Chapter 42

Herman Hawke sat in the darkness of Kelly and Sonny's front porch, watching the street as light rain splashed from the gutters and downspouts. He'd unscrewed the bulb in the porch light, just in case anyone inside flicked the switch without thinking.

The house anchored the corner of a vast lot. The developers had apparently been impressed with the emptiness of the Big Bend Region, and built the houses on two-acre plots. Light pollution wasn't a factor in the Big Empty, and the lack of street lamps made the neighborhood exceptionally dark, especially under thick cloud cover.

There were plenty of places to hide in the dark semi-rural neighborhood, and Herman felt as nervous as a cat in a doghouse. Lightning flickered in the distance beyond Ballard, and another storm fractured the clouds in the opposite direction. The wind freshened and he was glad he'd worn a flannel shirt.

He was thinking about the row that ate up too much time when Kelly found out that Jerry and Arturo had cut school and left for the national park to help in the search for his dad. She called Jerry's cell phone that rang until the automated voice said he was unavailable. Turning his phone off in such a crisis sent his schoolteacher mom into a tizzy, and Mary quietly suffered the lecture meant for both of them.

Jerry was just like his dad, and Herman couldn't help but grin, despite the situation.

A late-model sedan passed on M Street, traveling past the side of the house. The car California-Rolled the stop sign at the intersection. Taillights angling inward gave the shadowy car an irritated look, as if they were angry eyes. The driver wasn't much more than a silhouette. Herman wouldn't have seen anything at all, until the bright light from a cell phone below the level of the window came on and illuminated the man's face to reveal the driver's Hispanic origins.

Other shapes moved inside the car as it accelerated to the thirty-mile-per-hour speed limit and disappeared eastward. The retired Texas Ranger casually reached out and picked his shotgun up from where it leaned on a porch post. He laid it across his lap and waited.

Chapter 43

Calaka was gone, and I figured I'd pay the price for it. Pepito took off down the arroyo with a flashlight, looking for ol' Fat Face. I took the opportunity to lay there in the rain while everything throbbed, and that included my already broken nose that'd slammed against the ground while Calaka tried to climb my leg.

Asia and Javier squatted nearby. The anguished looks on their faces told me that despite being cold-blooded murderers, they still had a few human qualities. I lay still, hoping not to draw their attention, wondering how they were all connected.

Most of that particular storm had moved past when Javier stood and came over. He squatted beside me. "I know you're not unconscious."

"I was just laying here, enjoying the rain."

"*Humph*. You are lucky again tonight. I should be carrying your head to Chatto. Maybe if I had done that, Calaka would still be alive."

"You said Izel."

"Yes. We all have nicknames. His means skinny, or

skeleton, like little Pepito who is looking for Calaka's body, or Chino . . ."

"Who looks Chinese."

He looked surprised. "Yes. That is what Chino means. You are a funny man."

"What's your nickname?"

"I don't have one. I am more Mexican than *nnee*."

History was coming alive right there in the desert night. "That means *the People*."

"Yes. We are all related in some way."

"Mind if I sit up?"

Javier shrugged.

He didn't help, so it was a struggle to get my knees under me, then wriggle upright. Grinding my teeth, I blew hard through my broken nose, clearing a thick clot of blood, and finally breathed clearly.

I tilted my head up to let the rain wash my face and it was all I could do not to whimper or groan. I didn't want to give either of them the satisfaction, so I sat there for a long moment, just drawing air.

Javier nodded, as if I'd said something profound. *"Bien."*

"You're sure talking a lot all of a sudden."

He shrugged and met Chino's eyes. "You are a fighter. We respect that."

So they got talkative when one of them died. I hoped I'd get the opportunity again soon to get rid of another rat so this guy would spill his guts. "What's this all about?"

Chino perked up, telling me he knew a little English after all. He unloaded a string of complaints that I couldn't get the gist of. Javier answered back and their voices rose. Chino stood and jabbed a finger at me, then the arroyo, before turning and extending his arm with one finger pointed into the distance.

Their argument faded as quick as it had begun and Javier returned to our conversation. "It is nothing personal for us. It was for *him*, though, Abdullah."

I took a wild guess. "Because I killed his brother."

Javier was surprised again. "Yes. That is right."

You could almost hear my mind gear up, like a turbocharger. "I killed his brother and he killed three innocent people to draw me in so he could shoot me."

Javier nodded like a judge behind a tall bench. "Yes. But he missed and shot a bird."

"He didn't miss by much."

"It was too much. We are ready to return home to our green mountains. This desert was once the home of our ancestors, but today it holds nothing for us. Our roots have rotted here, but they thrive in the Occidental."

"Turn me loose and go home, then."

His face fell and the sadness in his eyes almost made me feel sorry for the guy. "We have made a promise to Chatto. He is the leader of our clan, but he is sick with the disease of money. He made a promise to the head of the Cervantes cartel. Two of our brothers remain behind as . . . what do you call it . . . insurance to complete the job. There is more at stake here than that *chiini* rotting back there. Chatto owes another in Houston."

The guy actually looked at me with pity. "That is another part of the story. The man who truly wants your head lives in how-stone."

"You mean Houston?"

"*Sí*, Hooston. A coyote keeps his word." Javier shook his head. "It is all we have left."

A flashlight beam pierced the darkness and the little guy, Pepito, returned. He rattled off something I couldn't understand and Javier put both hands to his head.

"*Aieee!*"

It was the damndest thing. I'd killed one of their guys back where this whole thing started, and from what I could tell, they hadn't given a fiddler's fangdang. But old Calaka drowned, and it was a tragedy.

For them anyway.

Chapter 44

Gabe Nakai waited in the deep shade of the porch, slumped in an antique shell-back lawn chair on the north side of Sonny's house. A Remington pump 870 lay across his lap. His running buddy Sonny was on his mind and he worried for his safety.

The old Ranger around the corner was as close as any of Gabe's relatives who still lived south of the border. He wondered how he'd gotten so lucky. He crossed the Rio years earlier, carrying his toddler daughter, Evangelina, to find a better life for the both of them after the death of his young wife. He was a youngster himself, still in his teens, but much more experienced in life than the American boys his age.

He hadn't used a coyote like most who crossed, but had talked to enough people in his small village not far from Parral to understand the dangers from both his own people and those he was sure to encounter on the Texas side.

The chances of being left alone in the desert by a coyote was too big a chance to take with a baby in his arms. Another danger of being robbed by thieves before he crossed was just as likely. Bandits prowled the wild country on the Mexican side like jaguars, preying on those who chose to cross.

Gabe waited for a dark, rainy night just like the one beyond the porch, and floated across in a makeshift raft made of empty plastic bottles. No one saw him slip out of his aunt's house with Evangelina in his arms and make his way to the river. The water was warm that night, and she delighted in splashing the dimpled surface with her tiny hands as they made their way into Texas.

A battered pickup truck driven by his distant cousin waited near Del Rio and took them to a friend's house. The street was dark and empty, and the house with all the windows open looked as inviting as his own bed.

He and Evangelina joined a group of migrant farm workers and soon made their way to Ballard. The first person he met there was Sonny Hawke, who introduced him to Herman, who hired him on the spot after being taken with the dark-eyed, expressive little girl. Gabe had been his top hand and adopted family member ever since, and was a natural-born cattleman.

Gabe tensed when a dark car without headlights appeared at the far end of the block and pulled to the curb. It was the same one with the distinctive taillights that passed earlier, going the opposite direction. *"Jefe."*

His soft voice carried across the silent porch with enough volume for the old Ranger to hear. His response was just as quiet. "Yes."

"A car at the end of the block."

There was a long pause, and Gabe imagined the old man leaning forward to peer into the darkness. "That'll be them."

Gabe rapped on the wall behind him.

Yolanda's voice came through the open window behind his shoulder. "We on?"

"Posiblemente."

"Great."

He heard a rustle as she moved away and knew her response was nothing but pure sarcasm.

Chapter 45

Showers came and went, while we just went.

Every step was excruciating, and I kinda wanted to ask Javier why they were keeping me alive if all this guy Chatto wanted was my head, but then again, I really didn't need to know that much.

I'd finally figured we were headed west, not by any frame of reference or outdoor skill, but by catching the Spanish word, *oeste*, in their mixed-language conversation. We'd eventually cut a road where we might be seen. It wasn't that I hoped to come across civilians, because those three would kill them as quick as a housewife stepping on a roach. I wanted to be seen, so it could get back to the command post I was sure they'd activated, where my buddies were probably working right then.

The heavy clouds cracked every now and then with lightning. For the next few hours, it was Pepito, Javier, me, and Chino in that order. I didn't like that murderous little bastard behind me with that long knife that he'd kept, but there wasn't anything to do about it.

At least he didn't keep whacking me in the back, trying to hurry me up. I was doing the best I could to stay up with the other two, and after a while, my brain disengaged and went off on its own.

I tried to imagine what Search and Rescue was doing. They'd have Hasty Teams already up and at 'em, experienced SAR pros who were the first boots on the ground. I figured they'd have finally found the truck. Ethan and the Old Man were most likely working together, and I prayed that they'd see mine wasn't a simple disappearance and figure out that something was up. Maybe Kelly and the kids were at the CP. I prayed for that. No civilian could handle a gang of assassins headed to the house.

The twins were close to being grown, and Jerry had developed into a stout young man. His problem was the temper that I'd cursed him with. Mary, on the other hand, was like her mama, quiet and thoughtful.

Even if they were home alone, I didn't think anyone could sneak up with the dogs in the house. Hell, they heard the refrigerator door open no matter how quiet I tried to be at three in the morning. Our lab, Buster, had a deep voice that could wake the dead if someone strange came to the house. And Willie, our little Shih Tzu, tuned up every time Buster barked, egging each other on until I had to holler at 'em to be quiet. I hoped they were watching, then I remembered Willie hated rain and thunderstorms, so he'd be on Kelly's bed, shivering hard enough to keep her awake.

Those two dogs might be their only chance.

With an effort, I yanked my thoughts back to the quiet desert. The rain had everything huddled down, and the only thing I heard was the ringing in my ears and the sounds of our footsteps. It was a lost time right then, like back hundreds of years when things with teeth ruled the night.

Or raiders.

Focus there, Boy.

Right, Dad. Thinking here.

Who are these guys?

Hybrid throwbacks. Part raiders from over a hundred years ago, and part gangster, cartel members, a mix from Hell itself. The desert has always been deadly, but they added an element that should have disappeared decades ago, yet it had gotten worse.

Javier said they were from the Occidental. That meant the Sierra Madre Occidental, the real wild west sitting right on America's back door. I could think of no mountains as rugged and steep as the canyon-slashed country south of the border of Arizona and New Mexico. That's where these guys called home, and it was a helluva long way off.

They weren't taking me there, even though we were walking in that direction.

The Lost Apaches south of the border had lived there for over a hundred years, raiding Mexican villages well into the 1940s. It was a way of life that predated the arrival of the Spanish Conquistadores.

I remembered the Old Man telling me of the last Indian raid in the United States. It was this same band who crossed the border into New Mexico back in 1924. They killed ranchers, stole horses and mules, and robbed everyone they could find, leaving them bleeding their lives out in the sand.

Posses formed and chased them into Arizona, and finally across the border into Mexico. That's where the pursuers stopped and the Indians never stepped back into the United States again, or at least best anyone knew.

My mind trailed off from there, following rabbit holes that did nothing but block out the forced march that was slowly killing me. I could feel my heart pumping in the gunshot wound that throbbed hot and angry. With each beat, I felt it pulse there, and in my broken nose.

Pepito stopped so suddenly I walked into Javier. He shoved me back with an elbow and I stood there, swaying. It took a few seconds for my mind to reset, and I realized I could see. Dawn had arrived.

The next thing I knew, Chino kicked my feet from under me and I hit the ground hard enough to knock the breath out of me. My three captors dropped just as fast, and I lay there, gasping for breath.

It took a while, but I finally got enough air to roll over. "What'n hell was that for?"

I didn't get to ask anything else, because Javier whirled and clamped his dirty hand over my mouth, hitting my tender nose in the process. My eyes watered and I tried to breathe, but he had his full weight on that hand. There was no way to get enough air through my once-again blood-clotted nose, and I thrashed like a fish on a hook.

The next thing I knew, Chino was laying across my legs and Javier whispered in my ear. "I will remove my hand. Make one sound and Chino will cut your throat. *Comprende*?"

It took more self-control than I thought I had, but I

finally got ahold of myself and nodded. He removed his hand, put a finger to his lips, and raised his head to stare into the distance.

From my position, I had to look between his ass and the ground to see a pair of headlights about fifty yards away.

We'd come to a road.

Chapter 46

Dawn defined the Hawke house on the corner. Afraid that his Silverbelly hat was going to reflect light and give away his position, Herman put it crown down on the floor under his chair. He moved to the corner of the house, the four-o'clock position if one considered the porch facing north to be the number twelve on a clock.

Rain pattered the porch roof above and dripped off the eaves. He'd told Gabe to cover the diagonally opposite corner, the ten-o'clock position. Lightning fissured the clouds, the flickering light strobing the yard and street.

Herman held the Remington 870 pump at port arms and backed into a pool of deep shadow created by the porch cover and a spreading Texas madrone, or Indian tree. He leaned against the wall, his shirt and jeans blending into the darkness. The house across the street was dark as well, because he'd spoken with the Wilsons earlier in the day, suggesting they stay at the Posada for the night, at his expense.

Kelly and Mary were there also, checked in under assumed names. He grinned at Jerry's impulsive action to cut school and go to help in the search for his dad. Jerry was Sonny made over, and Herman had seen his son do worse in the past. Much worse. Playing hooky didn't seem so bad at first, but now that they were concerned with the entire family's safety, having the youngster out of pocket was worrisome.

Herman took no chances. His longtime friend and owner of the hotel, Andy Clark, was under strict orders to deny any inquiries if someone should call for the Hawkes. The odd little proprietor would, too. He kept a Judge under the counter. The Taurus handgun was chambered for .410 bore shot shells and the .45 Colt cartridge. It would shred anyone or anything that forced its use.

The house on Gabe's side was empty. The Luciens were visiting relatives in Dallas. There was no house directly behind.

A surprising number of frogs croaked their conversations in the still air, drawn out by the wet weather. Thunder rumbled as a backbeat over an occasional cricket that joined in the chorus.

Herman taught all of his boys, and that included Gabe and Ethan, how to be still when hunting. He hoped Gabe remembered those lessons. Movement gives you away every time.

The only thing that moved on the old man were his eyes. He waited.

No other cars passed in the quiet pre-dawn shower.

Something caught his attention. A rustle. A scrape.

He consciously slowed his breathing, taking long, deep breaths through his mouth to remain calm. He flicked the safety off the twelve-gauge. A dark form

broke free of the house across the street and moved as
fluid as a lion to stop behind a cluster of yuccas growing near the street corner in the xeriscaped yard.

Herman became stone. The man was probably watching the house just as intently as the Ranger watched the
potential assailant, waiting for a signal of some kind.

The sudden report of Gabe's shotgun shattered the
night with a heart-stopping clap at the same time lightning cracked half a mile away, arcing down from the
low clouds and exploding a highline transformer in a
detonation of sparks that rained downward. He fired
the shotgun twice more in a rolling rumble of man-
made thunder similar to that coming from above.

Herman couldn't see Gabe's muzzle flashes on the
opposite corner of the house, but a second later the
flash from a different firearm from behind a car down
the street gave him a target that would have to wait because the man behind the yuccas raced across the street
toward the porch, edged steel glinting in his hand. He
must have seen the slight movement of Herman's head
as he turned toward the muzzle flash across the street,
because he ran straight at the old Ranger.

That moment brought back everything Herman had
learned about knife-wielding attackers. *The hell with
the twenty-one-foot rule.*

The shadowy form closed the distance with breath-
taking swiftness and frightening silence. The wraith
raised a machete in his right hand at the same time he
leaped for one foot to land on the top porch rail. Herman leveled the shotgun. The blade in his hand reflected a distant lightning bolt, warranting Herman's
response.

He pulled the trigger. Nine .32-caliber slugs shredded the man's chest at the same time his foot touched the wooden rail. Already dead before he landed on the porch, the limp body dropped onto the painted boards at Herman's feet. The gangster's foot twitched once, his sightless eyes fixed on the source of his death.

Herman shucked another shell into the chamber and waited.

A second muzzle flash from behind a parked car across the street gave the man's position away. Herman took a step back around the corner and dropped to one knee. Another shot split the air and a bullet splintered the corner of the house where he'd been standing.

Herman caught the muzzle flash in his peripheral vision. The shooter didn't stay still, though. Apparently thinking he'd hit what he aimed at, he charged the house, holding the trigger down on a machine gun that spit noise and death.

The old Ranger snugged the shotgun to his shoulder and acquired the moving target. He fired, pumped another shell into the chamber, and fired again as the man fell with a splash in the wet grass.

From inside the house, the shrill bark of the Shih Tzu Willie brought a deeper bellow when Buster the Labrador retriever opened up. The barking dogs gave Herman a half second of warning to register footsteps thumping on the wooden porch from behind. He snatched the 1911 from the Brill holster on his hip and spun. At least he would get one shot into the ambushing son-of-a-bitch who wanted to kill his family.

Window glass exploded outward when rounds from Yolanda's AR-15 caught the assailant as he rushed past. The impact of the 5.56-ball ammunition cut him down, and the lifeless body crumpled and slid to a stop. Gabe's shotgun spoke again from the other side of the house. A split second later the ranch hand fired as fast as he could pump shells into the chamber.

Chapter 47

Inside the house, Yolanda had a difficult decision to make. If they were attacked by people coming after Kelly and the kids, where should she be? Gabe was on the north side, near the northwest corner. He had a clear line of sight to M Street in front of the house, the empty Lucien place beside them, and N Street on the west.

There was no alley on the old, narrow block. Only houses facing east.

Herman was near the front door the last time she saw him, but she heard footsteps that told her he'd moved to the southeast side of the house, on the diagonal corner from Gabe. That gave him a clear view of M Street, the side, and down to N Street, if he looked that way.

She bet on the back of the house, and moved into the dining area, where they'd eaten spaghetti the night before. The open-concept kitchen, dining, and living areas worked to her favor. She pulled a chair away from the table and sat facing the back door. From there she could see through the window to the south side of the house on Herman's right. If someone came from that direction, she could cover for him. If they came through the back door or window of the dark house, she was in place to take them out.

Her instincts were right.

Gabe's shotgun blast jolted her upright and the next detonation made her think they'd brought explosives. Through the window she saw a distant light wink out, then heard the crack of lightning that took out a transformer somewhere.

Herman's twelve-gauge spoke. They were coming from two directions.

Buster's low growl told her a lot more than she could see was happening outside. As the "rover," her job was to move into position to back up the other two outside. She saw where Buster's nose was pointed at the same time Willie yapped at the sound of footsteps on the porch. Rifle shouldered and ready, she stepped to the window to check outside when a moving shadow caught her attention. Buster roared when a short man rushed down the porch, passing two of the four south windows.

She squeezed off a burst from her AR-15, cutting the man down in a fully automatic blast of lead and glass. Behind Yolanda, Kelly had an old-fashioned metal kitchen step stool chair at the end of the counter. A soft scrape told her she was no longer alone. She whirled in time to see a dark shape sidestep away from the chair.

Buster charged across the room, snarling. His white teeth startling in the dark.

A shadow stopped short at the sound of the rushing dog. *"Mierda!"*

He raised a stubby-looking weapon, but before he could fire, Yolanda emptied the AR's magazine into the shape. Strobelike, the muzzle blasts illuminated a short-haired, heavily tattooed Hispanic man who absorbed most of the rounds. He went down at the same time Buster buried his teeth in one arm.

Without uttering a sound, the limp body smacked into the tile. Changing the mag with the smooth efficiency of practice, Yolanda took a knee in the dark room. Not sure if the furious Lab would obey her command, she hissed an order anyway. "Buster, off!"

As if trained, he released his hold and waited for more movement, growling.

The moment Yolanda's knee touched the floor, Willie rushed over and leaned against her leg, shivering.

More gunfire came from Gabe's position, and confident that Buster would warn them of anyone else in the house, she cleared the utility room to find out where the man had entered.

Chapter 48

Javier and Chino were arguing in soft voices as I lay there in the darkness and waited. Pepito kept a lookout for more vehicles while a soft drizzle collected on the leaves and cactus pads around us.

The desert looked the same as before, with nothing recognizable in my sightline. I sure wished I'd taken the time to learn where the national park's most iconic landmarks were located. The rangers I knew could have glanced around and told within a mile of where they were.

I could have just as well been on the moon.

Heavy, gray clouds pressed down on the low mountains that seemed to squeeze out the moisture. The filtered morning light was hazy. It wasn't a fog necessarily, but the air was full of water.

I was lying on hardpan, and enough moisture had collected in a low place that I could turn my head and sip. The sandy-tasting water was delicious and it felt as if the tissues in my mouth were swelling like a sponge. The landscape around us defined itself on that cloudy morning. Continuous rain was uncommon in the Big Bend, and I figured the storms were about done.

At least I hoped it was true.

The gangsters whispered, their voices so low that I couldn't make out anything they said, but Pepito startled me when he rose and took off in a crouching run. I struggled to sit up and we watched him dodging the prickly vegetation as fast as a roadrunner. He reached the road in seconds and scrambled up a slight incline to a jumble of boulders. The little guy scaled them like a monkey up a palm tree and found a point where he could see up and down the road winding between rocky cliffs and still another deep canyon.

He waved, telling my captors that it was clear for us to follow. Javier rose and tugged under my arm. *"Vá-monos."*

"Look buddy, I'm about done. I couldn't run that far if there was a bear chasing me."

"Then we'll carry you."

I had a vision of hanging upside down over his shoulder. "I don't think there's enough of you to do it."

"I don't mean all of you."

That short little inspirational sentence brought me to my feet. Pepito waved again telling them it was all clear and we took off. Javier and Chino had a hand under my arms and they half-carried, half-pushed me along. Ten steps later I realized the whole support thing was a bad idea.

In places the cactus grew so thick that there was barely enough room to thread your way through them—they didn't care. Those guys had mountain goat feet, and they seemed to always place them in exactly the right spot to miss the cactus spines.

On the other hand, they didn't care if I stepped over or around them. The way they were carrying me, I was forced to run directly through some of the clumps. Thick spines pinned my jeans to my calves above the protection of my boot tops.

The pain from my shoulder and the fresh white-hot jabs were enough to make me holler out loud. I wrenched my good arm away from Chino and stopped. Javier turned loose then and pointed at the path leading to the road.

"All right." I bent, gasping from the pain and wishing I could use my dead hands to pull some of the spines from my legs, but Chino rattled something sharp and pulled that long knife free of his belt. It didn't take but a second to realize I was leaning over in the perfect position for him to take a whack at my neck, and I straightened up right quick.

"Come." Javier took off again and I followed as fast as I could, wincing and hissing every step of the way. Chino followed.

What I'd hoped was a road was nothing more than a two-rut dirt track. Since we were headed west, I figured it led down to the Rio Grande, but it wasn't well-traveled enough to be a main road to Boquillas.

I took a quick glance down at the ruts as we passed and saw only one set of tracks. No one was going to be coming back through for a while, and I doubted it was part of a SAR team. Half a dozen steps later, the opposite side of the road was mostly grass and short scrub, making walking easier.

Pepito was down off the rocks by the time we arrived. He motioned that we'd have to follow the edge of a line of low eroded hills. None of them seemed too enthused about that because we'd be in the open and be close to the road for far too long.

They shouldn't have cared, because the drizzle turned to a light rain, and then became heavier. Our tracks across the road were sure to wash away, and with that, any chance of discovery. Stumbling more than walking, each step was agony. The edge of the hill was dotted with rusty-colored boulders that had rolled down over the years. We hung close, just in case someone came by and we had to duck around behind them.

What seemed like hours later, we rounded a point, and a wide wash led in the direction we wanted to go. The runoff widened the stream zigzagging down the wash. Unconcerned about another flash flood, Pepito dropped down and led the way.

Half an hour later, I'd had enough. I stopped.

It's hard to believe that animals and plants can thrive in such a harsh environment, but they've learned to flourish. Life is tenuous in the desert, and plants have evolved to defend themselves because it takes so long to recover from any kind of damage. Almost all have some kind of weapon. Some have spines as long and stiff as darning needles, while others are soft with hair-like stickers. Some evolved into tough and wiry branches and sticky leaves, and it seemed like everything I encountered drew blood.

"Look. I can't do this anymore." I raised a leg full of cactus needles. My calf looked like a Chia Pet, and the only thing that saved me were the tall tops of my Luccheses that caught the worst of them. I'd found a new place in my head, and didn't give a shit at that particular moment. "I need to get these needles out of my leg, and now. If you wanted to kill me, you'd have already done it, so yank them out so we can move faster."

The look of surprise on Javier's face was comical. He translated for me, and Pepito nodded. Chino started to argue, but a long string of strange words cut him off. The truth was that I wanted to get this over with as soon as possible, with the distant thought that maybe I could get away from them and find a phone to call Ethan to see if my family was all right.

Chino's eyes were slits as he slid the pack off his shoulder.

"Don't move." Javier knelt in the wet sand and examined my legs. He reached out and yanked one of the larger cactus spines from the upper part of my calf. It had a small hook on the end that cut and tore on its way back out. I grunted at the sharp pain and held still. He yanked others while Pepito did the same.

Though it was a relief for them to pull them out, each was a jolt, like they were actually pushing the spines *into* my skin. Gritting my teeth, I stood still while they plucked them from my jeans, the same way I'd plucked porcupine quills from the muzzle of my cousin's dog way back when we were kids in east Texas.

The idea of kicking Chino in the face and trying to crush his neck was a pleasant distraction as they worked, but it would have done nothing but earn me another beating. While they worked, I wiggled my fingers, flexing my wrists as much as possible to restore circulation.

That my hands even worked at all seemed to be a miracle, but I was relieved to find the cuffs weren't as tight as I thought, and blood had continued to flow. My fingers tingled.

When they were finished, Chino opened his backpack and took out a thin roll of duct tape. He yanked off a strip and wrapped it around my jeans, pressing and smoothing the tape. Satisfied, he stripped it off and examined the sticky side. He held it up, and I saw it was covered with hundreds of tiny spines.

He repeated the process half a dozen times on each leg before rising and staring me in the eyes. He didn't say anything, but it was clear that he was through with my demands.

I winked at him, and the rage that filled that man's face was stunning. He stepped forward and shouted, only inches away. I wanted to turn my head, because his breath would gag a buzzard off a tub of guts, but I held in there to make some strange point. I just hoped he wouldn't hit me in the nose.

Javier moved in close without touching either of us. He spoke softly and finally Chino cooled off and backed up. Pepito threw in his two cents' worth and took off. Still mad, Chino swung his pack over one shoulder and followed, leaving Javier to ride drag so I wouldn't just stand there and let them walk away.

"Hey, do you have any aspirin or ibuprofen in your pack?"

His eyes followed his friends as they struck off across still another wash. "Why?"

"This infection in my side is getting bad. Anything to cut the pain will help."

He shoved my shoulder and pointed in the direction of his friends. "It won't make any difference pretty soon."

I went with the shove, because to push back would only irritate both him and my wound. I followed in Chino's footsteps and studied on what he'd just said.

Chapter 49

Morning light barely penetrated the thick cloud layer over Sonny Hawke's house. The rain turned to a light drizzle as sirens wailed in the distance. Herman double-checked the bodies on his side of the porch and drew a huge sigh of relief.

"Yolanda. You all right in there?"

Her voice came through the shattered window. "Best I can tell. I got one down in here. You hurt?"

"Nope. Two on this side." He raised his voice. "Gabe!"

"*Sí.*"

"You still kickin'?"

"*Sí.* I have a one down here, but he won't last much longer. Another is farther out, dead, I think."

Herman ducked around the corner of the house to find Gabe on his knees beside a trembling man lying on the painted porch. The old Ranger leaned his shotgun against the outside wall and knelt beside the bleeding gangster.

Gabe's weight was on the man's right arm, pinning it to the porch. The other arm was broken and useless, lying at an odd angle. The usually mild-mannered ranch hand's eyes were glassy and he had the gangster's throat in one bloody hand.

"Who sent you to this house?"

"No se. No comprendo."

Gabe hissed the question again in Spanish, almost throttling the wounded man and adding more to it than Herman could understand.

"Son, he can't answer with you choking the life out of him."

Gabe's eyes flashed when they flicked from the gangster to Herman. "He's dying anyway. I knew *pendejos* like this when I was a boy. They're nothing but *basura*, trash, who prey on weak and old people! They kill by . . . hiding."

"Ambush."

"Sí." Gabe inclined his head toward a razor-sharp machete lying only feet away. "This one won't be doing much of that anymore. And if he doesn't tell me what I want to know, I will use that machete to cut off this arm before he dies. *Pendejo,* I will send it to your family with a note."

The sirens wailed closer.

"I want some answers before *el diablo* takes the sorry soul of this amount of shit." He clamped harder, spittle on his lips. "Who sent you to kill my friends, *mi familia*?"

"Said he don't speak English."

Frustrated, Gabe asked again in Spanish. The answer was almost a gag. "Chatto."

"Where is he?"

"In a house in La Carmen, maybe across the river in Mexico in Paso La Carmen."

"Which one?"

The man's face turned red as Gabe ground tighter.

"Son, he can't talk with you squeezing his goozle so tight. Give 'im a little air."

"Uno momento." Confused by rage, Gabe forgot who he was talking to.

Herman understood though as Gabe let off on the pressure and asked his question again. *"Que casa o pueblo?"*

Which house or town?

"Paso La Carmen."

Herman picked out some of the conversation about houses on both sides of the river. Access to Paso La Carmen had been closed since 9/11, but families still managed to communicate. Locals organized an annual *fiesta protesta* with music on both sides of the shallow river focused on reopening the border. Called Voices from Both Sides, they shared music from the banks of the Rio Grande to protest the closing.

"Why did you say both?"

"Because he has a house on both sides."

"Mierda!"

The man's eyes lost focus.

A highway patrol car skidded around the corner and slid to a stop.

"You got about sixty seconds." Herman left his shotgun leaning against the wall, turned, and raised both hands. He stepped around the corner of the house. His Ranger badge flashed in the blue and yellow wig-wag lights reflecting in the puddles of water standing on the blacktop street. "It's me, Cloyce! Herman Hawke. Take it easy."

Cloyce Miller rolled out of the car with a Beretta M-9 in his right hand. An army veteran, he'd known the

Hawkes for years. Herman moved to the front steps, taking the officer's attention from the side porch. He didn't think Cloyce could see Gabe kneeling beside the wounded gangster.

"I see you, Herman. Keep 'em up and tell me what the hell's going on around here. Who's shooting who?"

Herman stayed where he was on the porch. "It was an ambush, Cloyce. Gangsters from across the river. You know this is where Sonny lives. He's disappeared in the Big Bend and it looks like bad business, but I don't know what it's all about. Some men came here after Kelly and the kids, it looks like."

"Are there any more?"

"Not that I can see."

"Where's Kelly and the twins?"

"I can't tell you that right now, but they're fine. We've got 'em hid." Herman kept his hands still until Cloyce could gather his thoughts.

Uncertain, the stocky officer stayed where he was beside the car. "Who was shooting?"

"I was, and Gabe Nakai over on the other side here with a wounded prisoner. There's two more dead 'uns on this side." He jerked a thumb to his right. "And from what I heard inside, Yolanda Rodriguez got another one or two. I don't know for sure. If you want to look to your right, you'll see their car still settin' there at the corner."

Keeping his eyes on the house, Cloyce spoke into the microphone on his shoulder. "All right, I want all your people where I can see 'em. No weapons, until I can figure this out."

"That'll be fine. I got a shotgun leaning over yonder around the corner, and my pistol's on my hip here.

Gabe! Yolanda. Y'all put your guns down and come on out now. I 'magine they're both still wearing their sidearms."

"You were *waiting* for this?" Cloyce holstered his pistol, but kept his hand on the butt.

"Had a hunch. We didn't know what we were waiting for. We just needed to be ready."

The front door opened, and Yolanda stepped outside with both hands in the air. Cloyce's eyes widened at the attractive woman in jeans and a tactical vest. "Howdy, Cloyce."

Gabe appeared around the corner at the same time, both hands raised, and bloody. "Right here."

Herman watched the deputy take in the blood on Gabe's hands and clothes. He frowned. "You hurt, Gabe?"

"No. It's not my blood. It belongs to that dead cow's ass back there."

Cloyce frowned, and Herman spoke up. "He means horse's ass."

"*Sí*. What *he* said."

"Fine." Cloyce relaxed, but was still on point. More sirens sounded in the distance. "Y'all have a seat there on the step until we get all this sorted out. Is there anyone else *alive* around here?"

The trio sat on the steps and exchanged raised eyebrows. All three shook their heads. Herman spoke for them. "Looks like that's a no."

Gabe chinned toward the sedan at the corner. "I think there may be a dead one in that car. I hit him and he ran back there and got in."

That announcement wound Cloyce up again and he went back to the radio. Cars arrived only a minute later and boxed in the sedan. Officers emerged, guns drawn. The radio crackled alive with the news that another gangster had bled out in the front seat.

Herman sat in the middle. He spoke to Gabe in a soft voice. He flicked his eyes over their shoulder. "He dead?"

"*Sí.*"

"You get what you wanted?"

"*Sí.* We need to call Perry Hale as soon as we can. I have an address in La Carmen that he needs to check out. And there's very bad news. It was an . . . ambush. They were to kill Sonny, but took him instead."

"Fine then. And it's piece of shit."

"*Qué?*"

"You said 'amount of shit' when you were choking that feller around there. It's piece of shit. I swanny, you'll never learn to cuss right."

Yolanda covered her mouth as she gave a yelp of nervous laughter.

Chapter 50

My mind went to another place as we made our way across the desert, and by the time we came to the base of a butte, I was wrung out. I snapped back to the world when the others stopped. The air was soft and damp, and there was no way to tell what time it was.

Javier pointed at the ground. "Sit."

"I'll get muddy."

His eyes lit for a moment, then hardened. "Sit or fall."

I sat, but not before seeing a thin ribbon of a two-lane highway in the distance.

They moved a short distance away and Javier dug a phone from his pack. The beefy, old-fashioned style told me it was a satellite phone, and I knew I was right when it connected without a glitch. Most people in the park spend half their time worrying at the reception bars on their iPhones, and waving them around in the air in the hopes of better reception.

This guy simply dialed and started talking, and it gored my ox when it was so easy for a gangster to communicate with his crooked friends and *my* phone wouldn't even *connect*.

His eyes flicked to me several times, and I knew I was the subject of discussion. His voice rose more than once, and he made several points by jabbing one forefinger at the muddy ground. I couldn't understand more than two or three words of the exchange, and they didn't help at all.

The other two made suggestions that Javier ignored. When they tired of interrupting him, they settled down to stare at me like I was a monkey in a zoo. I didn't really like the idea of being their focus, but there was nothing I could do but wait.

When Javier punched the phone and ended the call, I couldn't help myself.

"Did you order fries for me, too?"

He frowned and stepped closer. I tensed, ready for another attack, but he squatted a couple of feet away. "That was about you."

"I figured."

"Abdullah had orders to bring Chatto your head."

"I don't believe he's still in charge anymore, is he? And Chatto is someone I should know?"

"No, *amigo*. He is someone you *don't* want to know. But you won't be with him for long."

He paused and the others tensed when a pickup appeared on the highway. It moved as slowly as an ant, but only because of the distance. It didn't speed up or slow. It might have been a search vehicle, but I allowed it was someone else.

It was the first vehicle to pass and I suspected it was either because we were on one of the less traveled roads, or the weather. With all the rain that had fallen, some areas of the national park would likely be closed due to flash flooding that covered some roads, trails, and facilities. I'd had experiences with rainy weather in the park when the family and I visited in the past. We'd taken one short hike to the scenic drive south of the Mule Ears viewpoint and I recalled thinking that the runoff there after a hard rain would be impressive.

In addition, the wet, muddy conditions on the dirt backroads would give ground searchers fits. All the main park entrances were open for business. The truck proved that. I still didn't know where I was, but the sight of pavement was encouraging. They watched the truck as if were a snake until it was past.

Only then did Javier continue. "He is angry that you are still alive. He wanted to know why I wasn't bringing just your head, but I told him you are a fine fighter, and that he should look into your blinking eyes before you die."

The guy's speech patterns reminded me of the Indians I've known through the years. They didn't use the phrase Native Americans. I figured I'd better not bring that up right then.

"Chatto was angry at first when I told him you'd killed three of our brothers. But then I said we'd give you to El Molinillo and he laughed."

I translated and came up with The Grinder.

"El Molinillo is an expert in . . ." He searched for the word and started again. "We give him the bodies of our enemies and traitors, and he makes them disappear forever. Tomorrow we will give him a living, breathing Texas Ranger, and when he is done, you will be nothing but gone."

He looked into my eyes, and when I refused to say anything, he nodded

"He works outside in a leather apron some say is made of human skin. You will feel everything El Molinillo does until he tires of toying with you. Then he will take what is left of your body and wire it to iron rods hammered into the desert ground. Your meat will rot and be consumed by *aves de carroña*. How do you say, oh, *buitres,* vultures. They will eat what is left and shit it all over the desert.

"Then El Molinillo will put on his leather apron again and bring out his *piedras de molar,* his grinding stones, and will spend the next several days grinding your bones and teeth into meal that will feed the coyotes that hang around. They will lap you up like wet masa, the dough that is used to make tamales. That is what the remainder looks like when he is finished. You will then be nothing but a memory on the wind."

I'd heard about that guy, and had seen photos of his work. He was a little, gray-haired peckerhead that looked like somebody's granddaddy, but everyone south of the border knew his work.

Javier was right. If I got that far, I'd be nothing but molecules in a week.

Not much future for a guy with ambition.

Chapter 51

With their backs to the cold fireplace in the lobby of the art deco 1930s Posada Real Hotel, Herman, Gabe, and Mary listened as Kelly Hawke outlined what she'd do when she got her hands on Jerry for skipping school.

Andy Clark manned his registration counter where he could keep an eye on anyone coming into the historic hotel through the entry hall to his left, the main patio doors directly opposite, or through the lounge.

The odd proprietor with the habit of trailing off at the end of sentences with "... and ever'thing" kept one eye on the Hawke family gathered in front of the fireplace. A .45/4.10 caliber Judge handgun rested only a foot away, just in case anyone else tried to harm his friends.

Sitting ramrod straight, fingers laced in her lap, Kelly was in control of her emotions, but barely. "This is the wrong time for him to go string off down to Big Bend. Lordy mercy, as if I don't have enough to worry about as it is," she addressed her daughter, who refused to make eye contact, "and you, Sister Sue, are getting all this because he's not here. You should have told me up front that he cut school."

Chided, Mary studied the dark screen on her cell phone. "I didn't want to be the one to rat him out."

"And look where it got you. I'm going to pull his head off when I get my hands on that boy. He's going to be the death of me."

Herman chinned toward Andy Clark behind the registration counter. "Jerry'll be just fine. And to be on the safe side, I think y'all oughta stay here for a while longer."

Kelly nodded in agreement. Beside her on the leather couch, Mary woke her phone up and worried at the bright screen, running her fingers across the glass surface. Like so many young people with cell phones, her first response in any situation, benign or not, was to launch into a flurry of social media posts. The sight was so common the high school teacher didn't notice.

Herman tugged on his ear. "We also have news about Sonny."

Mary's fingers stopped at the statement. Both sat straighter as if their posture would help them hear what they wanted.

"One of those guys gave us some information." Herman didn't go into details about how they'd gotten the info. "Searchers haven't found him, but they told us that he's in the hands of a gang and they're probably taking him either to La Carmen or Paso La Carmen. He wasn't for sure which."

Sonny's still alive. Kelly Hawke's blood ran cold with the news that her husband was in the hands of Mexican gangsters. "How long ago was this?"

He glanced at his wristwatch and told her. "Why?"

"Because Perry Hale's down there."

"So are half of the police officers in this county."

"*They* have to follow protocol and answer to their superiors."

Gabe raised an eyebrow.

Mary returned to her phone in a flurry of thumb taps. Herman despised cell phones and often voiced his opinion that they were contributing to the coming downfall of society. "Honey, put down that phone until we're finished here."

Mary laid the phone in her lap. "I'm finished. Perry Hale knows."

"How?" Herman frowned.

"I have his number and Yolanda's. I just sent them a text. She says she's on the way to meet him."

"I reckon she was driving and texting." Mary shrugged. "Y'all should do as you say, and not as you do."

Kelly raised an eyebrow. "Careful there, Sis."

"We need to contact Sonny's commander with this news," Herman said more to himself than the others, ignoring their near-constant struggle between mother and teenage daughter.

"Can you wait another hour or so?"

Herman tilted his hat back. He squinted at Kelly. "Why?"

"To give Perry Hale a running start, and for Yolanda to get there first."

Chapter 52

Clouds thickened again two hours after we arrived. A late-model truck hitched to a bumper-pull aluminum camping trailer came into view and we watched him pass. Javier and his buddies kept an eye on the rig until it disappeared from sight. Dead tired and drained by the past several hours, I worried about Kelly and the kids instead of a passing tourist.

Worrying did nothing but increase the acid in my empty stomach, but I couldn't help myself. Here I was sitting in the desert with three hardcore gangsters, doing nothing but waiting. Thunder rumbled in the distance. The storm was far from over and was causing problems for my little friends, who had a specific destination in mind.

It was coming down in buckets somewhere in the higher elevations. The guy pulling the RV needed to get his butt out of there before the road flooded. I knew from experience that more arroyos than the one we nearly swam across were already impassable, and floodwaters rushing over low-water crossings took people and their vehicles every year.

Squatting behind a creosote bush, Chino fired up a cigarette he selected from a Baggie and wrapped his arms around both knees. Ignoring his blank stare that focused on my face, I adjusted my position and thought about laying down when the gangsters tensed, staring in the direction the truck and trailer had disappeared.

It popped up again over a slight rise. Was a bridge washed out below, or did the guy change his mind and find a place to turn around? Whatever it was, he had their attention.

Are these guys going to stop those folks and take their rig? The murdering bastards are more than capable of that, or worse.

A chill washed down my back when I realized I'd be in the prime seat to watch a possible robbery and murder. It was the perfect way to get out of the park, in the back of just one more camping trailer. No one would stop them, because tourists and campers were as common as the rocky outcroppings all around us.

Javier would probably have to drive if they stole the truck and camper. He had fewer facial tattoos than the others, giving him a chance at driving the rig out of the park. The others wouldn't be any use if they were stopped. The gang tattoos covering their arms, necks, and portions of their faces were neon signs to park personnel or law enforcement.

Old Javie wasn't much better, but his tattoos weren't as extensive. In the back of my mind I hoped he'd give it a try. Politically correct or not, he didn't look like the kind of guy who'd be driving a fairly new truck pulling a Jayco camping trailer. He simply didn't fit the profile, and I hoped the first lawman or park official that passed would act on their instincts and pull us over.

But then again, I didn't want to think about what the gangsters would do to those in the truck. I couldn't let that happen, so I struggled to my knees to warn the driver as he steered into a wide pullout not far away. Maybe they had the windows down on that cool day and could hear me shout. At least those folks might get away, even if the Coyotes behind me cut my throat.

Instead of shoving or knocking me back down though, Pepito and Chino used that momentum to grab me under my arms, and as soon as I had my stems under me, we all took off down a thin trail in the direction of the parked rig.

The driver got out and waited, looking up the slope in our direction until he found us. He waved and my heart fell. I was partly right. They were going to use the rig to get out of the park.

At least they aren't going to kill anyone to get it.

Unless they'd already done that earlier.

The closer we got, the clearer the driver became. My hopes that an officer would profile the driver went away when I got a closer look at him. The older guy had brown hair and was dressed in a nylon fishing shirt, shorts, and hiking boots. He could have blended in with any of the tourists in the park's visitor center down in Panther Junction.

He waited until we were within fifty yards before he opened the trailer door. Javier got there first and slapped him on the shoulder. They exchanged pleasantries as I was manhandled out of the scrub and onto the highway shoulder.

I got a good look at the light-skinned, blue-eyed Hispanic driver, who fell somewhere in his sixties, before they shoved me up the metal steps and into the interior.

My eyes slipped off his thick glasses to a woman of about the same age in the truck's passenger seat, casually looking at one of the free park maps from the visitor center.

Just before they pushed me inside the trailer, I glanced around. A highway sign was almost hidden behind the trailer, FM 2617. We were out of the park, on the northeast side. It took me a second to figure out which way the truck was pointed.

Good lord, I've been completely turned around. We weren't heading west into the depths of the park, but east *to the barren country and the Texas farm road running north and south beyond the park's boundary.*

We were exactly opposite of where they were searching for me. No one would think to look *outside* the park.

My head spun for a second as an internal compass righted itself. Our ultimate destination was south. It was the only direction that made sense. Going north would intersect with State Highway 385, which would take us either back into the park where we'd just left, and the other to Marathon, and that would be a mistake. There was a border check station south of that little town. They wouldn't risk it.

They're taking me to La Carmen, where the highway dead-ends at the Rio Grande.

No. *They want to* cross *the river into Paso La Carmen.*

I was thinking hard when they pushed me through the door and into the aluminum trailer. Pepito shoved past me in the narrow aisle running down the center and squeezed into the bedroom. He grabbed the foot of a queen-size bed and lifted.

It rose easily on its gas hinges, revealing an empty

cavity no more than eighteen inches deep. He pointed. "There."

"It's gonna be a little tight for me."

He got my attention pretty quick when he waved a finger to include him and the rest. *"Todos."*

Stopping in the door, my eyes widened. "All of us? In there?"

"Sí. Entran!"

The outside door slammed as I stepped over the box edge and ducked my head under the plywood base. Pepito and Chino manhandled me where they wanted on the floor. The rig pulled back on the highway as Javier made his way to the back and stepped into the base with us. He sat on the edge for several minutes, staring out the window at the passing hills.

The driver tapped the horn twice. At the signal, Javier motioned for them to make room and he settled in. My bad shoulder was already aching again in the cramped quarters when he ducked his head and lowered the bed.

It wasn't bad at first, but I was right. Things got pretty damned crowded with all four of us packed under there. Those guys weren't fans of bathing or deodorant, but I figured I probably smelled a little ripe myself. Relaxing best I could, every wound, cut, scrape, and bruise woke up, each screaming for attention. Stifling a groan, I wriggled around to find some relief, until Chino jabbed my cheek with a ragged fingernail.

"Silencio!"

I *silencio*ed as much as possible and thought about strangling him when I got the chance. The road was a roller-coaster ride of hills and valleys. The driver must have been kin to Mario Andretti, because he seldom took his foot off the gas. Sometimes centrifugal force slid me into Chino, and the next into Pepito. After what seemed an hour, but it could have been shorter or longer, the truck slowed and rattled. The trailer thumped over a line of potholes before accelerating. Sick and exhausted, despite my predicament, I dozed.

There was no telling how long I was out until something slapped the sole of my boot and I struggled back to consciousness. Javier pushed the bed upward and climbed out. The truck slowed on the smooth highway, and I struggled to sit up. Remarkably refreshed, I blinked my eyes clear and squinted through the semi-closed blinds.

Rough hills and valleys stretched toward a ridge of low mountains. I squinted out the other side to see scrub-colored hills in arid country that could have been anywhere in the Big Bend region.

We passed a sign for the La Carmen airstrip, a virtually abandoned dirt airstrip beside a tiny cluster of houses within spittin' distance of the Rio Grande.

Minutes later the driver pulled into a wide, bare turnaround that served as someone's front yard. I'd been to La Carmen a couple of times in the past and it hadn't changed a bit. Still nothing more than two or three empty houses overlooking the river, it was once a sister city to what's now a ghost town on the Mexico side, connected by an impassible one-lane bridge blocked from both sides by barbed wire, ten-foot steel panels topped by vertical bars and above that, chain link fence. A jumble of broken Jersey barriers made of crumbling concrete filled the surface from the highway to the fence.

Before 9/11, Paso La Carmen across the river was a bustling mining town that exported fluorspar to the United States. The government shut it down in the interest of national safety and it got progressively worse on the Mexican side as the cartels expanded their regions at the same time the mines shut down. By the time my little troupe of murderers pulled into the drive, the cluster of buildings across the river was no more than a ghost town with only a few residents and an abandoned white church gutted by the Mexican army in a misguided effort to push the cartels out.

Javier opened the camper's door and stepped out into a light shower, waving for me to follow. Stacks of lumber partially covered by blue tarps and assorted building materials were scattered around the house. Some had been there quite a while and had become part of the dust-covered landscape.

What we used to call a honey truck, a septic pump truck painted with the words: PANDO SANITATION SEPTIC SERVICES, was parked nearby. It was the least sanitary pump truck I'd ever seen, covered in brown goo that would have been crusty in dry weather. It had been rehydrated by the rain, and I caught a familiar whiff of an outhouse when we stumbled out of the camper.

I'm was glad it's not a hundred degrees or that stink would've taken off the top of my head.

The front door to the ranch-style house was unlocked. Javier led me into a large living room under renovation, but it looked as if the contractor had stepped out for a smoke two or three years earlier and never returned. The floor was rough concrete. Stacks of boxed flooring, a table saw, and other assorted tools were pushed against one bare wall of raw sheetrock.

Cheap furniture that could have come from a resale shop filled the remainder of the living room.

I got a glimpse of a patio under construction through a wall of windows overlooking Mexico before Javier shoved me down a long hall on the right and into a bedroom at the end. The floor crunched underfoot. Chino followed with his Cobra ready for use.

"Sit."

I turned so Javier could remove the cuffs. Hand resting on the Cobra's pistol grip, he shook his head and left, closing the door behind him. A padlock rattled on the other side and snapped shut.

"Hey, I gotta pee."

"No!"

A radio blared to life with Tejano music somewhere in the house, almost drowning out Javier's voice. I sat on the corner of a creaky bed and waited to see what would happen.

Impatience got the better of me half an hour later. I had to do something besides sit and look around at bad patch jobs in the grimy walls. "Hey, I really need to pee, guys, or we're gonna have a mess in here."

The radio was so loud I doubted anyone could hear me, but a few seconds later the padlock on the other side rattled. I was surprised to see a middle-aged Hispanic woman appear in the doorway. Her features reflected a distinct Indian ancestry. Her dark eyes roamed up and down from my head to my toes. "Stand up."

She was poor as a snake, with thick black hair pulled back and tied. She wore clothes from the same thrift shop the furniture came from. She motioned upward with her hands.

I stood. "Now what?"

She waved. "Come."

The bare floor under my boots was gritty with sand and fine caliche, reminding me of the time Kelly and I took the kids to Pensacola a year earlier and rented a house on the beach. The smooth floor under my bare feet was glorious in the first hour we were there. Seven days later, it felt like sandpaper and I preferred to wear my flip-flops as opposed to walking barefoot on the tile.

"Having a hard time finding a good housekeeper?" I passed a closed door, and she ignored my comment. We turned right down another hall. She pointed at an open door. "In there."

Though the bones of the house were in good shape, it appeared that no one had cleaned the filthy bathroom since the original builders left back in the 1990s. I caught a glimpse of a 5′10″ walking corpse that looked like me in the spotted mirror over the dripping sink. My dirty, bruised face, crooked nose, swollen jaw, and one black eye were the best parts of what I saw.

Past the mirror, a stained toilet told me it was obviously not a ladies' room, because the seat was still wet from the last customer.

I stood there and waited. She sighed and reached for my zipper. I stepped back against an empty metal towel rack. "No, ma'am."

Her eyes hardened. "That is how you are going to piss."

"No, it's not. Get these cuffs off."

"No."

"Piss your pants then."

"None of us want that."

She reached for my zipper again. "Be still."

I instinctively raised a leg, like we did as kids when someone tried to rack us in the nuts. "Look, the key to these cuffs is with my truck keys. Javier has them. He can come watch if he wants, but not you."

Indecisive, she shifted from one foot to the other. "Sit on the floor."

"I'd rather not touch it."

"Sit."

Instead, I sat on the edge of the crusted tub and waited. Bag Lady left and came back a minute later. My keys rattled in her hand. Javier appeared in the doorway behind her with a pistol and a nasty grin on his face. It was everything I could do not to lose it when I saw my badge was pinned on his shirt. *"Eres tímido?"*

"Not hardly. You can stand there and watch if you want to. My modesty extends to other people handling my business."

The grin slipped and he rattled an order. Bag Lady twirled her finger, telling me to turn around. The keys jangled again and the cuff on my right wrist opened. I don't know what felt the best, the cuff coming off, or my shoulders finally relaxing. My left arm dropped, pulling the closed bullet wound, and I winced.

I really wanted to rub my wrists, but all of a sudden, I really needed to use the bathroom. Ignoring my audience, I stepped up to the stained bowl and unzipped. They watched like spectators at a basketball game while I stood there and waited. As I've gotten older, it takes longer for my flow to start if I've been holding it for a long time, and for a minute I was afraid that I couldn't start at all.

Relief finally arrived with a trickle that increased in

a surprising volume. As it did, Bag Lady and Javier finally ignored me and leaned into each other, whispering. Taking advantage of the break I'd been looking for, I barely moved my right hand, twisted a couple of degrees away from them, and slipped a finger into the watch pocket of my Wranglers for the spare cuff key they missed. I knew from experience it can't be seen or felt by anyone patting me down.

It's not as easy as it sounds. My fingers weren't cooperating as smoothly as usual, and I was scared to death I'd drop it. I almost had a heart attack when Javier laughed. Watching through peripheral vision, I saw he was paying more attention to Bag Lady. Feeling that he had everything under control, he made another crack about how long I'd been going, then went back to whispering with her.

They were standing just outside the bathroom door, with her back to me and half hidden. He could see over her shoulder, but every now and then he'd shift his weight. When he did that, I lost sight of his head for a second, knowing he couldn't see me, either.

Looking at me.

Not seeing me.

Looking at me.

Not seeing me.

I popped the little key into my mouth and worked it between my cheek and gum like a dip of Skoal.

Looking at me.

I finally finished and sighed.

"Zip." It was the woman. She twirled her finger again. *"Manos."*

I tucked everything away and held my hands out. "Don't I get to wash up?"

"No. You only handled your own. *Giro de vuelta*."

It was worth a try. I put my hands behind my back. *"Atrás."*

She was really good. I followed her curt instructions and backed up to the door. There was no need to look over my shoulder to know that Javier had that pistol pointed at me. The cuff clicked back into place.

"Vámonos."

I followed her finger and returned down the narrow, gritty hallway, back to the bedroom.

"Esperas."

I sat on the edge of the bed and waited like she said. Bag Lady studied me for a minute, her head angled like a dog listening to a whistle. Javier stepped up behind her and dug his spurs in a little deeper.

"You like *mi insignia*?" He polished my badge with the palm of his hand.

"Always did." I tried not to change expression. "I'm going to get that back, you know."

"You can get it from me in Hell."

"It'll be long before that."

He laughed and closed the door.

I sat still for a long moment, wondering how long I needed to wait before it was safe to spit out the key and unlock the cuffs. About sixty seconds later the door blew open again and Bag Lady was standing there, eyes flashing. I waited a beat. "Sorry. I didn't flush."

She reached into the pocket of her baggy pants and pulled out a fresh bottle of water. Twisting the cap off with a soft crack, she crossed the room and held it out. I tilted my head and she poured some of the sweetest tasting water I've ever known into my mouth. A small stream more refreshing than sweet iced tea trickled down my chin. She instinctively wiped it dry with her hand. My heart almost stopped, wondering if she felt the key tucked away there, but her touch was so soft she missed it.

I dropped my gaze in thanks and saw the outline of a pistol in her other pocket.

"*Descansa*. Rest."

"Good idea."

She closed the door again and I waited, counting to one thousand. That done, I listened even longer. A familiar beetle-beep came to me though the closed door, telling me the house, and probably the windows, were electronically armed.

Car doors slammed somewhere outside. A burst of heavy rain drummed on the clay tile roof for several moments before slacking off. The volume on the music rose. I stood, worked the key from my cheek, and spit it onto the bed. I'd practiced the next move a thousand times, just in case I found myself in cuffs. I turned, sat down, and picked it up.

Practice makes perfect.

Chapter 53

I was shot, scraped, cut, beaten so badly I couldn't breathe through my nose, held hostage by at least four people with guns, and worn to a frazzle. My left side throbbed with heat from the infection, but at least I had a soft, full-size bed to sit on.

And my cuffs were off.

Things were looking up.

A cheap wooden headboard thumped the wall every time I moved. Hundred-year-old springs squeaked, reminding me of when I was a kid. Our kinfolk used those bedsprings until the mid-1960s, and it seemed like every smokehouse and junk room I was ever in had at least one or two sets leaning against the walls.

The room measuring maybe ten by fifteen made it easy to examine the windows from my position. I wanted to open one and crawl outside, but with a security system in place, there was no chance of doing it quietly. Raising a window equated to opening the bedroom door and yelling for room service. That possibility off the table, I studied my options and soon realized there was only one way to get out.

Hands still behind my back, I bounced up and down on the squeaky mattress a couple of times. The noise was loud enough to wake the dead. Setting my feet, I pushed myself to the edge of the mattress, trying to look like I wasn't ready to bolt.

The padlock rattled. Bag Lady came boiling into the room, flinging the door open. "What are you doing?"

"Trying to get comfortable."

She stayed by the door, studying me. "Stay still."

"I don't know if you noticed the hole in my shirt and all the dried blood, but I've been shot and I'm hurtin' like hell." I wasn't kidding. A fever was taking hold and at the very least I was on the edge of an infection that would lay me in the ground.

The old rock and roll song by the First Edition popped into my head, "Just Dropped In (To See What Condition My Condition Was In)." That's how I felt, with or without Kenny Rogers.

The frustrating woman didn't come any closer. Instead, she repeated herself. "Lay down and be still."

Her English was improving, probably through repetition. "Look, how about a couple of aspirin at least, and maybe some more water."

"No."

"Well, at least come over here and check this wound."

"No."

"It's too far back to lick it like a dog. Would you do it for me?"

I could see her trying to translate and frustration rose. She wasn't taking any of the bait I was throwing out. I ground my teeth. It was all I could do to keep both hands behind me. "You're not married, are you?"

She frowned. "Why?"

"Because no guy could put up with your negativity."

She tilted her head again, thinking. "You don't talk anymore."

"I don't talk any less, either."

"Qué?"

"You're backsliding." Dropping my head, I lowered my voice and tried to look pitiful. "Help me."

"Speak up."

"I'll pay you." I tried it in Spanish, hoping I was saying it right. *"Te daré dinero."*

"Qué?"

I breathed my answer. "Money."

"What?" She stepped forward. "What are you saying?"

"Gold. *Oro*." It was barely a whisper.

She heard *that*. "Gold?"

Anything over a solid quarter across the Rio was real money, and the word, even the idea of gold, was overwhelming to people who literally lived hand to mouth.

"Yes." The word was a breath.

She wrapped her hand around the pistol in her pocket and glanced toward the window, not back over her shoulder toward the rest of the house. That look spoke volumes. "Yes? *Aquí?* Where?"

"Coins, in pockets in my boots."

"Qué?"

"Oro cosida en mis botas."

Gold sewn into my boots, or at least that's what I hoped I was saying. I might have been proposing, though. We'd already gotten dangerously close to intimacy in the bathroom.

Rain intensified again on the roof, sounding like millions of soft hammers. The woman in cast-off clothes was easy to lure with the mention of gold. She stepped forward and unconsciously bent toward my feet.

I should have felt bad about nearly kicking her head off, but I didn't. My right foot snapped out and up, catching under the jaw. Her teeth cracked together and she flew backward, instinctively reaching for the battered dresser to catch her fall.

Instead, her skull slammed against the sharp wooden edge. Blood flew and her black hair exploded against the peeling finish. She collapsed onto the gritty floor without another sound. I yanked her onto her side and snatched the pistol free. She may have been dressed in cast-off, oversized clothing, but the gangsters had given her new technology in firearms.

It was a Glock 43, and the little 9mm fit my hand like it was made for it.

I eased back the slide to see the gleam of brass in the chamber. Thumbing the release, I dropped the magazine. It was loaded. I snicked it back into place and glanced out the open door, breathing hard.

A tooth was stuck on her bottom lip and blood ran from her mouth. Though the kick wasn't as hard as I would have used on a full-grown man, it was enough to put her lights out for a long, long time. I stepped over her still body and peeked into the hallway.

The radio blaring Tejano music came back into focus, louder with the door open. I was never a fan of accordions and brass, but didn't mind it right at that moment. It covered my crunching footsteps as I edged through the doorway, looking past the little pistol.

Chapter 54

The hallway was empty, but I was wound tight as a mainspring. It's one thing to clear a house with a SWAT team behind you, or with another professional. It's a completely different animal to do it alone and as beaten up as I was.

Despite Chino's tape technique in the desert, hundreds of tiny, hair-like stickers were still in my jeans, and in the skin of my legs, itching like fire. They were a distraction I had to grit my teeth and ignore, though. A closed doorway on the left was a problem. I could pass it by, but if there was a bad guy inside, he'd be behind me.

I couldn't have that.

Turning the knob as quietly as possible, I cracked it open and peeked inside. A cold chill ran down my back when I saw a naked young woman lying on the bed. One arm was duct taped to the metal bedframe that Teddy Roosevelt slept on, the other covered her breasts.

Eyes wide with terror, the Hispanic girl twisted sideways to keep me from seeing her business. She probably wasn't much older than my own daughter, and a hot rage took over, drowning the minor cactus issues that'd been plaguing me.

A quick glance down the empty hallway said I had a few seconds. I stepped inside and gently closed the door. The room was so dim I could hardly see her, which was both a blessing and a problem. Opening the blinds helped, but she squinted, moaned, and used her bare heels to push herself into a curl against the headboard in a defensive position.

"Shhh." The universal finger against the lips had an effect. She quit whimpering, but kept one eye on me. The room was thick with the odor of sweat, fear, and sex. I swallowed down rising nausea and crossed to her. "It's okay. *Está bien.*"

"No!"

"Easy, girl." I tucked the Glock into my back pocket and held out both hands. "I'll get you loose." Up close and in better light, her damaged and bruised face told even more of her story.

"No más!"

"That's right. *No más.* No more. I'm going to help you."

She struggled out of where she'd been hiding in her mind and finally saw an Anglo in the room. I probably looked worse than she did right then, but it was a lead-pipe cinch I wasn't one of the gangsters who'd been abusing her for God knows how long.

"You'll help me?"

"Shhh. Quiet. You speak English?"

"Probably better'n you. I'm from Midland."

A fire lit in her eyes and I knew that little gal had

spirit. "Good. Listen, it's me and you right now. Hang on while I get this tape off." It had been on for quite a while. Whoever had duct taped her to the bedstead had looped it several times around her raw wrist, and the metal. She was lucky in a way—it could have been wire. Several wraps spread out the pressure, but there was layer after layer.

"I tried to chew free a hundred times, but it's too strong." She bit at it as if to demonstrate. "Those bastards saw it and laughed whenever they came in here. I hated when they laughed at me."

"All right. Hang on." I dug out my handcuff key again and used the looped end to pick at the edges in a tedious process that finally gave me enough of a flap that I could peel the layers back. From there, it only took a couple of minutes to unwrap her wrist.

Thunder rumbled. She lay still, watching my face as I worked. "They beat you, too."

"They worked me over some." I took her upper arms and pulled her into a sitting position. "You good?"

"I'll be better when I'm out of here."

"That might be a few minutes." I palmed the Glock again. "I have to make sure it's clear to the door."

She stood, and I turned toward the door. Lithe as a doe, she tiptoed to the closet and dug around on the floor. I heard the rustle of clothing. "Do you have another gun?"

I turned around to find her in a pair of jeans that were obviously hers, and a sleeveless western shirt. Her question was a pleasant surprise. "Wish I did."

"Get another one so I can kill those sonsabitches."

"Easy, girl. I'd rather us just get away."

"You weren't raped."

I met her gaze. "No. I'd kill 'em all if I had the chance, but we're outnumbered and outgunned."

"Where'd you get that one?"

"Kicked some ugly gal's head off and she dropped it."

"Valeria! Hope you *really* kicked it off."

"Came damn close, but listen, we can't stand here and compare stories. We gotta go."

"Right behind you."

"Nope. You stay here and listen. I'm going to make sure the way is clear to the front door and then I'll call you so we can get gone."

She didn't like the idea of being left alone. "What if you don't make it?"

"Go out that window and run like hell."

"You'll call me when you get to the door?"

"Yep."

"My name's Phoebe. Holler it loud."

"Phoebe how much?"

She blinked for a second. "Oh, Yelverton. Phoebe Yelverton."

"Damn, that's a mouthful. Okay, Phoebe. Wait and listen."

I started out and she took my arm. "Hey, who are you?"

I sighed. "Sonny Hawke."

"Why'd they take you?"

"They don't like Texas Rangers, I guess."

"You're a baseball player?" She looked at me from head to toe. "Why would they work a *ball* player over?"

"I wouldn't shave points." I sighed again. "I'm a lawman. A *real* Texas Ranger."

Phoebe smiled with her eyes. "You don't *look* like a Ranger."

"Missing the hat. I've looked better."

"Badge, too, I see. I've heard of you guys. One riot, one Ranger. Right?"

"Yep, and they're about to find out. Right now, I'm feeling like they did back in the day."

Chapter 55

The music grew louder as I advanced one room at a time through the empty house. Two more bedrooms held backpacks and cast-off clothing, but no weapons. Each foot of real estate I covered gave me more confidence. By the time I reached the large open living room it looked like me, Phoebe, and Sleeping Beauty back there were the only ones in residence.

The living room would have been bright had the cloud cover not been so thick. A wall of windows overlooked the Rio Grande that began only yards beyond a covered flagstone patio. Water the color of chocolate milk roiled below. At one time the house was a showplace, built to take advantage of the view.

Two pallets of flat rocks told me someone was renovating the patio and matching fireplace. That clicked with the bare, open yard littered with construction materials.

Probably half the reason for the dirty floors.

Hope they ordered a new toilet.

I checked the front door to make sure it was unlocked, keeping an eye on the other end of the sprawling house I hadn't yet cleared. Tires crunched on the caliche outside.

Dammit!

Indecisive, I backed up against the wall, thinking I'd hide behind the door until they were all inside, and then shoot 'em in the back. No shame in that. The idea of a Hollywood fair fight was the last thing on my mind. I simply needed to kill 'em all so *I* could live and check on my family, but I heard the Old Man whispering in my ear.

That's a Glock 43, Son. Only seven shots. You may not have enough gun for the situation.

There it was again, a mantra he'd beaten into me throughout my life. Use enough gun.

I had two choices. Leave through the open sliding patio door and escape down the bank and follow the river, or use the unexplored hallway that probably terminated at a garage, or at least a carport exit that would get me out the side. Phoebe would have to tough it out a little longer until I figured out what to do.

The river it was. The bank was only twenty feet away, and if I ducked outside and angled away, I would put the house between me and the bad guys. I was halfway to the patio when my heart almost stopped. Someone was slumped down in a wide chaise lounge facing the Rio Grande.

They'd left a guard after all, but he'd been loafing under the overhang while it rained, instead of keeping an eye on me. He rose at the sound of his friends opening the front door. It was armed all right, and at the system's beetle-beep sound, he swung his feet onto the patio.

It was Chino. Asian eyes, sneer, and the trail of tears down his cheek. I was caught in the open.

He spun, reaching for the weapon, hard, black eyes as dark and depthless as the old Devil himself. *"Pendejo!"* The Cobra's muzzle rose.

Without thinking, I lined up the pistol's front and rear sights and fired at his center mass. His snap-front shirt jumped and puffed from the impact. Chino *oofed* and folded in the middle. He stumbled backward, collapsing over the lounge.

A shout from outside startled me. I made a little half jump, then whirled and threw a shot toward the first person coming through the front door. It was that little monkey Pepito. The round missed, gouging a chunk from the dark vanish and ricocheting off the heavy wooden door. He fell back with a holler and snatched a semi-automatic handgun from his waistband, sending a handful of random shots that spiderwebbed the patio doors behind me.

In the enclosed space, the concussions were deafening hammer blows to my ears. I fired again at the crack of cloudy daylight and rushed as fast as I could in my condition toward Chino's body.

He had my Grandaddy's Sweetheart pistol, and I wanted it back.

Chapter 56

Someone kicked open the front door, stuck a Cobra around the edge, and held the trigger down. The rounds shredded the living room, blowing huge chunks out of the cold limestone fireplace.

You're just adding to the renovation workload, buddy.

The patio glass doors and windows exploded behind me as the bullets walked from left to right. I half-slid, half-fell behind one of the pallets of rocks, landing hard on one hip and cussin' a blue streak.

Still not giving up the ghost like he would have if I'd shot him with enough gun, Chino rolled onto his side and came up with my Grandaddy's .45, swinging it in my direction. At least it seemed slow, but in explosive situations, time lags. My own little pistol rose and Chino absorbed two more rounds, one at the base of his throat and the second about six inches higher, entering just under his nose.

The pink spray from the back of his head told me my Chinese-looking friend was out of the game for good. I twisted toward the front door and emptied the

Glock's magazine toward half a body angling for a shot with a Cobra. The ugly little machine gun disappeared. I snatched my .45 from Chino's limp hand.

Goddlemighty that big ol' familiar pistol felt good. I steadied myself and pitched another round through the door, the heavy report telling those on the other side that the game had changed. There was more shouting from out front, but they'd changed their mind about coming in that way, at least for the moment.

Chino's backpack was lying beside him, along with his Cobra. A lit cigarette was burning a hole in the thick material when I picked it up by one strap and threw it over my good shoulder, hoping the extra mags for the pistol were inside. The guys on the far side of the house were quiet, and that meant they were planning something. I tucked the Colt into the small of my back at the same time a shot from the river almost parted my hair.

Despite the distance, the muzzle blast was a physical push and I ducked. The round whizzed overhead, passing through the broken glass patio door and knocking a gangster off his feet. He wasn't one of the original quartet and that told me I was probably *wayyy* outnumbered once again. The war opened up in the next few seconds with bullets flying through the broken doors and burying deep into a cedar support post only inches away from where I crouched.

Sonofabitch! There's more of 'em!

The rifle on the river fired again. I was in a crossfire. I had to get gone. The unexplored part of the house was the only direction that looked safe and led away from Phoebe. A voice shouted from the river, sounding like they were calling for reinforcements to cut me off. I slung the Cobra under my arm and sprayed the riverbank using the stream of bullets to drive the rifleman back down again. The small explosions stitched the muddy bank and I caught a glimpse of his head and shoulders at the same time he ducked.

Missed!

The gun ran dry and I ducked back into the living room and around the hallway to the right, fumbling for the eject button. I had some relief when I turned the corner, if only for a few seconds. The ill-fitting doorway at the end of the short hall offered just what I was looking for. Dim light came underneath and along one side, telling me it led outside. I stumbled into a side yard full of weeds, an abandoned car, and a rusty toolshed, all surrounded by a chest-high stucco fence.

Praying I had enough gas left to get over, I headed toward the river side once again, intending to use a stack of cinder blocks to launch myself up and over in a roll that would get me out of sight.

A rifle appeared exactly where I was headed. I still hadn't reloaded the Cobra and snatched the .45 from the small of my back at the same instant still *another* machine pistol opened up on my left. Rounds cracked through the air like snapping fingers. The River Guy missed me again and hit one of his own boys. I saw a pink mist explode from the back of the machine gunner's head before he dropped out of sight. I vowed I'd kiss River Guy on the lips before he died, if I ever got the chance to shoot him down.

They needed practice, but I was glad those boys were shooting each other instead of me. Unfortunately, more people popped up along the fence separating me from the caliche drive, followed by machine pistols spitting fire. The saving grace was that none of them were aiming, just sticking the guns over the top and pulling the trigger.

Even then the whole side yard was a kill zone. I stumbled back into the house through the hallway, and dammit, there was another gangster raising still *another* machine gun.

My sudden return startled him so much it gave me just enough time to level the Colt and crank off three rounds. The gangster fell back, dead as a dinosaur, and I saw the door crack open to my left. A bare arm waved at me. "In here, Ranger!"

The arm belonged to Phoebe, and I ducked inside what I expected to be a bedroom, slammed the door, and stopped, stunned at the sight of a billiard table tilted high on one end. I was looking at the bottom of a thin slab base held up by a hydraulic system that exposed a dark, rectangular hole in the concrete foundation.

I didn't know what to ask first, so I pulled Phoebe away from the door to the edge of the hole. "What are you doing in here?"

"Trying to get out of this damned place. You didn't holler and I heard all the shooting. I was going out the front door, but there's about a thousand mean-looking bastards out there, all of 'em with guns."

"You could have padded that information a little better." Out of habit I glanced through the clear inside Lucite grip on my 1911 to check the loads. I jerked my head toward the hole under the pool table. "What'n hell's this?"

"What these guys have been coming through ever since they brought me here. It's a tunnel leading to Mexico. I heard one of them talking on a cell phone in English. This opens up across the river. They use it to smuggle drugs and people back and forth, then they put 'em in that stinking sewage truck outside. One of the guys told me later they were trying to sell my ass over there to some guy named Chatto if they got the right price."

It made sense. No one was going to search that god-awful honey wagon parked outside when the owner went to work. I could see moving drugs in that nasty smelling container, but the thought of putting human beings down in there for any length of time almost made me gag, and I wasn't far from yakking up that water I'd drank.

A commotion in the hall told me our time was up. "Come on, kid. Looks like we're going to Mexico."

Chapter 57

The "hole" in the floor was sure 'nough the entrance to a tunnel, and I saw pretty quick where all the grit had come from. A white trail of limestone footprints showed where people had been in and out hundreds, if not thousands, of times.

Drug tunnels running under the border were nothing new. The Mexican drug lord Joaquín "El Chapo" Guzman had been the master of the conception and completion of what border agents had started calling "super tunnels." The only ones I'd seen up to then weren't much more than gopher burrows.

There wasn't much time before those guys shot their way into the room. Voices yelling both in the house and outside told me they were forming up, and things were about to happen pretty damn quick. I glanced into the hole, expecting to look into a yawning black void. Instead, the sophisticated tunnel was more than a burrow. Electric lights lit up the skim-coated walls and a substantial steel ladder led to the bottom way down below.

All right, buddy boy. This table don't go up and

down by itself. Find the switch and give yourself some time to get to the bottom of that ladder.

I'd read about agents finding a tunnel in Arizona that operated off the turn of a water faucet. Since there were no faucets in the room, I scanned the walls. Light switch by the door, five electrical outlets, and switch by the closet door. All pretty standard, except one of the walls had an extra outlet in a strange place, and it was smudged in the middle.

Javier's voice came through the closed door. "Ranger! Give yourself up. You cannot get out of that room. Do not cost me any more men or the Grinder will take even more time with you. I will have him keep you alive for days, so you can feel him peel off every inch of skin."

He obviously thought the billiard table was in place on the floor, and not above my head. Someone had fallen down on their job, and it was most likely the guy I'd killed in the hallway. That's why he looked so surprised. He'd come up in the middle of a gunfight, or maybe he'd seen Phoebe standing there where she shouldn't have been. Either way, it was a fatal mistake.

"Go." I pointed. "Shinny down that ladder. I'll be right behind you."

The slender little gal moved up in my estimation when she went down that hole like a rabbit.

"Hey, did you see a switch of some kind down there to close this up?"

She answered two beats later. "No."

I knelt by the wall outlet, the .45 pointed at the door, and felt around with my fingertips. "There's gotta be one somewhere." It didn't twist, but it made a slight click when I pushed in the middle. The hydraulics hissed and the table descended.

"Out of the way, gal!" I took two running steps and slid over the edge and onto the ladder.

Wrapping one leg around the ladder's side rails to hold myself steady, I aimed at the outlet, firing two shots. One looked as if it struck the plastic plate and it probably did, because the slab holding the table dropped the last few inches, almost hitting me in the head as I ducked and descended the ladder.

As usual, my idea seemed a little hasty in hindsight. After the slab landed with a thud, I wondered if there was a switch to get out at the opposite end. The odds were fifty-fifty I'd sealed my own grave.

Boy, sometimes you need to think things through.

Yeah, Pop, but there wasn't a whole lot of thinking time back there.

Another thought popped into my mind, leaving me hoping there wasn't some bad guy down below aiming a gun up at my nether regions.

Chapter 58

The shooting had subsided and Pepito peeked around the house. He pointed across the river toward the Mexico side. "Look over there."

Four Humvees full of Mexican soldiers in tactical gear appeared on the dirt road and turned into the ghost town. It wasn't unusual to see them in the area. They showed up from time to time, scouting for any sign of the cartels.

Chatto had bought off most of the officers through the years, but a few were still loyal to the country. Not all of Chihuahua's officials and politicians were on his payroll, but that number had increased in the past year as Chatto spent seemingly endless amounts of drug money to rebuild the dilapidated buildings, claiming Paso La Carmen to be his new project designed to provide job opportunities for the locals.

The only problem was there weren't many locals still in the area, and with no way of making a living, they weren't likely to return. It didn't matter. It was all a cover for his newest experiment in moving drugs by constructing tunnels under the border.

Two of his tunnels came up in El Paso, on the U.S. side of the border, but this new system of moving drugs through La Carmen was showing more profit with less chances of being discovered. After several years, he'd finally made contact with one of the border patrol agents who manned the permanent check station south of Marathon.

Border Patrol Lieutenant Rafael Fuentes had a pretty good side business going, finding thick packets of cash in his trash can back in Alpine on the first day of each month. His job for the past eight years, according to the cartel, was simple. Instead of checking the odiferous Pando Honey-Dipper each time it went north to allegedly service dozens of nonexistent septic systems, Fuentes made cracks to his men about the stench and waved the truck through.

Repetition breeds blindness and laziness. Even when he wasn't on duty, the Pando truck passed with the wave of a hand. It wasn't loaded then with drugs or illegals on those days, because the officer in charge might decide to break their routine and use the dogs.

Javier and Pepito, still numb from the loss of Chino, watched the heavily armed soldiers disgorge from the vehicles and scatter along the road running parallel to the river watching for whatever might come across. With all the gunfire on the Texas side, and the arrival of the Mexican army, the entire ghost town was sealed off. One man Javier assumed was an officer stood in front of a truck, holding binoculars to his eyes.

Dreading that he had to phone Chatto and explain that the very-much-alive Ranger had disappeared down their tunnel, Javier reached into his pack between his feet for the satellite phone. He jolted when his fingers wrapped around what was once a piece of high-tech equipment and now suddenly was a useless piece of plastic. *"Chinga tu madre!"*

"Qué?"

Javier held up the dead phone with a bullet hole through two sides. "We can't call Chatto."

Pepito glanced around the barren desert as if looking for a pay phone. A gray curtain of rain hid the low, barren hills to the west. "What do we do now?"

"Get in the truck and drive." Pepito slipped behind the wheel of a four-door Ford pickup registered to the owner of the house. He started the engine and flicked on the brittle wipers that threatened to break apart.

They pulled onto the northbound farm road, and Javier chewed his lip in thought as the tires hissed on the wet pavement. He flipped though his mental files, selecting and discarding a dozen scenarios in which they made phone calls from cell phones they'd take off tourists or unwary locals.

For the first time since he was tattooed, he wished the art on his face and neck was gone so they could move without notice. The extensive tattooing was ignored south of the border, where most people averted their eyes whenever he or the other gangsters passed. In the U.S., and especially the border region of Texas, the citizens often stared. Once he saw a woman taking his photo with a professional-looking camera.

There was only one solution he could see. "Drive until we're out of sight."

"We can't go into the park, and we can't risk the Border Patrol check station."

"We're not going that far. There's a dirt road that splits off from this one. We'll get out of sight and leave the truck. Chatto has two men in a house about five miles that way." He pointed over his shoulder toward Mexico. "We will get out of sight and cross. They will take us to a phone."

Hiking through the desert was no challenge for either of the Apaches, who grew up walking wherever they went. Javier thought of the distance they'd have to travel to reach the phone. It would take longer than he wanted, but it was their only option other than the hazardous trip to the pay phone in Stillwell's country store, which they couldn't chance, or Marathon, beyond the check station.

He hoped the river wasn't high enough with the recent rains to be a problem.

Chapter 59

Taking advantage of the most recent lull in the rain, Sheriff Ethan Armstrong and the three Texas Rangers gathered outside the CP. The sheriff pinched a dip from a container of Skoal and tucked it into his bottom lip. It was a habit he'd almost broken before the Ballard Incident. "There's a crop of people in there. It's good to get some air."

Major Parker unwrapped a cigar and stuck it into the corner of his mouth. "Too many for my money."

"I figure you have some men working on this, other than here."

"You figure right."

Ethan sighed. "Look, Major, I'm not supposed to know a whole lot about what I'm gonna say, but a little birdy told me something I'd like to talk to you about, alone."

Major Parker's eyebrow rose in question. The impassive Rangers adjusted their ties at the same time, either a signal or ingrained training, and left. Parker watched them drift away and then leaned toward the sheriff. "What are you referring to?"

Ethan spat to the side and smoothed his brush-pile mustache. "Sonny's Shadow Response Team."

The major's face hardened. His deep voice rumbled. "Who told you about that?"

"Doesn't matter. You need to remember, there are no real secrets in a small town."

"Ranger Hawke and I'll have a talk when . . ."

"It didn't come from Sonny. Higher up. But that's not the important part."

"There's no one higher in this but the governor."

"I won't say it was him or . . ." Ethan stopped talking when he recognized two young faces in the supply tent, sitting close to the coffee and donuts. Both Jerry Hawke and Arturo Alonzo saw the sheriff at the same time and froze like deer in headlights. Keeping an eye on the boys, the sheriff continued with his thought. He jerked his head toward FBI Agent Landon McDowell, who was on his cell phone. "You and I both know he was out here investigating that triple homicide, and even though it's on federal land, it ain't the FBI that's digging the deepest."

"Go on."

"Sonny and his wife were good friends with those folks, and it's personal to him. You need to know he has these gut feelings that usually turn out to be right. I think he stumbled onto something at the crime scene that led him away. In fact, I *know* I'm right, because I got a text telling me he's in La Carmen, or Paso La Carmen."

"Text from who?"

"It came a roundabout way from one of your former Rangers, Herman Hawke."

The major's face relaxed, and the deep crow's-feet in the corners of his eyes smoothed out. "How'd Herman find out?"

"You'll hear soon enough that gangsters tried to break into Sonny's house last night to kill his family. Herman was there with a couple of friends—one was Yolanda Rodriguez—and they shot it out. Dead bad guys were scattered all over hell's half acre when they got through with them. Nobody hurt on our side. But when it was over, they had fresh info about Sonny."

"So he drove to La Carmen? Good God, there's nothing but a blocked bridge there."

"Far from it. He was taken there by a gang called the Coyotes Rabiosos."

Parker used three fingers to reposition the still-unlit cigar. "I've heard of 'em."

"Well, I hadn't, but the info I'm receiving says they're some bad dudes."

"The worst. We need to get out there." Raindrops snapped on their hat brims and the taut canvas tent nearby. "Which La Carmen for sure?"

"We don't know. Perry Hale is out there right now, scouting around."

Parker chomped down on the cigar. "How'd *he* find out?"

Ethan wanted to grin at the confirmation about Perry Hale. Sonny had told him some, but not enough to know how their trio was to operate, just enough for Ethan to have a grasp on the Shadow Response Team if he was ever needed. "You'll have to ask *him* that question, but since he's part of the SRT . . ."

Major Parker pulled a phone from his back pocket and punched in a number. Lucky for him, the area's spotty cell phone service didn't include the area around the command post. The call went through, and he spoke for a moment before waving the other two Rangers over at the same time a light shower began to fall.

"Now I know. We're heading for Paso La Carmen."

"That's about sixty miles away. It'll take most of an hour."

The major adjusted the cigar in his mouth. "We won't be driving the speed limit."

"I figured you'd say that." Sheriff Armstrong glanced into the tent where the park rangers and rescue team were updating the search area. "I should tell them what we know." He wanted to go inside to see what he'd missed, but he also needed to speak to the boys, who'd obviously cut class and driven to the park. He completely understood why Jerry had come, and figured Arturo had tagged along for moral support, or worse, because he'd gotten a taste for excitement and adventure. "There's a possibility that all this info's wrong. We don't want to pull everyone off right now. Let's confirm first."

The volume from those inside the CP increased and they heard Park Ranger Rivera's voice over the others. "That's enough. Settle down. Search Team Six, Hector Robles and Vincent Taylor, found a body. The apparent gunshot victim is near coordinates . . ."

They moved back inside. Ethan stuck with his Rangers as they took up their original positions. A magic hole appeared in the crowd as everyone moved aside to make way for the Texas Rangers' presence.

Rivera turned to a park map they'd placed on an easel so everyone could see. There was so much crosstalk in the CP that she had to wave a hand and shout.

"Listen up!" She waited until the crowd settled down. "They've retreated from the body and will maintain a position here." She pointed at the map and reported the new coordinates. "This is now a crime scene . . ."

Ethan waved at his deputies who joined him and the Rangers.

Her radio awoke again. "Team Eight. We've found an individual who appears to have drowned. A Hispanic male who is caught in debris." The man gave her the coordinates and she marked it on the map. "They say he's covered in gangster tattoos."

"That's a long way from the first body." Ethan crossed his arms. "Maybe a hiker, or an illegal?"

Rivera shook her head. "Look at this arroyo. There's a hiking trail that crosses here, but it narrows down, making it hard for someone to cross while the water was high. I'd bet it's someone who got caught much further up."

"That expands the search area even more." The Major adjusted his unlit cigar. "You want to bet Sonny didn't have something to do with that?"

"I won't take that bet."

Chapter 60

Bare bulbs in the tunnel lit the way all the way down to the base of the ladder. The air was thick with dampness and mildew. Scrambling down the rungs using mostly my right arm and shoulder was a chore. I was so high, though, that I couldn't risk a fall, so my left hand went to work about a third of the way down, the needling pull of the wound adding to the workout.

I must have been making all kinds of grunting sounds, because Phoebe called up to me. "You all right?"

"Yeah." My answer was more of a gasp. "I got a lot of hurtin' going on up here."

Her voice was distant, telling me she was already on the ground. "You need help?"

"Probably, but there's nothing you can do. I'll be down directly. Gravity's trying to help more than I want."

Down safe. Down safe. Down safe, became my mantra as I descended. Both legs grew weak and quivered harder the farther down I got.

If this is such a sophisticated tunnel, why haven't they put in an elevator?

It wasn't fanciful thinking. Some of the super tunnels that border agents found in the past had elevators on both ends. One they'd found in Arizona was as well-engineered and finished as a subway. I hoped they'd followed the same blueprints and installed an elevator over on the Mexican side to help me get out.

The tunnel had electric lights and fresh air from a system of PVC pipes. Puffs of cool air from holes drilled in the PVC periodically caught me in the face as I descended. I passed another series of jets ten feet from the bottom, and then I was on solid ground. I glanced around. I'd seen that kind of workmanship before, but in professionally constructed public buildings. The curved ceiling three feet overhead increased the stability of the hand-dug tunnel.

Phoebe was waiting with a water bottle in each hand. "Here. You look like you need a drink."

The tunnel looked to have been made by a professional construction company and I saw that long booger was empty. Relieved for a minute, I unscrewed the cap and gulped the water down. "Where'd you get this?"

"Over there." She pointed at half a case of Ozarka water bottles only feet away, the plastic covered with dust. I grabbed half a dozen more and opened Chino's backpack to drop them in. I dug around a second and found the Colt's extra magazines. I really wished my badge was in there, too, but Javier was wearing it the last time I saw him.

Fighting a rising tide of emotions, I also came up with a satellite phone. Squatting with my back to the ladder, I turned it on and waited for the shakes to quiet down. The screen lit up, but the device couldn't connect underground. I sat back and saw Phoebe with her nose in the air like a bird dog winding quail.

"I smell grass. It's what the tunnel was built for. Grass is bulky, so a nice big tunnel like this one's the best way to get it into the country. I'd bet they store it down here for a while every now and then."

"You know a lot."

"I told you. I've been here for over a week. They took me just outside of Stillwell's store. I hitched a ride there and was on my way to the park when they pulled over on the side of the road and drug me into a truck. One of those bastards hit me and they pushed me down on the floor until we got here."

We sat there for another quiet minute before she started talking again. "I kept hoping someone would come looking for me, but who's gonna think anything's going on in a regular house somebody's renovating out in the middle of BF Egypt?"

The construction materials I'd seen out front were a perfect cover. Anyone watching the house would think a renovation project was under way with trucks and trailers coming and going for a year or two, or more if they could figure a way to stretch it out.

After that, a For Sale sign in the yard and advertisements in the paper would tell the locals that the house was up for sale again, and that would allow for more vehicles. Then after it "sold," and to the same shell company who owned it in the first place, more trucks could arrive for extra renovations, or another room, another wing, or even building up. It could work for years.

"You're right. No one knows where I am, either. They're looking forty or fifty miles to the west of here, in the park." I waggled the SAT phone. It was useless in the tunnel, but a lifeline once I emerged on the Mexican side of the border. "So that means we're on our own until we can use this to call for help."

I stood, feeling the angry throb under my arm. I thought the water I'd just drank was going to become public again and leaned against the wall. Instead, the infection sent a wave of feverish chills through my body. Cold sweat broke out and I shivered as it soaked my shirt.

"You gonna make it? You look like hell."

"That's 'cause I been through hell." I paused. "We both have, and we got a ways to go yet."

"You're bleeding through all the dried blood on your shirt."

The aching pain came back after she mentioned it. Climbing down that ladder hadn't helped it none. "Shot. It's infected, too, so that's probably why it's still open.

She built a slight grin that lit up her face. "We make a pair, don't we?"

"Yessum. We're something. What say we hie on down to the other end of this tunnel and find some help."

She gently took my good arm. "You can lean on me, if you want."

Those words from that little slip of a girl watered my eyes. She was likely damaged both physically and emotionally, but was willing to help me walk. She reminded me of Mary, and a wave of dread washed over me again, because I wasn't sure any of my family was still alive.

I let her hold my arm, more for the physical comfort than anything else, and we limped down the long slope, hoping to get to the exit before Javier could arrange for a surprise party on the other end.

Chapter 61

The well-lit command center was an oasis of light in the gathering dusk. Jerry kicked at a rock in the parking lot that skipped between two new pickups. He was mad as a Jap, as his Grandpa Herman would say. "Told me she couldn't use us!" He slammed the palm of his hand on the Bronco's hood.

Kick. Another rock went sailing, barely missing a game warden's truck.

"Said we were just kids and didn't have any experience! I told her who I was and she said the best thing I can do for him is wait right here. How's that supposed to help?"

Kick. That one bounced once and dented the rocker panel on a highway patrol car.

Arturo checked their surroundings, to be sure no one was watching. He didn't want trouble with the law, because he intended to become a Texas Ranger someday, and being part of a car denting was sure to get him in trouble.

"Look, calm down and let's decide what to do."

"Do!" Jerry kicked another rock and Arturo had the

feeling that the next time that hiking boot kicked out, a windshield was going to crack.

"Jerry. I might have an idea."

"About what?"

"About where your dad might be."

"Bullshit. How would you know?"

"Because while you were squared off in there with the commander, I was reading the maps they have out on the tables. Those guys like to write things down, and when they were pushing you outside, I heard one of the guys say he knew who you were and that they'd found your daddy's truck."

The anger disappeared and Jerry grabbed Arturo's elbow. "So let's get out of here. Where did they find it?"

"I don't know exactly where . . ."

"Then why did you tell me?"

"Well, at first because they found a body a ways off." Arturo saw the look on Jerry's face and held up a hand. "Hold it. That's why I didn't tell you, but it's not your daddy. It's someone else. Some park rangers and Texas Rangers went out there and said they think it's a gangster from across the river."

Jerry relaxed and the line between his eyes went away for the moment. "How would they know a gangster from a wetback? Do they carry signs, I'm a gangster?"

He saw the hurt look on Arturo's face and wilted a little. "Hey, I'm sorry I said that."

"Doesn't matter. You're worried and all."

"So where's the truck?"

Arturo repeated what he'd heard. "That area's going to be swarming with searchers. We can't go there. They'll have everything sealed off."

"We'll bluff our way through." Jerry was back on top with the good news. "Then we can join one of the search parties and . . ."

"Stop. Let's drive down to the visitor center and get us one of those topo maps they were looking at. I saw where they'd circled that area. If we get the same one, I can tell you where the truck was."

"Then what?"

"That Bronco has plenty of clearance. We can drive out on our own and come in the back way. You know your dad, maybe we can figure out where he went." Arturo saw Park Ranger Rivera and Major Parker leave the CP and stop beside five men in tactical camouflage, boonie hats, camo caps. AR-15s hung muzzle down across their chests. Prominent patches on their shoulders identified them as Texas Rangers, and it was the first time Arturo had ever seen them in anything other than their iconic western wear.

"Give me your phone."

"Why?" Jerry held the phone out even as he asked the question.

"Because I don't have one." Arturo took it and drifted back toward the huddle of men behind Rivera, tapping at the screen and scowling. It was the same performance the boys had seen over and over that day with frustrated responders. Cell phones seemed to have a mind of their own in the remote park, sometimes working, sometimes not.

The youngster turned one ear toward the group and listened as Rivera spoke softly with the Texas Rangers. None of them paid any attention to the familiar sight of a youngster intent on a cell phone. He angled himself and lifted the device as if trying to find a signal, and with the ears of youth, heard enough to make him want to dance.

Arturo waved Jerry over and led the way toward the impromptu parking lot when the group dissolved and Rivera returned to the CP.

"Where are we going?"

"La Carmen."

"La Carmen? Why there? That place is nothing but a dead end in the desert."

"Because that's where your daddy is. We're following those guys. I'll tell you on the way."

They broke into a run as a rumble of thunder seemed to jar even more water from the sky.

Chapter 62

Frustrated at the lack of news and equally aggravated that she hadn't heard from her brother, Mary Hawke sent a flurry of Snapchat photos to her friends, complaining that she was going nuts in the Posada Real Hotel and wished she had some news about her dad.

In his sprawling house in Houston, Chavez gave a child's giggle of glee as Mary's Snapchat photos popped up on his screen. "Gotcha!"

He adjusted the mouthpiece on his headset and tapped a couple of keys on the laptop squared up with the edge of his light granite counter.

The gruff voice on the other end of the call answered with a thick Spanish accent. "What?"

"I'm pleased to inform you that I have some excellent news."

The man on the other end sighed as if a great weight had been placed on his shoulders. "What?"

Taken aback by the Chatto's gruff tone, Chavez almost declined to give the gangster his news. However, the thought of taking his revenge on the Hawke family overcame his childish reluctance. "Fine fine fine, if you want to dispense with social courtesy"—he licked his lips in anticipation—"the Hawke targets that your people missed are now securely ensconced in the Posada Real Hotel. You may complete your contract there."

"You still owe me that package."

"I'm sure you know that it's in hand and on the way to your location at this moment."

"That man you had so much faith in probably failed. I should have sent my own man along with the Apaches."

"Issues arose beyond my grasp."

"You and I are finished."

"I expected as much. Just do what I paid you for." Chavez clicked off and sighed. Dealing with people of such low class was frustrating. If this project failed as he expected, much like the last in Ballard, he planned to take a different tack on the next one. He'd forget the Hawkes, charging both failures to experience, and contact his disillusioned mercenaries in EmCorp. Those guys were professionals and would do as he asked without fail.

Bolstered with the idea, Chavez clicked the keys on his computer again and sat straighter when a woman's soft voice answered.

"Hello?"

"This is . . . Ed."

"Well hello, honey. Are you lonely today?"

"Yes. Can you have someone here in say, two hours?"

"Of course. Now, don't get started without us."

* * *

Sheltered in the cool darkness of the Americana Bar de Vista, in Paso La Carmen, Chatto handed the cell phone back to his number one man, who slipped it into the pocket of his linen slacks. "Ernesto. Send Rodriguez and some men to Chavez's house in Houston. Our association has come to an end. Wrap this up before the sun comes up tomorrow."

"Sí." The gangster pulled a second burner phone from another pocket and pushed a button. *"Ernesto aquí. Terminar el contrato de Chávez en Houston."*

Ernesto here. Terminate the contract with Chavez in Houston.

"Cuándo?"

"Inmediatamente!"

Immediately.

Chatto nodded and walked across the grimy floor. He stopped at the open doors and sighed in satisfaction at the soft rain falling on the darkening desert. "The Ranger's family is in the Posada Real Hotel in Ballard. I want this finished."

"Instructions?" Ernesto's face was impassive.

"Kill everyone there, and then burn the hotel down."

The gangster's eyes glittered. He surveyed the room full of local cowboys, gangsters, and the Mexican officer in fatigues. "That will take an army."

Chatto shifted his feet, and leveled his response to Captain Perez of the Mexican Army, who leaned forward and laced his fingers on the table, listening. "It is time to go to war."

Ernesto made another call on his burner phone. *"Ernesto aquí. Es hora de ir a trabajar."*

Ernesto here. It's time to go to work.

Chapter 63

"I'm all boogered up, but we can't stay in here."

Our feet were wet from half an inch of water that covered the floor. It was an eerie feeling to walk down the long tunnel lit by bare bulbs and know that the Rio Grande was flowing not far above our heads.

Long gray electrical cables attached to the wet walls sagged like bunting. I limped along best I could, with Phoebe holding my arm like I was a hundred years old. Honestly, I could have used a walker.

Like I'd expected, there was no elevator at the end of the tunnel. I eased up to see past the ceiling and into the shaft leading upward. The metal ladder set into the wall was exactly the same as the other, and a bare yellow bulb showed me the closed door above.

I pulled Phoebe back. "Listen, kid. I have a bad feeling about this. You wait until I find out what's up there. I'll call you when I know the coast is clear."

"Or when everyone is dead?"

My eyebrow went up at her question.

"I saw your work back there."

"Look, I was lucky as hell. That's all. The odds are

against me if I get into another altercation with those guys."

"Altercation?"

"You know what I mean. They've had plenty of time to call their friends on this side. They're probably waiting for us up there."

"The cops back at the house will figure things out. Why don't we wait until it's safe?"

"More than one reason." Now that I was still and thinking about it again, the infection pressed down like a weight on my shoulders. I almost sagged and put one hand on the wall as my head spun. It took a moment to rally. "Mostly because I might be unconscious from this bullet wound by morning, and second, there'll probably be someone from this side who'll open the door at any time. They have product to move, and we're smack dab in the way."

"Fine then, but don't get yourself killed. I'm beginning to like you."

"You'd like my daughter better. She's about your age."

Trying not to groan out loud, I worked my left arm through the backpack's straps and settled it on my shoulders. Climbing up was going to be harder than going down, but I figured out how to keep my left arm as still as possible.

Things got a little complicated when I reached the top. That little thing called gravity gave me trouble. I had to loop my good arm through the ladder to hold steady while a couple of deep breaths gave me the strength and courage to reach way out with the other. The wound shrieked and light flickered in my eyes.

A large white garage button pushed by many dirty

hands lifted the door above my head. It moved with a growl and hiss of hydraulics. Expecting light to come pouring in, I was surprised to see I'd come up in some kind of pit in the floor of a metal building. A lone yellow security light directly overhead showed me the grimy floor.

Any other time I'd have peeked out with the .45, but essentially being one-handed on the ladder presented a problem. I swiveled my head like an owl, scanning what I could see of a long narrow concrete trench. Feeling disoriented by the fever, I wondered if I was hallucinating. A steel grate four or five feet above my head explained everything.

The trap door came up in an oil-changing pit. It was something I hadn't expected to find in Mexico, but I figured it was a relic of the days before 9/11 when the area was booming. Someone must have had more money than sense back in the 1980s or '90s to put in an oil-changing station, and the owners must have been betting on an economic upturn.

After the attacks, the border was closed and Paso La Carmen withered away to nothing.

I waited, listening. The building was empty, so I pulled myself upward and rolled onto the pit's floor with a groan.

Silence.

"Hang on. It's going to take a minute or two more."

Instead of listening, Phoebe came up the ladder like a monkey, apparently glad to get out of the tunnel. I was wondering if she was claustrophobic when something scraped in the metal building. It was so late in the day that a dim glow around a large rolling steel door on one end was all I could see. I used the concrete trench as cover and stretched my arm with the cocked 1911 above the floor. I was waiting for my eyes to adjust when Phoebe squeaked like a mouse.

I spun to find two armed men pointing guns at the same time something the size of a calf landed on my shoulders. More bodies dropped into the pit like falling fruit, and their weight took me to the ground.

Chapter 64

Yolanda Rodriguez was in the Posada Real Hotel's colorful art deco lobby when her cell phone vibrated. Guided by a strong sense of responsibility, she'd stopped by on the way out of town to check on the Hawke family on her way to join Perry Hale. Beside her on the dark leather couch, Kelly Hawke raised an eyebrow in question and Yolanda nodded. "It's Perry Hale."

The Posada's lobby went silent at the announcement. Yolanda answered. "Hey you."

"Good to hear your voice."

"You sound great, too. You're coming through loud and clear. You must have a good signal wherever you are in the park."

"I don't know how. I'm not there. I'm in La Carmen Hacienda, where we spent the weekend a couple of months ago, and that's what I wanted to talk to you about. Sonny's alive, and the last time I saw him he was in a house down below the bed and breakfast, overlooking the river."

Yolanda saw the anticipation in everyone's faces

and rose, shaking her head that Perry Hale didn't have anything new. They went back to their discussions as she left the lobby and crossed the red Mexican tile floor. She pushed through the double French doors out onto the patio. It had stopped raining for the moment, and the streamer flags crisscrossing overhead hung limp. The bubbling fountain covered her voice and she faced the arched entrance to the street, talking freely.

"I remember the place. You can see all the way to that little church on the Mexico side from our room. You're in there now?"

No phones, no television, and no Wi-Fi, the remote Hacienda was for people who wanted to get completely off the grid for a while. It was so remote, they opened only when someone reserved a room, which meant the rental was empty and closed most of the time.

"Yep. That's where I am. I've glassed both sides of the river. There's a few locals over there with what looks like a squad of Mexican soldiers."

"Do they have Sonny?"

"He disappeared back into the house with me hollering at him. I worked my way down the river so no one could see me coming in, and the minute I got behind the house, here came Sonny, boiling outside, shooting at everyone in sight. The whole world went to shit. I tried to cover him, but he must have thought I was one of the bad guys. I kept yelling at him, but he couldn't hear me. He ducked back inside and things got too hot. I had to slip back down the riverbank and split.

"But here's the deal, the war ended and them that could walk took off without him. It's quiet now, but with those people across the river watching I don't dare go down there to look."

"What does that mean?"

"It means he's still inside, or something else. I'm voting for something else. While I was watching all this down below, I checked out the houses and buildings on the poor side of town."

She grinned at the reference. One of Perry Hale's favorite songs was Johnny Rivers' "Poor Side of Town," and she immediately knew he meant the hardscrabble cluster of buildings in Mexico that made up the Paso La Carmen ghost town. "That's politically incorrect, *tonto*."

"You just spoke my middle name, and it ain't *dummy*. There's a locked metal building over there when I first looked at it. Called *Camiones Cisternas*, River Bend Trucking. An open business in a ghost town. An hour after Sonny shot up all the gangsters on our side of the river, a pickup pulled up and left a few minutes later with a tarped load."

A knot formed in her stomach and Yolanda turned so those in the lobby couldn't see her face. "You're leading up to something."

"Yep, but the truck over there didn't go far. I figured they'd take off south and we'd never see it again, but I watched it follow a dirt road east along the river and stop at a nasty-looking little bar I can see from here. They pulled Sonny and a woman out of the back and walked them inside. That boy has more lives than Carter has little liver pills. When it gets full dark, I'm going in after him."

"The soldiers are still there, right?"

"Yep."

"You need me, then."

"That's my girl."

"I'm on my way."

Chapter 65

It was early evening when six men living in the trailer within sight of Gary Collins' house outside of Ballard received a phone call at the same moment Perry Hale and Yolanda were talking. Three of them were slouched in front of a tube television, watching an snowy, overacted Mexican soap opera with scantily dressed women.

Two others were asleep in the bedroom, and Tiburón was on lookout. He snatched the phone off the 1960s-era coffee table and answered, scratching at the tattoo on his bull neck. "Yes."

"Is it all quiet?" The question in Spanish was code for those waiting in the house for the next load of cocaine.

"Of course it is." The response allowed both men to relax.

"Is everyone with you?"

"Yes."

"You have a job. Miguel failed. The Ranger's family is alive and at the Posada Real Hotel. Chatto wants this finished."

"When?"

"By dawn."

"How?"

"The way we took out the Alejandros."

"It will bring every policeman in Texas."

It wasn't an overstatement. They'd killed the Alejandros family by simply walking into the Mexican restaurant in Progreso, just across the Texas border, before it closed one night, and gunning down everyone in the building. In addition to the family that had insulted Chatto by refusing to pay him for protection, they executed the staff, several customers in the family-owned restaurant, and two off-duty Mexican police officers who'd stopped by for a free meal.

It was the murder of the officers that angered the Mexican officials the most and Chatto paid dearly to calm them down. It cost fifty thousand dollars and the lives of the four shooters to soothe the hurt feelings of the Mexican police. The shooters were given to El Molinillo, the Grinder, in apology for the attack.

Tiburón peered out the fly-spotted window. It wasn't raining at the moment, but puddles of water were scattered across the rugged landscape. Clouds almost seemed to rest on the roof of the Collins' house in the distance. "We will have to leave."

"Yes. I chose you because I want people there who know the area. Chatto wanted twenty men, but you and the others can do it."

"We are worth more than twenty men." Tiburón stuck out his chest. His pride had always gotten him into trouble.

"When you are finished, go to El Paso. We will send fresh brothers to take your place in Ballard."

A smile split Tiburón's face. He was tired of being

cooped up a house in the middle of the desert. The only excitement they had was when the sheriff and an old man came to the trailer after their dogs attacked an old woman walking down the road.

Guns in hand with the safeties off, Tiburón and his men sat motionless in the trailer as the sheriff banged on the door. When he received no response, they watched him and the old man through cracks in the plastic Venetian blinds as they circled the house to check the dog pen. Tiburón expected the sheriff to shoot the guard dogs. *He* would have, but instead, the old man blocked the hole and left them alone.

Americans had no guts for doing what was necessary. The cowards hadn't been back since. He'd hoped to someday kill the sheriff with the thick mustache, who walked around like he owned the country. The old man wouldn't have been any trouble at all. He felt old men should sit in the shade and talk about life gone past instead of irritating younger people trying to make a living.

Well, the death of the *alguacil* would be someone else's pleasure.

"We will go there after dark."

"*Sí.*"

Tiburón punched the receiver icon and ended the call. "*Amigos! Levantate!* Get up. We are going to kill some *traidores*! Get your belongings. We aren't coming back."

He pointed at the back door. "Let the dogs out, too. Those lazy *perros* need some exercise."

Maybe they'd finish the old woman off this time.

* * *

Just south of the Galleria shopping mall in Houston, a lowered silver Nissan Sentra filled with young career gangbangers from the Barrio Mafia pulled out of the Latino neighborhood. A second car, this one a maroon Nissan Altima, followed closely. Long shadows from blooming crepe myrtles and apartment buildings stretched across the street.

A light breeze shook blue, white, and red petals on the cars as they cruised down the once-bustling neighborhood with the Latino song "Ginza" filling the air. Thirty years earlier, the suburb was called Swinglesville, an up-and-coming area full of career-oriented Anglos looking to make their mark on the world.

Now the cars passed decaying apartment complexes with huge banners advertising free move-in specials. Old men sitting in cast-off plastic chairs and drinking beer watched cars go past. As the sun went down, women gathered in the courtyards beside cracked and empty swimming pools, holding babies and chatting in the cooling air.

The tattooed young men in those same cars were dressed alike in starched pants, either jeans or khakis, T-shirts, bandanas in their pockets, and crosses or rosaries. All wore short, dark hair. None of them expected to reach thirty years of age.

Angel was driving the lead car. His hand rested across the silver Nissan's steering wheel, revealing the gang tattoo on his wrist of five small wavy lines. "Where are we going?"

In the back seat, Margarita, a young Latino girl with big dark eyes, elbowed the men on either side of her. "Maybe to the Galleria? I need to get a new rosary for my mother."

They smiled, because Margarita was always talking about her gangster mother who'd been killed in a drive-by when she was only two. It was a joke only she understood.

Ricardo, the oldest and their leader, watched out the side window, his head bobbing to the loud music they had to almost shout over. "We have a job in River Oaks."

Everyone in the car laughed at the thought of the most affluent neighborhood in Houston.

Angel kept his eyes on a police car that passed going the opposite direction. "It will be the only job we ever have there."

Ricardo thought about the machetes, baseball bats, knives, and two semi-automatic handguns in the trunk that had come dearly. "It will be one everybody will remember." He crossed himself and touched the gold cross hanging around his neck.

Marc Chavez waited impatiently in his sprawling River Oaks home for the escort service's *representative* to arrive. He'd learned his lesson months earlier when his much older live-in companion left after taking more than a quarter of his money with her. Now he paid for companionship provided by high-end escort services who never advertised, but came highly recommended by satisfied clients.

Chavez never knew who would arrive at his door after he called. The young women varied in size, appearance, and hair color. Sometimes they looked like housewives, one time a rodeo girl, and once an innocent-looking black woman whose specialty was role playing. They stayed all night, leaving the next morning with a thick envelope full of cash.

He paced the house as he waited, worrying over the progress of Chatto's assignment. Frustrated that his hopes had been pinned on Abdullah, who was now feeding the carnivorous wildlife in Big Bend National Park, he couldn't stand the wait for word of the Ranger's death.

He smoothed his perfectly combed black hair and talked to himself. "This is too much, too much, too much. I should have waited until Chatto contacted me that the deed was done. Maybe if I'd told her to arrive at nine tonight it would have been better, much better, better."

He toured his house, adjusting a perfectly straight photo on the wall, mumbling in frustration that the carpet in the bedroom revealed his footsteps from an hour earlier, and debating on whether or not to get out the vacuum. Waiting for the doorbell to ring, he moved a book to just the right position on the shelf beside the fireplace. "Maybe it'll be another Latino." His breath caught at the memory of the last time. "Yes. A slender Latino girl with big dark eyes."

Dusk arrived in La Carmen and so did Yolanda Rodriguez. She met Perry Hale at his room high above the Rio Grande and dropped her backpack on the bed. "This place looks closed."

"It is."

"How'd you get in?"

"Experience. Remember, I grew up in South Oak Cliff."

She grinned at the reference to a rough, primarily African-American, Dallas suburb.

Perry Hale wrapped his arms around her. "You don't have to come with me."

She smiled with her eyes, and his stomach clenched as it always did. "You need me."

"More than you know."

"How are we doing this?" She gave him a squeeze and stepped back.

He pointed at the river and the crumbling bridge she couldn't see. "They've blocked the bridge with Jersey barriers. Those are the easy part. Then comes a nine-foot-tall steel wall topped by another six feet of bars that look like what you'd find in a jail cell. But above that is how we get in. There's another barrier angling toward the Mexican side made of chain link. We cut through that and we're in."

"We could get caught." Her words were a warning but the twinkle in her eyes told him she was looking forward to getting across and finding Sonny.

"We won't."

"Why?"

He cut his eyes toward the bed covered with his equipment and weapons. "Because I won't let that happen."

Chapter 66

The truck stopped suddenly and rocked on its springs. We hadn't gone more than half a mile from the metal building, maybe less. Phoebe and I lay face-to-face in the truck bed under a tarp that smelled like carrion, our hands duct taped behind us. I had a good idea what was going on.

The gunfight at the house across the river had attracted attention from both sides. Anyone who heard the gunshots would have drifted down to watch the action and see if it had any chance of spilling across the river.

Folks all over the world are drawn to accidents and violence and gawk at the slightest incident. I was always one of those highway patrol officers who went nuts when onlookers created traffic jams to eye car wrecks, large or small, looking for bodies under sheets. I'd written more than one ticket for impeding traffic, interfering in an investigation, and generally being a dumbass. Well, that last one wasn't real, but I always wanted to write it.

Heightened awareness by the local law increased

the danger of transporting kidnap victims in the open, unless the law was paid off, so moving us to an alternate location until things settled down only made sense.

There was a lot of conversation beside the tailgate after we stopped. My limited Spanish was useless because they were talking so fast. Lucky for me, I was lying on my right side or I don't think I could have taken it. Someone finally yanked on the handle and let the tailgate down. Hands grabbed our feet, and they drug us out like deer carcasses. I couldn't help but groan, and Phoebe gasped at the rough handling. Two mean-looking characters used our shirts to pull us upright.

"Levantate."

We wriggled around to get our legs over the tailgate and stood up like the thick guy with a shaved head told us. From what I could tell, we were on a dirt road in front of the Americana Bar de Vista, halfway up a ridge overlooking the Rio Grande. Any other time I would have snorted at the name. Some American vista, just that house I'd been in and another on the ridge above, but hell, what's in a name?

Bars in rural Mexico were far from fancy, but in a ghost town, this one was downright creepy. It was a mix of *The Texas Chainsaw Massacre* and that Quentin Tarantino vampire movie *From Dusk Till Dawn*, only much, much worse.

Not even a neon sign glowed in the gathering dusk, just a faded, painted plank with the bar's name. A bare bulb on a single wire dangled over the sign, the only illumination.

I'd been in some rough places in my life, including

honky-tonks with sawdust on the floor to soak up the blood, but the American Vista Bar was downright nasty looking, and that was from its *good* side, the exterior.

"Caminen." The thick guy shoved us toward the door.

The neon lights were inside, and I wondered if it was to avoid gaining attention from our side of the Rio. The multicolored lights, some in Spanish, advertised Corona, Modelo, and Sol mostly, with a few for Patrón and Jose Cuervo tequilas.

Above, a pressed-tin ceiling looked original, telling me the joint had been there a long, long time. The sagging pine floor was dark with filth, grease, spilled drinks, and what I suspected to be blood. There was something missing, but I couldn't put my finger on it.

Old Blackjack Pershing might have had a drink there way back when he crossed over to chase Pancho Villa, but the guy that met us sure wasn't either of them. "Well, amigo. I've been wanting to meet you."

A shape sitting in the dark corner farthest from the door was all I could see. Waiting for my eyes to adjust, I moved around to relieve the stress on my side. Phoebe shifted closer and I felt her tremble. She was as terrified as me. But I wasn't going to show it.

The infection rose up hot and wet again, making my head reel. I broke out into another cold sweat, and it pissed me off because they'd think I was scared. My knees were weak all right, but not from fear. I'd 'bout reached the end of my rope, and I wanted nothing more than to sit down, or better yet, lay down and sleep for a week.

The last time I was that bad off, I told Kelly I wanted

to close my eyes and die, but that comment hit a little too close to home right then. I was fed up with being pushed around. "You Chatto?"

"Sí."

"Like I told ol' Javier back in the States, you're under arrest. He still is, too, when I find his ass."

"I don't find you amusing, Ranger, and to me, Javier is no longer a man. He is a ghost walking on this earth."

The voice made me shiver and I was glad I wasn't in ol' Javier's shoes, but then again, the boots on my feet weren't exactly in a convent and my future looked pretty bleak. "I can't find you at all, hiding there in the shadows. Can someone turn on another beer sign or something?"

"Release them."

A man with bad teeth in a pressed western shirt yanked us around and set us free. He grabbed Phoebe's arm and shoved her toward the bar occupied by several others wearing Taco Hats who watched with blank faces. They were Mexican cowboys for the most part, locals who came in to spend their hard-earned pesos drinking skunky beer and listening to music. I didn't think they were part of Chatto's gang.

The guys surrounding the cartel's enforcer were a different breed, shaved, tattooed, and looking mean as hungry rattlesnakes. None of them wore hats. There was a flat-brimmed cap or two, but the rest were uncovered. I couldn't tell much about their clothes in the dim light, but that wasn't important. We weren't there for a fashion show.

My eyes were becoming accustomed to the light

and it was easier to make out Chatto's features. The man had spent a lot in ink. His face and bald head were tatted in a confusion of words, symbols, swirls, and patterns.

The words *Coyotes Rabiosos* started under his right ear, followed his jawline, and ended under the left. His hooded eyes were dead. There was nothing in there at all. Once you saw that guy, you'd remember him until the day you died, and I wasn't sure how long that'd be for me.

Chatto was one of those people who looked at you down his nose, like a man peering through the bottoms of bifocals. "I'm looking at more of you than I contracted for."

"Yeah, well, good men are hard to find."

He traded looks with a guy sitting beside him, and my eyes adjusted to the dimness to realize he was dressed in a Mexican soldier's camo fatigues. Another soldier sat beside him, but he didn't look as confident. I figured the first guy as a crooked officer, one of the many people in the Mexican military that Chatto had bought off.

"Those *Indios* didn't do their job. They are only, what do you call *la leyenda* in his country?"

The general or whatever he was spoke so softly I could barely hear him. "Legend."

"Ah, *sí*, legend, with no true basis. The descendents of Geronimo are nothing more than weak kittens who couldn't do their job, and now I have to do it for them."

Chatto inclined his head and Thick Guy punched me in the left kidney. The next second I was on my knees, gasping in pain. I've hurt before, but never from anything like that. I heard Phoebe yelp, but there was no strength in my legs to push upright. Blood roared in my ears and I couldn't do anything but suck air.

Beyond that, there was no other sound. That's what was missing. I was in a bar with no band or jukebox. On one hand, it was positive because I hated their music, but it was eerie. Silent bars are not normal.

Warm blood ran down my side as the wound broke open still *again*, and I shook my head to clear the stars from in front of my eyes. Bile rose and I spat a yellow fluid onto the already filthy floor.

The general leaned forward and rested one elbow on the scarred, rickety table. "You, too, are a legend, *guardabosque*. Maybe one of real . . . substance. We have heard of you even over here, after you killed so many people when *la nieve* covered the ground."

"If you mean when it snowed, yeah, I was cold and that made me crabby."

A foot kicked me in the side again and I screamed. From a distant place, Chatto's voice penetrated the pain. "Ranger. I would have them take your head now, but you have a date with El Molinillo. You will face him when he gets here, and will do it alive. I want you to look at him before my men cut your throat."

The pain was so great I didn't even try to think of another smart-ass comment. The beer signs spun, and I fell into darkness.

Chapter 67

It was dark when Kelly Hawke stood in the second-floor hotel room window overlooking the Posada courtyard. There were only two rooms on the top of that horseshoe shape with a western view of the courtyard lit by bare-bulb patio lights. Two dozen streamer flags crisscrossed the open area, fluttering in the breeze. The flagstone was still damp, but the skies overhead offered an occasional view of a flickering star.

Filled to the brim by the incessant rain, the fountain in the middle of the courtyard splashed unsuspecting people passing by. A uniformed sheriff's deputy occupied a metal chair in a hidden corner beside the arched entrance. A pump shotgun leaned against the wall beside him.

"Mom, when are we going to hear something?" Mary was propped against the headboard, tapping endlessly on her phone's screen.

Already almost ready to scream in frustration, Kelly forced herself not to turn from the deputy assigned to protect them. To do that would unleash a response the high school student hadn't earned. Kelly was scared to death because no one had contacted her in the last hour. Her eyes flicked to the phone on the desk charger. It was dark.

"You know as much as I do."

"Why do we have to stay here? Let's go to Alpine at least. It's closer if anything happens."

"Because everyone who needs to get in touch with us knows we're here." Kelly paused. An itch somewhere in her subconscious told her she'd said something important, but she couldn't figure out what it was. "This is where they can find us if they hear anything new. We don't need to be running all over West Texas."

"Well, I'd like to have someone with us. How about we call Evangelina and ask her to come over? Her dad's downstairs. I bet Gabe'd like to have his daughter close so he could keep an eye on her, too."

Experienced with manipulative high school students, Kelly ignored the convoluted logic and turned to her daughter. "If it's dangerous for us, it would be just as bad for her." She realized that since Gabe was downstairs with Herman, her daughter's best friend might be home alone. "Where is Angie anyway?"

Mary rose and sat cross-legged, still tapping at her phone. Kelly remembered when she was that age, dating Sonny and talking endlessly on the house phone that had a cord just long enough to run under her closed door.

"Staying with Gillian. They've been texting me, asking if they can come over. Angie said we could keep each other company."

Kelly wondered who was keeping an eye on the

girls with Gillian's dad, Sheriff Ethan Armstrong, out of pocket in Big Bend. "The answer is no."

There was that niggle again. Something, but what?

Mary's thumbs flew over the screen. It was the way their generation traded information and kept in contact. Social media was fast taking over face-to-face conversation and it worried Kelly and Sonny. They'd spent endless hours sitting on the porch, Kelly drinking red wine and Sonny with a Bombay Sapphire gin and tonic, discussing the trend where people conversed by text, even in the same house or sitting side-by-side on a couch.

Kelly glanced at her phone again. *Maybe I need to check my Facebook and see if anyone is talking about the search. Maybe there's something there . . .*

She froze with a hand over her mouth.

"Mary, have you told any of your friends where we are?"

She didn't glance up. "I haven't called any of them, but I've posted on Snapchat, why?"

"But the girls are texting, too, about what's going on, right?" Kelly'd seen how the kids interacted with several people at the same time. She'd tried it once, texting to her building principal Victor Hernandez about one subject and Sonny on another. That experience failed miserably when she signed off with Sonny, texting an "I love you" that went to the principal instead.

It took a while to explain how she'd made that mistake.

Mary nodded, barely listening. "Probably." She listed six other friends by name.

Kelly snatched her phone off the table and thumbed it alive, suddenly realizing how the gangsters knew they were home alone, or thought they were. Social media. Their whole lives were wide open for anyone to see.

Her Facebook page showed over seventy comments on Kelly's post that she and Mary were not at home, so don't bother to come around. They were staying somewhere in town, she said, and she knew they were all concerned. All the comments were from friends who sent condolences or concerns.

She flicked the screen and gasped. Instead of posting "Private," Mary had put it up for "Public" comments.

"Mary. Shut it down."

"I will in a sec. I'm checking to see if Perry Hale got back to me. I can't wait any longer. I sent him a text to see what he found out. Maybe he'll tell us something."

"Did you say anything about us being at the Posada?"

"Sure. Perry Hale won't tell."

Kelly whirled and looked out onto the courtyard. It seemed the same at first glance, and then she saw the deputy leaning back in his chair, arms hanging limp by his side. His face was turned toward the sky, a huge gash across his throat. The blood had already stopped pumping and covered the front of his shirt, running down into a dark pool at his feet.

She lunged across the bed, knocking the phone from Mary's hand, and rolled to her feet on the other side. She slapped the lights off and grabbed her purse containing a Ladysmith .38 revolver just as the shadow of someone's feet broke the beam of light coming under the door.

Chapter 68

Marc Chavez's doorbell rang at half past midnight. He started upright, stomach clenched in anticipation. He'd turned down all the lights and lit candles throughout the house, giving it a soft ambiance that the young lady would surely appreciate.

Already in silk pajamas covered by a soft robe, he answered the door with a crystal glass of wine in his hand. "Good evening. I'm glad to have you here with me to celebrate."

The dark-eyed young woman standing on his doorstep didn't look like anything he expected. Instead of the soft, voluptuous type of woman he typically hired, she was a lean, hard-looking Latino. Chavez's heart flipped at the sight. This was something new, exotic, and exciting.

He held out the glass. "This is for you. Come in and let's get acquainted."

She blinked for a moment before her white teeth flashed in the candlelight spilling through the door. *"Seguro, mi amor."*

My sweetheart.

Chavez's insides went soft and he fell instantly in

love. He stepped back for her to enter and spoke in fluent Spanish. *"El baño está a la vuelta de la esquina. Estoy seguro de que querrás lavarte antes de empezar. Lo siento, pero soy exigente con la limpieza.* I'm sorry, but I'm picky about cleanliness."

She threw her head back and laughed at the mention of the bathroom and her need to wash up before they start. "I'll need it more when we're finished."

His heart fluttered at the sound, a sensation he hadn't experienced in months. *"Hablas* English?"

"Sure do."

"Good, I won't have to concentrate so hard on my Spanish."

The young woman stepped inside and Chavez got a good look at her, immediately recognizing the gangster clothing and the bright blue bandana hanging from her back pocket. "What's this, a little role-playing game you must have in mind?"

His ardor as well as his blood went cold when a crowd of young, hard-looking gangsters materialized behind her with edged weapons and guns.

Chapter 69

The soft tap outside Kelly Hawke's hotel room was as startling as a gunshot. Her eyes flicked from the shadow under the door, then back up to the peephole. She knew better. If someone heard her speak, the obvious place for her eye to be was behind the tiny round lens.

Mary rolled off the bed to answer the second knock. Kelly went cold. Her voice was nothing more than a hiss. "Mary, no!"

With the maddening stubbornness of a high school junior, the young woman argued as she stepped into the small vestibule. "Why not?"

Kelly grabbed her daughter's arm and yanked her back at the same time Mary saw the pistol in her mother's hand. Her eyes widened and she allowed herself to be pulled back around the corner. "What is it?"

"It's bad."

The soft rap came again, this time accompanied by a familiar voice. "Kelly. Mary. It's Herman."

Weak with relief, Kelly held her daughter against the wall with one hand. She whispered. "Stay here.

There still may be trouble." Her palm was sweaty on the pistol butt. Just in case Herman had a gun to his head, she cracked the door, leaving the brass hasp in place. She peeked through the one-inch gap.

Herman held up a pump shotgun so she could see he was armed and not a hostage. "S'okay."

She closed the door and removed the hasp. "Herman, the deputy is dead out there!"

"Yep. Saw it myself." He stayed where he was, watching the elevators to his left. "Y'all come with me."

Knowing better than to ask questions, Kelly waved to her daughter. "Mary, let's go."

Once in the hall, she glanced around and saw Gabe positioned where he could watch the elevator and stairwell. He held a black poly pump shotgun and she knew why at once. Shotgun pellets are less likely to penetrate walls and doors in the event of a fight.

She reached back and took Mary's hand. "Where?"

Herman pointed. "Back there's another staircase. It goes down to the kitchen."

"Where are the other deputies?"

"Don't know, and that's why we're gettin' out of here." Herman took her arm, and Kelly allowed him to guide her away from the elevators.

She carried the little .38 with the muzzle pointed toward the floor. Mary followed with her retrieved cell phone. "What about the other people staying here?"

"Nobody's after *them*." Herman released Kelly's arm and cracked a door marked "Employees Only." After making sure the room was empty, he urged them inside and positioned himself half in and out of the utility closet. He rapped the wall, the sound just loud enough to be heard down the hall. "Gabe."

Instead of the answer Kelly expected to hear, Gabe's shotgun hammered the still air with a hard thump followed by the immediately recognizable sound of another round shucking into the chamber. He fired twice more, fast.

Herman backed into the tiny room and shut the door. He pushed past the women and yanked open a skinny door partially hidden by shelves jutting from the wall on their left.

"Come . . ."

A man wielding a large knife lunged from the darkness of the stairwell. Herman instinctively blocked the thrust with his left arm, earning a deep cut above his elbow. He grunted and fell back, yanking the Colt 1911 from the holster on his hip. The big .45 came to life, spitting out three quick rounds that deadened Kelly's hearing in the small room. Their assailant vanished into the darkness, tumbling downward.

Mary screamed. Herman fired twice more and slammed the door. His left sleeve was already turning red. "Cut me with a big ol' knife, dammit! Might've been another'n behind him, but I couldn't tell, it was so dark in there. How the hell'd he find them stairs?"

Directly across from the doorway sat a gray metal utility shelf full of cleaning supplies. Herman yanked it away from the wall and the heavy shelf toppled at a forty-five-degree angle, spilling chemicals and blocking the doorway.

Kelly grabbed a thick hand towel from another set of shelves and pressed it over the wound. "It's bleeding, but not pumping. He didn't hit an artery. We don't have time to do much more." She picked up the shotgun he'd dropped.

His face white as a sheet, Herman holstered the .45 and held the improvised compression bandage against the wound at the same time Gabe rapped the door.

"Hell and damn. It's me. They coming in here, too?"

Kelly opened the door, knowing good and well it was Gabe by his odd cussing. She held Herman's shotgun across her chest. "Yep. Sounds like the same thing happened with you."

"A *cholo* popped out of *el hueco de la escalara* with a machete, I mean the stairwell. He would have taken my head off if I'd been closer. There was another one behind him, but the first one got in his way. How many?"

Herman put himself between Mary and the door, turned so she couldn't see the white hand towel turn red. "One. You?"

"Dos."

"Wonder how many they sent?"

Gabe shrugged. "More than that."

"I'm afraid you're right."

Kelly pulled Gabe's shirtsleeve with two fingers. "Where are we going now?"

"I think back to your room."

"That's my think." Herman licked his lips and shivered, either from pain or the thought of what could have happened if the man with the knife had been successful

Their options were limited. "We hole up there until more help arrives. With all this shootin', it won't be long."

Chapter 70

Soaked by a hard, steady rain, Javier and Pepito arrived at the banks of the Rio Grande that rushed past with a force far beyond what they were expecting. Pepito flicked on a flashlight and skipped it across the roiling surface. A mesquite limb rose and submerged. "We can't cross this."

"You're right, but the rain is on our side. We're not far from the bridge. It's just around the bend. We cross there."

"But you said it was too dangerous."

"It wasn't raining when I said that. The soldiers are going to be inside where it's dry, not watching a closed bridge in a storm." He shrugged. "Once we're over there, we wait inside the Americana Bar de Vista and I will call Chatto. They have a phone there."

"What about the Ranger?"

Javier wiped at the rain in his face. "I don't care anymore. This has been nothing more than death for us. We go home to our mountains and be done with this business as soon as the soldiers leave."

"They will come for us. Chatto will never leave this alone. We failed him."

"They will never find us. The *norteamericanos* couldn't find our ancestors after Geronimo left them. Our country is too rough." He touched the tattoo on his neck, exactly tracing the four wavy lines even though he couldn't see them. "Our people won't let anything happen to us anyway. Chatto knows better than to come into the Sierra Occidental. It is our home."

Chapter 71

Also taking advantage of the heavy rain, Perry Hale and Yolanda knelt behind the thigh-high red-and-white-striped concrete Jersey barriers blocking the unused two-lane bridge. Both wore MOLLE packs they'd checked and rechecked before leaving.

"There's four more of these, like hurdles on a track." Perry Hale kept his voice low. "Then it's a chain-link fence built against a steel wall." He held up a pair of heavy-duty bolt cutters. "We go through with these."

Yolanda peeked over the barrier at the tall security fence high above, using a small flashlight with a red lens. "Tell me that's all."

"Yep. Then we just walk on across."

"Getting back with Sonny might be an issue."

"We'll cross that bridge when we come to it."

"Funny." She sighed. "You're liking this *wayyyy* too much."

"That glint in your eye tells me you're glad to be back in action, too."

"Yep. Let's go get him."

Holding the heavy two-foot bolt cutters in one hand, Perry Hale adjusted the AR battle-slung over his chest. "Yes, ma'am."

Chapter 72

Jerry Hawke and Arturo passed Stillwell's dark general store and kept going, though at a slower pace. The windshield wipers slapped hard and fast. Jerry checked the odometer. "We shut off the lights in fifteen miles."

"Why?"

"Because the river is another five miles past that. I don't want to drive up there with them on. They'll see us."

Arturo frowned at the pitch-black world beyond their dry car. "You won't be able to see. It's too dark."

"We'll drive slow and feel our way with the tires."

"We'll be screwed if we get struck."

"We won't."

"Then what are we gonna do?"

"I haven't figured that out yet. I just want to be there before the Rangers show up. They'll be less likely to make us leave than if we drive up behind them. They'll probably close the road and won't let anybody through."

"You dad's gonna blister our butts."

Jerry checked the odometer again and did the math in his head. "I hope he gets the chance."

Chapter 73

I woke up on the floor, laying with my hands cuffed around a scarred wooden post holding up the Americana Bar de Vista's roof. The good news was that the cuffs were loose on my wrists. The bad news was there were too many people around for me to try and fish out the key I'd put back in my watch pocket.

Rain drummed on the tin roof and I heard water dripping somewhere behind.

There's no telling how long I'd been out. I raised my head and saw men gathered around the tables, talking quietly. There weren't as many as before, and it took a few minutes to realize the guys with the cowboy hats were gone, all except for one in a blue pattern snap-button shirt. I'd have been as afraid of those gangsters as a snake, but he didn't seem to pay them any attention.

Makes sense. They were probably locals who got caught in the bar when Chatto and his gang rolled in. They came for music and beer. Instead, they watched the place fill up with snakes. That guy left must be a tough mother.

Phoebe was nowhere in sight.

Trying to be as inconspicuous as possible, I saw Chatto sitting at his same table in the far corner with three other men. One was the Mexican officer from before. They were playing cards and not paying any attention to me.

My back was to the entrance. I dropped my head for a minute, listening. More rustling came from the bar. Turning with glacial speed, I peeked right to find people scattered around the tables and floor. Some were sleeping, others occupying themselves in some way. One I could see clearly was picking his nose. They were all drinking beer, and I bet they hadn't paid a dime for one single bottle.

Though it was still pretty dim in the corners, my eyes were accustomed to the light. My chest and shoulder were against the support post and with my head hanging low, I saw it was chipped and rotten where they'd nailed it to the floor. I put some pressure against the 4x4 with my shoulder and watched as it gave a lot more than I expected. I stopped and listened.

The soft murmuring and slap of cards continued. Someone behind me pitched an empty bottle on top of a pile with a rattle of breaking glass. The jukebox by the front door was dark, maybe broken, maybe unplugged. Either way I wished they were playing that lousy music of theirs right then, the louder the better.

The nails in the post's base weren't angled in properly and had split the wood. After being kicked by countless boots and shoes for decades, the corners were worn smooth. I leaned again, this time pushing a little harder, and a big chunk of pulpy wood broke loose on my side, revealing a single nail. I knew in an instant that if I shoved hard enough, the missing chunk would provide enough room for me to pull the post away from the floor.

Then I could slip the cuffs' chains free.

Someone pushed back from a table. The sudden loud sound of the legs scraping was abrupt. It was surprising enough for the murmuring to momentarily stop before starting again.

A car door slammed outside.

"El Molinillo." The name was whispered in awe. The speaker's exóópression was a mix of fascination and fear.

My heart fluttered at the last name I wanted to hear right then.

Chapter 74

Wounded by the man with a black shotgun, Tiburón fled down the Posada's stairs and into the empty lobby. The registration desk was unmanned and he rushed down the short hallway toward the front door. A display of colorful western bandanas in the first-floor gift shop caught his attention. He grabbed two blue scarves off a table to stop the bleeding in his chest and arm.

He glanced out the front windows as sirens wailed through the streets of Ballard, Texas. The sheriff's office was only two hundred yards from the Hotel Posada, but the only person there besides the on-call deputy was the young lady in dispatch. For that reason, Tiburón thought he and his men could get in and out before anyone realized they were under assault. His plan went out the window not long after they arrived.

Killing the two guards outside the doors was easy. The deputy sitting in the corner of the patio had been looking at his phone, his night vision destroyed by the bright light in the palm of his hand. Tiburón's number-three *cholo*, Fortunado, simply reached through the ornate iron fence and cut the man's throat.

The other deputy watching the front entrance was more alert, but leaning against the wall inside the alcove was his mistake. The inset blocked his sight line down Broadway toward the Ballard Courthouse. It was easy for one of the gangster's men to move as quiet as a mouse, his sneakers making no noise on the concrete sidewalk.

Tiburón watched from the shadows in the alley across the street as his man Angel simply stopped against the wall and whipped a machete around the inset. The keen blade nearly took the deputy's head off and they were in.

They bypassed the main entrance, rounding the corner, and slipped through the arched patio gates. It was a simple matter to force the doors to the closed hotel bar, and they were inside in seconds. Luis and Fortunado disappeared into the kitchen with instructions to find a way to the second floor where the Hawke women were hiding and come into the hallway to catch the room in a pincer movement.

Tiburón and Angel waited until the desk manager went into the office and crawled past the registration counter. From there it was nothing to take the stairs that bore their weight without a creak. They were surprised to find a Hispanic *jornalero*, farm hand, at the top of the stairs with a shotgun. Angel waved at the same time he charged the man, expecting him to freeze in fear at the sight of his frightening tattoos and bloody machete.

Instead, the farm hand leveled the shotgun as if were part of his body and pulled the trigger. Tiburón ab-

sorbed some of the shot that hit Angel full in the chest
and draped him across the top steps.

Now bleeding in the gift shop, Tiburón saw a shape
limping down the hallway and recognized Luis.
"Amigo," he whispered.

The gangster's face went white and he jumped at the
sound. Recognizing Tiburón, he ducked into the dark
shop. "You are wounded."

"Not bad. Where is Fortunado?"

"He bled out in the kitchen after that old man shot
him three times."

"Which old man?"

"The one that came out to the trailer."

Tiburón wondered how his plan could have failed.
He should already be bragging about how easy it was
to kill the Hawke family and burn down the hotel. Now
those people were still somewhere inside and the
building was undamaged.

Tiburón was in trouble in more ways than one. He
glanced around at the shelves full of souvenirs, candy,
drinks, and T-shirts, as if there was something there
that would help him decide what to do. His T-shirt was
wet with blood that seeped from the holes in his chest.
His breathing was wet and labored. "We need to leave.
Those pellets went deep, and I'm losing a lot of blood.
La policía will be here soon."

Their driver Erasmo waited in the car parked across
the railroad tracks. Tiburón had an idea. He whispered
so low it was barely a breath. "We set fire to the building and get out through the back."

Luis held out a bloody hand "What will you start the
fire with? You have a can of gasoline in your pocket?
I'm shot, too, *cabrón*!"

Tiburón scowled into the darkness at the same time blue lights appeared on the street as a highway patrol car skidded to a stop near the entrance.

"They'll see that dead deputy," Tiburón said. "They won't come inside for a few more minutes."

"Do you hear those other sirens? They're coming from all directions. We need to get out *now*."

"We can't go out the front. How?"

Luis pointed. "Past the counter and through that big room there. The back door opens onto the inside pool. There's another door on the other side and we come out in the alley. From there we run to the next street over and that takes us to the car."

Impressed, Tiburón slapped him on the shoulder. "Lead the way!"

Running in a crouch, they rushed out of the gift shop and turned left, intending to charge through the lobby that had already proven empty. The door to the office behind the counter opened and a man stepped into view. Tiburón shouted to frighten the manager. "Stay back or we will kill you!"

Their charge ended when something that sounded like a cannon exploded in the darkness. Luis went to the floor without uttering a sound at the same time the cannon fired again. This time Tiburón's entire chest and face felt like a swarm of bees had attacked all at once, stinging him everywhere.

They writhed on the floor in pain as a shrill voice filled the air. "Stay down or I'll give you the other loads! Help! They're down, I need help in here!"

A flashlight pierced the darkness and through the increasing fire in his body Tiburón heard a deputy's voice at the entrance. "Andy! Don't shoot again. I see them. You two stay down! Show me your hands! Show me your hands!"

Writhing in pain, Tiburón refused to listen, covering his bloody face with both hands. Luis would never move again.

"Do what he says. The next time I shoot this ol' Judge, you won't get .410 loads. The rest are .45s . . . and ever'thing."

Chapter 75

The eastern sky was gray and the rain had stopped by the time Javier and Pepito arrived at the barricaded bridge. Their trip downriver was uneventful until then. The gangsters were surprised to find a ragged hole cut high in the chain-link fence blocking the La Carmen bridge.

It was barely light enough to see the blocked bridge and high above the surface, a folded-down flap of chain link pushed toward the Mexican side. Pepito pointed. "Someone made a hole for us to cross."

"It wasn't for us, and it goes *into* Mexico. No one crosses in that direction." Javier rubbed his forehead in thought. They were crouched against the concrete barricade. He scanned the low scrub around them, wishing he could see over the bluff and down over the riverbank steep and deep enough to hide a hundred men. The high water gurgled and splashed down below. "We have to go now. It'll be too light in ten minutes."

Desperate to get into their country before the sun rose any farther behind the clouds, he led the way and they scrambled over the barriers and climbed to the fence high above.

Jerry rose upright in the car seat. They were parked in a wide turnout fifty yards from the river. Both windows were open, admitting cool air. "Is that Perry Hale and Yolanda climbing up through the fence?"

Arturo shook his head. "I don't think so. One of them is the right size, but the other one is too big."

Frightened, Jerry thought about flicking on his headlights, but settled back instead. "What do we do now?"

"You keep asking me that."

"Hey, this part was your idea."

The shapes paused at the top, and scampered back down. Arturo was the first to figure it out. "They went through a hole up there. Those are people crossing *into* Mexico."

"Then we can, too."

"Oh hell no. I'm not going over there."

"Look." Jerry pointed at a cinder-block building and two shapes that were barely visible. "That's Perry Hale and Yolanda. I can tell by the way they walk."

"You have to be kidding."

"No, when Dad took us out in the desert to shoot with them, Perry Hale showed me how to move. That's them. I know it. Man. I want to help. Let's figure out what to do on this side."

"And what'll that be?"

"I don't know yet."

Chapter 76

Dark clouds still held the sky despite the rising sun.

On the Mexican side of the bridge, Perry Hale and Yolanda made their slow, quiet way toward four battered Humvees parked bumper to bumper at Paso La Carmen's only three-way intersection. The cluster of abandoned roofless buildings were all that remained of the ghost town. South beyond the vehicles was nothing but desert.

The second dirt road cut to the left, eastward, past the metal building bearing the sign Camiones Cisternas, River Bend Trucking, and followed the serpentine river until it dead-ended at a bar.

Perry Hale tapped Yolanda's shoulder, pointed at his eyes, and then at the trucking building.

Keep an eye on that one.

Their weapons were at high ready and pointed at the silent Humvees full of sleeping soldiers in front of the trucking company building. Though the two veterans practiced working in tandem out in the desert for the past few months since they'd met, Perry felt a difference. Their training came back with surprising ease, and it felt like old times across the water in the Sandbox. He knew she'd make the right moves at the right time and his confidence level rose with every step.

They'd discussed their dangerous new lives as Sonny Hawke's Shadow Response Team. Both had come to grips with the idea they'd be moving along the fringes of right and wrong back in the states. Neither had entertained the idea they'd be on foreign soil, though, armed invaders who could spark an international incident. If they were captured with the weapons, they'd probably never see each other, or their home country, again.

Ten feet separated the couple to present more difficult targets and divide their opponents' fire if they were spotted. They were past the Humvees when Yolanda froze in mid-stride. Perry Hale caught it in his peripheral vision. He stopped, ready. She made eye contact and jerked her head down at the way they'd just come. She pointed at the ground at the tracks they'd left. Two distinct sets of footprints were the only marred places in the otherwise untracked mud.

She twisted her lips into an expression of *yikes, we're in trouble now.*

Perry Hale answered by widening his own eyes, *whadda ya gonna do?*

Simultaneous shrugs put a period on the silent conversation, and they continued on their way. The trucking company was completely buttoned up, the door padlocked. Perry Hale continued past the dark building and covered their advance.

Yolanda made a clicking noise with her tongue and

he stopped, waiting for what might come next. She inclined her head at the same time the sound of an engine approached from the south. Caught in the open, Yolanda pointed at a missing door in the nearest abandoned building to her right. He nodded and ducked across the muddy road. She led the way into a gaping black hole and Perry Hale followed, swinging the muzzle of his rifle one more time to cover the street before backing inside and out of sight.

Her voice came soft and low in the darkness. "Here." She'd ducked around the right side of the door. The enclosure was dark and shadowy but open to the lightening sky. Her boots crunched on gravel and broken glass.

Perry Hale sidestepped so they could cover the road from two different angles. The engine slowed as the driver entered the ghost town. "He's turning this way." He waited, knees flexed and the rifle at his shoulder. His eyes grew accustomed to the dim light coming from above.

A black Suburban turned onto the muddy two-lane track and passed the empty building. They relaxed only for a moment as the car made the slight incline and stopped in front of the American View bar. Doors slammed and distant voices came without definition.

Yolanda whispered. "That's not going to help."

Voices arose from the direction of the Humvees. Someone hawked and spat. Doors slammed. Another voice laughed, and the sounds of men moving told them the soldiers were up.

"New game." Perry Hale chewed his lip. "We stick right here for a minute."

"It's about to get too light to move."

He glanced up at the gray clouds. "Pray for more rain."

Footsteps came their way. She shouldered her rifle. "We're gonna need more than that."

Chapter 77

Raging with fever, I felt like death warmed over on the floor of that nasty bar. Everything hurt, even my eyeballs. The infection was tearing me up, and it was everything I could do to keep it together.

I hadn't realized how hot and thick the bar had become with cigarette smoke, body odor, and musky testosterone. The door pushed open, bringing in dim morning light and fresh, rain-washed air. Gathering what strength I still had, I twisted around to see who was coming inside.

It was a skinny, gray-haired guy in baggy old-man clothes who reminded me of someone's grandfather. Several people spoke his name again, El Molinillo, in hushed tones, as if a priest or famous athlete had arrived. Most of them stood, whether in respect or fear I couldn't tell. Chairs scraped and one fell over, its clatter loud in the silence.

The little guy didn't react to anyone standing straight and quiet, as if presenting themselves for inspection, or to show they weren't holding weapons. Instead, his eyes locked on me and he walked inside like he'd just gotten home. Ten paces later, he slipped both hands in his baggy gray pants and tilted his head, like a scientist observing a rare specimen.

"Este guardabosque nunca ha visto a un demonio como yo."

If he thought I was going to be afraid and quiet, he had another think coming. I was too tired and sick to care what happened next. As usual, I still couldn't understand everything he said, but I picked out one important word, *demonio*. "You'll *see* the demon if I can get my hands free."

His face split into a wide grin revealing yellow and rotting teeth that hadn't seen a toothbrush since his first baby tooth came in. He spoke in English. "This one is going to be a pleasure."

"It'll be a pleasure to kill *you*."

Audible gasps behind me said I'd probably gone too far. The truth is, he could have shot me in the head right then the way I felt and it would have been a relief.

Chatto's voice came over my shoulder, almost filled with pride. "I told you this one was different."

"No." El Molinillo's voice suddenly took on a different tone and his face fell, as if overwhelmed by a flood of sad memories. "They are all the same when they feel the blade. He will cry at first, then scream himself silent." He brightened. "It is a pleasure by then, because their cries hurt my ears."

Chapter 78

Javier was the first to see the boot prints in the mud, leading from the bridge, around the Humvees, and toward the bar. Snores coming from the transport vehicles sent them in another direction to find a way around. Neither wanted any type of interaction with the Mexican soldiers.

Javier whispered and pointed. "Who do you think this is?"

The little gangster shrugged. *"No lo sé."*

Javier nodded. "Possibly a *fuerzas especiales* team. But there are only two sets of tracks, and look how small those are compared to the others. Do you think it was them who made the hole?"

Pepito started. Both men were afraid of American Special Forces and hoped they'd never have to face them. "They lead down this road."

"It's quiet." Javier raised his face, almost sniffing the air for trouble the same way his ancestors did generations earlier.

Pepito's eyes were full of fear.

The gangsters swiveled in place, scanning the empty buildings. The faint sound of a car engine came to Pepito. He cupped one ear and faced the southbound road.

"Someone's coming."

Javier pointed at the doorless, roofless ruin of a building. "There."

"No. I don't want to get trapped inside with no way to shoot our way out. Behind the *compania de camiones*." They trotted around the side of the metal River Bend Trucking building, rounding the corner and out of sight from the road.

A black Suburban passed and drove along the riverbank to the bar. Seconds later, one of the lead Humvee's doors popped open and someone coughed.

Chapter 79

Things in the bar went downhill fast when the Mexican officer spoke. "We have been waiting for you. I thought you were nothing more than a legend that parents used to frighten children."

El Molinillo's eyes hardened. "You have found me." His hands went back into his pockets as if he were shiftless, or lazy. "Or I have found *you*."

Chatto shifted his position, clearly uneasy. The gangsters sensed his mood, setting their feet.

The officer ran fingers through his greasy hair. He scanned the room and shrugged. "I did not say I was looking that hard, were we, Lieutenant?"

"No, Captain Perez."

The tension eased and El Molinillo removed his hands. I wondered exactly what was in his pocket. Whatever it was, it worried the hell out of everyone in the room.

No one but me saw Captain Perez and his lieutenant exchange looks. The captain's head gave an almost imperceptible move before returning to Chatto. "We will withdraw outside of town until you are finished."

The gangster's leader didn't respond. Instead, he left the table and stopped beside the Grinder. "Where?"

El Molinillo shrugged. "I don't know this area."

Chatto flicked a hand at the cowboy with a taco hat and patterned blue shirt. His face didn't have the same look of malice as the others, and I figured he was still in the wrong place at the wrong time. Probably had outstayed his welcome. "Yes."

"You know this area. Where can we do this work?"

"Work?"

"Where El Molinillo can work without being seen . . . or heard."

"There's a thick tangle of arroyos back there that widens into nothing." He waved toward the back of the bar. "No one will find you."

"Bien." Chatto dismissed the man. "Is that satisfactory?"

"Yes." The Grinder nodded. "But first, he had something I've heard about. I want the pistol with the *apreton de novia*."

Chatto kinda deflated and reached behind his back. He came out with my granddaddy's .45. He handed it over, but it looked like it hurt his heart to give up the Sweetheart Grips. The Grinder brightened and he took the pistol, turning it this way and that to admire the photo of my young grandmother and toddler dad under the Lucite grips.

"I have always wanted one of these. And it belongs to this *guardabosque*?"

Chatto nodded and frowned at the captain, who scowled at him. It was apparent he wanted the pistol, but wouldn't stand his ground. The Grinder must have been their boogeyman in the flesh.

The Grinder slid it down into the waistband at the small of his back. "More?" He held out his hand and Chatto produced a spare magazine. The Grinder hefted it, then dropped it into the left-hand pocket of his pants. He turned to the man who knew the area. "You. Go to get my leather apron from the back of the car. I have one more thing to do before we get started. The *guardabosque* must be anchored."

"He is handcuffed, and to that post." Chatto came forward and nudged my leg with his toe.

I sure didn't like the direction their conversation was taking. They were standing directly over me and discussing what was about to happen with the same sense of boredom businessmen have when trying to decide where to eat lunch.

From my position on the floor, a brief burst of soft light lit the Grinder's worn shoes as the lieutenant slipped out the door along with the local. There were dark stains on them shoes and I instantly knew it was blood. He needed an apron to keep the blood off his clothes.

"That is not what I mean." The Grinder pointed at my boots. "You will have to uncuff him. I do not want to take any chances here or out there. *Manea lo*."

Their entire discussion had been in Spanish, but I picked out enough to know what they were talking about, but that last short sentence stumped me. It was slightly familiar, but I couldn't put my hand on it. Something Gabe had once said.

Chatto grinned.

The Grinder wants my boots?

"Take them off." He pointed to a table of men who

hurried over. Something wasn't right. You don't steal a man's boots when he's alive and kicking.

Cuffed and on the ground, fighting back was hard when they dropped on me like vultures. One of them sat on my legs and they yanked my boots off seconds later. They were grunting and breathing hard, like men at work.

As they yanked at my boots, I remembered exactly what Gabe had said a year earlier when he told me he had to hobble Dad's horse one night when the corral gate was broken.

Manea lo was hobble.

My boots were gone, but those guys stayed on me. The looks on those sonsabitches' faces told me I wasn't going to like what happened next very much. I knew exactly what it was when the old man pulled out a wicked-looking knife.

He was going to cut the tendons on the back of my ankles.

Chapter 80

Hiding behind the metal building, Javier saw a soldier stroll down the muddy road and meet with his comrades loafing in the street. Smoking and at ease, they stared across the river at the old Bronco parked in a turnaround fifty yards from the bridge.

A man with a lieutenant patch on the sleeve of his fatigues joined them and spat into a mud puddle. "The captain will be out here in a moment. We will stop south of town and hold the road until those men in there finish their work." He jolted his men into action. "Load up. He does not want to wait when he gets here."

One private hesitated. "I need to pee."

"Go ahead."

"You know I can't with everyone watching me."

"Go around there, then."

Javier wished he could see the men. He started when an armed soldier with barely a wrinkle on his forehead appeared around the corner. All three froze for a second before the startled soldier in his twenties fumbled with the Heckler & Koch assault rifle slung over his shoulder.

"Hold it!" Pepito held out both hands to show he was unarmed. "We mean no harm."

"Halt!" The smooth-faced private finally pulled the strap off his shoulder and held the H&K aimed at the two gangsters. "Put up your hands!"

"They're already up, brother." Javier's breath caught when the frightened man's hands trembled. "Easy. We're with Chatto." The sounds of running feet made him swallow.

"Then why are you out here? Why aren't you in there with him?"

Javier felt the blood drain from his face. "Chatto, here?"

"Yes."

Others rounded the corner, drawn by the loud voices. Javier and Pepito suddenly found themselves staring down the barrels of even more automatic weapons.

The lieutenant arrived and waved for his men to lower their weapons. "Don't shoot. Look at their ink. These men are Coyotes Rabiosos."

The experienced soldiers were stunned to face living legends and lowered their weapons before the two gangsters killed them all with their bare hands. Two crossed themselves. The lieutenant surveyed his frightened men and sighed. "Take them to Chatto, and tell Captain Perez we are ready when he is."

"Sheeeit." Perry Hale whispered. The commotion between the gangsters and soldiers was mere feet away, just on the other side of a cracked cinder-block wall.

"See anything?" Yolanda's view was to the east, away from the metal building.

"No. But they're all out there."

"This is about to go bad."

"Not about to." Perry Hale stepped back when he saw the lieutenant point at the hole they cut in the fence. "It already has."

Javier and Pepito led the way toward the bar with three soldiers trailing behind. The last thing they wanted to see was Chatto, and Javier was trying to think of something to say that would keep them from going inside.

His opportunity came when he saw that same two sets of tracks leading across the road. The Suburban's tires cut them off in the muddy road, but the footprints continued up a slight incline and into a deteriorating building on their right.

"We saw those earlier. Do they belong to your men?"

The officer shrugged. "How would I know?"

"They came from across the river, like us."

The soldiers stopped, uncertain what to do. The lieutenant slipped a hand into the pocket of his fatigues as if looking for the answer there. Bareheaded, he scratched at his hair. He glanced over his shoulder at the barricaded bridge and his eyes widened when he saw the gaping hole high in the chain link. "Someone cut through."

His men tightened their grips on the H&Ks. The fresh-faced private stepped back, surveying the criss-crossed footprints in the mud. The lieutenant watched the man work out the tracks in his head.

The private stiffened and swept his arm from the

bridge, up the road, and into the nearby collapsed building. "Sir, I think maybe they're in there."

The officer drew his sidearm, a Sig Sauer semi-automatic. "Check it out."

Across the river, the boys in the Bronco watched the soldiers milling in front of the cinder-block structure to the left of the metal building. Despite the drizzle, Arturo saw one of the soldiers point at the empty doorway.

"They're going inside."

The only thing Jerry could do was lean on the horn and hope Perry Hale knew what to do.

When he saw a young private point toward their position, Perry Hale sighed. "Here we go." He had no intention of fighting a defensive action inside the building. The rising sun had revealed the interior tangled with splintered beams and boards from the collapsed roof. Though there was a warped wooden door still standing at the back, he had no idea what lay on the other side.

A car horn on the Texas side surprised the soldiers. To a man they turned toward the source, giving Perry Hale a half-second lead on the men standing in the road. Thanking whoever had honked the horn, he took advantage of their inattention and stepped outside, rifle at his shoulder, and aimed at the officer in charge. "Hands up, now!"

They'd been speaking Spanish, but he had no intention of trying to communicate in a relatively unfamiliar language.

Yolanda followed, covering the startled soldier and gangsters. She spoke fluent Spanish. *"Manos arriba!"*

Heads snapped back around at the two people in camouflage who suddenly appeared, aiming automatic weapons at them.

Perry Hale swept the group with the muzzle, giving them a good look down the black tube. "Good, now boys, y'all put those guns on the ground."

Yolanda repeated the order in Spanish and shouted at those sitting in the Humvees. "You in there. Come out without weapons or we shoot your officer and these men!"

Those under the muzzle of the AR-15s disarmed themselves, gently laying their rifles on the ground. Perry Hale turned his attention to the lieutenant. "Y'all do what she says, then back away." He stepped forward and pushed the rifle a couple of inches to urge them to move. They backed up a step, then another with a second jab.

The problem was the men in the line of parked Humvees. Several had been loafing in the road. They froze in their tracks, shocked into immobility. One stepped back behind the huge vehicle and out of sight.

"Perry, we have a problem."

It came when still *another* man rolled out of the second Humvee and snapped a shot at Yolanda at the same time the guy hiding behind the first vehicle popped up like a jack-in-the-box and fired.

The standoff went to hell.

Chapter 81

Gunfire from outside started the ball rolling in the bar. The bad guys forgot about me and rushed toward the door like water pouring down the drain. I waited until the Grinder followed them through the door and gave that post I was chained to a hard yank.

Another gun fired out there, and it seemed like a dozen weapons went off at the same time, all on full automatic. The support post came loose just like I expected and I slid the cuffs free at the same time the ceiling groaned and something cracked way overhead. I crab-crawled to the door and stood to the side.

Quick as a wink, I dug the key from my watch pocket and had the cuffs off. Another groan and snap in the rotten roof overhead told me bad things were fixin' to happen. The next thing I knew, the Grinder popped back inside like his ass was on fire.

I hit that mean little bastard in the jaw as hard as I could. He seized up, already unconscious on his feet. I grabbed his arm and snatched my .45 from his pants. Two gangsters pushed through behind him, trying to get away from the firefight, and must have thought the

Grinder'd tripped or something, because they did their best to climb over him.

The big .45 roared as soon as I shoved it against one guy's side. He gasped and fell sideways and I shot the other, then put one square in the chest of a third man following them inside. With gunfire coming from both inside and out, the gangsters were confused and terrified. Shouts and screams came through the door at the same time bullets cracked past and buried themselves in the walls behind me.

Crouched on the floor, I dug my spare magazine out of the Grinder's pocket. With three bodies blocking the door, I couldn't close it and I sure couldn't get out that way. Another crack came from above when a corner of the ceiling sagged dangerously low.

A closed door at the back right-hand corner of the bar was my only option. I shot the Grinder in the side of the head to save someone else's life down the road, and took off across the bar in a sprint. A small war was going on outside by the time I turned the knob.

It led outside, and I popped through as the ceiling completely collapsed with a splintering of wood. I glanced over my shoulder to see it take down half of the building's front wall and then there was nothing but a gray cloud of dust.

Chapter 82

Bullets snapped between Perry Hale and Yolanda. They instinctively ducked as the soldiers behind the Humvees laid down covering fire for the men who whirled and raced for their lives toward the Humvees, leaving their rifles in the mud.

Perry Hale threw a triple-tap at the soldier behind the big vehicle who started shooting first. He swung toward the retreating men, but held his fire. He'd always considered himself a lot of things, but being a murderer wasn't one of them. Some of those men might be crooked, but they were brothers in arms and had not, to that point, threatened him with harm.

Shouts from behind gave the Americans just enough warning to know they were under attack from the rear. The gangsters pouring outside began firing as soon as they saw the Americans. Some carried automatic weapons and they chattered to life, mixing with those of the military.

He and Yolanda fell back, squeezing off three-round bursts, and ducked around the abandoned building, putting it between them and gunfire coming from two different directions. She kept her rifle pointed at the corner. "Whadda ya think?"

"The bar. That's where Sonny is."

A gangster rolled around the corner of the bar, spraying the world on full auto. Yolanda dropped him with a double-tap. She glanced back and forth between the Humvees and the bar to their right. "That's right into the teeth of the lion."

"That's where he is."

"Then let's go get him." She shouldered the AR and led, looking down the sights with both eyes wide open. "I have the point."

Perry Hale mirrored her posture and covered their rear. They were still protected by the decaying building. The soldiers were unloading with everything they had at absolutely nothing. Bullets pulverized the corner of the empty cinder-block building. Ricochets whined off and Perry Hale wondered if the soldiers' tactic was to throw enough lead to keep them from firing back. It didn't matter, because they suddenly found themselves facing even heavier gunfire from the Suburban parked in front of the bar.

To their left was the empty dirt track bordered by knee-high scrub brush. To their right an open area with the same scattered brush and small cedars. Bullets cracked past, and they separated to present a wider target area.

"Too hot!" Perry Hale shouted and returned fire. "Around back!"

Maneuvering from the line of fire, they rushed to put the American Vista Bar between themselves and the heavily armed gangsters. Caught between two groups, they could no longer try to reach Sonny, if he was still there.

A small wooden shed sat off the back corner of the bar. "Around there!" Perry Hale dodged a clump of prickly pear.

Rounds cracked past again and Yolanda ducked. "Soldiers!"

He dropped to one knee and put two shots into a uniformed private who tempted fate by stepping into the open and spraying on full auto. Yolanda twisted at the waist and squeezed off a short burst in response at the same time Perry Hale double-tapped the man. The firing stopped and they rounded the shed. "Reloading!" She dropped the empty magazine and slapped in a fresh one.

"Hey, you guys speak English!"

The voice came from inside the warped shed. Perry Hale sighted on the leaning structure. "Who's there!"

"Phoebe. Can you get me out of here?"

"Shit." He pivoted back to the bar and caught a glimpse of an arm and pistol pointed at them from around the corner of a building. He fired. The arm bloomed red and the pistol fell. "Get away from the door. Yolanda! Reloading. Cover fire!"

A chain threaded through holes in the sun-bleached planks held the door closed. Yolanda knelt and squeezed off controlled bursts, keeping the Mexican army at bay on the left, and the gangsters on the right.

He kicked at the door and one of the boards cracked. He kicked again, trusting Yolanda to keep him covered, then again. The dry, brittle board shattered and he yanked the door open to find a young, dark-haired woman with two black eyes staring out at him, her hands duct taped behind her back.

"Jesus! Come on."

"That's not my name. It's Phoebe." She turned. "Cut this!"

Responding to her curt order, Perry Hale snatched the razor-sharp MK-3 Navy knife from the sheath strapped onto his pack and sliced her bonds like butter. She was out in a flash, ducking between Perry Hale and Yolanda and heading for the open ground to the south at a dead run. The distinctive crack of breaking wood caught his attention and the entire roof of the bar collapsed from front to back, disappearing behind the cinder-block walls. Stunned, he missed Phoebe's escape.

"Hey!" Yolanda shouted. "Where you going?"

Phoebe threw the answer over her shoulder, black hair flying. "Away from here!"

Another flash of movement from the back of the bar caught Perry Hale's attention. A wooden door slammed open a moment before the last of the roof disappeared, and a man popped outside with a pistol in his hand. Perry Hale almost shot him, but having both eyes open saved Sonny Hawke's life.

Despite the situation, Perry Hale laughed. "Sonny!"

Yolanda's voice was full of wonder. "No way."

Chapter 83

The last thing I expected to hear when I got outside was Perry Hale's voice. He was beside a poor excuse for a sun-bleached shed twenty yards away. I caught a glimpse of Phoebe hauling ass toward the wide-open country behind it, and Yolanda on one knee, firing one short burst after the other at what looked like half the Mexican army maneuvering along the shallow drop-off beside the dirt road. Beyond that was the Rio Grande sixty yards north of a cluster of dying buildings and the La Carmen Bridge.

Socks aren't made for running across the desert, but the wet ground felt good under my feet as I sprinted toward my friends. Okay, the way I felt and the shape I was in didn't lend itself to a real sprint, more a walking-dead-zombie stagger/shuffle, but I had bullets nipping at my heels, and that overcame everything for the moment.

Perry Hale squeezed off three shots that cracked past going the other direction, only feet away. The muzzle blast was a physical presence, but I didn't care. His return fire slowed them down some and probably made more than a few guys dodge back out of the way.

He shook his head in disgust. "If you'd listened to me at the house on the other side of the river we wouldn't be in this mess now!"

"That was *you*?"

"Yeah, and you almost shot me." The shooting fell off as the three of us ducked around behind the scant protection of the shed.

I leaned back against the wall to blow for a minute and realized it was Perry Hale with the rifle, shooting the bad guys off me in the house. "Y'all are a sight for sore eyes. What took you so long?"

"Like I told you, I've already tried once to get you out of this." Perry Hale gave me a squint. "By the way, you look like hell." I got that head-to-toe look, and figured all the mud, blood, swelling, and grime really *was* a sight. "You gonna live long enough to get across the river?"

"Screw you. I've been under a lot of pressure."

We were in a lull, and they chuckled. Yolanda reached out a hand and barely touched my shoulder with manicured fingernails. I looked down at the red polish and choked down a sob that rose quick as a geyser. I had to blink my eyes clear. "What's the plan?"

Yolanda turned her back to me and scanned the scrub-covered landscape. "There isn't one."

"Y'all had to have something in mind."

"To get the hell out of here is the first thing I can think of. Reloading." Perry Hale slapped in a fresh magazine.

A female voice floated from where Phoebe'd disappeared. We couldn't find her at first, but then I saw only her head and waving arm. "Is she standing in a hole?"

"Arroyo, I'll bet." Perry Hale grinned. "That's a better idea than I had."

No one was shooting at us when we pushed away from the shed. Perry Hale grabbed my good right arm to give me something to lean on and we lurched toward Phoebe's hidey-hole.

Chapter 84

Kelly Hawke sat on the bed with Mary in their Hotel Posada room, listening to sirens converge on the area. Herman was in the room's only chair watching the door. The pump 870 shotgun rested across his knees. Gabe stood against the wall, peeking down at the patio through curtains barely cracked enough to let in the dim light of a cloudy sunrise.

There had been gunfire downstairs, but now everything was quiet. So quiet they could hear phones and soft voices through the walls as the hotel's terrified guests spoke to the outside world.

A soft knock at the door was an electric jolt to the Hawkes. Gabe barely moved.

Kelly gasped and was angry at herself for such a reaction. She picked up the little .38 from the bed beside her leg and waited.

Herman leveled the shotgun with his good arm. "Who is it?"

"Deputy Frank Malone, Herman."

"All right. Frank, you stay out there. You alone?"

"Sure am. Y'all all right?"

"We're good."

"Nobody hurt? I hear there was a lot of shooting up here, and if I'm right, it was y'all who left a few of these bodies out here. It's over now."

"Fine."

There was a pause. Kelly raised an eyebrow in question. Herman shook his head and mouthed "Wait."

Malone tapped the door again. "Y'all can come out now. There's deputies downstairs."

"Frank, I know you and you know me. We're gonna stay right here until I see more badges down there in the patio."

"Herman, how do I know y'all ain't in there at gunpoint? Let me in to check on you, and then I'll leave and you can stay right there until we get things tidied up out here."

"How do I know the same ain't going on out there and somebody's got a gun on *you*? Me and Gabe are going to stay right here for a little bit longer."

"Are Kelly and Mary all right?"

Kelly licked her wet lips. "We're fine, Frank. We tried to come out a little while ago and ran into those guys."

"I can see that." The floor creaked as the deputy shifted his weight. Another siren approached. "I'll get some men down in the patio for you."

Herman nodded, as if Deputy Malone could see him. "A'ite. But wait until it's full light."

"That's overkill, ain't it?"

"Damned sure is."

"Fine then. I'm gonna post some men at either end

of this hall, and Herman, there are people in these other rooms. We're gonna get them out of here, so y'all'll be the only ones on this floor."

"Good. We'll come out at full light."

"Mary, I need to hear both you and Gabe right fast here."

"We're fine." Mary spoke first.

"Me, too." Gabe's voice was steady. "We shot the damn hell out of those guys."

Kelly saw the crow's-feet appear in the corner of Herman's eyes. "Shot the hell out of them, Gabe."

Malone chuckled outside the door. "Now I *know* y'all are all right. Holler when you're ready."

Footsteps walked away and Kelly listened to make sure it was only one person. "Herman, let's leave when they get the other guests."

"Nope. I have complete control in here. I want an army of men in this hotel before I even *think* of taking y'all somewheres else. Gabe, what do you see down there?"

He parted the material with one finger and peered past the narrow balcony and into the patio below. "Not much yet. The body is still on the chair in the corner. Lots of blue lights flashing. A highway patrol car down on the street and fire truck farther down."

"See much of the patio?"

"Some." Gabe pulled the curtain back even farther and adjusted his position to look past the balcony rail just outside the French doors.

Mary'd had enough. She pushed herself off the bed. "Guys, this is too much. Mister Frank's outside. It's over. I'll show you." She stalked across the room and yanked one side of the curtains open. The sheer behind it fluttered and she snapped the thumb lock open on the wooden doors to prove all was well.

The glass doors exploded inward as two men with gleaming blades charged inside.

Chapter 85

Javier and Pepito found themselves all alone behind a Humvee as the soldiers pressed forward toward the two armed Americans. All four doors were open, and the interior was a gangster's dream of firearms and explosives.

Javier crawled half-inside and emerged with a pair of H&K rifles. He handed one to Pepito, then collected a handful of loaded magazines for each of them. Pepito grinned. "I feel better now."

"Me, too. Let's go."

"Where?"

"Home." Javier waved to the southwest. "We're going home."

The gunfire ended for the moment and Chatto rose from behind the Grinder's shot-up Suburban. "Are they dead, Captain?"

Shaken, Captain Perez surveyed the bodies lying in front of the American Vista Bar and several others in the street. He snorted. "My men, your men, or those *norteamericanos*?"

Chatto's face reddened and it made him furious to feel that way in front of an inferior. "The Americans."

Perez shouted the question and his second in command, Lieutenant Oscar Hernandez joined them. "They disappeared into that arroyo. I have men following."

"Call them back."

"Sir?"

"They're coming around. They can't afford to stay on this side of the river and the water is so high they will need the bridge to cross."

Hernandez relayed his orders as Captain Perez turned to Chatto. "Most of these bodies are *your* men."

Chatto shrugged at the carnage. Only a handful of his men had survived. "They know what can happen. Alvar, where is El Molinillo?"

The dazed gangster who had miraculously gotten by unscathed gestured toward the building and for the first time Chatto realized what had happened to the bar. "He's in there, dead." Alvar pointed at the collapsed building.

The gang leader's face reddened. "*Americanos*. I'm going to hang their bodies from that bridge."

Jerry and Arturo watched Perry Hale and Yolanda emerge from the empty building and force some of the soldiers to drop their weapons.

Arturo relaxed. "I think we're good."

The boys jolted when gunfire erupted across the river. More weapons joined in, and the volume swelled.

"Dayum!" Jerry breathed.

Less than two hundred yards separated the boys' car across the river from the abandoned buildings. Their young eyes made out their friends in the gray light of dawn.

"Vato, do you think we should back up?"

Jerry glanced down at the steering wheel, as if debating whether or not to put the Bronco into reverse. "They won't shoot at us across the river. That's illegal."

Arturo snorted. "That won't stop them." He paused when a man in a blue shirt popped up behind the Suburban and sprinted toward the river. There was only one person who ran like that, with his head ducked impossibly low and his forearms tight against the side of his chest. It was his step-dad, Santiago Estrada. "That *pendejo!*"

"What? Who?"

"That guy over there in the blue shirt, who's running like a rabbit. That's my step-dad."

"What's he doing with those guys?"

"How should *I* know. He was deported a few months ago."

"Where's he going?"

Arturo flashed Jerry a disgusted look. "Dude, I don't have any idea."

Estrada reached the raging Rio Grande and leaped over the edge onto a thin strip of muddy riverbed. Losing his balance, he windmilled his arms for a moment before regaining his feet.

He ducked below the bank and made his treacherous way upriver.

Chapter 86

Phoebe's arroyo was wide and chest deep on the 5'2" girl. A stream of water cut through the middle, but there was enough space on either side for us to run in a crouch.

That's what we did.

Yolanda led the way and set a hard pace that I could barely manage. I was sucking air and wanted to tell her to slow down, but we needed to make hay while we could. Phoebe was hot on her heels. Perry Hale was last, twisting this way and that to make sure nobody popped up behind us.

My socks were soaked, and I came down on something that cut my foot. I hissed, wanting to sit down and cry like a baby, but there was no way I'd do that in front of those three.

Yolanda stopped. "There's a low-water crossing here. Perry, this must be the road going south."

He moved up past me, then turned to face back where we came. "We've come around behind them." He pointed to the right. "The bridge is that way. Let's get over there before they realize what happened."

I'd seen that bridge before and there was more wire on that thing than the impound lot. "How are we going to get over?"

"We've cut a hole in the wire."

"The wire *above* the steel panel and bars? That's twenty feet in the air."

"More like twenty-five."

I looked down at my bloody socks. My blisters woke up when I started thinking about them. "I don't think I can climb a chain-link fence in these."

Perry saw my feet for the first time. Half a beat later, he knelt and unlaced his boots. "Wear these."

"I can't . . ."

"You can. I'm fresh. Besides, by the time it's my turn to go through the wire there'll be so much adrenaline pumping I'll probably fly over the top." He dug in his pack and pulled out a second set of thick socks that he pulled on over those he already wore.

The combat boots were a size too large, but I didn't argue. They felt like a feather bed on my feet and I rallied. "Phoebe, hope you're good at climbing."

A tiny smile was her only response.

"We gotta go." Yolanda started forward. "I don't hear a thing, and that worries me."

Perry Hale pushed past her. "I lead this time. Sonny, you and Phoebe listen to us and do exactly what we say."

"Got it." I was in way over my head. "Let's go."

We'd been crouched in an area protected from the ghost town by the head-high bank of the arroyo. The road crossed on a plank bridge fifty yards ahead and continued north to the river. The recent floods had cut a deeper channel in the middle of our arroyo, and the water gurgled, splashing around a small dam of debris.

Perry Hale led us to the steep cut in the wet, muddy bank at the same time two armed men suddenly slid to the bottom, heading west and away from us. We would have let them go, but one checked over his shoulder and saw us. He whirled.

Perry Hale barked a soft order. "Drop them!"

I stopped in shock when I saw it was Javier and Pepito standing there in the open, bigger'n Dallas. They registered Perry Hale and Yolanda in their tactical gear first, then Phoebe. I stepped out from behind Perry Hale and Pepito noticed me.

Javier was a beat behind. Their mouths popped open in recognition and their weapons came up at the same time I raised the big Colt and shot Javier in the chest. The bullet snapped past Perry Hale and he flinched, then pulled the trigger on his shouldered rifle. Pepito soaked up half a dozen rounds before he dropped beside Javier's body.

Though I had enough gun in my hand, I anchored Javier with a second shot. Yolanda raised an eyebrow, then checked behind us. Those shots had obviously been heard by the others and they'd be coming along pretty soon.

Perry Hale raised his cheek from the rifle's stock just long enough to comment. "Did you owe them money?"

"Those are the two that started all this."

"Good deal."

"Hang on." I limped over to the bodies, confident the others would keep an eye out.

Yolanda's voice rose and the fear and frustration she carried came out clear as a bell. "Sonny, we need to move."

"I know it. But this guy has something of mine." I knelt beside Javier's cooling body. I slapped his right pants pocket and pulled out two full magazines for the machine gun lying beside his hand. I tucked them into my back pockets. It was his shirt I was most interested in. My badge wasn't there, but a slight bulge in the snap pocket showed me what I was looking for. I unsnapped the flap and fished out my Ranger badge.

I held it up for them to see. "I told this sonofabitch I was gonna get this back." I pinned it to my shirt and the familiar weight made me feel a little taller.

"You've never said nothin' you didn't follow up on. Let's go." Perry Hale led us up the road at a run. I picked up one of the gangster's weapons and followed as best I could.

Chapter 87

A line of official vehicles rolled down FM 2627, the two-lane farm road running from the bridge to civilization. Jerry saw them in his rearview mirror.

"Uh oh. Cavalry's here."

Arturo looked over his shoulder through the Bronco's back glass. "They're gonna be mad."

"I don't care. This is a free country. We can go anywhere we want and don't have to ask. Besides, my dad's supposed to be over there."

Had the ground been dry, the air would have been full of dust when the tires squalled off the pavement and slid to a stop on all sides of the kids' car. The sound of gunfire from across the river met Sheriff Ethan Armstrong when he popped out from behind the wheel of his Dodge Durango and dropped down behind the open door.

"You boys get out of there. Get behind the car and under cover!"

It hadn't occurred to Jerry that they were in danger either from stray or aimed bullets. He and Arturo shared frightened looks, then bailed out to join the grown-ups behind the cars. More vehicles arrived, disgorging armed law-enforcement officers ranging from local deputies, park police, highway patrol, the lone FBI agent, and a Suburban full of Texas Rangers in combat gear.

Jerry recognized his dad's boss, Major Parker, when he stepped out as if he'd pulled up in the parking lot of the grocery store. He stood behind his open door, one foot still inside the Expedition. "Nick."

The Ranger on the other side was just as unconcerned. "Yessir."

"Get that long lens out of the back there and put it on your camera. I want video of what's going on over there."

The tailgate popped open on the Expedition when Major Parker pressed the key fob. Ranger Nick Delgado trotted around back as gunfire continued across the river. He quickly locked a 600mm telephoto lens onto a digital 35mm Canon camera body. He added a tripod to the bottom of the camera that could shoot both still and video. Such a long lens demanded a firm foundation despite its automatic stabilization feature.

Major Parker pointed. "Video that. Bad guys only. Zoom in and get as many faces as you can. You see what I see?"

"Yessir."

"Get it."

Jerry rose from cover and watched the action across the river.

Chapter 88

"Not gonna work." Perry Hale dropped to one knee. I looked past him and saw the Mexican soldiers scattering out on both sides of the street. "They're moving up to the right."

Three collapsed buildings that we could see were once downtown Paso La Carmen. Now they were home to rodents and snakes. The opposite side was fringed with tall cedars, abandoned and rusting cars, mounds of dumped rock, and thick stands of prickly pear. A mix of gangsters and soldiers took cover wherever they could find it.

"Scatter." Perry Hale flicked a finger toward both sides of the muddy road. He and I went left. Yolanda and Phoebe split right. Phoebe moved up close behind Yolanda.

"Leapfrog?" Yolanda called across the dirt road. She wasn't indecisive or scared. She simply deferred to Perry Hale because he had more experience under fire.

"Yep. I want one of those Humvees. Sonny, you

stick close behind me. Don't go western on me here. We have a plan."

"Any plan is better than what I can think of right now."

Perry Hale rose. "Moving!" Weapon shouldered, he sighted down the rifle. I stepped slightly to the side so I could shoot around him and we started forward at a crouch. We stopped fifteen yards later behind a rusted-out Dodge pickup. Perry Hale took a knee. "Move!"

"Moving!" Yolanda matched his style and pace, creeping past us and ducking behind a hummock of land screened by scrub. She kept her rifle aimed. No one had yet fired a shot. She and Phoebe stopped beside a crumbling adobe wall. "Move!"

It was our turn again and that's when someone poked a rifle around the corner of the River Bend transport building at the far end of the street and opened up on full auto. Even though we'd already been shot at, it shocked the hell out of me, and I jumped twice. The second time was when Yolanda hosed that corner of the building before sweeping her rifle across the narrow dirt road to force the others down.

Perry Hale dropped behind a thigh-high cut of dirt and opened up. "Move!"

"Moving!" Yolanda rose and I joined in with the unfamiliar H&K. It woke up with a sewing-machine chatter and we threw enough lead to push the soldiers down. Yolanda rushed forward to the next available piece of cover. Phoebe had one hand on her pack and followed as tight as a tick.

Chapter 89

A bullet cracked overhead, fired from across the river, causing everyone on the Texas side to duck again. Ranger Nick Delgado swung the long lens. "That came from our people. They're shooting this way."

"That's because they're headed home." Major Parker waved at one of the Rangers who'd been in the command center with him. Ranger Gasch had changed into SWAT gear. "Bill, they're going to be coming across somewhere. Y'all check that house over there and that other one up top of the ridge. Get the folks out if they're home. I don't want civilians to get hurt by stray bullets. Send 'em on back to the store till it's clear here. Once they're gone, get ready to move."

Ranger Gasch glanced across the river. "You're not telling us to shoot into Mexico. That'll be an act of war."

"Just get ready."

"Yessir."

Chapter 90

We were doing more shooting than the bad guys, but that's what Perry Hale's maneuver was all about. The only way to advance against overwhelming odds was to force their heads down. We moved forward in increments. The only problem, we were getting damned close to the muzzles of their guns.

"Sonny, burn 'em down on this side of the Humvee. Moving!"

We covered Yolanda with a barrage from behind a collapsed adobe shack. Perry Hale found a target and fired. "Move!

"Moving!" Yolanda broke cover and advanced, walking her way north, toward the river.

She stopped. It was our turn to leapfrog again. Perry Hale shouted. "Moving!"

"No, stay!" Yolanda's command was flat. "Reloading!"

We dropped back down. The slap of metal. Another clap. "Loaded. Move!" She opened up.

We stopped again behind another half-melted adobe

fence. "Yolanda, cross behind us when we get set. Sonny, pour it on 'em! Move!"

"Moving!"

We filled the air with lead. This time Yolanda cut across the road behind us and kept going, angling farther to our left, keeping enough distance between our two teams so the bad guys didn't have a concentrated target. We swept our fire to the left also. Perry Hale squeezed off three burst groups, but I was never a great shot, so I took my time aiming.

People fell, both gangsters and Mexican soldiers.

The truth was, I didn't feel bad about shooting those guys. They were all in cahoots and every one of them wanted to kill us. I'd finally gotten past that stomach-clenching idea that I was killing men. Maybe it was the distance between us, maybe because I was sick as a dog, but I emptied the magazine, slapped in my last, and continued firing.

Our continuous rate of fire pushed them down as we leapfrogged forward, and the next thing I knew, our side of the Humvee was quiet and all four of us were running like striped-ass baboons for the two open doors on the nearest vehicle on our end.

"Sonny! Drive!"

We dove inside as gunfire rose again when they realized we'd taken their transportation.

Yolanda went first, followed by Phoebe, then Perry Hale. I already had the engine going and shoved it into gear, steering around the other Humvee and taking off for the bridge. The back window on the passenger side went down and Perry Hale's arm flashed outside.

We were a dozen yards past the lead Humvee when

it exploded. I couldn't help but look back over my shoulder. Perry Hale grinned. "Found a grenade on the floor. This is a whole 'nother country."

I turned back forward to see the top half of a man in a blue shirt waving two empty hands from behind the steep bank of the Rio Grande. He looked familiar and I was pretty sure it was Arturo's daddy, Santiago Estrada.

Chapter 91

The cleaning crew who arrived every other day at Marc Chavez's sprawling Houston home were surprised to find the front door unlocked. Lupe Hinojosa replaced the house key in her pocket and lightly tapped the solid mahogany door.

She opened it a crack. "Hello?"

When no one answered, she shrugged and picked up her bucket and mop. Two other cleaning ladies followed with an assortment of buckets, stepladders, and supplies. They filed into the entry. From there most of the open-concept layout revealed the living room, kitchen, and dining room.

The office to their right was just as they'd left it forty-eight hours earlier, all the way down to the vacuum marks in the carpet. The youngest of the Hispanic ladies flicked a rag at the French doors. *"Terminado!"*

Done.

They laughed and walked into the living room. Lupe headed for the kitchen, but a gasp from the other two caused her to spin around and find a sight that would haunt her until the day she died.

Marc Chavez's naked and bloody body was tied at the wrists and ankles in front of the fireplace. His tongue and genitals were arranged on either side of his head, the floor thick with congealed blood. Splatters on the wall and ceiling told a horrific story about how he'd died.

The rest of the house was pristine.

Chapter 92

The stressed observers on the Texas side watched from cover as their friends fought their way toward the river. Every man and woman there had already identified Sonny, Perry Hale, and Yolanda by name.

To a person they yearned to open up with everything they had across the river to force the bad guys down. The Americans needed help, and all they could do was stand around and watch. Almost too much, it was like seeing the choreography of a movie unfold after the director shouts "action," but much deadlier.

Major Parker leaned over to Ranger Nick Delgado. "Who the hell is that skinny little gal with them? The one behind Yolanda."

Squinting into the viewfinder, Delgado kept the camera rock solid. "No idea, sir."

Sheriff Armstrong grinned. "Leave it to Sonny to be involved with blowing things up and rescuing maidens in distress."

Ranger Gasch trotted up from his recon of the house on the river. "Major."

Parker plucked a cigar from his shirt pocket. "Huh?"

"That house over there's full of bodies. No one else. We pulled back to preserve the crime scene. The place is shredded from a firefight."

The Major grunted and stuck the cigar into the corner of his mouth. "Bet that was Hawke's doin', and if it was, it was sure 'nough a war, one that moved across the border." He pointed to the west. "There's an oxbow over there. I bet that's where they're headed. Set up out of sight from all these people. Help 'em if they need it."

Gasch cocked his head in a silent question.

"You heard me."

The order had been given. "Yessir."

Chapter 93

When the two remaining gangsters crashed through the balcony's French doors, they brought the heavy drapes in with them. One with strands of barbed wire tattooed around his shaved head charged Gabe, growling like an animal. The heavy material fell across the ranch hand's arms and shotgun, preventing him from pulling the trigger but blocking the man's furious attempts to slash with a razor-sharp machete.

The other gangster tripped on the drapes, dropping to his hands and scuttling forward like a crab. Bare from the waist up, his body was nothing but one mass of inked words and drawings.

Mary fell back, screaming.

Kelly recoiled at the disturbing sight, the pistol in her hand momentarily forgotten.

At Herman's age, and wounded from the knife slash, his reactions were slower than the rest. It took several moments to register the sudden burst of activity.

Bad guys with machetes.

Kelly raising her revolver.

Gabe not giving an inch, driving forward like an offensive lineman, using the temporarily useless shotgun to push Barbed Wire off balance.

Herman's thought processes shifted into high gear at the sight of the tattooed face. Words, symbols, crude pictures—it was a vision of lawlessness, cruelty, and death. It was that crabwalking man with spiderwebs inked around his eyes who dropped the tangled machete and pulled a pistol free. He fired.

The bullet whizzed past Herman's head and buried itself in the wall. The 870 twelve-gauge shotgun lying across his lap was pointed the wrong way. Rapidly coming up to speed in the fight, but still behind the action, his left hand on the pump's grip yanked the barrel toward Spider Eyes, who seemed stunned that he'd missed at such close range.

Kelly was in the line of the swing. Herman lowered the muzzle.

Still struggling with Gabe, Barbed Wire also dropped his machete and yanked a cheap .38 pistol from his pants and fired at the same instant Gabe yelled in terror and planted his feet. Holding his impotent shotgun at port arms, Gabe shoved, stepped back, and fired. The range was too close and the blast missed the gangster by a hair. He chopped the stock at the man's head, forcing him back toward the broken French doors.

Herman finished the swing and pulled the trigger on Spider Eyes, who slapped at the barrel with his left hand. The load of #4 buck nearly severed the tattooed gangster's left leg. He went down, but raised the pistol toward the old Ranger.

Catching the fight from the corner of his eye, Gabe shucked another shell into the receiver and shot Spider Eyes in the side. The full load of buckshot from only three feet away dropped him to the floor.

Barbed Wire regained his balance and tried to bring his pistol to bear. With a roar, the work-hardened ranch hand lowered his shoulder and charged like a bull, trying to shove the gangster back out and over the balcony rail.

The fight occurred with breathless speed, but Kelly finally responded, sticking the five-shot Airweight under Gabe's arm and into Barbed Wire's chest. She pulled the trigger three times on the hammerless revolver as fast as possible in a roll of muffled thunder. The gangster went limp, and Gabe pushed him out and over the rail. The body landed with a hard splat on the flagstones.

Kelly backed away from the window, left hand over her mouth.

Gabe took the pistol from her fingers. "I killed that man."

She tore her eyes from the shattered glass doors. "No, I . . ."

His voice was firm. "I picked up your pistol and shot him."

"That's what I saw."

Kelly whirled to see Herman nodding his head. The wound in his arm had reopened and blood soaked his sleeve. "Gabe shot him and that's what you gals are gonna say. High school teachers ought not shoot people."

Herman held both hands into the air as Mary unlocked the hotel's door that slammed open, nearly knocking her into the wall. "Clear here, boys. It's over."

Deputy Malone and two other deputies poured into the room, filling it with big men and guns.

Chapter 94

Lordy, the seat in that Humvee felt like pure heaven even though it was worn to a frazzle, but it was the most comfortable thing I'd felt since I climbed out of my truck what seemed like a year ago.

One-handed, I turned the Humvee left and slowed beside Estrada, who by then had gained the top of the bank. The vehicle was between him and the guys that opened up on us with everything they had left. Rounds slapped the sides of the vehicle, and I hoped none of them had smarts enough to aim for the tires.

Taking my foot off the accelerator, I slowed enough for Arturo's dad to jump up on the running board. "Hold on!"

He probably couldn't hear through the thick glass and steady shooting, but he got the idea as we followed the ragged edge of the riverbank. We rolled right over scrub brush and short cedars that scraped the under-carriage, the Humvee bouncing and jumping like a bronc.

We hit an open spot and the ground smoothed. By then I steered around some of the bigger clumps of vegetation and sped up to get out of range. Estrada yelled, but I couldn't hear him.

"Sonny, slow down for a minute and let him get in." Perry Hale leaned forward and slapped my shoulder. "We have enough distance now."

I glanced into the side mirror and saw no one was following. Knowing better than to hit my brakes and throw our passenger off, I slowed enough so he could take two fast steps off the running board and yank the door open. He jumped inside and I accelerated again.

Without taking my eyes off the riverbank to our right, I put a little distance between us and the four-foot drop-off to frothing muddy water. "You're Arturo's daddy, right?"

He was shocked that I recognized him. "*Sí, Santiago Estrada.*"

He cut loose with a lot more in rapid-fire Spanish, and I didn't understand more'n two words. Yolanda leaned forward and translated. "Arturo's *step*-daddy. He says we can cross up ahead."

"Where? I know for a fact there's no bridge anywhere in this direction, and the water's too high to drive across."

They had another jabbering session, and I vowed to take Spanish lessons when I got to feeling better. "He says there's a narrow horseshoe bend up ahead. He has a boat there."

"A *boat*?"

She grinned. "Him and some other guys were going to use it last night to cross. Figured it was the perfect time, but then Chatto showed up at the bar and his friends ran off."

Made sense.

"Where? *Dónde?*"

He showed me a mouthful of gold teeth in a smile that spread from ear to ear.

I accelerated and the big tires threw up fat chunks of mud in a plopping rooster-tail behind us.

Phoebe'd been watching out the back. She finally turned around. "We're leaving ruts deep enough to plant corn. They won't have any trouble following us."

"Aquí! Aquí!" Estrada gripped the hard dash with both hands and braced himself.

I hit the brakes and we slid and slid until there was nothing in the windshield but river and Texas. Now that it was light we could see the churning, chocolate-milk-colored water flowing past. We'd come to an oxbow, a horseshoe bend in the river that brought Texas a hair closer where the water choked to a narrow point. Only problem was, that increased the velocity in a Venturi effect.

We detrucked in record time and gathered on the edge of the steep bank. This time the water was more of a deep, thick chuffing sound. I didn't like that noise one whit. "Where's that boat?"

Estrada pointed to a clump of sagebrush. Behind it was a johnboat that looked as if it had gone through a trash compactor.

"That's not a boat," Perry Hale said. "It's a promised drowning."

Estrada picked up a splintered oar made from tacked-together slats of wood. A pile of one-gallon plastic jugs were tied together in the middle of the boat. *"Se filtra, pero es suficiente para llevarnos a traves de."*

Perry Hale and I both raised our eyebrows, waiting for Yolanda to translate. "He says it leaks, but he thinks we can get across."

I pointed at the jugs. "And those?"

She asked and Estrada answered. She seemed to deflate at the answer. "Flotation devices, just in case. Lifejackets."

Perry Hale turned back to the ghost town and set his sock feet. "I'd rather take my chances fighting those guys."

Chapter 95

Major Parker finally lit his cigar in frustration as they watched the battle across the river. The Humvee driven by Sonny Hawke sped away as both gangsters and military personnel sent a storm of bullets after them.

Seconds later, a man he recognized as Chatto, one of Juárez Cartel's leaders, rose from behind the shot-to-pieces Suburban with a pistol in his hand. His men commandeered an undamaged Humvee, and the gangsters' leader piled in, along with two of his men.

The sight caused Parker to unconsciously bite down on the end of the cigar. "Just what I thought."

The military officer in command of the Mexican soldiers stepped out from the same cover and pointed at the dead Suburban parked in front of the Americana Bar de Vista. The dusty paint was dimpled with bullet holes surrounded by brighter metal and gray primer.

Major Parker tilted his Stetson back on his forehead. "Nick, dig that megaphone out of the back there."

Ranger Delgado was back in a second with a black

battery-operated bullhorn. He flicked the On switch and handed it to Major Parker, who plucked the cigar from the corner of his mouth. "Hello across the river!"

The surviving soldiers and gangsters rose from cover, turning toward the river as if they hadn't seen the men and vehicles gathered on the Texas side until that moment. The commanding officer took his time turning in that direction, as if to prove immediate response wasn't required. From the major's position, he watched the officer stroll over to one of his men.

Major Parker lowered the bullhorn and stuck the cigar back in his mouth, chewing rather than smoking to tamp down his rising frustration.

Sheriff Armstrong joined them. "You don't need to stand out here in the open by yourself."

Parker looked over to see the Ballard sheriff with an AR-15 cradled in his arms. "Little out of your jurisdiction, you know."

"Yep."

After a lengthy exchange between the Mexican officer and his subordinate, the commanding officer waved his arms and shouted at his men to tend to their wounded and dead scattered on the muddy street.

The officer finally walked to the riverbank and waited with both hands on his hips, facing the Texas Ranger across the Rio Grande. His face was red either from anger, fear, or high blood pressure. He had to shout across the distance and rushing water. "I am Captain Perez, and this was an armed invasion of my country by your military!"

"Major Chase Parker, Texas Rangers. You need to

stop right there with that and listen to what I have to say. How's your English?"

"Not good." Perez shrugged and waved one of his men over. They spoke for a moment.

Major Parker called Ranger Delgado over. "C'mere and bring that camera."

"Sir?"

"We're gonna get that pompous ass' goat. Hold the camera where he can see it."

"Yessir."

"Watch and learn." Parker puffed at the cigar to keep it alive and raised the bullhorn again. "This is going to be short and sweet between the two of us. There will be no negotiations after I've said my piece."

Perez propped his fists on his hips again, listening.

"My men have been shooting still photos and video since we arrived."

Ranger Delgado held the black Canon aloft.

"I have an accurate and true record of you and your soldiers colluding with Chatto, the El Machete enforcer for the Vincente Gonzales Flores Cartel. That means your involvement with him makes you a criminal to both the American and Mexican governments.

"This will end right here. You will not pursue this issue, or those people who just fled, from this moment on. If you do, I will release these photos and video to the American government, your government, and the media in both the United States and your country. You'll wind up in front of one of your own firing squads by the end of the week."

Captain Perez listened as his translator repeated what Major Parker had said.

Major Parker thought the Mexican officer's head was going to explode. He shouted at the cowed soldier beside him, first gesturing toward the Texas side of the river, and then back southward.

The man answered and pointed at the Texas lawmen. The Mexican officer railed even more before his translator relayed the message with both hands around his mouth. "The captain says you will not do that! It will be an attempt to cover up this invasion of our country!"

Major Parker turned and waved at the armed men still standing behind the vehicles they'd used for cover. "I need all the border patrol agents up there." He located the FBI agent. "Landon, come up here with me. I need to use you as a visual aid."

Frowning, the FBI agent came around a Suburban and joined the heavily armed agents who gathered on both sides of the tall Ranger. He handed the bullhorn to Ranger Delgado. "Nick, repeat this in Spanish so that sonofabitch can hear it in his own language.

"We also have the FBI here, as well as Border Patrol agents that recognized and also recorded what just went on across the river. The images we have do not show anyone other than the military and cartel members meeting, colluding, and then acting together to fire upon others."

Ranger Delgado repeated the statement with the bullhorn as the major spoke.

Perez threw up his hands and stalked back and forth, raging up and down the riverbank. Major Parker replaced the cigar and crossed his arms, waiting for the man to calm down.

The officer finally came back to the private, who wilted under a long verbal onslaught. Finally, Perez calmed down and gave his man instructions. The soldier cupped his hands again, clearly irritated that he had to shout to be heard.

His voice wasn't as strong as it had been. "Captain Perez asks you to repeat your demands."

"Nick, tell him we'll do better than that. What we saw was his men engage members of the cartel and fight with bravery and honor. This is over as far as we're concerned. That is the end of my statement and word on this matter. Do. You. Understand?"

Ranger Delgado grinned as he relayed the message. A burst of gunfire from upriver caused the men on both sides of the river to pause.

Perez crossed his arms and squared his shoulders at the sound.

"Nick. Repeat this. Those are my men bringing the others back home. This is over."

Perez stared across the roiling water for several long moments before finally nodding. Raising one hand, he spoke to his translator, then spun on his heel, shouting orders to his men.

"Captain Perez says that is exactly what happened and you can disperse your men. We have the situation well in hand, and Texas is once again safe from this cartel."

The world across the river blew up. Captain Perez's men knew their commanding officer enough to almost move as one. As the Texans watched, almost as spectators at a music venue, the Mexican soldiers turned on the surviving cartel members.

Guns rose on both sides, but the overwhelming firepower from the military's fully automatic weapons dropped the few remaining gangsters like wheat before a scythe.

Major Parker laughed. "Boys, I believe this is over."

The Texans chuckled.

Chapter 96

"C'mon, buddy." Yolanda jumped down to the narrow slice of solid land between the drop-off and boiling water. Estrada built a smile full of gold teeth and dropped down beside her.

I slapped Perry Hale on the shoulder. "Hey, it's only a few feet across." Not about to jump four feet down, I sat on my rear and slid off, favoring my left side.

"I think my plan was better," Perry Hale said as he landed beside me. "Y'all get in, but you get in the middle, Sonny. Yolanda and this guy can paddle. I'm gonna shoot some more people, because getting scared makes me mad and that's what's gonna happen when we get out on that water."

I started to respond when several men materialized from the scrub on the Texas side of the river. I recognized my Rangers. Perry Hale reached back over the high bank and grabbed the aluminum johnboat. He leaned backward, dragging it over the edge.

Yolanda pushed past me to help drag it to the river. They couldn't shove it into the strong current that would have pulled it away. She asked Estrada a question and he answered. Her face fell.

The change in her demeanor was obvious. "What?"

"His plan is to push off and let the current take us around the horseshoe. He thinks it'll push us up against the far bank." She pointed to the riverbank at the other end of the horseshoe not fifty yards away.

"This thing's already leaking like a sieve."

"It won't make any difference. If we float past that curve, it'll take us under the bridge where we'll be sitting ducks." Yolanda climbed in first, moving to the far end. Water seeped in through a dozen holes. Phoebe followed.

Perry Hale swung the pack off his shoulders and dropped it in our end of the boat. "You're next."

I stepped over the first bench seat and settled into the next at the same time the boat broke free in the violent current. Perry Hale launched himself over the bow, landing on his stomach with a thud. Yolanda and I were already trying to control the out-of-control boat with the homemade paddles.

It wasn't working.

Seconds later we were floating backwards in the raging river that had taken control of our lives. Yolanda's paddle snapped. I passed mine to Perry Hale. "Use this one. I can't control it from this seat!"

He grabbed it and dug in, trying to turn the boat and gain enough control to reach the bank only thirty yards downstream, but the river had us. Desperate, Phoebe grabbed the gunnel and leaned over to paddle with her hands.

All we needed was a couple of people with rifles to appear on the Mexican side of the riverbank and it'd be all over but the cryin'.

Chatto thought it was the second miracle of the day, when his only surviving Humvee stopped behind the Americans' stolen vehicle. He'd been given a present. "Quick, the river. They are trying to cross. Kill them!"

The two bodyguards exchanged glances, but obeyed their leader. They split up and rounded the car from both ends, guns ready. Chatto followed with a Beretta 92 he'd taken from a dying young private with smooth skin who clutched his hand and asked for absolution.

Chico and Emilio approached the riverbank in a crouch and quickly rose when they saw their quarry halfway across the river. They opened fire, not seeing the camouflaged Texas Rangers on the other side.

Flat-bottom boats don't cooperate with paddlers, and especially in high, fast water. Perry Hale was fighting a losing battle. Four inches of water was already sloshing around our feet, and we weren't a quarter mile from where we wanted it to go.

"Ranger! Here!"

Several men shouted at once and their combined voices were loud enough for us to hear over the river and all our activity. It was a team of Texas Rangers moving in a flurry of action. We were in too much of a battle with the swift river to see what they were doing, but whatever it was, I had complete faith.

We were moving fast, and I hoped whatever they had in mind would work.

"Grab one!"

We were almost on them, but still in the middle of the river. Three lines simultaneously flew in our direction. One fell short, but two went completely across the boat and weights splashed into the water.

We grabbed at the blue and red nylon climbing ropes. The short one was on Yolanda's end, but Perry Hale and I snagged the other two. The Rangers on the other end set their feet and wrapped the ropes around their hips like cowboys holding a fighting steer.

Perry Hale and I did the same and the ropes tightened. We didn't expect the boat to skip around on the surface, slinging one end around like kids playing snap the whip. We were almost yanked completely out, and would have been if we hadn't planted our feet against the gunnels. The force pushed Yolanda and Phoebe toward the stern and they held on for dear life.

The Rangers on the other end held tight and we played a deadly game of tug-of-war against the current. Red water poured over the sides, threatening to sink the boat before we could reach the bank.

Two of the Rangers raised M4 carbines and took careful aim at the gangsters shooting at those in the boat. Bullets flew across the international border. Chico took two high in his chest and dropped backward, the pistol flying from his hand. The back of Emilio's head exploded in a red and gray mist. He didn't know he was dead until he woke up in Hell.

My side shrieked and I lost my grip on the rope that sizzled through my hands. With the tension released, I fell back and rolled into the bottom of the boat. Water filled my mouth, and it was all I could do to roll over, gagging for breath.

Yolanda lunged across Phoebe for the rope, but her reach was too short.

It was all up to Perry Hale, and he did his best. The boat shipped more water and it flipped, throwing us toward the Texas side. Guns roared overhead, and I reached out a hand to swim.

Someone grabbed that hand and my head went under. The next thing I knew, more hands grabbed hold and I was in Texas with the rest of my crew.

The Texas Rangers had come through.

Chatto crouched behind the Humvee and watched his men fall as the flat-bottom boat spun out of control in the river. The Rangers set their feet and roped the sinking boat in as if it was a wild horse. The johnboat swung with the current and shipped water. It overturned, throwing all four passengers into the river.

They were close enough that their rescuers could drop down the bank and plant their feet on the two-foot strip of solid land above the high-water mark. The Americans in tactical gear grabbed at both the young woman Chatto had wanted to sample and the Texas Ranger. Others rescued the man and woman in military clothing.

He stepped around the Humvee as they pulled all four people ashore and stretched them out on the bank. The two men in tactical gear who'd shot Chico and Emilio watched over their rifles, waiting to see what Chatto would do. Suddenly tired, he laid his pistol on the hood and contemplated the long drive back to his home one hundred miles south.

I wasn't out for long, and when I came to, Ranger Bill Gasch and his men were gathered around us. I coughed up some water and sat up. For a moment, it felt as if I were looking through a telescope. I blinked a couple of times to clear my vision and saw Chatto standing there as if he were shopping for cars. He stepped around to the front bumper and rested his hand on the hood.

That man who was responsible for so many deaths and so much pain grinned across the water. It was more than I could stand. "Bill, give me your rifle."

"I can't do that, Sonny." Bill laid the rifle on the muddy ground beside me and knelt facing the opposite direction. "My boot's untied again."

The others waited to see what I was going to do. I picked it up with one hand because my left side had almost given up on me. The weight was too much. Still sitting, I bent my left knee and propped it there.

"Need some help?" Perry Hale sat with his back against mine.

Yolanda backed against my bad side and together they kept me stable and upright.

Ranger Gasch's voice floated out soft, but firm. "Hey boys, who's that coming from behind us?"

Men and gear rustled as they turned away from Mexico.

I adjusted the forepiece on my knee, snugged the butt to my shoulder, and found Chatto in the scope that wavered around, then steadied for a moment. It hurt like hell when I made myself use that left arm one last time to help steady the AR.

"Dad!"

Jerry's voice startled me so much I almost pulled the trigger. He was still far enough away that I could do it, but I couldn't shoot a man simply standing beside a vehicle while my son watched, no matter what Chatto had done. Lowering the muzzle, I felt my human braces move aside.

A hand reached out to take the rifle at the same time Jerry slid to a stop on his knees, hugging me as hard as he could. My eyes watered and I returned his embrace at the same time an AR opened up on full auto. Startled, I glanced up to see Phoebe on one knee with my rifle at her shoulder.

Chatto dropped where he stood behind the Humvee and she lowered the rifle. "I was in fear for my life because I'm sure he recognized me." She addressed the openmouthed Rangers. "My daddy's a cop. He taught me to shoot."

"Well, you sure killed that Humvee," Perry Hale said.

Yolanda squeezed my arm.

His boot retied, Ranger Gasch took his rifle back. "You boys police up all this brass. Every single hull."

Those Rangers gathered around me, and they looked to be ten feet tall.

Something stung Chatto in the shoulder, then he lost his breath at the same time a huge blow knocked his head backward. He suddenly was on his back, staring at the clouds breaking overhead. The sun peeked through for a moment, then darkness.

Chapter 97

Major Parker looked past Ranger Delgado and re-moved the cigar. "Looky over yonder. I believe I see the end to this little situation."

They turned upriver to see Sonny Hawke, Yolanda Rodriguez, Perry Hale, and a stranger, all four soaked to the bone, followed by Ranger Bill Gasch and his squad. Sonny walked with the aid of his son Jerry and Perry Hale, but shrugged off their hands when he neared the cluster of lawmen.

Hatless, with his hair standing on end, the ashen-faced Ranger looked to be on the edge of death. Badge haphazardly pinned onto his shirt and his signature Colt .45 stuck in the waistband of his torn jeans, Sonny stuck out his hand and shook with his commanding of-ficer. "Thanks, boss." Sonny scanned the crowd. "Ethan, have you heard from Kelly and Mary?"

"They're all right." Sheriff Ethan Parker joined them. "There was some trouble, but everyone's just fine. Her-man was there. He was injured, but he'll be fine."

"Well, he's a tough old hide." That short sentence

seemed to take the last of his strength, and Sonny's knees went week. He sagged against Jerry, who helped him settle to the ground as two emergency medical responders pushed through.

Sonny wasn't through. "Ethan, how's my horse? Did anyone find Red?"

"Yep. Just heard on the radio he was fine and dandy, found trotting down the road."

Major Parker made eye contact with Ranger Gasch. "All clean?"

"Yessir."

The major nodded a response and watched Arturo and his step-dad Santiago Estrada talking beside the kids' Bronco. The angry youngster jabbed Estrada's faded blue shirt with an index finger, clearly telling him off. The man listened, his head hung low. When Arturo ran out of steam, Estrada wrapped his arms around the boy, who finally relaxed and returned the hug.

The clouds broke and a single shaft of sun broke through, landing somewhere in the national park to the west.

Major Parker turned to look across the river. "Glad to have you back, Ranger Hawke."

ACKNOWLEDGMENTS

There are always people to thank when a book finally comes to completion. Of course, friends and family are always there to support this writing endeavor, but there are a few others from outside the circle that I need to recognize.

Thanks also to Jennette Jurado, Park Ranger, CUA Coordinator, and Public Information Officer for Big Bend National Park. She offered a number of valuable suggestions on the locations both inside and outside the park, and they completely changed the ending for the better. I took a few liberties with the topography of the northeast corner of the park itself in the interest of entertainment. Also, the real topography of the Rio Grande itself is a little different from what I described, especially both ends of the blocked bridge at the end of Highway 2627, and the real ghost town of La Linda, Mexico, that I renamed Paso la Carmen.

Thanks to the folks in Marfa for letting me use their town (also under the name Ballard), and especially Vicki Lynn Barge and the folks at the El Paisano hotel for the same. West Texas folks are salt of the earth, and y'all've proved it over and over again.

Some names keep turning up, and those are folks who are always there to read, offer suggestions, or answer questions. Thanks to my sister-in-law Sharon Reynolds, my boy Adam McKay (USMC), Sgt. Chris Grall (former Special Forces Operations, U.S. Army), Steve Knagg, and Steve Brigman. Joe Lansdale, C. J. Box, Jeffery Deaver, Craig Johnson, Marc Cameron, and Sandra Brannan have all offered advice and friendship. I'm honored to call you friends.

Thanks to my outstanding agent and good friend Anne Hawkins, who continues to guide me in this bewildering world of publishing.

My editor, Michaela Hamilton, is so full of energy and enthusiasm that she makes everyone else look like pikers. Thank you, ma'am, for believing in me and Sonny Hawke. Working with you and Kensington is an absolute pleasure.

And you'll see this name over and over again as I continue to thank my brother from another mother, John Gilstrap. Thanks, my good friend, and I'm looking forward to the next of our many adventures together.

The love of my life, Shana, is always right there for me. Thank you, babe.

Don't miss the next Sonny Hawke thriller

Hawke's Revenge

Coming soon from Kensington Publishing Corp.

Keep reading to enjoy a sample excerpt . . .

Chapter 1

The eastbound desert highway shimmered under a hot afternoon sun. I thumbed off the Dodge's cruise control at the sight of the blocked two-lane up ahead. The opening riffs of "Gimme Shelter" by the Rolling Stones were too loud at the slower speed, so I cranked the volume down a couple of notches and studied the backup of vehicles.

Over in the shotgun seat, Buster frowned when I lowered the volume. He likes that song, and especially ZZ Top, that little band from Texas, which was up next on my playlist. Buster's my black Labrador retriever.

The engine brake growled, slowing the dually pickup, but the sound was so familiar neither of us paid it any mind. It was the cars overflowing from the Marfa Lights viewing area's parking lot and lining both sides of the table-flat highway that had my attention.

"Again?"

Buster turned his brown eyes toward my side of the cab and woofed.

"You're right. Ethan's gonna be right in the middle of this one, too. It looks bigger'n the last."

I slowed to a crawl when I reached the clot of cars. A few people were hanging around the packed parking lot, sitting in the viewing center's shade and smoking. They were a mix of our part of the world out there in far West Texas—white, brown, and American Indian. I figured they were there to protest the existence of the Trans-Pecos pipeline for the second time in a month.

Trying to be friendly, I raised two fingers from the steering wheel in a wave, because that's what Texans do, but no one lifted a hand in return. At least no one used a similar gesture to tell me I was number one.

They watched with impassive faces as we rolled through the corridor of vehicles. Once past, I mashed on the foot-feed, knowing that in less than two miles I'd find the drivers, and the action.

The highway ahead was completely blocked with protestors who had the light traffic choked down to a standstill. Half a dozen sheriff's department and highway patrol cars idled with their lights flashing both on the shoulder and the pull-out in front of the BranCo's pipe yard, an enclosure full of pipe and drilling equipment, scraped clean of vegetation by bulldozers. A handful of pipeline workers watched from behind the chain-link fence.

Since the road was blocked, I pulled onto the dusty shoulder and crept past the line of cars until it too was blocked by highway patrol cars and other vehicles I figured belonged to the television and news crews. There was an open space between clumps of prickly pear and yuccas. I steered onto the hardpan and stopped at a knot of people milling between the highway and a bob-wire fence that ended at the pipe and continued into the distance on the opposite side.

My cell phone rang. I would have ignored it, but it was Major Chase Parker, my commander. I pushed the screen. "Yessir."

"I need you to come to the office. We have a little situation that's gonna be your baby."

"I'm feeling fine, thanks."

He was silent on the other end. "Okay. I get it. How're you healing up?"

"Like I said, fine. What's up?"

He sighed like he usually does when we talk. "We have someone crossing the country, executing people who've gotten off murder raps on technicalities, or out on pardons. It looks like he's gonna be here in Texas any day now, from what we've been seeing. This one's right up your alley."

"You want me there today?"

"If you can get here."

I scanned the chanting crowd. "I'll do my best."

"Fine. See you at three o'clock."

"Hey . . ."

He hung up. I pitched the phone onto the dash in frustration and opened the door. Riding shotgun, Buster rose to follow me out of the truck, but I shook my head. "I'm gonna leave this AC going for you, but don't get over here and lock the doors on me."

He woofed an answer and sat back down to stare out the windshield.

He'd locked me out a year earlier when I left the big dummy in the truck cab with the motor running. Annoyed that he couldn't go, Buster pawed at the driver side armrest and hit the electronic lock. After Ethan finally showed up with a Slim Jim, a thin piece of metal he inserted between the glass and car frame to pop the lock, I took the spare key from the fob and kept it in my pocket from there on out.

Even with so many people around, I wasn't worried about leaving the truck running. Nobody was going to get inside with those white fangs of his showing.

Once outside I was met by angry looks from both the trapped travelers in their automobiles and the protestors between them and the yard gate. A dozen or so activists turned at the slam of the truck door and stood shoulder to shoulder with the intention of blocking my way.

Knowing better than to show any emotion to the angry collection of anti-pipeline marchers, I locked eyes with an American Indian demonstrator in a blue bandana, who looked to be ten years younger and sixty pounds heavier than me. Ignoring the man's ALL LAND IS SACRED poster, I headed directly toward Big Boy, maintaining a steady pace.

His glare held solid until I was close enough for him to see the *cinco peso* Ranger badge on my shirt. Big Boy's eyes flicked up to my new straw O'Farrell hat, then down to the hand-tooled double-rig belt holding the 1911 Colt .45 semi-automatic.

I was banking on the Texas Ranger reputation to work its magic, and when I was close, he waved a turkey-wing fan. "You Rangers think you're something."

"We just represent the law."

"*Your* law is allowing this!" A young woman spat in the dirt beside my black Lucchese boot. She held a sign saying, Save our Land! "It isn't *our* law."

"I don't like this pipeline any more than y'all, but I have my job to do, just like you." I waved a hand toward a local news crew filming the protest. "They got what you wanted. Let's just do it without any real trouble, how 'bout that?"

Big Boy took my measure for a beat before stepping back to let me pass. I nodded my thanks. "Much obliged."

I kept walking, ignoring a barrage of comments thrown at my back, and hoping none of those folks were violent. I couldn't hold my own right then because I hadn't fully healed up from a bullet wound on my side.

There was more rattling and yelling behind me, but it was for the benefit of the camera that swept in our direction. A cluster of officers gathered around half a dozen demonstrators who'd chained themselves to the pipe yard's access gates.

Looking cool and collected, Presidio County Sheriff Ethan Armstrong knelt on one knee, talking to a female protestor. Gathered in a semicircle around them, the demonstrators of varied races in bandanas, feathers, and matching T-shirts were all waving signs, flags, and Indian totems. Seeing me, Ethan rose and tilted his Stetson back. "Howdy, Sonny. Somebody call you?"

Despite his calm voice and demeanor, I saw the fire in my high school friend's eyes. "Nope. I's headed to Alpine when I came up on this little demonstration." I scanned the ring of shouting protestors. "Most of these folks are strangers."

"Might near everyone." Ethan leaned in close so I could hear over the noise. "We've sent for some bolt cutters." He shrugged. "Loaned mine out, and then I'll clear this bunch out."

"You taking any of 'em to jail?" I didn't see anyone in cuffs.

"Not yet. I'm gonna get these dummies free and give 'em a chance to leave on their own. If they don't, *then* I'll cuff 'em up."

Just like the last time, the crowd was there protesting the new pipeline going through our county and under the Rio Grande, a hundred miles away. In a way I was kinda with them. The pipeline was an eyesore, and we'd already seen that those kinds of cleared dirt highways through the desert brush were custom-made for illegal immigrants who simply followed them to the interstate and beyond.

The easement made it easier for drug smugglers to travel north from the Rio Grande. Both drug smugglers and illegals follow landmarks, traveling dry creek beds, power lines, and even railroad tracks to disappear into the American fabric.

We'd already caught a red Chevy Avalanche packed full of marijuana following one of the temporary access roads. One of the BranCo construction crews called it in and the bust made national news. The 500 pounds of grass had a street value of over a million dollars and was the first time we'd caught drug runners using the new "superhighway" over the buried pipeline.

I took a good long look around. The mixed group waited on the shoulder and in the highway to see what would happen next. A couple of the deputies were urging them to clear the highway while the drivers caught in the protest were getting increasingly irritated.

Ethan held a hand up to a shouting demonstrator who shook a sign. DEFEND THE SACRED! "Hold your horses, bud. We're gonna be here for a while yet." He turned back to me. "You look like you're feeling better. I guess you're still riding the desk?"

I rolled my shoulders in answer. "Better. Still a little stiff. I'll be on the desk until the major turns me back out."

"You're doing a lot of that lately. You're the only Ranger I know who spends more time off-duty than on. Maybe you need to stay out of trouble."

"Well, I'm trying. I've been out of circulation for a while, but then again, when I'm on, it's intense."

He chuckled and scanned the crowd, which hadn't stopped chanting from the moment I arrived, "Stop the lies, water is life, stop the lies, water is life!" That one was about the threat of oil leaks and the pipeline's potential to contaminate the water table. Water is precious anywhere, but in the arid high desert north of Texas' Big Bend, its value rose even more.

I studied the crowd that was growing angrier by the minute. "How long ago did you send for the bolt cutters?"

Ethan shrugged. "Half an hour."

"I have a pair in the truck."

His eyes lit up. "Good. We can have them loose by the time Malone gets back." He whistled through his teeth and waved the highway patrol officers back to the gates. I went to the truck. The crowd around us parted like water around a rock as I cut through the pack. A DPS helicopter clattered overhead, circling the blockade.

Like I figured, no one had bothered the truck and

Buster was looking cool as a cucumber sitting there behind the wheel. He was keeping an eye on two young men who were leaning against a nearby car half on and off the shoulder. I knew if they so much as stuck a finger inside the truck, they'd draw back a nub.

They'd already figured that out for themselves.

I was reaching for the back-door handle when I looked past the young men's vehicles to see a silver four-door Ford F-150 caught in the traffic jam. The windows in the back seat were blacked out, but I had a good view of the passenger through his open window. He looked familiar and I ran through my mental files, trying to remember where I'd seen him. It took a moment to recollect he'd been on a wanted poster.

We don't get the old-fashioned paper posters mailed to us anymore, but Ethan's secretary always prints those that come through email and pins them to the bulletin board in the sheriff's office. I also get them through email from the FBI and other entities, as well as from Major Chase Parker, my commander.

The driver saw me looking in his direction. His head snapped back so fast I almost heard his eyeballs click. The passenger with a nose that looked to have been flattened with a shovel stared straight ahead. Raising his right hand to adjust his cap, the guy kept it against his cheek way too long.

A name popped into my head. Miguel Torrez. Wanted for armed robbery, drug trafficking, and assault with a deadly weapon. I suspected the driver to be Eric Navarro, his cousin.

"Buster, you have the truck."

I swiveled to find Ethan, but he'd knelt back down to speak with one of the people chained to the gate.

The rest of the deputies were turned away from me, and I couldn't catch anyone's eye. Luck was on my side, because Navarro had stopped close to the Nissan in front and couldn't back up because of a jacked-up white Chevy pickup right on his back bumper.

Or so I thought.

Torrez said something to his cousin behind the wheel, then swung back around to see if I was paying any attention. My eyes were still on the truck and that's all it took. He snapped something to Torrez and reached down for what I assumed to be a weapon. Navarro shifted into reverse and slammed against the Chevy with the lift kit. The crunch of collapsing metal floated over the crowd as the Ford's tailgate caved in under the Chevy's high bumper.

There was no subtlety at that point. "Ethan!"

The people nearest me quit chanting. Their silence spread like ripples across the crowd and nearly every head there focused on the apparent accident. Navarro dropped his truck into gear and hit the gas, crunching the Nissan coupe's back bumper and shoving it into a sedan in front.

Navarro jammed the Ford back into reverse to make a three-point turn. I was fifty yards closer than any of the other lawmen who were rushing to converge on the scene. From those circling in the helicopter, it must have looked like filings drawn to a blue Ford magnet.

I drew my .45, the smooth Lexan-covered Sweetheart Grips familiar in my hand.

The entire situation was a nightmare. Too many cars, too many civilians, and a possibly armed felon who didn't care about anyone but himself. That *possibly* armed qualification evaporated when Torrez stuck his arm through the open window and swung a Mac 11 subcompact machine pistol in my direction.

My stomach dropped. "Everybody down!"

He squeezed the trigger, streaming a burst of .380 caliber rounds in my direction. At the same time, Navarro spun the wheel to U-turn into the open lane and escape back the way they came. He stomped the gas, burning rubber. The truck jerked forward when the back tires shrieked on the concrete.

I zigzagged between the parked cars as the truck's rear end slewed. Centrifugal force jerked Torrez's arm and widened the arc of spraying bullets. Hot lead punched holes in half a dozen vehicles between me and the escaping felons, spiderwebbing windshields and side windows. People dropped like wheat before a scythe. There was no way to tell if they were ducking, like me, or falling with wounds.

A deputy opened up with his service weapon at the same time Navarro centered the truck in the westbound lane. I raced around the tail end of the white Chevy pickup, close enough to see Navarro behind the wheel, swinging a pistol around in my direction with his right hand. He fired three times over his left bicep as the truck accelerated.

My .45 came up, the sight picture lining up on his ear. Planting my feet, I fired three fast times. Two of the three missed, but the third caught him at the tip of his shoulder. He dropped the pistol and slumped forward. The angle was such that I no longer had a clear target, so the next best thing to do was empty the magazine into his left front tire. It exploded with a dull pop, wrenching the wheel from Navarro's hand at the same time Deputy Frank Malone roared up in his cruiser in the open lane and hit the Ford head-on.

Navarro slammed into the expanding airbag, disappearing from view.

At that point lawmen appeared from between the stopped cars. With nothing on the right side of the Ford truck but empty desert they opened up with a fusillade. I dropped my empty magazine, slapped in a fresh one, and hurried toward the steaming car at the same time the passenger door on the truck popped open and Torrez slid out, taking cover behind their now well-ventilated pickup. He stuck the machine pistol over the bed and held the trigger down, spraying rounds in still another deadly arc.

The passenger door to Malone's cruiser opened and he fought free of his deployed airbag, crawling across the front seat to roll out on my side with a shotgun in his hands. Once outside, he crabbed toward the rear of his cruiser. "What'n hell!!!??"

I ducked down behind the car and joined him at the rear. "Bad guys."

His face was red from the airbag. "No shit!"

"Driver's dead, I think. There's another one."

Gunfire rose.

"I saw him just before we hit."

I pointed toward the passenger side of the wrecked truck. "He might pop up over here."

"Hope he does."

Staying low, we duck-walked behind the cruiser, and I peeked up through the back glass. Thinking himself protected from the deputies' gunfire by the open passenger door, Torrez was changing magazines beside the truck's right front fender.

"Move now!"

Struggling to insert a fresh magazine in the little machine pistol, Torrez was intent on the weapon when Malone's 12-gauge joined in with my .45. Torrez dropped to the hot, sandy shoulder.

I rose and saw Navarro slumped over the steering wheel. "Clear!"

Ethan and the deputies eased around the truck, not really taking my word for it, but I didn't blame 'em. I watched Ethan kick the MAC-10 out of the dead man's reach. The sound of screams and crying filled the silence. The helicopter circled overhead and I realized my side was on fire.

Holstering my pistol, I felt around to see if I was shot again, but it was only the half-healed wound that had woken up.

Shaking his head, Ethan joined us beside the wrecked cruiser. "What'n hell was that all about?"

"There was paper on them yesterday and they saw I'd made 'em."

Taking his Stetson off, Ethan wiped the sweat from his forehead with a trembling hand. "Looks like you're back on the desk again, and I think I'm gonna recommend that Major Parker keeps you there for the rest of the year."

"Can I count on you for that?"